THE KITCHEN MARRIAGE

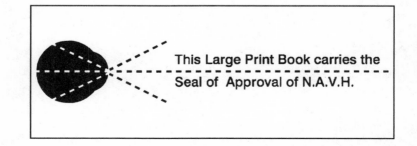

This Large Print Book carries the
Seal of Approval of N.A.V.H.

A MONTANA BRIDES ROMANCE

THE KITCHEN MARRIAGE

GINA WELBORN
AND
BECCA WHITHAM

THORNDIKE PRESS
A part of Gale, a Cengage Company

Farmington Hills, Mich • San Francisco • New York • Waterville, Maine
Meriden, Conn • Mason, Ohio • Chicago

Copyright © 2018 by Gina Welborn and Becca Whitham.
A Montana Brides Romance.
Thorndike Press, a part of Gale, a Cengage Company.

ALL RIGHTS RESERVED
Thorndike Press® Large Print Clean Reads.
The text of this Large Print edition is unabridged.
Other aspects of the book may vary from the original edition.
Set in 16 pt. Plantin.

LIBRARY OF CONGRESS CIP DATA ON FILE.
CATALOGUING IN PUBLICATION FOR THIS BOOK
IS AVAILABLE FROM THE LIBRARY OF CONGRESS

ISBN-13: 978-1-4328-5703-5 (hardcover)

Published in 2019 by arrangement with Zebra Books, an imprint of
Kensington Publishing Group, a division of Penguin Random House LLC

Printed in the United States of America
1 2 3 4 5 6 7 23 22 21 20 19

Mothers are a force to be reckoned with. Mothers teach, counsel, and guide. They impart wisdom. They comfort. They reflect the heart of God. We are blessed to have mothers who, to this day, still use their compassion, joy, wounds, wisdom, and skills for the good of others.

This story is for our mothers for leaving a legacy of peace, patience, kindness, and goodness, of faithfulness, and of hope. Oh, and for teaching us how to cook. Our families are most appreciative.

ACKNOWLEDGMENTS

In addition to the same people who helped us with *The Promise Bride* — our agents, Dr. Ellen Baumler of the Montana Historical Society, everyone at Kensington Publishing, and our families — we also want to thank:

Stephanie Miller who offered Becca, whom she'd only "met" via Facebook, her air-conditioned home and a Wi-Fi connection when Becca's power went out a week before this story was due.

Valir Physical Therapy and Ferrara Chiropractic for helping Gina recover from the damage she did to her arm and shoulder after falling out of a bed. (It was a really, really small bed.)

AUTHOR'S NOTE

Today's average American has heard of William Shakespeare. His works have been performed on countless stages, read in countless classrooms, and spawned countless movies and TV shows, including *Clueless, 10 Things I Hate About You, Lion King, Warm Bodies, House of Cards, and Sons of Anarchy.* Let's not fail to mention the Broadway hit *Something Rotten!* which my (Gina's) husband took our family to see in Tulsa, OK, while *The Kitchen Marriage* was being written. Until the early 1700s, the prolific English bard was unknown in France. French playwrights eschewed corpses, bad language, violence, sex, and subplots. In their opinions, his plays had "too many characters, too much variety of speech and action, were morally ambiguous, and (worst of all) were written in blank verse" ("French Hissing," *The Economist,* 31 Mar. 2005). Those Shakespearean plays that did reach the French stage were gutted and sanitized of their "lusty Shakespearean vitality — and meaning." (Harriss, Joseph A., "The Shocking Monsieur Shakespeare," *The American Spectator,* 23 May 2014). You can learn more about Shakespeare in France in John Pemble's book, *Shakespeare Goes to Paris and Conquered France.*

Throughout our story, we have interspersed real people, places, and events to interact with our characters. One of the real people is Joseph Hendry, whom we introduced in *The Promise Bride.* We alluded to his death in the epilogue of that story, then elaborated on it more in this story. Per *The Livingston Enterprise* newspaper, Joseph Hendry died of typhoid fever on December 13, 1887, at the age of twenty-eight. According to the news article, he was "fearless as a Roman gladiator" and was "not afraid of death, but sought to live to continue his manly work." The writer of the obituary then says: "Death has silenced his pen and his work is done; but his memory will never die in the hearts of those who knew him and his fame will be known in history for all time to come. In this we know his life will be everlasting."

We brought him into our story to honor

him. We hope he will forgive us for exaggerating the cause of his death.

. . . a fact that all women who ever answered a matrimonial advertisement, or ever intend to answer one, should remember: No man who has the ability or means to support a wife in comfort needs to advertise for one.

— CHICAGO DAILY TRIBUNE,
28 December 1884

What strange creatures brothers are!

— JANE AUSTEN

Courtship consists in a number of quiet attentions, not so pointed as to alarm, nor so vague as not to be understood.

— LAURENCE STERNE

Certainly, a good cook will manage to

make an agreeable dish of a material a bad one would reject as unpresentable. The most skillful agriculture is not always found in the richest districts.

— MRS. TOOGOOD,
Treasury of French Cookery

So let's not get tired of doing what is good. At just the right time we will reap a harvest of blessing if we don't give up. Therefore, whenever we have the opportunity, we should do good to everyone — especially to those in the family of faith.

— GALATIANS 6:9–10 (NLT)

Prologue

Helena, Montana
July 4, 1887

Jakob Gunderson lifted his chin to acknowledge friends as he marched, pie plate in hand, across the lawn in search of a solitary tree. Normally, he loved everything about the Independence Day church picnic: spending hours chatting with friends, the band playing military marches, the children bouncing inside potato sacks racing against one another toward a red streamer, and the patriotic banners draping tables burdened with food. Oh, how he loved ice cream and fruit pies! But this year, nothing he loved could cut the bitter taste in his mouth.

He sat down and leaned against a pine tree, the bark's ridges gouging into his back.

"Are you over here pouting?" Yancey Palmer strolled up to him, her dress the same color as the vanilla ice cream mounded on her tin pie plate. "Because if you are, I'd like to join you."

Jakob scooted over despite his grumpy mood. "Hale ignoring you again?"

Yancey sighed. She plopped down on the grass beside him. "One of these days, Mr. Hale Adams is going to regret how much time he wasted ignoring me." She spooned a bite of ice cream but didn't eat while staring across the church lawn to where Hale stood. "Do you see how the Watsons are giving me the stink eye?"

"Never mind them." Jakob focused on eating his second helping of ice cream and pie while she picked at her dessert. Despite both the sheriff's office and the city marshal's office confirming Joseph Hendry's salacious article, Jakob still struggled with believing his friend, Finn Collins, had worked with Madame Lestraude, one of Helena's richest brothel owners, to lure mail-order brides out West and sell them into prostitution. Word on the street put Yancey on Lestraude's payroll because she had stood in as a proxy bride for Finn's first victim, Emilia Stanek Collins. If that was true, Mac — the county sheriff and Emilia's betrothed — had to be on Madame Lestraude's payroll, because he was her son.

Jakob would stake his life on *that* not being true.

The only thing that made sense was Finn alone working for Lestraude. Emilia, Yancey, and Mac were unwitting victims. However, Hendry's article had stirred up a hornet's nest in the community. Helena's citizens weren't sure who they could trust. Finn had been a faithful church member and helped dozens of local area ranchers recover after the blizzards of '86. Finding out he'd lied to everyone — even his closest friend, Mac — made people distrust their neighbors and certainly anyone with a connection to Finn.

It would be a while yet before the Watsons and people like them stopped glaring. Jakob looked their way and smiled, which was how he'd handled all the censuring glances and questions over the past month. Soon enough, a new scandal would swing attention somewhere else. In the meantime, let them talk. That wasn't what was bothering him.

Jakob peeked over at the source of his sour mood. Emilia stood beside Mac. They were well suited, but Jakob had hoped to pursue the lovely Emilia for himself not so long ago. He wasn't bothered so much by Emilia's disinterest in him as he was in the general female population of Helena. There were plenty of girls willing to fall in love with him, but they all saw him as Isaak Gunderson's irresponsible twin brother. Jakob refocused on his ice cream. It'd be nice to find someone who would see him as his own man.

"Mail order worked out pretty well for Mac and Emilia. Maybe I should give it a go."

He didn't realize he'd spoken aloud until Yancey sat up straight and twisted around so fast her spoon fell off her still-full tin plate. "In Luanne's last letter, she mentioned a lady in her church is — are you ready for this? — a matchmaker."

Jakob didn't know whether to laugh or take her seriously. He opted for the latter. "How does her business work?"

"Luanne didn't say. I could telegram her tomorrow and ask."

"Let me know what she says."

"Are you really interested?"

He nodded. Emilia was proof a man could meet a girl through mail correspondence who was kind, intelligent, and pretty.

Yancey's smile faded. "Maybe I'll answer an advertisement myself."

Her woebegone tone of voice told him what she was thinking before he even asked. "Is this about Hale?"

"Unfortunately, it always rolls back around to him." She fiddled with the fabric of her skirt for a long moment. "Why doesn't he like me? Everyone likes me."

"Joseph Hendry certainly does." Jakob shifted his gaze to where the reporter stood holding a tin plate and looking their way. "Might be time to give another man a chance to see what a gem you are."

"Maybe you're right." She placed her hand over his fingers and squeezed them tight. "Sometimes I wish I could fall in love with you."

They'd tried once. A few years ago. Before they both realized they were much better suited to a type of brother-sister relationship.

Jakob tilted his head and gave Yancey his most charming grin — the exact one she always teased could make grown women swoon. "But what will my mail-order bride have to say about that?"

CHAPTER ONE

Manhattan Island, New York
Wednesday, February 29, 1888

Her future rested upon one flawless meal.

Zoe de Fleur maintained a leisurely pace as she walked home from Central Park. Remains of last week's snow were still nestled in rooftop crevices and frost blanketed the grass. Birds chirped, on the hunt for food. Smells of roasting chestnuts. White plumes of smoke rose from newly stoked hearths. An icy breeze nipped at her likely reddened cheeks, reminding her that winter — and February — enjoyed an extra day this year.

The perfect leap year day for the perfect dinner.

She exhaled, creating a puff of cloud. How could she capture the morning's beauty in food? Not for tonight. She had no time to experiment. But for Easter. Meringue certainly.

And what else?

She strolled along the marble wall that encircled Mrs. Gilfoyle-Crane's Fifth Avenue mansion, pondering future dessert ideas. While construction of new mansions could be seen up and down the avenue, this five-story white marble home on the corner had been for the last decade considered "almost too splendid for comfort."

Or so Zoe had been told.

Although she had spent her childhood and youth living in numerous European castles, the Crane house surpassed them all, in her estimation, because of its spacious and modern kitchen.

Meringue, marzipan flowers, and . . . cake.

But what kind?

"Hey, Miss de Fleur, you want a paper?" Up ahead, Nico — and his red-tipped nose — stood on the street corner with his daily stock of newspapers in his cart . . . and with that flat beige derby of his cocked jauntily to the side fitting his devil-may-care attitude.

"Not today," Zoe said as she always did. As she stopped next to him, she eyed the bandage on the fourteen-year-old's right hand. His knuckles were swollen. His face, though, bespoke no bruises, nor did he stand in pain as he had after last week's beating. "How are you zis morning?"

He grinned. "All to the merry, I say."

"Nico," she said, stretching out the vowels in his name to convey her displeasure.

"What?" came with a big cloud of breath.

"You know I dislike . . ." She paused, trying to think of the right words in English. Façade faces? Emotion masks? "Fake cheer. Be honest with me about" — she pointed to the bandage — "zat."

His smile fell. He fisted his bandaged hand. "I fought back, all right. You told me I had to stand up for myself."

That she had.

Her advice had also come with encouragement to be the bigger man and walk away from the argument before it became physical. Or, even better, start a conversation to bring harmony, to understand the other person's feelings. Become friends. Not fight back. Never fight back, because fighting brought pain. Brought scars. Not all of which were physical.

"When I was a child" — she unwrapped the woolen scarf about her neck — "my papa said embarrassing a bully with words can be as effective as responding with fisticuffs. I did what he told me, and I was horrified because of how my words made ze other girl cry." She draped the scarf around

Nico's neck. "How did hitting zat boy make you feel?"

"Strong."

Zoe clasped her gloved hands together. "Were his feelings hurt?"

Nico shrugged. "Don't care. I wanted him to stop pestering me." He shoved his hands in the pockets of his brown corduroy coat. "I'm not ever going to see him again anyway. I'm never going back to the orphanage. With all I've saved, I can buy a train ticket to California and . . ."

Zoe nodded as he rambled on and on about his grand plans to start over out West. Open a saloon. Become a blacksmith or a trapper. Maybe even dig for gold. Or marry some rich old lady about to die. The poor boy had hopes and dreams enough for a score of orphans. If only half the stories he told about life in the orphanage were true, she would hate living there. In the last three years of Nico trying to sell her a paper, he had vowed at least twice a month that he would never return to the orphanage. And yet he had.

As he would today, too.

"Find me after you have sold your stock," she said, interrupting Nico's description of his future house and its six floors.

His blue eyes widened. "Can I taste what

you're cooking for tonight?"

"Some."

"With wine?"

"No," she said, and then smiled and patted his shoulder. "Come to ze kitchen around eleven. I will make you hot cocoa, but you must be gone before Chef Henri arrives or he will have both our heads." She swiped her hand across her throat.

Nico's upper lip curled, enough of an action to clarify to Zoe what he thought of the renowned and current president of the *Société Culinaire Philanthropique,* who had an exclusive contract to cater any and all of Mrs. Gilfoyle-Crane's parties. Unlike Papa and Chef Henri, Zoe could never become a member of the Société because she was female, a rule Mrs. Gilfoyle-Crane called "a medieval practice." It bothered her greatly that Zoe could not claim the respectful title of chef, despite her French blood, despite following European tradition and apprenticing over a decade under her father's tutelage, and despite taking over Papa's job as chef for the Gilfoyle-Crane household.

If anyone should be offended, Zoe should be. And she was not. Changing the Société rules was tantamount to changing her sex. Impossible. Complaining would accomplish nothing.

Mrs. Gilfoyle-Crane paid Zoe a salary equal to what Papa had earned, even though, at twenty-two, she had less than two years' experience managing a kitchen on her own.

At that thought, Zoe smiled. "Life is good here."

"For you it is." Nico's brow furrowed as he studied her. "Why are you always so happy?"

"I have much to be zankful for. God is good to me." She tugged his derby down over his red-tipped ears. "Be not late for lunch."

"You're swell, Miss de Fleur."

"Zis is true."

He laughed. "Don't let Chef On-ree convince you otherwise."

Zoe waved as she walked away. She turned down the alley behind the homes lining Fifth Avenue. As the BEZEE'S FLOWERS delivery wagon waited in front of the steps leading to the Crane house basement, which was only a little below street level, similar to the other nearby brownstones, the hired florist and her workers unloaded the profusion of flowers.

Zoe breathed in the fragrant air. Tonight's dinner guests would enjoy an ethereal and fragrant floral feast.

While the florist issued orders to her workers, Zoe silently slipped past them. She hurried down the five steps to the servants' entrance. Electric sconces brightened the narrow hall that, even in the full light of day, received no outside sun.

She stepped into the kitchen.

Mrs. Horton was adding a tea set to a tray. Nothing but crumbs remained of the breakfast scones, coddled eggs, and ham Zoe had prepared for those on staff.

"Good morning," she said, removing her gloves. She shrugged off her hat and winter cloak, then hung them on a wall peg. "Is zere anything I can do to help?"

To Zoe's relief, Mrs. Horton shook her head. "You have enough to do before Chef Henri and his crew arrives," she said with a fair amount of pity in her tone. She finished preparing a tea service. "The Nephew has requested his morning tea."

Zoe sighed. Mrs. Gilfoyle-Crane's oldest nephew had a name — Manchester Gilfoyle IV — but, in private, the rest of the staff simply called him the Nephew. If Zoe were Mr. Gilfoyle, she would feel crushed to know she was so disliked. Of course, if she were Mr. Gilfoyle, she would be a more considerate person.

Mrs. Horton picked up the service tray.

"I'll be back to check on you later."

"Zank you." As Mrs. Horton left the kitchen, Zoe claimed her freshly washed white apron from the peg next to her coat.

She looped the apron over her head, then wrapped it around her serviceable gray work dress. From the apron pocket, she withdrew a white kerchief, folded it into a triangle, and draped it over her curly black hair, knotting the ends at the base of her neck. Her uniform failed to testify to her skills. But if she were to wear Papa's double-breasted chef's coat and *toque blanche* . . .

Chef Henri, in affront, would banish her from the kitchen.

She breathed deeply and slowly, as she always did to focus her mind on work. Tonight could not fail. She owed it to Mrs. Gilfoyle-Crane.

After a quick cleaning of the remains from breakfast, Zoe sat at her office desk in the small room connected to the kitchen. In the center of her desk was the dinner menu Chef Henri had created with Mrs. Gilfoyle-Crane's approval. Embossed gold font on Egyptian linen parchment. The writing was in French, even though the hostess could barely speak the language.

Zoe sighed. Oh, the irony.

Four dishes in the twelve-course meal

28

were Zoe's creations. Not to Chef Henri's pleasure. He had conceded to Mrs. Gilfoyle-Crane's request, although his outrageous fee would remain the same.

Chef Henri was greedy and arrogant and —

Worth none of Zoe's thoughts.

She opened the notebook Chef Henri's assistant, Chef Gerard — who constantly boasted he used to be a *pâtissier* in a shop near the Palais-Royal in Paris — had given her a month ago. He had listed what *she* needed to purchase, what *she* needed to have prepared ahead of their arrival, and what *she* needed to do during the four-hour meal to aid them as they cooked. Though detailed, his list was inefficient. Nor did it allot her time to prepare her four dishes. Why would anyone consider doing something in a way so obviously cumbersome and impractical?

Zoe grabbed her fountain pen. A few adjustments were necessary for a better flow for all. Content with the changes, she put down her pen. "Tonight will be a success," she muttered.

And then she went to work.

That evening
"You are a genius in the kitchen" came a

husky voice, soft enough for Zoe to hear over the yelling and cooking noise from Chef Henri and his assistants.

She looked left and flinched in shock at how close the footman, Robert, stood to her. As she continued to whisk the egg whites, while holding the bowl at the perfect fifteen-degree angle, she took a step back to put more space between them. That she was an excellent chef was true. A genius? That had been her father.

Now was not the time to disagree with Robert's praise.

Every second of this evening mattered. Every second increased her taut nerves. She hated cooking in the same kitchen as Chef Henri, whose every look in her direction was icy and critical. Because he refused to allow the windows open, the kitchen temperature neared unbearable. He was quicksand to all the joy, pleasure, and beauty she usually experienced while cooking.

As long as he and his assistants continued to ignore her, she could endure the heat.

Zoe smiled at Robert, then nodded toward the platters of hors d'oeuvres to begin the dinner's third course. To achieve a successful twelve-course dinner in four hours in *service à la russe,* courses must be brought to the table in sequence. At the precise time.

Precise.

Or else.

Robert leaned against the counter as if he had all the time in the world. "While I was clearing the oyster platters, the talk was about the vinaigrette you'd made. The banker you asked me to observe wholeheartedly agreed."

Zoe's curiosity perked up. "Oh. What was said about ze soups?"

He shrugged. "What does it matter? You didn't make any."

"I wish to know."

"No one seemed overly impressed with any of them."

Not surprising. None of Chef Henri's soups had ever impressed her. If Papa were alive, elephant consommé would never have been put on the menu.

Zoe moistened her dry lips, then glanced down at the upside-down watch pinned to her apron's bib. One minute left to whisk the eggs and then she —

"Girl, where are the truffles?" Chef Henri bellowed in French, and Zoe flinched. He never spoke to her while catering a dinner. Nor had he said a word to her when Papa introduced them four years before.

Because Chef Henri behaved as if he was entitled to respect — but mostly because there was no person she disliked more — Zoe responded in English. "On ze supply shelf." *Where all is organized alphabetically.* Despite the ache in her arm, Zoe kept whisking the eggs into a stiff froth. "Go," she ordered Robert. To convey urgency, she motioned with her eyes to Mr. Peterson, the ever-punctual butler, who carried the third-course wine selection.

That was all it took to prod Robert into action. He grabbed two platters of hors d'oeuvres.

Zoe checked the time. Almost finished whisking.

"Find them for me!"

She jerked her attention to the center of the kitchen, where Chef Henri stood at the chopping block counter, preparing the filling for the roasted fowls. She waited for one of Chef Henri's assistants to aid him. Doing so was their job. At this point of the evening, her only responsibility was her three remaining dishes.

No one moved to help.

Zoe stopped whisking. She peeked at her watch and then at Chef Henri's glaring face and then to the bowl of perfectly stiffened egg whites she held. Now was the exact moment to add them to the cooled coffee mixture. Chef Henri was closer to the larder than she was. In three steps he could grab the truffles from —

He punctuated his "Now!" with fists pounding the chopping block. "Or you will never work in this city again!"

Every assistant stared at Zoe.

If she helped, her soufflé would be ruined. If she disobeyed —

It is better to give an artist what he wants than to argue with him. Papa's admonishment echoed louder in her mind than any of the kitchen sounds.

Thus she set down the bowl of stiffened whites and went in search of truffles.

Sometime after midnight

Zoe dropped the scrubbing brush and covered her mouth with the back of her hand, shielding anyone from seeing her yawn. Not that anyone would. For the last hour, Chef Henri's assistants, in their bundled coats and scarves, sat outside on the benches under the basement windows, looking up to the street level, smoking, and sharing the remaining food and several bottles of wine from the dinner. They had no more concern for the evening temperature than they did for helping her clean the kitchen's disarray. At least the two footmen had helped with removing the trash.

She gripped the kettle in the sink and closed her eyes, taking a moment to rest. The dishwater was lukewarm. Once she finished washing the last of Mrs. Gilfoyle-Crane's copper kettle, she needed to . . . needed to . . . to —

Her chin hit her chest. Zoe gasped and jolted awake. She stretched her eyes open, slapping her cheeks with her wet palms and shaking her head until the drowsiness passed. Now was not the time to fall asleep. She withdrew the last copper kettle from the dishwater, rinsed it, and then grabbed the drying towel.

The kitchen door opened.

"Miss de Fleur?" came Mr. Peterson's reserved voice. "Your presence is requested in the drawing room."

Zoe looked to where the impeccably dressed butler stood next to the kitchen's propped open door. How did he manage not to look tired? Like her, he had been awake since before dawn.

Leaving the kettle on the counter next to the plethora of washed dishes, she followed Mr. Peterson out of the kitchen.

They climbed the stairs to the main floor on ground level, then made their way down the marble hallway to the front of the house. Light from the crystal chandelier shone brightly in the drawing room. Mrs. Gilfoyle-Crane sat in a chair by the crackling hearth. Brilliantly arrayed in diamonds and a pale oyster gown from the House of Worth, she looked as beautiful and pristine as she had when the dinner had begun — six hours ago!

Chef Henri sat on the gold velvet settee in front of the heavily draped double windows.

Zoe stepped into the room.

Chef Henri stood.

Zoe found her place on the Persian rug's center medallion.

Mrs. Gilfoyle-Crane motioned for Chef Henri to leave the room.

He dipped his head in acknowledgment. As he passed Zoe, the corner of his mouth indented.

"I expected better from you," Mrs. Gilfoyle-Crane announced the moment they were alone.

Zoe blinked, confident she had not heard correctly.

"Chef Henri explained everything, specifically your interaction with the footmen." Mrs. Gilfoyle-Crane sighed.

That one breath conveyed all Zoe needed to know.

Disappointment.

"Did my cooking meet your expectations?" Zoe asked, and hoped her tone did not sound desperate and insecure.

"Of course it did" — Mrs. Gilfoyle-Crane shifted on the chair — "and that is why it devastates me to have to ask you to leave."

Leave?

Zoe stared in shock.

Mrs. Gilfoyle-Crane strode to the hearth. Her gaze focused on the crackling flames, her hands clasped tight. "Your unimposing nature causes you to be overlooked and overpowered by others. Your father knew this . . . and believed you had the skills to be one of the finest chefs in the country. Before he died, he asked me to help you rise to your potential." She regarded Zoe. "That is why I have put up the collateral you need to secure a loan for your own restaurant. I know your cooking rivals Chef Henri's."

"You zink too highly of me."

"And you think too poorly of yourself." Said in a manner more firm and decisive than anything Zoe had ever heard her employer speak. "You need someone to believe in you so you can learn to believe in yourself."

Zoe studied her clenched hands.

"Tonight wasn't a failure." Mrs. Gilfoyle-Crane's words drew Zoe's attention. "Your dishes impressed Mr. Soutter. You will go to the bank at two o'clock tomorrow afternoon to sign the loan papers and discuss available locations for you to rent. Mr. Soutter is expecting you."

Managing a restaurant was beyond her expertise. Papa had never worked in a restaurant either; he had only served as a private chef. To those of noble blood. To those of nouveau-riche blood.

And yet Zoe nodded at Mrs. Gilfoyle-Crane's command.

"You may stay here through the end of the week. I have done all I can to help you build your reputation. However, I cannot continue to employ a household cook who fraternizes with the men in my service when she should be focused on her work." Mrs. Gilfoyle-Crane gave a sad shake of her head. "I'm sorry, Zoe. I know you did nothing of the sort, but Chef Henri will say otherwise."

Zoe regarded the crackling fire, mesmerized by how it flickered and moved on its own. Nothing forced it. Yet it stayed confined to the hearth even when it had the power to consume this room, this home. It stayed because it had no mind of its own. It stayed because it was as subjugated as Chef Henri's assistants.

She looked at Mrs. Gilfoyle-Crane. "When

I was at ze critical point of my soufflé, if I had explained zat to Chef Henri, would he have asked someone else to help him?"

Mrs. Gilfoyle-Crane was quiet for a moment. "I am quite aware of his attitude toward women chefs. Despite his medieval and misogynistic views — and I am disgusted at the position in which he has put me — I must behave as if I believe his word over yours."

Tears blurred Zoe's vision.

"Please tell me you understand why I must do this," Mrs. Gilfoyle-Crane said.

Zoe nodded.

Mrs. Gilfoyle-Crane's reputation in society would be impugned by standing beside a lowly female's word over that of the esteemed president of the Société Culinaire. She needed Chef Henri catering her dinners more than she needed Zoe to be her household cook.

"Why does he hate me?" Zoe asked. "I am insignificant to him."

"As I would be, were it not for Mr. Crane's bank account. Men like Chef Henri —" Mrs. Gilfoyle-Crane waved at nothing. "Enough about him. I see greatness in you, Zoe de Fleur, but you need someone to push you out of your complacency."

"You do zis for my own good?" Zoe could

not help but ask.

"Yes, dear girl, I do." Mrs. Gilfoyle-Crane walked to Zoe. "You will become a great chef once you learn to stand firm for what you know is right. Don't let any man limit your success."

"I shall never forget all you have done for me . . . and for Papa," Zoe managed to say despite the tightness in her throat. "I will make you proud."

Mrs. Gilfoyle-Crane smiled. "You already have. I'll be here for you if you need me. Now go conquer the world."

CHAPTER TWO

Later that morning

Zoe trailed her gloved fingers along the marble wall surrounding Crane house. She strolled with no need to hurry. In three days, she had to leave the only home she had known since emigrating with Papa to America. But she was also free of the incessant competition between Mrs. Gilfoyle-Crane and her sister, *the* Mrs. Marsden — the designation hers — to prove which one of them hosted the best dinner parties. Why did it matter?

A party should never be a means to affirm status in society or lead siblings into a verbal battle.

A party should be about spending time with loved ones.

Into Zoe's mind popped the memory of Papa sitting at a table with her, enjoying the tea and pastries she had prepared. Vision blurring, she stopped walking. Tears slid down her cheeks. She sniffed and wiped them away in time to see a rock skipped across the sidewalk. It landed exactly where her next step should be. She looked up.

Ahead on the corner was Nico, waving and grinning broadly.

Zoe trudged forward.

He had not been on the corner when she left the mansion to walk to Central Park. He seemed more interested in her than in waving papers at the carriages, hackneys, and wagons moving as slowly down the street as she was.

"How was the dinner party?" he called out.

As she neared Nico, she eyed the space between him and the marble wall. She could easily slide past him and turn down the alley, but before she reached the servants' entrance, he would have caught up to her. Such an action of hers would only incite his curiosity. As much as she wished to avoid him — avoid everyone — the wisest thing would be to behave as usual.

Which was why she stopped at the corner and said, "Ze dinner was a success."

"I knew it would be." He tipped up his cap and frowned. "You don't look well. I've never seen your face so blotchy. You sick?"

"Ze night was long and my sleep fitful."

41

Of the five hours she had lain in bed, she may have slept an hour. She glanced inside his cart. Four papers comprised what was left of his stack.

"You want a paper?" he asked.

Zoe hesitated. If she had a newspaper, she could ask Mrs. Horton to help her find a boardinghouse or an apartment in the classifieds.

She nodded. "Wait here. I will go find a nickel."

He gave her a sheepish look. "Uh, you wouldn't have any leftover dinner, would you?"

"Zere is some." She tried to smile, but her heart ached too much to put on a mask of false cheer. "Why do you ask?"

"How about a trade?" He looked hopeful. "A paper for lunch."

On the tip of her tongue was *When did you eat last?* She suspected his last meal had been the one she had served him yesterday.

Instead, she said, "Come with me."

She turned down the alley. Once they reached the basement stairs, Nico stored his cart beside the Crane house's servants' entrance. He grabbed a paper, then opened the door. She led him down the hallway to the kitchen. After their coats and hats were hung on the wall pegs, she pulled on her apron and wrapped the kerchief around her head. Mrs. Horton, whom she expected to see in the kitchen when she returned from her walk, was nowhere to be seen. The dear woman must be managing the housecleaning . . . or meeting with Mrs. Gilfoyle-Crane. A new household cook would need to be hired. If Mrs. Horton failed to find one, she would be responsible for the cooking until one was employed.

Which did not have to be. Zoe could stay and cook.

Tears again blurred her vision.

Blinking them away, Zoe pointed to the table in the far corner of the kitchen. "Sit."

Nico obeyed.

Zoe then focused on her work. She warmed the oven, collected a pot of stew from the icebox to feed her fellow servants, set it on the cookstove for it to reheat, grabbed a dinner plate, and then descended to the cellar to study the contents. The remains of last night's banquet would be enough for Nico. She filled his plate with salted petit fours and a few dry and glazed ones, leaving what was on the platter for the rest of the staff to enjoy with their stew.

She eyed the shelves. The cellar needed restocking after last night's dinner. She should go after her meeting at the bank and —

Her chest tightened, her pulse raced, her heart pounded, and she suddenly felt moisture on her forehead. The ceiling had no leak. Could it be . . . ? She touched her face. Why was she perspiring? She shivered. The cellar was nippy, even more so in the winter. It was so cold down here that fine hairs on her arm verily stood tall. Verily? A panicked bubble of laughter slipped across her lips. Why did she laugh? She had nothing to laugh about. And yet another panicked bubble of laughter slipped out.

Unsure of what was happening to her, she grabbed a half-filled bottle of milk, pulled the string to turn off the light, and then hurried up the steps to the kitchen. She closed the cellar door. Leaning against it, she drew in a deep, calming breath. The strange panic that had washed over her began to lift.

"You all right?" Nico asked.

Zoe nodded. She walked to the table. "Please say grace," she said, setting the heaping plate of food and the milk bottle in front of him. She waited until he bowed his head before she closed her eyes.

"Come, Lord Jesus, be our Guest, and let these gifts to us be blessed. Amen."

"Amen," she echoed. Leaving him to eat,

she stepped to the worktable in the center of the kitchen. She lifted the fine cloth covering the rolls she had prepared before leaving for her walk to the park. Perfect. She slid them into the oven to bake.

After making herself a cup of café au lait, she sat across from Nico.

He frowned. "Aren't you going to eat?"

She shook her head. Truth was, she had no appetite.

Where was Mrs. Horton?

Zoe glanced at the kitchen door, then at the watch pinned to her apron bodice. The time for the housekeeper to prepare Mr. Gilfoyle's breakfast tray had passed. Zoe had little time to spare to wait around to help her. In an hour and four minutes, she must leave for the bank. She must change clothes. She must —

Her lungs tightened, restricting air, and her heart pounded like horses racing down a track. What was this happening to her?

Hearing a noise from the hallway, Zoe glanced again to the kitchen door. She waited.

It stayed closed.

"You worried about someone finding me here?" Nico asked.

"No. Everyone knows I feed you from time to time."

"Then why do you keep looking at the door?"

"Mrs. Horton should be arriving soon with Mr. Gilfoyle's meal request."

"Ah, the Nephew." Nico returned his attention to his food. "I've seen him come and go with that odd dog of his."

Zoe lifted the teacup to her lips. As she sipped the warm café au lait, the kitchen door was flung open.

"Miss Difflers, I —"

She froze.

Manchester Gilfoyle IV, in a three-piece gray suit, stepped into her kitchen, clenching his black derby in one hand and the leash of his three-legged dog in the other . . . and looking decidedly annoyed. The door closed. His dog lay down and released a low-pitched "awrrr-oomph."

Mr. Gilfoyle's mouth pressed together in an angry line. "You have a guest," he said, glaring at Zoe.

"Nico sells papers on ze corner. Your aunt encourages her staff to show kindness to all." She looked from Mr. Gilfoyle to Nico, then back to him. According to the staff, Mr. Gilfoyle called all servants "you there." He had called her Miss Difflers this time. Better than when he called her Miss de Flowers. She set her teacup on its saucer.

46

"Is zere something you need?"

He quirked a brow. "My aunt told me what transpired. I've heard the servants laud your kindness, so I am surprised you would attempt to sabotage such a great chef."

The sabotaging had been Chef Henri's. She would never!

Mr. Gilfoyle tapped his derby against his thigh. "Before you leave my aunt's employment on Saturday, you will prepare me a five-course meal which will include poulet à la crème and mille-feuille."

"Why?" Nico put in. "She doesn't work for you."

Mr. Gilfoyle's blue-eyed gaze narrowed upon Nico, and Zoe had the distinct impression he was weighing and measuring the boy and his impertinent comment.

"Who are you?" he asked.

Nico's chin lifted. "I'm Miss de Fleur's friend. Close friend. Almost a brother."

His answer was enough — or possibly more — than Mr. Gilfoyle sincerely wished to know, because he turned his annoyed attention to Zoe. "Inform Mrs. Wharton to deliver the food at two-fifteen Saturday afternoon. Not a minute later."

"You mean Mrs. Hor—"

"Shh." Zoe hushed Nico before he impolitely corrected his — their — superior. She considered Mr. Gilfoyle but then paused, taking time to choose her words. "It has been an honor to cook for you."

He stared at her blankly before blinking and saying, "Of course." After he gave a minuscule tug on the leash, his dog rolled onto its feet. The pair left the kitchen.

"I don't know what all the fuss is about," Nico said. "The man is a bad egg."

Zoe ignored the insult.

Nico gulped the last of the milk. He set the bottle on the table. "I take it Mrs. Gilfoyle-Crane sacked you because of Chef On-ree?"

Zoe nodded, then pulled the newspaper in front of her.

"I don't mean no offense," Nico said in a most caring tone, "but can you read any of that?"

"*New York Times.* March 1, 1888." She pointed at a paragraph. "Zis, no."

"You speak pretty decent."

"I understand English when I hear it, most of ze time, but words written —" She shrugged. "English has too many conundrums, too many exceptions, too many inconsistencies with pronunciations. Why is *trough* pronounced *troff, rough* pronounced *ruff, bough* pronounced *bow* to rhyme with *cow,* and *through* pronounced *throo*? All too confusing."

"Like reading Shakespeare."

"I have never read his work," Zoe said with pride. "Before leaving France for America, Papa took me to a performance of *Romeo and Juliet.* Adulation for ze play confounds me. It was a pleasant story with an expected ending."

Nico's eyes widened. "You expected *that* ending?"

She nodded. "A romance always ends with a happily ever after."

"You must have seen a different play than I did."

"I wish I had not seen it at all."

"Sometimes I think you're strange." Nico grabbed the paper. "So, what are you looking for?"

"I need work and zen a place to live."

His brow furrowed as he studied her. "Why stay in the city? If I were you, I would start over somewhere new, where people appreciated my cooking. I'd also want to cook for someone who doesn't believe the worst of me when he hears criticism like the Nephew did."

Zoe opened her mouth, but the back of her throat tightened and closed, hindering her from speaking. Leave the city? Start over somewhere new?

At that thought, the tightness in her throat abated.

If she found employment in a private residence as a household cook, she would oversee the kitchen her way. She could make a home there. Perhaps she would marry the butler or gardener. They could live in a little cottage beside the grand house and start a family. She would no longer have to have a job. She would no longer have to work. She could be a wife and a mother. Everything could be perfect again.

If she started over somewhere new.

If.

When.

When?

Needing a moment to ponder this new possibility, she sipped her lukewarm café au lait. She liked to try new things. She liked to experience new things. She had loved the anticipation she felt each time she and Papa moved from one castle in France to another. When Papa suggested they move to America, she happily agreed to another exciting adventure . . . because they were together. She now had no one to journey to the unknown with. No one.

Could she do this on her own?

If Papa were here, he would say she should never leave the future to chance, and instead do all she could do today to make her future better. That was how he had lived.

"Carpe diem," she whispered.

"Here's something!" Nico slapped the folded newspaper on the table, then turned it to face her. He pointed at an eight-line advertisement. " 'Finest kitchen west of the Mississippi seeks trained chef. Only women need apply.' "

Zoe studied the words. The only words she recognized were *fine* and *dining,* which must also mean *kitchen* in the English language. As for the Mississippi River, she thought it divided the country in half, but she was unsure. That the river was not next to New York she knew with confidence.

She looked at Nico. "Where is zis kitchen located?"

"Denver, Colorado."

"Colorado is in ze middle of ze United States, yes?"

He nodded.

"Zat is too far to travel."

"No. It's barely over the Mississippi." He leaned forward. "I heard Denver is called the New York of the West. It's an exciting town, Miss de Fleur. Here in New York, you are one of dozens of French chefs. Denver — well, I doubt they have more than one. If that. Move there and you'll reach stardom."

"Stardom?"

"You'd be a celebrity."

"Ah." Zoe moistened her bottom lip as she considered being a cook in Denver. Any job would be temporary until she fell in love and married. "Is zis kitchen in a hotel?"

"Does that matter?"

"I have never worked in a restaurant, but I know zey are loud, smoke-filled, and busy." She leaned forward and lowered her voice. "I fear I will abhor it."

Nico turned the paper and read the advertisement. His brow furrowed. "I'm pretty sure this is a private residence. It also says chefs will be required to demonstrate their skills. That shouldn't be a problem. You're the best chef in all of New York." His lips parted, and he hesitated a moment before saying, "I could go with you, if you'd like. Help read things. I don't suppose you can write English, either."

She shook her head.

"You really need me to go with you."

Having him along would be convenient.

Zoe beheld the spacious kitchen and sighed. This was no longer her home. If she left now for Denver, Colorado, she could miss the meeting at the bank. She would spare herself the discomfort of explaining to Mr. Soutter why she did not wish to take out a loan or even open a restaurant. If she left now, she could avoid Mrs. Gilfoyle-Crane and her vocal disappointment that Zoe had refused a loan. If she left now, she would not have to cook a meal for a man who was too full of himself to learn another person's name.

She wanted to create delicious food for people who appreciated her skills.

And she could.

In Denver.

Where she would meet the man of her dreams.

She smiled at Nico. "We shall go West."

Capitol Hill, Denver, Colorado
Tuesday, March 6

Zoe rested her gloved hands atop the blue-beaded reticule in the lap of her blue-striped dress as she waited for Mrs. Archer to return to the parlor. The woman's two-story wood-framed home paled in size to the Crane house, but the ornate carved mantel and the wall paneling looked to be made of mahogany, Zoe's favorite wood. Sunshine streamed through the windows framed with yellow silk curtains. The room smelled of roses. Likely from the four arrangements about the room.

She breathed deeply.

Her future home would have fresh flowers. Brought home by her husband.

She loved the house's dollhouse-style architecture. She loved the porch that wrapped around the front and sides. She loved that the house had been painted the same shade of yellow as the parlor curtains, while the spindles and fish-scale shingles under the eaves were a vivid peacock blue. Most of all, she loved how the parquet de Versailles in the hallway flowed beautifully into the parlor. Were she to ever own a home, she would choose warm wooden floors over cold marble flooring like in the Crane house, which was exquisite to look at yet required constant washing.

Nico bumped his arm against hers. "Why are you smiling?"

"Zis could be my new home."

His mouth indented in one corner. "Could be." He patted her arm. "Thanks for inviting me to come with you to Denver. This is a new opportunity for both of us."

Zoe nodded, yet felt as if his words held an additional meaning. What could it be? He had offered to join her, had he not? Or had she done the inviting? She could not recall.

What mattered was that he had been gracious in helping her purchase tickets for her travel in a ladies' Pullman car, while he happily traveled in third class. He even found them a lovely hotel next to the cable line. He had secured directions to Mrs. Archer's home. Even though Zoe disliked his insistence at the depot and to every conductor on the journey that they were siblings, Nico had been a true friend.

"Ah, here we are," Mrs. Archer said cheerfully, sailing into the room with a thick folder in her hand, her lime-green taffeta skirt rustling. "I apologize for making you wait. You are the first prospect to arrive in person." She sat in a chair opposite Zoe and Nico. "This isn't how I usually do this. Everyone else has sent a letter, per the dictates of the advertisement . . . but because you're such a beautiful young woman, well-mannered and well-spoken, I'll adjust." Her brown-eyed gaze lowered to the coffee table's bare surface, her smile dying and her brow furrowing. "Antonia didn't bring refreshments?"

Zoe exchanged a glance with Nico.

He shrugged.

She looked at Mrs. Archer. "No one has seen to us."

Mrs. Archer glanced at the grandfather clock in the corner, farthest from the crackling fire in the hearth. "She may have left already to visit Luanne, so I shan't complain about her absentmindedness. In the last nine months, Luanne has taught my daughter more about behaving as a lady should than I've been able to accomplish in twenty-four years. Antonia even joined the Ladies' Aid Society at church. I know she only did so because Luanne had. I choose to see this as Antonia finally moving past her grief over her father's unexpected passing. He died eighteen months ago."

Zoe smiled to be polite.

Mrs. Archer rested the file on her lap. "Mrs. Luanne Bennett is a few years older than Mr. Gunderson —"

Mr. Gunderson?

"— but their families are close." Mrs. Archer took a breath. "Luanne highly endorsed him. If you wish to interview her, I know she will agree. She confirmed everything in his letters, as well as those letters from his three references — a judge, a reverend, and a prominent widow. My standard practice when an unfamiliar man secures my services is to seek out additional references. My clients, except Mr. Gunderson, live here in Denver."

Clients? Had Mrs. Gilfoyle-Crane been this detailed prior to hiring Papa? Zoe could not remember. Unsure if Mrs. Archer expected a response, Zoe continued to smile

And Mrs. Archer continued to talk. "I subject them to intense interviews to ensure their motivations are sincere. Jakob Gunderson is" — she gazed heavenward for a long moment — "let's say he is less affluent than my regular clients, not that he is poor by any stretch of the imagination. His family owns an exclusive resale shop in Helena and is working toward opening a second store, which Mr. Gunderson will manage. Of course, I don't know why a man of his ilk isn't already married." She sighed.

Zoe shifted in the chair, trying to make sense of the woman's treatise on her client, Mr. Jakob Gunderson. Could he be the one who wished to hire a chef? "Madame Archer, where is Helena?"

"In the Montana Territory," Mrs. Archer answered.

Zoe looked to Nico.

"The state above Colorado is Wyoming," he said with devastating calm, "and Montana Territory is far north of here. It's uncivilized. You don't want to go."

Upon the first opportunity, Zoe was going to buy a map of America.

Mrs. Archer's confused gaze shifted from Nico to Zoe. "My dear Miss de Fleur, Montana sounds farther away than it is.

Helena is quite civilized. Over ten thousand people live there." Mrs. Archer opened the file. "Let me find you Jakob Gunderson's photograph. Once you see it and read his letters, you will understand my willingness to help him find a bride."

"A bride?" Zoe interjected. "I wish to apply for ze chef's position. Ze one posted in ze *New York Times.* Zat is you, yes?"

Mrs. Archer blinked a few times. Her gaze then shifted to Nico.

Zoe turned on the settee to face Nico, who sat there with a strange, smug grin. "Is zere something you failed to tell me?"

"I lied, Zoe, about the newspaper ad. It wasn't for a chef. It was for" — he shrugged — "a mail-order bride. Tell Mrs. Archer you aren't interested and we can leave."

Men ordered brides to be delivered by the mail? She had never heard of such a thing.

Zoe opened her reticule. She withdrew the folded advertisement she had clipped out of the newspaper, then offered it to Mrs. Archer. "Will you read zis to me?"

Mrs. Archer took it from her. " 'WANTED: Correspondence with a refined lady aged eighteen to twenty-three with a view to matrimony. The Montana Territory gentleman, aged twenty-two, conducts business in the city, enjoys an active routine, including the theater and fine dining, and faithful church attendance. Send inquiries and references to the Archer Matrimonial Co., Denver, Colorado.' "

Zoe looked at Mrs. Archer in confusion. "Zere is no 'finest kitchen west of ze Mississippi?' "

She shook her head.

"No chef wanted?"

She shook her head again. "Miss de Fleur, I would be remiss if I didn't ask if you can read English."

Zoe opened her mouth to confess her limitation.

"I made it up," Nico blurted out. "It was all I could think of to convince you to leave New York. Besides, you didn't want to stay there and open a restaurant anyway."

Zoe stared at him, stunned. "I fail to understand why you would lie about such a zing."

"I had to." A shadow fell across his features, literally from a cloud, perhaps, blocking the sun, and yet he looked weary and repentant. "Grand Central Depot refused to sell me a ticket. Said children had to travel with an adult. I was desperate, Zoe. Life will be so much easier for me if you keep pretending to be my sister. Please, please believe me when I say I did this for your own good."

"And yours," Mrs. Archer murmured.

He raised his chin. "Zoe, you said it yourself — carpe diem. You have to admit we've had fun. We're a good team."

Zoe moistened her bottom lip. What fun it had been, meeting Nico at Grand Central Depot, and then starting West in hope of a grand future. It had been the first time she had felt eager expectation since Papa's death.

Carpe diem.

She *had* seized the day and loved every minute of it.

Her sketchbook contained drawings of the ladies who had traveled all or part of the trip to Denver, of a ferry boat on the Mississippi, and of bison in Kansas. She had seen the most glorious sunsets and sunrises over the plains. The farther they traveled from New York, the greater space between towns and homes and any sign of civilization amid the rolling hills and expansive grasslands. And the Rocky Mountains —

Oh, to explore them as she and Papa had explored the Alps and Pyrenees and Vosges.

After all the serenity she had seen — *felt* while traveling West — she refused to return to New York. Maybe this was how God was answering her prayers. Ever since Papa died, she had been alone. Until this trip. It would be nice to have a family of her own, where Nico could live as her brother.

She wanted a husband. And children. And a pet dog . . . and a bird that talked.

But to marry a man who ordered a bride like one ordered a dress from a catalog? To marry a stranger?

She waited for her lungs to tighten, for her pulse to race, for the panic to strike her as it had at the Crane house when she thought of going to the bank to secure a loan.

She felt no panic. She felt —

Intrigued.

"I wish to see Mr. Gunderson's photograph."

Mrs. Archer placed the advertisement in the file, then withdrew a photograph. She gave it to Zoe, who immediately sighed with pleasure. With his light hair and strong jaw, Mr. Gunderson was a handsome man. Had he or his parents emigrated from Scandinavia?

"Zis man is impressive."

"Indeed he is," Mrs. Archer put in.

Nico bumped against her shoulder. "He doesn't look that impressive to me."

"His eyes are happy," Zoe noted. Just like Papa's had been.

Mrs. Archer smiled. "Interesting description, and fitting. Jakob Gunderson's references all described him as a happy man. Would you like me to read his letters?"

Zoe hesitated, her cheeks warming with embarrassment. She was unable to correspond with him without dictating her letter to someone else. "Is writing to him my only option?"

Nico stared gap-mouthed at her. "I can't believe you're considering this."

Zoe ignored him.

Mrs. Archer did as well. "Written correspondence is usually the first stage in courtship. Seeing that you appear refined, intelligent, and have an interest in cooking, I believe we can move on to the second stage, whereby the potential bride — that would be you — moves to the client's hometown, where he secures reputable boarding for sixty days, during which the two of you engage in a proper courtship. I would need to telegraph Mr. Gunderson first to see if this change is acceptable to him."

This seemed reasonable.

"What if your client is a bad egg?" Nico asked.

"That, young man, is a fair question." Mrs. Archer looked at the grandfather clock, then at Zoe. "If at any time the potential bride, whom I shall refer to as you, feels pressured or threatened or realizes my client has not been forthright, you may return to Denver using the train ticket I will give you. I will then help you secure reputable employment. However, do know I have several other clients, men of great means, with whom you would be suitable. One of whom speaks French."

Nico pressed his lips into a peevish expression. "This all sounds fishy."

Zoe nipped at her bottom lip. Maybe she should be warier, like Nico.

Mrs. Archer laid Mr. Gunderson's file on the table between them. "I am an honest businesswoman. If necessary, I can supply references, including ones from the city marshal and the regional judge."

"I'd like to read them," Nico answered, "*if* we were taking your offer seriously. But we aren't." He stood. "Come on, Zoe. I saw several chef openings in the newspaper."

Zoe stayed seated.

"I'm serious." Nico's voice rose. "If you do this, I won't help you. There's no future for us in Montana."

Zoe studied Mrs. Archer. Nothing about the older woman seemed dishonest. But then, neither had Zoe suspected Nico had been anything but honest. He had lied repeatedly and too easily. Although she never would have left New York were it not for Nico. This *was* a new opportunity for them both.

Jakob Gunderson might become a wonderful husband.

She should give him a chance. If his courtship failed, she could return to Denver. She had options. Best of all, this was her choice. Not Mrs. Gilfoyle-Crane's. Not Nico's. Hers. To seize what she truly wanted — a husband, a home, a family for her to love, feed, and cherish.

She studied the photograph of Jakob Gunderson and his happy eyes. "Mrs. Archer, I would like zis man to court me."

CHAPTER THREE

Helena, Montana
Friday, March 9, 1888

Isaak Gunderson bounced his fingertips against his thigh while he waited in the wedding reception line to congratulate his employee, Emilia, and her new husband. What was taking so long?

He tilted his head to the side. Emilia and Mac were nodding and smiling at Mrs. Simpson, a widow, who was holding up the line with a long discourse. Seeing her reminded Isaak to check on Mrs. Johnston, one of the widows in his church. He pulled a notebook and pencil from inside his coat pocket and added the task to his ongoing list. Perhaps he should have given up chairing the Widows and Orphans Committee when he decided to run for mayor of Helena, but the heavy campaigning wouldn't kick off until May, and he didn't want the church committee to return to its haphazard and inefficient ways.

A quiet, "About time," came from the man ahead of Isaak in the reception line.

It took considerable effort not to reprimand the older gentleman for allowing a rude comment to pass his lips in the presence of ladies, but Isaak held his tongue as he took a small step forward. To answer rudeness with rudeness did no good.

Isaak tucked the notebook and pencil back inside his coat while glancing around the basement reception hall. His eyes snagged on Madame Lestraude standing near — but not against — a wall. Even though she was the groom's mother, she didn't belong here. Given the wide circle of open space around her, the other wedding guests agreed.

Everyone except Emilia's father, who stood chatting with the brothel owner who'd nearly succeeded in selling both of his daughters into prostitution. Mr. Stanek clearly ascribed to Emilia's philosophy of showing forgiveness in the same measure as Christ meted out. Isaak honored them for their charity, but wasn't sure he could be as forbearing given the same circumstances.

The line moved again.

He stepped forward to greet the bride. Emilia McCall glowed in a gown of creamy satin and lace.

"Mrs. McCall." Isaak lifted her hand with his right hand and bowed over it per custom, but he laid his left hand over the top and gave it an extra squeeze. "It was a beautiful ceremony. I wish you and Mac every happiness."

Tears filled her caramel-colored eyes. "Thank you, Mr. Gunderson. And thank you for everything you've done to make this day possible."

"It was nothing." He took another step and greeted her husband. "You're a lucky man."

Mac's smile was filled with awed pride, and his handshake was stronger than usual. "I'm well aware."

Isaak wanted to say more, but his throat constricted with sudden emotion. Even though Mac was four and a half years older, he and Isaak had forged a tight bond over the past year. In fact, lately it felt like Mac was more a brother than Jakob was. Isaak squeezed Mac's hand tighter in lieu of words. Based on the way Mac sobered and tightened his grip in return, he understood all the things Isaak wanted to say but couldn't.

"I'll take good care of her." Mac let go of Isaak's hand and smiled at his bride.

Emilia turned her gaze to her husband, and the look of love that passed between them twisted Isaak's heart with unmistakable envy. He didn't want to be married. Not yet anyway. He was only twenty-two with a long list of things he needed to accomplish before taking a bride, but the rationale didn't loosen the knot in his chest.

Isaak moved away from the formal reception line to where Luci Stanek was waiting for him. Like her sister, Luci was petite. Unlike her sister, she looked older than her years in a cotton print dress with a pink silk sash and small bustle in the back. Emilia had chosen it to make Luci feel fancy without being too sophisticated for a thirteen-year-old, and because it could be worn to parties at the Truetts' or to church sometimes. Quite a practical choice.

Luci threw her arms around his waist. "Hi, Mr. Gunderson."

He patted her back, then pulled away. "I hear you will be staying with the Truetts while your sister is on her honeymoon."

Luci nodded, her brown curls bouncing against her shoulders. "But not until next week. Roch is staying for a few more days before reporting to Fort Missoula. He and Da are going to ride there together, so I get to stay with Melrose until Da gets back."

Luci's gaze traveled across the reception hall. "It's a nice turnout, isn't it?" She twisted her neck to look to her far right. "Even the mayor, the city marshal, and that other judge — the one that made Emilia and Roch stay in jail last year — are here." There was a tiny hitch in her voice.

Was she still affected by what her sister's first husband — a man she'd never met — had almost done? Or by Edgar Dunfree's near molestation of her? Both men were dead, and the scandal had died when a more sensational news item monopolized the front page: the murder of Joseph Hendry who had been a reporter for the *Daily Independent.*

Isaak patted the girl's back again to offer some consolation. He was about to ask if there was anything he could do to help, but Melrose Truett bounded up to Luci, pulling her arm and whispering in her ear about whatever thirteen-year-old girls found fascinating.

He turned his attention to greeting friends and acquaintances, all of whom were eager to hear what he planned to do if he won the mayoral election in November. Mr. Palmer wanted less horse dung on Helena Avenue by making all the streetcars steam powered; Mr. Watson wanted part of the proceeds from the annual Harvest Festival to go to the school district; Mr. Truett wanted to get rid of the steam-powered streetcar already running because it belched smoke and was so loud it spooked horses; Mr. Cannon wanted stricter punishment for counterfeiters; Mrs. Danbury wanted to know when the red-light district was going to be shut down for good. After about ten minutes of informal campaigning, Isaak went in search of his brother.

Jakob was near the back of the reception hall, pulling coins and penny candy from behind the ears of a small crowd of boys.

Desiring a moment alone with his brother, Isaak turned the boys' attention to the wedding cake and they all scampered off. "Seems like yesterday we were that young."

Jakob offered Isaak a piece of candy. "And Ma and Pa always made us wait until everyone else was served."

"I was thinking the same thing." Isaak placed the candy in his mouth, tucking it between his teeth and cheek. "How are things going down at the new store?"

Jakob reached in his coat pocket and withdrew a second piece of candy for himself. "Great. In fact, things are going so well, I'm taking tomorrow morning off."

Isaak crushed the candy between his teeth.

This lack of focus on Jakob's part was exactly why he couldn't be trusted to make sure the new store opened on time. Isaak swallowed the shards of sweet. "I don't recall you saying anything about needing to be gone before now."

Jakob looked out over the crowded hall. "It came up a bit ago."

"A bit as in an hour or a week ago?"

"Does it matter?" Jakob's tone was clipped.

Isaak's temper heated. "It does when it affects the schedule for the grand opening of The Import Company." He dislodged a stray piece of candy from behind his molar with his tongue while telling himself to remain calm. "You're barely keeping to the schedule as it is. How can you afford to take a whole morning off?"

Jakob started walking, tipping his head to indicate that Isaak should follow. Once they reached a more secluded corner of the church reception hall, Jakob stopped.

"This thing . . ." He paused and, for a flickering moment, looked nothing like his usual confident self. "It might not end up being anything."

Isaak took a slow, deep breath. "When you" — *begged* — "asked to be in charge of The Import Company's build and grand opening, you promised to follow it through to the end. This past week you've spent more time with Roch Stanek than at the store, which set your work crew back by three days. Last week, you held things up for two whole days because you couldn't decide on stain colors. And now you want more time off? I can't keep covering for you, Jake. You have no idea how much work I have to accomplish in one day. I can't afford to keep checking up on you to make sure things remain on schedule at The Import Company, too."

The tips of Jakob's ears turned red. "First of all, it's not your job to check up on me. Second, by your own admission, I'm still on schedule. And third, I don't need your permission to take the morning off to meet someone." His gaze shifted away.

Isaak turned to see who his brother was looking at.

Emilia.

What did the bride have to do with meeting someone on a Saturday morning?

Isaak tensed. No! It couldn't be, could it?

They'd talked about this. Months ago. After the Independence Day picnic when Jakob had asked what Isaak thought about a correspondence courtship. It was a nonsensical idea, which they'd both agreed on;

at least Isaak *thought* they'd agreed on it because the topic never came up again.

Until this morning at breakfast.

Isaak looked back at Jakob. "I wondered where all your talk about how lucky Mac was that Emilia answered that mail-order advertisement was leading. You've ordered yourself a bride, too. Haven't you?"

"And what if I did?" Jakob patted his own chest "Why can't I have my chance at love?"

"Because what happens if" — Isaak lowered his voice to keep the rest of the wedding guests from overhearing — "she turns out to be like one of those women who are out for money? The newspapers have been full of warnings for years."

Jakob smirked as though Isaak was the lunatic here. "I've been in contact with a matchmaker in Denver."

Was that supposed to make it better? Whether a bride-finding service was called mail-order or matchmaking didn't change the basic fact that they were all scams. "How much did you have to pay this so-called Cupid?"

Jakob pressed his lips together in a tight line.

Isaak shook his head. "That much, huh? What if this woman shows up and she's entirely unsuitable?" And she would be. In cases such as these, either the bride or groom turned out to be dishonorable — sometimes both. For proof, Jakob need only look to Emilia's near-disastrous proxy marriage to a man who intended to sell her and her sister into prostitution, or to Mrs. Wiley, their housekeeper — who'd lied about her four children to a groom who'd lied about his *prosperous* farm.

Typical Jakob — never considering the ramifications when it contradicted what he wanted to do.

Isaak raked his fingers through his hair. "You'd better not expect me to clean up after you."

"And you'd better not pull your big-brother act and mess this up for me."

"There won't be any need because tomorrow morning, when you meet this mail-order bride of yours, she'll be closer to fifty than twenty. She'll also be dragging along a relative she's never mentioned who happens to need a little money to get back on his feet."

Jakob studied the floor. After a long moment, he raised his head and spoke in a composed voice. "In which case my contract states I can put her on the train, send her back to the matchmaker in Denver, and receive a full refund."

The rationale did nothing for Isaak's temper. He glanced around the reception hall to give himself a moment to calm down. Hale Adams was looking their way with a censorious frown on his face.

Isaak turned back to his brother. "We will continue this discussion at home."

"No, we won't." Jakob tugged on the lapels of his suit coat. "I love you, Iz. You're my favorite brother, but I'm a full-grown man who can make decisions on my own."

"The wrong ones."

Jakob looked Isaak in the eye. "In your opinion."

"If you think I'm wrong, why did you hide this correspondence courtship?"

"I don't necessarily think you're wrong, I just don't think you're necessarily right either."

"What does that mean?"

Jakob opened his lips, closed them again, and huffed. "I haven't told you about any of my correspondence courtships because, after every one of them failed, I would have heard an *I told you so.*"

There'd been more women before this one?

Isaak stepped closer. "You think this next one will be any different?"

"Right there's the difference between you

and me. I *hope* it will be different. You prepare for the worst." Jakob gripped the side of Isaak's arm. "I know you always look at things to see what could go wrong so you can avoid mistakes, but that isn't always good. It closes a man off to countless possibilities. Sometimes you need to jump into something and see what happens."

The convoluted logic stopped Isaak's next argument in his throat. If Jakob believed his own nonsense, there was no reasoning with him.

Jakob released his grip. "I'm going to Ming's Opera House tonight with Yancey, Carline, and Geddes. Don't wait up for me." With that, he turned on his heel and rejoined the wedding guests.

Isaak watched his brother's progress through the crowd as he joined his friends. Both Yancey and Carline lit up the moment Jakob appeared. Of all the many reasons this mail-order or matchmaking or whatever he wanted to call it scheme was a bad idea, at least one of them should have penetrated Jakob's thick skull. And why was he in such a hurry to get married? They were only twenty-two.

This better not be another of Jakob's it'll-be-fun ideas. Courtship was a serious business. A man didn't go into it unless he was prepared to marry.

At least he *shouldn't*.

Hale walked across the hall to where Isaak stood. "In light of the fact we are celebrating a joyous event, I should be polite by not mentioning that I wasn't the only one who noticed the disagreement between you and Jakob."

Isaak grimaced. "Think I lost any votes?"

Hale pushed his wire-rimmed glasses up on his nose with one finger. "Voters have short-term memories. Anything I can do to help?"

"Actually, you might." Isaak paused for a moment to frame his question. "Have you ever run across a matchmaking service that offers a refund for a bride who doesn't turn out to be as advertised?"

Hale's eyes narrowed. "Indeed I have."

Something in his tone of voice made Isaak look closely at the man he considered an older brother and had always admired for his unflappable good sense. "You already know about Jakob and the Denver matchmaker, don't you?"

Hale's expression didn't change.

"You should have talked him out of such foolishness."

"Not my place. Not yours either, in point of fact."

Isaak groaned. Had the whole world gone mad?

He strolled through the reception, keeping a look out for important people he'd need to greet. He lifted his chin to acknowledge J. P. Fisk, the man who'd sponsored his membership to the exclusive Montana Club in downtown Helena. He'd worked hard to carve out a place beside the millionaires, elected officials, and powerful men of the territory. Sometimes his conscience said he'd gone too far, but every compromise of his integrity was for a greater purpose. A man couldn't wield power and influence for the people he served — and for those he loved — if he wasn't in a position of authority.

Regrets over things like Finn Collin's unintended death and inciting wrath against Joseph Hendry until he was also eliminated were useless at this stage of the game. His only option was to keep moving forward with his plans.

He checked his pocket watch. Fifteen minutes before he needed to leave for his meeting about the November election and the Gunderson problem. Bribery was out. With Hendry dead, so was any chance of putting a nosy reporter on the hunt for a skeleton in the closet.

But something needed to be done. Isaak Gunderson was too good as a candidate . . . and too likely to win with the Honorable Jonas Forsythe backing him. However, there was trouble brewing between the twins. Two men fighting over a woman always ended badly.

How might he use that to his advantage?

CHAPTER FOUR

Northern Pacific Railway Depot
Helena, Montana
De Fleur-Gunderson Courtship Contract,
  Day 1

His photograph failed to capture his true appearance.

For a long moment, and since fellow passengers continued to stroll past, Zoe took her leisure in staring at Mr. Gunderson's impressive profile. His blond hair, from what she could see under his black hat, looked neatly trimmed. He was as tall as Mrs. Luanne Bennett had described, taller than anyone else on the platform, and stocky, although not corpulent based on how closely fit his black suit was.

He stood on the train platform a car's length away from Zoe, both hands clenching a bouquet of yellow roses as he scrutinized the train windows.

Likely looking for a woman who fit an

"eminently suitable" description.

Zoe chuckled under her breath. The vagueness of Mrs. Archer's words continued to amuse her. The telegram Mrs. Archer had shared yesterday during tea with Zoe, her daughter Antonia, and Mrs. Luanne Bennett had been brief.

UNEXPECTED ARRIVAL OF EMINENTLY SUITABLE WOMAN IN DENVER STOP ADVISE YOU MEET IN PERSON IMMEDIATELY STOP WIRE FUNDS FOR TRAIN TICKET BY FRIDAY IF YOU APPROVE STOP

The three ladies had insisted that Mr. Gunderson's wiring of the funds within hours of the telegram being sent boded well for Zoe. She wanted to be hopeful. Mrs. Bennett had repeatedly raved about him, calling him her little brother because of how close their families were. While Mr. Gunderson and his brother were not the richest of the rich in Helena, their stepfather had made a significant amount over the years. Thus Jakob and Isaak Gunderson were, in Mrs. Bennett's estimation, two of the most eligible bachelors in town.

Good, respectful, considerate, God-fearing men.

Zoe moistened her lips in nervous anticipation.

Mrs. Archer's follow-up telegram conveyed Zoe's full name and when to expect her arrival in Helena. Nico had called her decision rash. She preferred to think of it as adventurous.

Mr. Gunderson tugged on the bottom of his blue brocade vest, then pulled on his suit coat lapels one at a time.

Zoe drew in a breath, took a step forward, and stopped.

He turned.

His gaze met hers, and Zoe smiled, hoping she looked eminently suitable to be his future bride. To increase the likelihood, she had worn her midnight blue traveling dress with an underskirt in brown and cream stripes and a matching straw hat adorned with feathers. She had also ruthlessly tamed her black curly hair into a modest bun at the nape of her neck.

His mouth gaped.

Zoe took his response as affirmation that he was pleased with what he saw.

She weaved through the crowd and extended her gloved hand. "Mr. Gunderson, I am Zoe de Fleur."

He shook her hand, his blue eyes focused

on her. "I never expected you to be this pretty."

Zoe felt her face warm. "Zank you. I am most happy to —" Her words died as a youth darted around a cluster of men. Nico? She leaned to the right to get a better look, but no dark-haired youths were in view on the platform.

"Is something wrong?"

Zoe looked up at Mr. Gunderson, his brow furrowed with concern. "No, no. My eyes tricked me into zinking I saw a friend from home."

He thrust the yellow roses at her. "Welcome to Helena."

She raised the bouquet to her nose and inhaled the sweet fragrance. "Zey are exquisite."

"Just like you."

A throat cleared.

Mr. Gunderson's gaze shifted to the conductor. That moment looking away from her was all it took for Mr. Gunderson's composure to steady, his shoulders to straighten, and his awkwardness to leave him. He smiled at her. And Zoe's breath caught. He truly was a strikingly handsome man.

He took her gloved hand and drew it over his arm. "We need to leave."

Zoe noted the number of glances their way as Mr. Gunderson escorted her toward the luggage porter, where a crowd of people waited to claim the trunks, cases, and hatboxes being unloaded from the train. While they waited their turn, Zoe looked for Nico . . . or at least the youth resembling him.

People moved.

Mr. Gunderson stepped forward.

". . . suggested I borrow a surrey," he was saying, with no realization she had been distracted, "so we don't have to walk to the boardinghouse I've secured for you. Once we drop off your things, we can go to lunch. Or you can take some time to refresh yourself after your journey and we can share a meal this evening."

"Will zis make trouble with your family?"

"Trouble?" He snorted a laugh. "Oh, Miss de Fleur, the last thing you should fret about is my family. Someday they're all going to thank me for bringing you to Helena. I'm glad you're here. So glad." Mr. Gunderson inched forward again as the crowd around the luggage porter thinned. "I've already made reservations for both lunch and supper at a new restaurant. It has the best food in town."

Zoe felt dazed. "You made reservations

for both lunch *and* supper?"

"I wasn't sure which meal you would prefer to have." He gave her a sheepish grin. "I didn't want to take a chance on inferior food on your first day in town."

His words warmed her heart.

"Next!"

The luggage porter's shout jolted Zoe out of her admiration of Mr. Gunderson. She handed the bouquet back to him, then dug inside her reticule for the baggage tickets.

The porter took her claim tickets. He called out the numbers to the men inside the luggage compartment.

Mr. Gunderson returned the bouquet to Zoe.

She stood patiently while he hefted, loaded, and strapped down each of her wood-and-leather trunks into the surrey. Her four hatboxes were added last. With the same ease he had used to load her luggage, he lifted her into the surrey, spacious enough to seat four adults comfortably, and then walked to the other side.

"It's warm for March," he said, climbing in. He pointed to the floorboards. "There's a quilt under the bench if you get cold. Good thing for us the breeze is from the south."

"I will let you know if I am cold."

As his eyes — a lovely robin's egg blue with specks of brown near the center — focused on hers, the seconds stretched into minutes. The silence deepened.

Zoe moistened her bottom lip, unsure whether she was expected to speak.

His lips twitched. "I'm glad you're here."

"You have already told me zis."

"I hope you're not tired of hearing it, 'cause I'm not tired of saying it." He flicked the reins and the surrey started into motion, his action relieving her of having to utter a response.

Zoe clasped her hands together in her lap, smiling to herself. She liked his ability to make her feel comfortable, as if they had known each other for years, not minutes.

Truth was, she liked every bit of Jakob Gunderson.

As they made their way up the hill, heading toward the cluster of buildings southwest of the train depot, Mr. Gunderson shared the history of Helena. The dirt-hardened roads here were hilly and crooked, reminding her more of the roads in France than in New York. The buildings were shorter, less grand. But the air carried a sweetness not found in New York or Paris. Or even Denver. The pedestrian and horse-drawn traffic on the road increased, and Mr. Gunderson slowed the surrey's pace as he continued to speak.

Based on his numbers, with over ten thousand residents, Helena had a fraction of the populace of Denver, but his beloved town had plenty of entertainments and the modern conveniences Zoe had grown accustomed to in New York City — the streetcar line, telephone service, and electric lighting.

"I love ze theater," she said when he paused to take a breath.

"I do, too, but I should warn you, if a building in Helena is called a theater, it's likely not the type for a lady of good breeding. Ming's Opera House always provides wholesome entertainment. The Helena Orchestra is performing all this week. I'll buy us tickets." The hopefulness in his voice — joy, wonder, and anticipation — drew her attention away from the scenery.

Zoe studied his chiseled profile. How was it he was not already married? "I would like to attend ze opera with you."

As they approached a two-story, triangular-shaped building on their right, she noticed the business's name was painted in black near the flat roof. They stopped at the Y-shaped intersection, where the road they were on merged with two others. A group of Indians crossed in front of them, walking west. Each man wore blankets wrapped about him. The women carried baskets strapped to their back. The group entered the building, the same words painted in black also etched into the shop's wide front window.

Zoe recognized THE and CO., which could be pronounced *Ko* or *So,* depending on whether the C was soft or hard. Before she could sound out the middle word, Mr. Gunderson flicked the reins. The surrey sprang to life again.

"This October will be our third annual Harvest Festival," Mr. Gunderson said, glancing at her. "Have you ever ridden in a hot-air balloon?"

Zoe admired the blue sky sprinkled with random puffy clouds. To fly a mile or more above the ground . . .

She shuddered.

He chuckled. "I'll take that as a *no.*" He lifted his brows and grinned mischievously. "Would you ever ride in one?"

"I would if I felt safe," she admitted.

"Challenge accepted. Trust me, it'll be fun." His gaze returned to the road, and before Zoe could respond to his comment, he spoke again. "Mrs. Archer's telegram said you *arrived* in Denver, not that you were from there. Where is home for you?"

"Paris."

His eyes widened. "As in Paris, France?"

"I was born zere." She clenched her hands together and rested them on her lap. "For ze last four years I lived in New York City."

"The farthest I've ever traveled from where I was born was Denver. I never —" He broke off, his expression no longer seeming happy.

"What is it, Mr. Gunderson?"

"Please call me Jakob," he said absently, his attention on driving the surrey. "Mr. Gunderson is my brother."

After four years of living in America, where people were laxer in etiquette, she still could not use his Christian name after so short an acquaintance. Calling him — any male — by his first name implied a certain familiarity.

She turned on the seat to face him. "I am most interested to meet your twin," she said, because it was the truth, but also because she hoped changing the subject would improve his spirits.

"Isaak and I aren't identical, so you don't have to worry about not being able to tell us apart."

"You are much blessed to have a sibling." She paused for a moment before adding,

"My papa passed away a year ago. We traveled many places and saw many wonderful sights."

He rested a hand atop her still-clenched ones. "I'm sorry for your loss."

"Zank you."

He clicked his tongue twice, then pulled on the right rein, directing the horse to pull the surrey into the alley behind a two-story wooden building in dire need of a whitewashing. He halted the surrey, tied off the reins, and shifted on the bench to face her. "I'm glad you're —"

Zoe held up a hand, silencing him. "I am glad I am here, too."

He chuckled. "Welcome to Deal's Boardinghouse. It's the finest one in Helena . . . and farthest from the parts of town a woman like you needs to avoid."

A stately man stepped into the alley. "Jakob! I see you have our newest guest." The man smiled at Zoe. "Miss de Fleur, I am Alfred Deal. My wife and I are honored to have you stay with us."

A raggedly dressed boy younger than Nico pumped his arms up and down as he came running down the alley. He had sunken cheeks and a pinched expression in his brown eyes.

Mr. Gunderson jumped from the surrey

to block the boy's path. "Slow down, buddy!"

The boy scrambled to stop. He slipped and fell back onto the cobblestones. "Sorry, sir. I didn't mean nothin' by it."

Mr. Gunderson helped the boy to his feet. "What's your name?"

"Timothy Sundin the Third" — he peeped at Zoe, then at Mr. Deal, then back at Mr. Gunderson — "but most folks just call me Timmy."

"Well, Mr. Timothy Sundin the Third, because you're here and I could use some help, how'd you like to earn yourself a dollar?"

The boy's eyes widened. "A whole dollar?"

Mr. Gunderson nodded. "And if you do a good job of it, I'll hire you to help over at that new brick building going up on Lawrence Street."

"That's your building?"

"It sure is."

"Whoa! It's grand!"

Mr. Gunderson grinned in obvious pleasure over the boy's words. He grabbed two of the four hatboxes off the floorboard between the front and second surrey benches and handed them to Mr. Deal. He then grabbed the other two and offered them to the boy, who took them.

"Follow Mr. Deal," Mr. Gunderson said before walking to Zoe's side of the surrey.

The boy gave Mr. Deal a nervous look. His gaze lowered. "Uh, sure, sir."

Mr. Deal motioned for the boy to enter the boardinghouse first.

Mr. Gunderson waited to speak until the boy and Mr. Deal were inside. "Helena has some sundry elements I wish I could shield you from, but I can't. You'd be shocked to know what some children — girls, in particular — are conscripted into for the sake of a measly dollar. That boy is likely the child of a prostitute. I hope you don't mind that I asked him to carry your hatboxes inside."

Zoe studied his face. "Your photograph did not tell ze whole story of you."

"My photograph?"

"I saw ze happiness in your eyes, but ze photograph failed to capture your kindness. And I do not mind zat he is helping. Zis is a wonderful zing you have done."

He grinned. And she grinned, too.

After a long, comfortable moment, he helped her out of the surrey.

The next half hour was taken up with carting luggage up to Zoe's room on the ladies' side of the second floor and meeting Mr. and Mrs. Deal and their niece, Janet, the only other female residing in the boardinghouse. The Deals dutifully shared how, for being a frontier town, Helena had theaters, restaurants, hotels, and a variety of shops, which they vowed Zoe was sure to enjoy.

She fingered the key to her room as she listened to the Deals yet watched Mr. Gunderson kneel in front of little Timmy Sundin, the pair speaking too softly for her to overhear.

Mrs. Deal touched Zoe's arm. "Please, Miss de Fleur, have a seat in the dining room. I'll bring you some tea and cake."

Tea would be nice. So would cake. Breakfast had been hours ago. As much as she would also enjoy a nap, her heart's strongest desire was getting to know Jakob Gunderson. The question of why he had yet to marry lingered in the back of her mind. If he was hiding something, she wanted to find out before her heart grew too attached.

She smiled at the older woman. "Zank you, but Mr. Gunderson is taking me to lunch." And . . . because he had reservations, maybe supper, too.

Four hours later
The Resale Company
Isaak checked the clock in his office. Two-

thirty in the afternoon. Was Jakob back to work? He'd promised to only take the morning. Assuming the train was on time, he'd picked up the woman over four hours ago.

Plenty of time to realize he'd made a terrible mistake and buy the woman a ticket straight back to Denver.

Knock, knock, knock.

"Isaak?" Carline Pope, who was filling in for Emilia McCall while she was on her honeymoon, opened the door to his office without waiting for an invitation to enter. "Mr. O'Leary is here to see you. He says it's important."

"Send him in." Isaak sat straight in the ladder-back chair. What had Jakob done — or, *not* done — to prod the foreman of the work crew up at The Import Co. into running here for help?

Carline disappeared, and O'Leary took her place in the doorway.

He held his cap in both hands, wringing the brown tweed like it was a piece of laundry. "I'm sorry to bother you, Mr. Gunderson, but the men are ready to hang windows, only we don't got any."

"Where's Jakob?"

O'Leary twisted his cap tighter.

"You haven't seen him all day, have you?"

"Not since nine this morning, sir. After we had our crew meeting, he said he was gonna meet someone at the train station and then go to lunch."

Isaak's jaw muscles tightened. "Did he say where?"

"No, sir, but Moses said he saw him at the Grand Hotel around noon."

Isaak stood. "I'll go get him."

"What do you want me and the men to do in the meantime?"

"Whatever you can so we meet the May 4 grand opening."

O'Leary's eyes flitted to the floor.

"Is all construction at a standstill until the windows go in?"

"No, sir. We can still work on the upper floors."

Isaak's fingers curled as he imagined wrapping them around his brother's thick neck. "Do what you can."

"Yes, sir. Thank you, sir." O'Leary didn't turn to leave.

"Was there something else?"

"Yeah. A lad by the name of Timmy showed up an hour ago. Said your brother hired him to clean up wood shavings and the like. You know anything about that?"

"No, but it sounds like Jakob." Isaak took his coat off the back of his chair. "Is the boy working hard?"

O'Leary nodded.

At least Jakob had done one good thing today. "Then let him stay on."

"Very well, sir." The foreman nodded again, then turned and left the office.

Isaak followed, slipping his arms into the sleeves of his coat as he hurried to the hat rack and retrieved his black bowler. He walked into the retail portion of The Resale Co. Carline was behind the counter ringing up some books and a pile of tapered candles for Mrs. Snowe. Isaak greeted the woman and chatted with her about her husband's carpentry designs for The Import Co. while her items were wrapped. He walked her to the door, turned around, and told Carline he'd be back in an hour.

"You're leaving me?" Panic laced her question.

"You can manage." He checked his inside coat pocket to be sure his notebook and pencil were inside. "If anything comes up that you aren't comfortable handling, write it down."

She twisted her hands in the skirt of her blue calico dress. "What if I suspect someone of giving me counterfeit money?"

Carline and Yancey Palmer were best friends. Yancey's fiancé, Joseph Hendry, had been killed right after returning from Dawson County, where he was investigating counterfeiting. Everyone knew Hendry was killed by angry brothel owners because his inflammatory articles stirred up sentiment against the red-light district, resulting in raids and more stringent laws against prostitution, but Yancey and Carline connected his death to the counterfeiting. No amount of rational argument could dislodge the association.

"If you suspect something, put a little star or dot by the name when you record their purchase in the ledger. Then put the money in a separate place, and I'll deal with it when I get back."

Carline regarded him solemnly.

He smiled. "You'll be fine. You know what's on the shelves better than you think you do."

A bit of wariness faded from her blue eyes. "I've shopped here often enough." She glanced down at the ledger, then back at Isaak. "All right. As long as you aren't too worried about counterfeit money, I suppose I'll be fine until you get back."

"I'm certain you will." He put on his hat and walked into the sunshine.

He held himself to a steady pace while walking the five blocks to the Grand Hotel.

Despite how irritated he was with his brother, he managed to greet people with a smile and chat with them. A few white clouds hovered above, the kind in which he and Jakob used to find shapes. They'd lie in the grass and point to the various clouds, trying to outdo each other by coming up with more and more outlandish likenesses. Isaak stopped and put a hand up to hold his hat in place while picking out a sideways pear and a soup pot with a whiff of steam escaping the top. Funny how it only took a second for him to find the shapes even after years of not playing the cloud game — one he didn't have time to play anymore. Unfortunate, but a fact of life.

He dropped his hand and started walking again. At Jackson and Sixth, the sight of Hale's law office reminded Isaak that he needed to reschedule their dinner at the Montana Club, but he didn't have enough time to stop now. The Grand Hotel was the next building, and he could see his brother through the window. Half curtains blocked his lunch companion except for a tall brown hat trimmed with feathers.

How could a woman who was desperate enough to become a mail-order bride afford such a stylish hat?

Isaak yanked his attention away from the

window and schooled his features before nodding at the man holding the door open for him.

"Good afternoon, Mr. Gunderson."

"Afternoon, Abe. How's the family?"

"Can't complain, sir. Can't complain."

Isaak dug a dollar coin from his pocket and tipped the man. With six mouths to feed, he needed it. "Give your lovely wife my best."

"I will, Mr. Gunderson." Abe touched the brim of his red cap and opened the door an inch wider.

Isaak stepped into the hotel lobby. He crossed to the restaurant and told the _maître d'hôtel_ he wasn't there to eat but to talk to his brother, looking to where Jakob sat for emphasis.

Jakob was laughing at something, his face filled with . . . what? More than the polite disinterest Isaak expected — no, hoped — to see.

Confound it all, his brother was taken with the woman! Her dark blue dress, with a gold-and-brown-stripe underskirt was made of silk. A potted tree hid her figure, but as best Isaak could tell, she was slender. None of which fit his mental picture of a distressed or otherwise unacceptable female who would be hopeless enough to become a mail-order bride. She turned her head toward the window, and Jakob stared at her with a silly grin on his face.

Jakob looked up, his expression melting into irritation when he saw Isaak.

Isaak answered Jakob's scowl with one of his own.

Jakob shook his head and looked pointedly at his companion.

Isaak jerked his head toward the lobby.

Another shake of Jakob's head.

Knowing Jakob wouldn't want his precious mail-order bride to overhear their upcoming conversation, Isaak stepped through the archway separating the lobby from the dining area.

Jakob jolted to his feet and appeared to excuse himself from the table. His entire demeanor turned sour as soon as he was out of his companion's view.

Isaak stepped back, squared his shoulders, and braced for their confrontation.

CHAPTER FIVE

Zoe waited until Mr. Gunderson was beyond the table before turning her head just enough to watch him stroll toward the potted plants framing the arched entrance that led to the restaurant lobby.

Goodness, the man was impressive!

Mr. Gunderson's laughter reminded her of Papa's — deep-chested and ending in a snort. When she spoke, his gaze never veered from hers, his lips curving in a you-fascinate-me smile. She considered mimicking his smile. She wanted to, but she had never been good with flirting. This man she wished to flirt with. And yet her mind had thought of nothing coquettish.

She was clearly more like Papa than *Maman*.

Zoe sighed.

She turned back to the table, her gaze catching on the coffee cup next to Mr. Gunderson's half-eaten chocolate cake. Coffee with breakfast she understood. But during a dinner meal? Mrs. Gilfoyle-Crane had insisted upon coffee after the solids had been removed from the table because she favored the way the bitter brew paired with sweets. Zoe agreed. She also knew coffee was a less costly alternative to liquor or wine for aiding digestion.

For someone who drank four cups of coffee with his meal — if this was normal behavior for him and not merely nerves — Mr. Gunderson should have sallow skin in addition to intestinal issues; his tanned complexion could disguise sallowness. It was no wonder he had to leave the meal in search of a washroom.

Poor man.

Embarrassed for him, Zoe focused on her dessert, which, upon her first bite, was as disappointing as the main dish. The flavor of the chicken fricassee would have been improved if the chef had added some thin-sliced, cold-boiled ham during the stewing. She picked up her spoon, uncertain whether she wanted another bite. The crème brûlée was too eggy. The pâtissier should have layered in another half cup of whipping crème. A pity, for the brûlée was perfect.

She tapped her spoon against the toasted sugar, cracking off another piece. Her spoon hovered over the ramekin. If she slid the spoon under the sugar, she could avoid the lackluster custard. She ought to eat it; Mr. Gunderson was paying for the meal. She should. Especially because she had managed to endure only half the main dish.

To her relief, at that moment Mr. Gunderson slid back into his seat, grinning. "It's an unseasonably warm day. Let's go for a walk. It'll be fun."

"Zis is true, but what about ze surrey?"

"I'll fetch it later."

He was gazing at her with an unnerving intensity. The sun streaming through the restaurant windows brightened the heavenly blue of his eyes.

Zoe laid down her spoon. "I would enjoy a walk." She considered asking, *Where to?* but how much more fun it was to be surprised.

While Mr. Gunderson paid the bill, Zoe sought out the washroom. He was waiting for her in the hotel lobby, holding the bouquet of roses, her leather gloves, and her winter cloak. He draped the cloak over her shoulders, then gave her a moment to pull on her gloves before handing her the bouquet.

She had not felt so treasured since Papa passed away. But this was different. Jakob

Gunderson was not her father.

A voice cleared.

She turned to the sound.

The doorman held open the door. "Hey, Jakob, would you tell my brother to come by here after work?"

Mr. Gunderson patted the side of the man's shoulder. "Will do, Abe. Give your wife my love."

The doorman chuckled. "And give her a reason to regret marrying me? Not on your life." He looked at Zoe. "Ma'am, we appreciate you visiting the finest hotel in Helena. We hope you'll come back again soon."

"Zank you." And then she stepped outside.

Mr. Gunderson motioned to the right. "This way."

A pair of horse-drawn wagons drove past. Several men on horses rode by, too.

Zoe partially listened as Mr. Gunderson acknowledged fellow pedestrians and talked about the businesses they passed. How pleasant not to be the one required to carry the conversation. She also enjoyed sensing how much he loved this town and the people in it. Yet he was still unmarried. Why? The question had nagged at her during the drive from the boardinghouse and throughout the meal. It still nagged.

As they passed another business, which had old barrels filled with soil on either side of the entrance, Zoe brushed her fingers over the green shoots peeking through the rich brown dirt. In another month, flowers and greenery would brighten this main thoroughfare through town.

While buildings lined both sides of the street, to the northwest, white-topped, rugged mountains peppered the view.

The largest — Mount Helena.

Of all the letters and references Mrs. Archer had read to Zoe, the one from the reverend had been the most descriptive of God's created majesty surrounding Helena. She had been wary of his narrative. She now agreed with the words he had chosen. Nothing obstructed the vast blue skyline. On Manhattan Island, the best view of the sky came when standing on the Crane house rooftop, Papa's favorite place to watch the sunrise. Yet even there, the sky was partially obstructed by the taller buildings blocks away.

A streetcar bell sounded as it stopped at the upcoming intersection. Zoe smiled with optimism about creating a future here as she watched passengers climb off before others climbed on, including a mother with her three identically dressed, stair-step little girls.

"In the next few years," Mr. Gunderson boasted, "the streetcar line will extend beyond this one line direct to the train depot. There will be tracks through neighborhoods."

Zoe looked up at Mr. Gunderson and listened as he spoke. She had never expected to feel such an instant compatibility with a stranger.

He enjoyed hiking in the mountains. She did, too. He enjoyed sunsets. She did, too. He enjoyed helping those less fortunate, attending worship services, and spending time with friends and family. She did, too! Her favorite story was of how his stepfather had agreed to raise twin babies as his own, even though they would bear their real father's last name. A lot could be understood about a man in how he spoke about his parents. Jakob Gunderson clearly treasured his.

By the time they reached the intersection, the streetcar had moved on. They crossed the street, the sound of hammers against wood growing louder as they walked.

"Here it is!" Mr. Gunderson said. "The Import Company."

They stood there, looking at a grand three-story, red-brick building with stone accents under the window frames and around the double-doored entrance. Zoe admired how THE IMPORT COMPANY had been carved into stone over the third-floor windows in between the brickwork.

When a person was looking for a business —

She gasped. "Oh! Zis is your building. You wrote about it in your second letter."

He smiled with pride, as if presenting her with his greatest treasure.

"I like it," she said. "When will ze construction finish?"

"We've had an unexpected delay on the windowpanes, so they won't go in until next week. The interior work will be finished by the middle of April. That leaves us two weeks to arrange displays and price the goods before the May 4 grand opening."

Six arched window openings on each of the second and third floors. Two wide ones on the ground level. She leaned to the right and counted the side window openings. Eight . . . no, ten.

"Is your papa's other business in a building zis grand?"

"No. The Resale Company could fit inside this one's first floor," he said in a curious voice, as if he had never realized the difference in the buildings' sizes. "The plan is to rent the second floor as office space."

"And ze third floor?"

"Storage."

When he said no more, she looked up at him. "That whole floor only for storage?"

He swallowed, his Adam's apple shifting in his throat. "There's also an apartment for me and my future family." He motioned to the building. "Shall we?"

"Certainly."

Five minutes later, they stood in the center of what would be The Import Company. Sunshine streamed through the window openings and cast elongated rectangles on the unstained floorboards. Hammering sounded on the upper floors.

Zoe eyed the handful of different tin tiles adhered to the ceiling. She favored the one on the far left with the *fleur-de-lis.*

Mr. Gunderson touched her arm, and she met his gaze. "Stay here. I need to check on today's progress, and I don't want you on our makeshift staircase."

"I am content to admire ze view."

As soon as he disappeared through a doorway in the back wall, Zoe strolled around the wide, open space — empty save for sawdust, six support pillars, and her. Everything about Helena smelled earthy and new. She imagined the register near the front and display racks abounding with merchandise. If she were arranging the store, she would segregate the merchandise by the regions where they were made, so that when customers moved around the store, they would feel as if they were traveling the world in eighty steps instead of in eighty days. And she would sell scented candles and oils.

How nice it would be to have cookbooks of recipes from different cultures.

A whistle drew her gaze to the doorless entrance.

Nico?

Zoe stared, unable to believe he was there. After her first meeting with Mrs. Archer, Nico had broken Zoe's heart when he refused to support her decision to allow Mr. Gunderson to court her. She had believed Nico to be her friend. But a true friend would never desert her as he had. Once they had returned to her hotel, he had thanked her for helping him reach Denver and wished her well. She had not seen him since.

But she *had* seen him. Earlier, at the train depot.

Nico motioned her to walk his way.

Zoe hurried over. "Why are you here?"

"You need my help."

She gave him a look to convey exactly

what she felt about his claim.

"You do," he insisted. His brow furrowed. He looked tense . . . and a bit worried. "That man you came here with isn't what he seems."

"How did you come by zis belief?"

"I just know."

Zoe released a weary breath. Nico had also insisted courting a stranger was a bad idea. If he had returned to Mrs. Archer's house yesterday morning as Zoe had, he would have listened to the matchmaker read the reverend's reference letter. Mr. Gunderson and his brother were pillars of society, their parents some of the earliest settlers of Helena. Mrs. Luanne Bennett, a charming woman four years older than Zoe, had also confirmed everything written in Mr. Gunderson's letters and in those written by his other references.

Amid all these truths, there was one lie: Nico's, about the advertisement.

She had no cause to trust him again.

Except . . .

None of Mr. Gunderson's family had sent a letter of reference. She understood his parents because they were still away on their tour of the country. But why not his twin? Mr. Gunderson had said little about his brother during the meal. Perhaps his family was not as perfect and loving as he claimed.

Nico was here because he was concerned and worried about her. He had lied because he had no other way to escape New York. He needed her help, needed her to be his friend. Not to forgive him would make her an unkind and ungrateful person. The most gracious and wise thing she could do was give a listening ear to his concerns.

Zoe gave his shoulder a little squeeze. "I am pleased to see you."

He enveloped her in a hug. "I'm sorry, Zoe, for getting angry and leaving you." He choked up. "I love you. You're the only family I've got."

She rested her chin atop his head. He was the closest she had to family, too, but she had signed a contract agreeing to a two-month courtship. She had to — no, she *wanted to* — give Mr. Gunderson a fair chance to woo her.

She drew back. "Go to Deal's Boardinghouse and I will pay for you a room."

"Thanks, but I found somewhere to stay." The moment her brow rose, he added, "It's reputable. Trust me. I met someone at the depot who gave me a job making deliveries."

That was Nico — ever resourceful. During the train ride to Denver, he had convinced the conductor to hire him to work in the passenger cars, selling sandwiches, cigars, and newspapers.

She gripped the lapels of his coat and tugged until it rested properly on his shoulders. "Zen come to ze boardinghouse in ze morning at eight. I will buy you breakfast and tell you all I have learned about Mr. Gunderson. You will see he is a good man."

Nico grimaced. "You'd better have a plan for what you're going to do if this courtship doesn't turn out like you're dreaming it will. 'Cause I know it won't. He's not the man for you."

Zoe held her response. Now was not the time to try to convince Nico to be optimistic.

"See ya tomorrow." He gave her a quick hug, then dashed away.

Minutes passed before the hammering stopped.

She glanced around the empty store. Mr. Gunderson was still upstairs. On the second floor? Or was he examining the work on the third floor, his future living quarters? To have her own home would be another dream come true.

But if things did not go as she hoped —

Zoe nipped her bottom lip. That grand lady who had sat next to her on the train

112

from Butte to Helena had mentioned a new luxury hotel and hot springs resort "unlike any other in the world" set to open in a year. The exclusive Broadwater was exactly the kind of place that would desire the services of a French chef. Or she could apply to work in the Grand Hotel restaurant, for they could use someone with her skills. In a town of ten thousand people, Jakob Gunderson could not be the only decent bachelor interested in marriage.

Tomorrow she would explain to Nico the number of other paths her future could take, if she chose to leave the one leading her to Jakob Gunderson.

Her gaze fell to the bouquet of roses.

She inhaled the sweet scent . . . and remembered how Mr. Gunderson had gazed upon her at the restaurant. And smiled.

No other paths were needed.

This courtship would end with a marriage. She was sure of it.

Chapter Six

The next morning
De Fleur-Gunderson Courtship Contract,
  Day 2

Isaak cracked an egg into the bowl and dropped the shell into the bin beside the stove. In two more months, Ma would be home and take over the cooking and gardening again. While he was looking forward to having her here, he wasn't sure he wanted to give up cooking. Turned out he liked it. Plus, food didn't talk back or wander off or tell you it was going to do one thing and then do the exact opposite.

Unlike a brother.

He cracked another egg to make an even dozen in the bowl. After dropping that shell in the bin, he took up the whisk lying on the soapstone counter and started beating the eggs. He checked the clock. What was taking Jakob so long this morning?

As if in answer to his question, footsteps

thudded down the stairs. "Breakfast ready?" Jakob's morning cheerfulness sounded somewhat forced.

Isaak poured the scrambled eggs into a heated cast-iron skillet. "It will be in a few minutes."

"Great." Based on the crunching noise that followed, Jakob had helped himself to a bacon strip. "I need to wolf down breakfast if I'm going to make it over to Deal's Boardinghouse in time to pick up Miss de Fleur for church."

Miss de Fleur? Was that a French-sounding type of *nom de plume,* the same way Mac's mother had gone from being Mary Lester to Madame Lestraude?

Isaak turned over the eggs. "What are you doing after church?"

"I thought I'd take her out to eat, show her around town a little, and then . . . I don't know. We'll see." Another crunch and a whiff of bacon on the air.

Isaak held in a retort about how that would have been nice to know on Friday, before he purchased four lamb chops for today's lunch. He didn't want to start Sunday morning with an argument.

Pa often said, "Give Jakob some credit. He doesn't plan things the way you do, but he almost always lands on his feet." Isaak doubted Pa would give that same advice if he knew Jakob was shirking his duties at The Import Co. to squire a woman around town. Sure, he'd gone back to work after Isaak forced the issue yesterday, but Jakob had come home and refused to talk about the woman. Or about what he accomplished at the store, saying only that everything was on schedule.

On Jakob's schedule.

Isaak was certain it wasn't the one he'd written out last December, or any of the ones he'd altered in the months since then. Some of the changes were to be expected. Building a new business from the ground up was certain to involve adjustments. They didn't need additional, unnecessary ones because Jakob couldn't keep his focus.

Isaak's grip tightened on the wooden spoon. "Grab us some plates."

Some footsteps against the wood plank floor, a whoosh of air, and the scrape of crockery. "Here."

A blue plate appeared in Isaak's peripheral vision. He scooped fluffy yellow eggs on the plate.

"That's enough." Jakob pulled away his plate and held out the other one.

Isaak piled the rest of the eggs on his plate, then set the skillet in the sink. He turned to pick up the bacon, pleased to find that Jakob had left him a full four strips. Isaak added the bacon to his plate, then grabbed the teapot. "Bring the coffee to the table."

"Sure." Jakob held his plate with one hand and the coffeepot with the other.

They sat down at the small kitchen table, said grace, and began eating.

Jakob ate quickly, eager to be on his way.

Isaak sipped his tea, added more sugar, and sipped again. He reached for the cream. Over the past year, he and Jakob had developed a breakfast routine. They would take turns reading the newspaper, occasionally commenting on something they found interesting or important, then head out to work or church. Any silence between them was comfortable.

Today, tension scraped through the silence.

Isaak didn't even reach for the newspaper because, although Jakob was clearly intent on eating as fast as possible, Isaak feared that one of their friendly tussles about who read which section first might turn ugly. Instead, he focused on making his tea perfect. By the time it was, Jakob was done eating.

He stood. "Thanks for breakfast. I'll see

you at church." He carried his empty plate and coffee cup to the sink and hurried out the back door.

Isaak huffed. "Miss de *Fleur.* What a fraud."

Jakob opened the door and poked his head inside to say, "I heard that," before slamming the door behind him.

Somewhat chagrined at being caught speaking ill of a woman no matter how much she deserved it, Isaak crumbled the bacon over his eggs, took a bite, and reached for the Sunday edition of the *Daily Independent.* There, on the front page below the fold, was yet another article exposing a ring of females who had bilked a whole slew of men out of thousands of dollars by posing as European mail-order brides in need of money to travel. The interesting thing — what made it front-page news — was the erstwhile grooms. They were bankers and business owners, lawyers and landlords. In other words, men who weren't easily taken in under normal circumstances, yet they'd fallen for a mail-order bride scam all the same.

For European women. As in *French* women.

Isaak tossed the paper on the table. Ate his breakfast. Pushed the paper farther away. Drank his tea. Dragged the article back to the side of his plate and reread it.

Twice.

Zoe noted the number of people looking their way as Mr. Gunderson drew the little two-seater carriage to a stop next to a fringe-topped surrey that had been painted a shockingly bright shade of yellow. Was it traditional in western America to mingle outside the church before services commenced? At the New York church she attended, regardless of the weather, people arrived and immediately found an empty seat or, for the wealthier members, found their name-plate-designated pew.

The number of people standing outside the white-painted church neared a hundred. The building itself, while similar in size to the other churches she had seen in town, appeared to be able to house about that many. They should all be inside where it was warmer, away from the chilly March breeze, away from the tumultuous gray sky that Mr. Gunderson said looked as if it would rain but, in Montana, looks could be deceiving.

That made no sense.

In her experience, gray clouds always preceded rain.

Yet instead of looking at the sky, everyone was looking at her. Zoe twisted one gloved hand around the other, her stomach in knots.

Mr. Gunderson had warned yesterday that she would draw attention when they arrived for church together. As much because she was a new lady in town as because she was with him. Her silk crimson dress and matching bonnet were no more or less fancy than the clothes the other ladies wore, but her crimson paisley mantelet, with its chenille fringe and wooden beads looked foreign compared to their plain woolen ones.

She must look foreign to them, too.

"You do that a lot."

She turned to her right to see Mr. Gunderson standing there, smiling at her. "I did not realize you had climbed out of ze carriage."

"I could tell."

"What is it I do?"

His eyes fixed on hers with an expression of amusement. "When you're lost in your thoughts, you will" — he motioned to her mouth — "lick your bottom lip."

Zoe felt her cheeks warm. "Is zis an unflattering zing?"

"Unflattering?" He muttered something too softly for her to hear. And then he lifted her to the ground as if she were as light as a bird. He grinned. "Are you ready to meet everyone?"

She opened her mouth, then closed it, unsure if she should admit her worry. There were so many strangers, so many people staring at her, curious about her. And about her and Mr. Gunderson together. If that were not intimidating enough, the one person she wished to meet was nowhere to be seen. Had he stayed home to avoid her, as he had yesterday?

"What is it?" Mr. Gunderson asked softly.

"What if he dislikes me?"

"Who?"

"Your twin."

A look of utter dread crossed his face. He looked to the side, staring at nothing, and she knew he was thinking about his brother.

If they were close, as stated by his references and by Mrs. Luanne Bennett, why had his brother failed to greet Zoe at the train station yesterday? Or at The Import Company after lunch? Or joined them for a second meal at the Grand Hotel restaurant? Not once this morning had Mr. Gunderson spoken of his twin, unlike yesterday, when occasional mentions of *my brother Isaak* had peppered their conversation.

Something had occurred this morning

before Mr. Gunderson arrived at the boardinghouse to claim her for church. Something unpleasant between the brothers.

If their relationship was strained because of her —

Mr. Gunderson abruptly smiled. "Isaak won't dislike you, although it might seem that way at first. He's been under more stress than usual because he's running for mayor and his employee, Emilia McCall, is away on her honeymoon, leaving him to manage The Resale Company without her help. He says I don't understand all the work he accomplishes in a day."

"*Do* you understand?"

He shrugged. "I couldn't live with his schedule and maintain my sanity. Life should be about more than just work. Life should be enjoyed, especially with" — he looked at her intently — "people who matter to you, because one day you may wake up and that person you love is gone."

Zoe's eyes blurred. She gave his gloved hand a gentle squeeze. "Zis I understand." She had experienced that loss twice in her life already.

His gaze fell to where their hands were joined. He looked at her. "Thank you."

She waited for him to explain his reason for thanking her, but when he stayed silent, she asked, "For what?"

"For many things." His look warmed her down to the tips of her toes. "For listening attentively when I talk. For being straightforward about why you left Paris and then New York. For being warm, sensitive, and kind. But mostly, Miss de Fleur, for answering my advertisement. You are a brave and adventurous woman to come out West all alone."

She tilted her head and smiled. The sheer joy she felt was too much to be contained. Papa had been the only other person who had ever told her she was brave. "Zank you, Mr. Gunderson, for not insisting upon a letter correspondence."

"It's nice to hear someone appreciates my spontaneity," he quipped.

"It is one of ze many zings about you I appreciate." Zoe knew her cheeks were pink, but this time she did not look away in awkwardness or embarrassment. She held his gaze.

Something about Jakob Gunderson made her feel bold.

She looped her arm around his left one. "I would like to meet your friends."

"And my brother?"

"Oh. He is here?"

"Isaak has never missed a Sunday service

in his life."

"Zat is" — she paused to think of the right word — "exemplary."

He laughed. "Not the adjective I would use."

As they strolled toward the church, Zoe smiled in anticipation.

"Morning, Jakob!" someone called out.

People began to crowd around them.

Zoe eased closer to Mr. Gunderson, who shook hands with each member of the Watson family as he introduced her to the president of the Helena Public Schools board of trustees, his wife, and their five children. The oldest son looked to be near Zoe's age, early twenties, while the youngest was two and proud of his ability to stick his whole hand into his mouth and not gag.

One by one, people took turns welcoming her to Helena.

The Palmers were related to Mrs. Luanne Bennett of Denver. Miss Yancey Palmer hugged Zoe as if they were intimate friends. Mr. Geddes Palmer politely shook her hand and then smiled, patted Jakob's shoulder, and murmured, "Lucky dog," before walking away.

After the Palmers, Zoe lost track of the overwhelming number of names.

Between moments of being introduced,

she glanced around in hopes of seeing Nico. Why had he missed breakfast? He needed to eat. He could be making a delivery for his new employer. Or perhaps he was hawking newspapers. When Mr. Gunderson had driven by the newspaper building, Nico was not among the handful of newsies filling their wagons. Perhaps he had found employment elsewhere.

The church bell rang.

The double doors opened. Two men, similar in size to Mr. Gunderson, stepped outside. Neither were smiling. While both wore black three-piece suits, the dark-haired, heavily bearded man looked as if he hadn't visited a barber in several years. The blond —

Her heart leaped.

It was him! It had to be. Alike but not identical.

The old-enough-to-be-her-father gentleman on Mr. Gunderson's right said, "Let me know if Tuesday doesn't work. We would be happy to reschedule."

"Tuesday is perfect, sir," answered Mr. Gunderson, drawing Zoe's attention. He smiled at the man's wife. "Aunt Lily, I sure do like your apple pies."

"Oh, Jakob, you know you just have to ask and I'll make you one. I can never say no to you." She looked at Zoe. "Miss de Fleur, I'm looking forward to visiting with you more over supper."

Supper? Zoe felt her stomach drop. Oh no! She had missed part of the conversation.

She smiled at the woman. *And* hoped her initial expression had not conveyed her confusion. "I am looking forward to it, too."

The woman — Aunt Lily — stepped closer, and Zoe breathed in the familiar orange-blossom cologne, the same delicate and expensive perfume Mrs. Gilfoyle-Crane favored.

"Meeting so many new people at once can be overwhelming." The elegant woman's voice softened with motherly concern. "That's why I insisted to Jonas that we have you and Jakob over for a more relaxed time on Tuesday to get to know one another. Meals are easy moments to build friendships." She hugged Zoe. "Marilyn and David will be so pleased."

Marilyn and David? The names were familiar.

The dignified gentleman tipped his black top hat at Zoe and gave her a nod, small and polite. He then escorted his wife on to the church. This well-dressed, gracious couple should be a part of Mrs. Gilfoyle-

Crane's social set, not residents of a frontier town. Who were they?

"The Forsythes," Mr. Gunderson whispered, even though he and Zoe were the only two remaining on the church lawn. "Your wondering is all over your face."

"Is zis unflattering?"

He chuckled. "Nothing about you is unflattering." Before Zoe had time to ponder his remark, he added, "Jonas Forsythe is one of four Montana territorial judges. And he's my godfather."

Judge Forsythe? She knew that name. Oh! He had written one of the letters of glowing reference for Mr. Gunderson. The words of his wife now made sense. Marilyn and David were Jakob Gunderson's mother and stepfather and were bosom friends with the Forsythes. Love for one another had proliferated every letter Mrs. Archer had read Zoe about Jakob and his friends and family.

If only she had taken notes . . .

All in Mr. Gunderson's file would stay in Mrs. Archer's possession until he married or canceled his service with her.

Zoe looked up at Mr. Gunderson. "I would like to share a meal with ze Forsythes."

"Is Tuesday all right?"

"I zink my schedule has an opening."

He let out a little laugh. "I hope so."

Zoe looped her arm around Mr. Gunderson's, then fell into step with him.

As they walked, she tilted her head and studied Mr. Gunderson's face. His gaze stayed fixed ahead. A growing scowl replaced his smile; unlike before, his pace seemed slower, the muscles under her palm tense. Something had soured his joy.

The most logical thing was —

She focused on the two men atop the church steps. Neither smiled. They exchanged words, their gazes on her, and then the dark-haired one disappeared inside the white-washed building.

"Zat is your brother, yes?" she said and wondered if she sounded as breathless to Mr. Gunderson as she sounded to herself. "Zere on ze church steps?"

He regarded her with a peculiar, steady gaze before looking to where his brother stood greeting church attendees. "That's him."

The church bell rang again.

A trio of redheaded boys raced around the building. They stopped abruptly at the bottom of the steps and lined up according to height.

"Ollie!" one yelled.

A fourth child — a girl with strawberry-blond braids to the middle of her back — skipped around the building, dangling a rag doll in her left hand and wearing black stockings with a hole in one knee. She slid between the second and third boy. In a sedate fashion, the four marched up the steps and took turns shaking Mr. Isaak Gunderson's hand.

He then withdrew something from a waistcoat pocket, laid it in the girl's up-turned palm, and curled her fingers around it.

She nodded.

He said something to the three boys.

This time they nodded.

". . . find you after the service," he was saying when Zoe and Mr. Jakob Gunderson reached the church steps.

"Mornin', Jakob," the tallest boy called out before ushering the other three children — presumably his siblings — into the church.

Mr. Isaak Gunderson said nothing.

His green eyes fixed on Zoe, and her breath caught. He looked at her exactly as Chef Henri always had. It took all her fortitude not to lower her gaze, as she had four years ago and every other time she had been in Chef Henri's presence. She held still. This man was not Chef Henri.

She lifted her chin and smiled. "*Bonjour,* Mr. Gunderson."

"Welcome to Helena, Miss de Fleur." He glanced over his shoulder into the church, then looked back and said, "The service is about to start."

"This is the moment" — Mr. Jakob Gunderson squeezed Zoe's hand, which lay on his arm — "when you should start calling me Jakob or things will get confusing. Trust me, if you say Mr. Gunderson, everyone in town will think you're talking about *him.*"

Zoe looked from brother to brother. Two Mr. Gundersons. Jakob, with his happy eyes and easy grin, was the more attractive.

And charming. And likable.

Although Mr. Isaak Gunderson's dislike might not be aimed at *her,* he was glaring at his brother with bristling hostility, and Jakob's smile seemed forced. Twice in her life, she had awoken to discover a parent was gone: her mother, when she left to live in Italy, and then the day her father died. The Gunderson brothers needed to be reminded of the importance of family.

She must do something to help. But what?

Meals were easy moments in which to build friendships. Zoe had no kitchen to prepare a meal. Perhaps a good solution would be to ask Mr. Gunderson to join them for lunch. Surely the hotel restaurant could accommodate a third person added to their reservation.

"Jakob," she said, and instantly liked the way his name sounded on her tongue.

"Yes?"

"I zink we should invite your brother to share a meal with us."

The woman was everything Isaak feared she'd be: exotically beautiful, speaking with a fake French accent, and already bossing his brother around. He didn't see the poor relative but had no doubt one would turn up in a day or two.

And she'd made her first big mistake.

Isaak stared down at her from his superior height. "I think a shared meal is a wonderful idea. I'll cook."

The woman turned her chocolate-brown eyes on Jakob, who was too busy staring daggers at Isaak to notice.

Isaak smirked. Perhaps the vixen didn't have her claws in quite as deep as she thought. He raised his eyebrows and continued to meet his brother's glare.

"Zat will be lovely." There was a bit of uncertainty in her voice, which should have thrilled him.

It didn't. Isaak slanted his gaze to her,

surprised and annoyed at the prickle in his soul warning that he'd done something to upset her.

Oh, she was good. No wonder Jakob couldn't see past that pretty face and perfect figure.

"Church is about to start." Isaak stepped back to let them pass. "Meet me at home after service is over."

Miss de Fleur looked between him and Jakob before stepping across the threshold.

Jakob leaned close to whisper, "You can't invite a woman over to the house without a chaperone."

Isaak stiffened. As if he didn't already know that.

"I'll take care of it." He patted his brother's shoulder to move him along. Too bad Mrs. Hollenbeck wasn't back from her European tour. The conversation would have turned to travel, and then the de Fleur vixen would be caught in her own trap. Isaak doubted she knew anything about France except what could be gleaned from books.

Windsor Buchanan returned from wherever he had gone and closed his side of the double doors. "Thought you said she'd be ugly and at least fifty."

Isaak shut his door and turned to look at

the pew where Jakob and Miss de Fleur stood chatting with Yancey Palmer. "I was wrong about that, but I'm not wrong on the whole." Sure, her appearance wasn't what he'd been expecting, but Miss de Fleur was too pretty, with her curling black hair that refused to stay pinned up so little ringlets framed her heart-shaped face and danced along the curve of her shapely neck. Had he not read the article about the intelligent men taken in by women claiming to be foreign brides, he might have fallen for her himself.

Windsor crossed his arms over his chest. "Whatever you need, I've got your back."

Isaak thanked him with a nod and surveyed the church attendees who were gradually taking their seats in search of anyone who had taken a European tour or had relatives in France. Only Edward Tandy fit the bill, and a third man around the dinner table with a lone woman was not appropriate.

If Isaak couldn't have Mrs. Hollenbeck as a chaperone, the next best person was his godmother, Lily Forsythe. Uncle Jonas was taking her to Paris for their tenth wedding anniversary, and she was a voracious reader. She'd know if something Miss de Fleur said about her supposed homeland was wrong.

Isaak turned to his right and made his way down the aisle to the third row, where the Forsythes were sitting.

Murmuring his apologies, Isaak scooted past the Watson family. He reached the vacant seat next to his godmother just as Reverend Neven called for everyone to rise for the first hymn. Isaak took the hymnal from the pew back in front of him and opened to hymn number 323, "Blessed Assurance." He held it low so Aunt Lily could share it with him.

She chuckled. "Can you see the words from that great a distance?"

Isaak's lips twitched and the tension in his gut eased. "Shall I sit down so we're the same height?"

"That would help." The voice was Yancey Palmer's and came from behind him.

He craned his neck to look at her. "Sorry, Yance. I'll slouch during the sermon."

She grinned at him, and he was glad to see the humor reached her eyes. After Joseph Hendry died — and their engagement along with him — her parents had sent her to Denver for a long visit with her sister, Luanne. It had done her a world of good.

Isaak returned his attention to the hymnal for the duration of the song, but as they were sitting down, he leaned close to Aunt

Lily and whispered, "Would you be available to come for lunch after church? I need a chaperone for Jakob's Miss de Fleur."

She placed a gloved hand at the side of her mouth. "I'm sorry, but we're promised to the Cannons this afternoon."

"I can come," Yancey spoke again. "And I'll bring Carline and Geddes, too. We'll have a merry time."

Isaak groaned.

CHAPTER SEVEN

"*Zat* is why your brother is upset with you?" Zoe whispered back in shock as she and Jakob stood in the foyer of his parents' home, still wearing their outer garments. She had been right to suspect a conflict between the brothers. "Oh, Jakob, do you not see how keeping your contract with ze Archer Matrimonial Company from your brother was most hurtful?"

"It wasn't Isaak's business to know." His expression grim, Jakob shrugged off his greatcoat. He laid it on the mirrored hall tree bench, atop the other coats and cloaks of those who had arrived before them. "Besides, Zoe, his feelings don't get hurt like a normal person's."

Zoe held back her retort. Everyone had feelings, even his brother.

She untied then removed her bonnet. "Are you ashamed of me? Is zat why you kept me a secret?"

"How could I be ashamed of you?" He hung her bonnet and his black hat on empty hooks and then continued to speak softly so no one in the drawing room would overhear them. "The only thing I knew about you was your name and that you'd arrived in Denver because you wanted to be my mail-order bride."

Zoe grimaced. Becoming his bride had never been a consideration until Mrs. Archer revealed Nico's falsehood about someone wanting to hire a chef for the finest kitchen west of the Mississippi. She opened her mouth with the intention of finally telling Jakob about Nico, but this moment was about Jakob and his brother, not her and Nico.

Instead she said, "Zat was a misunderstanding."

"And I for one am quite thankful. What brought you to me matters little in light of the fact you are here." A smile lifted the corners of Jakob's lips. "We covered at least three months of correspondence with all the talking we did yesterday."

She nodded in response. Yesterday had been one of the best days of her life. Never before had she met someone with such an effortless ability to fill silences. Most of all, she appreciated the way he never pressured her for information she felt uncomfortable sharing.

She removed her gloves, then handed them to him before she unbuttoned the mantelet covering her crimson dress.

Jakob slid it from her shoulders. He added her belongings to the mirrored hall tree. "I'd planned to tell Isaak about you — or whoever answered my advertisement — when the time was right." He shrugged. "Things went faster with you than I expected. Don't look at me like that. I know . . . *yesterday* was the right time."

"Zen why did you not confess all?"

"It's a brother thing."

"What is a 'brother zing'?"

"If you had a sibling, you'd understand."

Zoe winced at the sting his words brought. Her life would be different had she had a sibling. Or a mother. Or if Papa were still alive.

Jakob rubbed the back of his neck. "Isaak and I are each other's best friend and worst enemy. We say and do things to each other that we'd never let someone else do. Does that make sense?"

How could something be both good and bad? Oh!

"You are salt," she said with a smile. "Too much ruins a dish. Ze right amount makes ze meal — *parfait*!

"Par-fay?"

"It means perfect in French."

"Isaak and I are both salt." He chuckled. "All right, I like that comparison. It makes us equals."

Zoe gripped his hands. "My heart breaks knowing you and your brother are at odds."

His hands moved to cradle hers. "You think *now* is my new right time to talk to him?"

She lifted her shoulder in a noncommittal shrug. It was not her place to force her opinions or views on anyone. But she wished harmony upon the twins. She could only hope in time they would repair the rift between them, preferably sooner than later.

His troubled gaze shifted to the drawing room, where the other guests were waiting. "Now isn't the right time anyway. I need to stay and help you socialize. When Yancey and Carline are together, they can be overwhelming, especially to people who are shy, like you are. Geddes will find something to distract himself from their loquacious exuberance."

Unsure of how to respond, Zoe stood there and waited. Clearly, he had to talk himself into a decision.

He released her hands, then gripped both

lapels of his black suit coat. "The problem with discussing this with Isaak right now is that, when he's cooking, he doesn't want anyone talking to him." His shoulders slumped as he let out a long, loud exhale. "Seems to me the 'right time' would be when it's a good time for both people."

Zoe lifted her shoulder in another non-committal shrug.

He groaned. "That's easy for you to say. You don't know Isaak like I do. Nothing I say will make a difference," he argued aloud, as if trying to convince himself. "Once Isaak believes he's right, he doesn't change his mind."

He fell silent.

After a long moment, and several paces around the foyer, he remarked, "If my parents were here, they would say, 'A kind word chases away wrath.' "

"It does."

He shook his head helplessly. "I really don't have a choice."

Zoe sighed.

"I need to go talk to Isaak anyway," he continued. "He ought to be warned that you're a highly trained chef —"

"Household cook," she corrected.

"— since he's so proud of his cooking," he finished with more conviction than anything else he'd said since their arrival at the house. He sighed wearily. "But first I'll apologize to him for keeping him in the dark about my contract with the Archer Matrimonial Company."

For a moment, she was struck dumb. Jakob Gunderson was *such* a good man to admit he had been in the wrong.

He stepped closer to her. "I probably ought to ask you this officially, instead of just depending on the contract you signed." He drew her hand to his chest, resting it palm down over his heart. "Zoe de Fleur, would you do me the honor of allowing me to court you for the next sixty days?"

"Fifty-nine," she corrected. "Ze contract began yesterday."

"Indeed it did."

She smiled. "Indeed you may."

Isaak was stirring potatoes on the cookstove when Jakob strolled into the kitchen and announced, "Zoe is worried that we're fighting."

This morning she was *Miss de Fleur* and now *Zoe*! Typical of Jakob to remove respectful status boundaries after so short an acquaintance.

Isaak kept stirring, letting the rest of what his brother said sink in. "What did you say that made her think we were?"

Jakob leaned his hip against a cupboard. "She just sensed it. She wanted me to come in here and apologize to you for not saying anything about her before she arrived. I'm sorry I didn't."

Isaak stopped stirring. Clearly, the woman had figured out that, despite their current disagreement, both brothers would need to be persuaded into this crazy matrimonial plan.

Not going to happen.

Jakob crossed one ankle over the other. "I don't want to argue again. It seems it's all we've done for the past few days. I'm sorry I didn't tell you sooner about my contract with Mrs. Archer, but I'm not going to have you treat Zoe with disrespect because you don't agree with how she ended up in Helena."

Isaak didn't care about her being in Helena; it was her being in Jakob's life that was the problem. "Whatever possessed you to bring a woman all this way, one about whom you didn't even know the barest of facts?"

Jakob held Isaak's gaze for a moment before shrugging. "I guess that's a fair question. We were supposed to correspond by letter first. That's how it usually works. Mrs.

Archer has never had a prospective bride show up uninvited, but after the interview, she realized Zoe was eminently suitable. Even you have to agree she is. She's smart. She's cultured. She's also tenderhearted and shyer than any girl we've ever met."

The change in Jakob's tone of voice on the last sentence said he expected Isaak to keep from questioning her too closely given her gentle disposition.

Ha! Her disposition was more coy than shy.

Isaak set the wooden spoon on the soapstone counter and removed the potatoes from the heat. "She may not be who she says she is."

"I have sixty days to figure that out before she's contractually free to walk away from my courtship." Jakob shot a glance toward the kitchen door. "I like her. I like her a lot."

Isaak was afraid of that.

"Please be nice to her."

"Of course I'll be nice." But that didn't mean he wasn't going to ask some pointed questions.

Jakob let out a huff of relief, then looked at the cookstove. "Need any help?"

Isaak shook his head. "As soon as I finish the potatoes, I'll warm the green beans and make gravy. The lamb chops are already cooked. I just need to cut them up and add them to the gravy."

"You're making gravy?" Jakob made it sound like the worst idea in the world.

"Of course. Mashed potatoes need gravy." And what else was Isaak supposed to do about only having four chops for six people?

Jakob rubbed the back of his neck, shifting awkwardly, as he always did when he knew he needed to 'fess up. "Um, this may not be the best time to tell you, but . . ." His gaze shifted again to the kitchen door.

"Say it." Isaak carried the kettle of potatoes over to the sink to drain.

"Zoe's a chef."

Of course she was! Just like she was French and the perfect wife for a man she'd never met as decided by a woman in Denver who made matches to make money — the more the better, at least for her.

Isaak inhaled through his nose and let out the air in a slow exhale to keep from stating his thoughts. "What do you mean, a 'chef'?"

"I mean exactly that. She's culinary trained. She's cooked for those rich guys, Vanderbilt and Astor. Her father used to be the secretary of the Society of Culinary Philanthropy in New York City."

Isaak focused his attention on draining

the potatoes to give him time to figure out what to say. He was proud of his cooking, something Jakob knew full well, so ignoring the woman's supposed skill wasn't an option. On the other hand, Isaak didn't want to appear to believe the obvious lie. A quick telegram to this society was all it would take to disprove her story — assuming the organization even existed.

"Why didn't you tell me that before I invited her to lunch?"

Jakob's hand appeared, holding the butter plate. "I didn't know myself until yesterday, and we didn't talk this morning about Zoe and me coming back here after church."

"Fair enough." Isaak took the butter and dumped all of it into the pot. He'd made a huge batch of potatoes, hoping people would fill up on them and not notice how little meat they were getting. "Grab the milk out of the icebox and then ask Yancey to come in here."

"You must be desperate if you're asking Yancey for cooking help."

Isaak mashed the potatoes, the extra quantity requiring greater force. He *was* desperate, at least about getting a telegram sent, something Yancey could help him with because her family owned both telegraph offices in town. As for the cooking, she'd improved once her mother forced her to stay in the kitchen and learn for an entire summer.

He added a large amount of salt to the pot. "There's nothing difficult about making gravy."

Jakob set the milk bottle on the countertop. "If you don't mind lumps." The usual note of teasing was absent from his voice. Was he worried that a hearty meal would scare off a woman claiming to be a chef?

Ridiculous. Miss de Fleur would probably eat sparingly in front of everyone for appearance's sake, but then she'd ask to take the leftovers back to the boardinghouse, where she'd shovel them down fast enough. Or share them with the relative who had yet to make an appearance.

Isaak added the milk and finished mashing. He tasted the potatoes. A little too much salt. He'd add less to the gravy, and once it and the potatoes were stirred together, the flavor would even out.

Jakob hadn't left the kitchen yet. "How are they?"

"They're fine." Isaak kept hold of the spoon to keep his brother from taking a bite. "Send Yancey in."

"Right." Jakob pivoted and sauntered out the door.

Isaak crossed to the stove to start the green beans. Doubt nipped at the edges of his confidence. A trained chef?

From her spot on the velvet-covered settee, Zoe glanced around the parlor that Mrs. Pawlikowski had decorated with damask wallpaper from baseboards right up to the cream-painted crown molding. One would think the burgundy rug and burgundy silk curtains next to the olive-green wallpaper would make the room seem like one was celebrating Christmas all year long. Instead, it looked exquisite. In her crimson gown, Zoe blended in perfectly.

She breathed in deeply. The house smelled wonderfully of bergamot and lemon oil . . . and of fresh-brewed coffee.

Miss Carline Pope sat at the upright piano, expertly playing a soft tune. Beethoven, Zoe guessed. She loved music, but she never listened to it enough to distinguish composers. *Maman* would know. There was not an instrument *Maman* could not play. Geddes Palmer sat in one of the Queen Anne chairs opposite Zoe reading a book.

Zoe smiled as she studied the pair. Someday she would have friends and family with whom she could sit in a room and not feel obligated to entertain the other.

Alone yet not alone. It sounded wonderful.

"Miss de Fleur?" came a gentle voice.

Miss Pope stopped playing. Mr. Palmer closed his book. Zoe followed their gazes to where Yancey Palmer stood on the drawing room's threshold.

Miss Palmer looked apologetic. "Please believe me when I say we tried our best."

Although confused by the vague statement, Zoe nodded.

"Follow me," ordered Miss Palmer. She turned around, raised her right arm, and waved in a circle. "To the dining room we go."

Mr. Palmer stood. "Ladies first."

Upon reaching the dining room, Miss Palmer led a pointed discussion with the Gunderson brothers over where everyone was to sit. Miss Pope and Mr. Palmer sat, only to be ordered to move by Isaak Gunderson, who claimed head of household status. Finally, Zoe and Jakob sat next to each other on one side of the rectangular table. Mr. Palmer and Miss Pope sat opposite them. Mr. Isaak Gunderson sat at the end of table between Mr. Palmer and Zoe. Miss Palmer sat on the other end between Miss Pope and Jakob, who asked the Lord's blessing on the meal.

"Amen," was said in unison.

Except by Zoe, who had not known she was supposed to join in.

When they had lived in France, she and Papa had taken their meals alone. The hierarchy among servants was strictly adhered to. After they settled in with Mrs. Gilfoyle-Crane, there had been more socializing, and only in English because doing so was, in Mrs. Gilfoyle-Crane's opinion, the best way to help Papa and Zoe become fluent. Meal prayers, if spoken, were always formal.

She liked the ease with which Jakob asked God to bless the food and their fellowship.

"Miss de Fleur?"

She turned left, toward the man who had whispered her name.

Mr. Isaak Gunderson offered her a bowl of coarsely mashed potatoes. He said nothing more as his intense gaze fixed on hers.

While his eyes were green and Jakob's blue, they both had stunning flecks of brown in the center. Why did Mr. Gunderson look at her so disapprovingly? Her skin next to her black hair must look pasty white compared to the soft bronze glow the Misses Palmer and Pope had, a lovely contrast to their blond hair. Zoe's crimson silk dress must seem pretentious next to the modest calico dresses the other ladies wore. She was nothing more than a blackbird amid these five popular — and astoundingly beautiful — canaries.

Zoe swallowed awkwardly, then accepted the bowl of potatoes. She added a scoop to her plate before passing the potatoes on to Jakob. Keeping her gaze lowered, she accepted the different bowls and platters Mr. Gunderson handed her. Soon the room filled with sounds of silverware clinking against china plates.

Miss Pope spoke first. "Jakob, how's work coming along at The Import Company?"

Before Jakob finished answering, Miss Palmer asked him a question. And then Miss Pope did again. Jakob had been right when he said the two ladies were overwhelming. They laughed and carried on as if everyone understood what they found amusing; they barraged him with questions, not once including Zoe in the conversation, although she minded not.

How nice to watch and listen.

She preferred to just watch and listen.

Mr. Palmer spoke to Mr. Gunderson, who nodded as he listened.

His handsome face was more square than rectangular, as Jakob's was. They both had the same strong jaw, the same heavy dark

blond brows, the same ash-blond hair —
no, Mr. Gunderson's hair was a shade or
two darker. Or perhaps Jakob's hair looked
lighter because his skin was tanned from
the greater amount of time he spent out-
doors than his brother.

"Miss de Fleur," Mr. Gunderson said as
he buttered a slice of bread, "tell everyone
what you think of Helena so far." His
pointed look contrasted with his added,
"Please."

CHAPTER EIGHT

Zoe looked down at the fork in her hand and her food-filled plate, which she had yet to take a bite from because she had been enchanted with the effortless conversation among everyone else at the table. She raised her gaze to see Miss Pope, Miss Palmer, and Mr. Palmer, who all looked sincerely interested in her response.

She smiled softly, while keeping her gaze away from Mr. Isaak Gunderson. "It is all so much more zan I could have hoped to find. Zis morning I saw a woman in a cart being pulled by a bison."

Miss Pope nodded. "That was Mrs. Nanawity. She owns the icehouse. I can introduce you to her if you like."

Zoe hesitated. She was unsure if she wished to meet this Mrs. Nanawity. Thankfully, she was spared from answering. Miss Palmer leaned forward in her chair, smiling broadly. "What's your favorite thing so far?"

Her amused eyes flickered to Jakob in a silent I-know-you-will-say-*him* look.

While Zoe liked Jakob, of all the things she had seen in Helena so far, what made her heart sing the most was — "I like how ze Montana sun awakes with a gentle crawl and yet sets with all ze power of a raging fire but none of ze destruction."

A *humph* slipped from between Mr. Gunderson's lips.

Zoe ignored him. "I watched last night and zis morning from ze balcony outside my room."

"Where are you staying?" Miss Pope asked between bites.

"Deal's Boardinghouse," Jakob answered. He gave Zoe a doting look before speaking to Miss Pope. "I wanted Zoe to stay in the one closest to The Import Company."

"And closest to you." Miss Pope sighed wistfully. "Oh, Jakob, that's so romantic."

Another *humph* came from Mr. Gunderson. Exemplifying the difference between himself and his brother were the smile lines on Jakob's face and the vertical crease Mr. Gunderson wore between his brows. Likely from scowling, as he was doing now.

Mr. Palmer's fork stopped halfway to his mouth. His brow furrowed, eyes narrowing. He looked at Mr. Gunderson. "Isn't Alfred

Deal supporting Kendrick in the mayoral election?"

"Isaak is running for mayor," Miss Pope put in before Mr. Gunderson could answer. "We're all so proud of him. If you need a man to lead the masses, to charge into battle, to change a town for the better, Isaak is that guy."

"Hear, hear," Miss Palmer cheered.

Out of the corner of her eye, Zoe saw Jakob slide his left arm under the table, but not before she noticed the fist he had made. She scooped a bite of potatoes and gravy into her mouth . . . and managed to swallow the unsavory food. Meals at the boardinghouse were about as tasty.

"Deal *is* supporting Kendrick," Mr. Gunderson finally answered in that voice of his that was slightly deeper than his brother's, drawing Zoe's attention to him again. "So are Charles Cannon, J. P. Fisk, and most of the brothel owners in town. Including Lestraude." He said the latter with an inflection that must have meant something to everyone else in the dining room.

Zoe drew in a breath to inquire who Lestraude was, but Mr. Gunderson turned her way, saw she was looking at him, and proceeded to stare. Zoe shifted uncomfortably in her chair. She moistened her bottom lip, but when his hard gaze lowered to her mouth, she pressed her lips closed, holding in her response, holding in her breath. With his jaw clenched, he looked as if he wished to be anywhere but sitting next to her.

Now that he was looking directly at her, she could see he was a more refined version of Jakob.

They are equally handsome. A bizarre flutter began in her heart and spread to her belly. Zoe ate her green beans in response. Never had overcooked, under- and over-seasoned food bothered her insides as this meal was doing.

"Salt," she whispered to Jakob.

He handed her both the salt and pepper shakers.

"Zank you." She peppered the potatoes and salted the beans.

"Right now, Isaak's campaign is un-official," Miss Yancey Palmer said, because clearly silence was something she found dull. "He plans on making a formal declaration on May 4, during The Import Company's grand opening."

The men continued to eat while Miss Pope and Miss Palmer took turns explaining to Zoe what Mr. Gunderson's reasons were for running against the corrupt, according to them, mayor. Their conversation then turned to disagreements over what could help his campaign.

Paying no heed to their discourse, Zoe forced down the potatoes, lamb gravy, and green beans. The only way to keep from starving to death here in Helena would be to purchase her own home so she could do her own cooking. Or she could find employment until she married. Nico would say either option was too permanent and too soon. She needed first to open a bank account. The gold coins she had hidden away in her trunks needed to be safely secured in a bank.

". . . that's because *every* politician hosts a barbeque," Miss Palmer said in a loud voice. She slid her fork onto her empty plate. "We need to do something unexpected — something *different* — to set Isaak apart."

"Good point, Yancey." Mr. Gunderson was silent for a moment, just long enough for Zoe to finish chewing a piece of overcooked lamb, before he said in a cheerful voice, "Let's ask Miss de Fleur for her opinion."

Zoe swung her gaze to him. Why would he draw her into the discussion? She knew nothing of politics.

She settled on, "Zis is none of my business."

"She's right," Jakob said in a crisp voice. "It isn't."

"Surely she has an opinion," Mr. Gunderson prodded.

Jakob looked her way. "You don't have to answer him."

"I know." To his brother, she said, "On American politics, I have no opinion."

Mr. Gunderson's green eyes focused solely on her with unnerving intensity. He was studying her, looking for something. She was about to believe he had given up on his inquiry when he asked, "Do you have an opinion on the food?"

Zoe wet her lips. She could not think, not with him staring at her as if they were the only two souls in the dining room. He kept looking at her in clear expectation of a reply, but she was speechless. And warm. Strangely warm.

"Isaak, stop," Jakob ordered.

"I think we all are interested in her culinary-trained chef's opinion." Mr. Gunderson motioned to Zoe's dinner plate, to the remaining food she had yet to force herself to eat. "Go on, Miss de Fleur. Speak your mind."

Zoe looked about the table; everyone had stopped eating.

In her peripheral vision, she could see

Jakob's left hand had balled into a fist again. What was she to say to his brother? She would not lie, but no man wished to hear criticism of his cooking. Of course, Mr. Gunderson could have intentionally sabotaged the meal.

"Why are you doing this?" Jakob asked his brother in an almost malevolent growl. "You promised you'd be nice to her."

Mr. Gunderson smiled at Jakob. "How am I not being nice?" he said in a genial tone. "If she *is* a real chef, she will have an opinion about this meal." He rested his left arm on the table. "Well, Miss de Fleur? You are a chef, aren't you?"

"Household cook," she said weakly.

His brows rose. "You told Jakob you were a chef."

She looked to Jakob for help.

"A chef, a cook." He glared at his brother. "What does it matter? They're the same thing and you know it."

Mr. Gunderson nodded, as if that made sense to him, and yet he said, "*Are* they, Miss de Fleur?"

Zoe moistened her bottom lip. This meal was supposed to make friends. It felt more like an inquisition. "Zey are similar, but not ze same."

"Explain," he ordered.

The others at the table looked at her with curiosity. Except Jakob. He continued to glare angrily at his brother, who seemed unperturbed. Oh, how she wished she could flee the room and Isaak Gunderson's disconcerting presence.

Zoe lowered her gaze to where she could see nothing but her dinner plate. "Uh, men are chefs. Women can only be household cooks."

"Where did you live in France?" His tone sounded genuine and interested. "Your accent has a strange R-lessness."

She studied his intense gaze. "What do you mean?"

"You drop the R sound in words like people born and raised in New York do, like my godfather does. Instead of saying *pow-er* or *A-mer-i-can,* Uncle Jonas says *powah* and you say *A-meh-i-can.* No R sound. Just like your accent." He leaned closer. "Where did you say you hail from?"

"Isaak, stop!" Jakob tossed his napkin on the table. "Zoe isn't one of those mail-order bride schemers you've read about in the papers. She doesn't deserve this." He stood and looked to their other guests. "Excuse us. I promised Zoe a tour of Helena."

Isaak stood out of politeness when Miss de

Fleur rose and left the table.

Yancey popped up to chase after Jakob and Miss de Fleur. "Don't go. Please." She glared at Isaak, as if to say, *Apologize,* on her way out of the dining room.

But he'd done nothing wrong, and he wasn't sorry about asking a few questions. He pressed his lips together. He wasn't opening his mouth, because if he did, he'd yell that the woman was a fraud and *somebody* needed to ask questions until she admitted it or — more likely — disappeared one day, leaving a note with a fabricated emergency that took her back to Denver.

Carline's gaze flitted between him and the archway, as if she didn't know whether she should follow her best friend or remain where she was. She was still sitting at the table when Yancey returned with a blunt, "How could you be so rude?"

Isaak sat and placed his napkin in his lap. "Is asking questions considered ill-mannered now? How fortunate I am to have you to point that out to me."

"Don't get snippy with me." Yancey pointed her index finger at him. "You weren't asking questions; you were making accusations."

"I was acting in the best interests of my brother, and you aren't going to make me feel guilty about that." Isaak swirled his remaining potatoes and gravy together. "We know nothing about this woman except what she's told us, and I find even that suspect."

Yancey huffed, sat down, and stabbed her fork into her green beans. "You're impossible when you get on your high horse."

Carline laid her napkin beside her empty plate. "I don't know, Yancey. Isaak has a bit of a point."

Yancey dropped her fork onto the side of the china plate with a clang.

Carline lifted one shoulder and leaned her head sideways at the same time, the gesture an act of contrition for disagreeing with her best friend.

Yancey looked to her brother. "What do you think, Geddes?"

"None of my business." He reached across the table and took another helping of mashed potatoes. "Carline, would you please pass the gravy?"

Jakob stormed back into the dining room. With a fire in his eyes that Isaak hadn't seen in years, Jakob leaned over Isaak's chair, one hand on the armrest, the other on the table. "How could you be so rude?"

Isaak wiped his lips with his napkin. "We can discuss that at a more appropriate time."

"Like you chose an appropriate time to interrogate Zoe?" Jakob shook his head. "I've never been ashamed to be called your brother until today." He pushed himself upright and stomped out of the dining room. The front door swooshed open and then slammed shut.

Isaak laid his napkin beside his plate. "I apologize for my brother's behavior. Would anyone like dessert?" He looked around the table for a response.

Carline's blue eyes couldn't get any wider.

Geddes was holding his fork aloft and swiveling his head between Isaak and the archway as though watching a tennis match.

Yancey covered her lips with a napkin, but hilarity pinched the corners of her eyes together. "You deserved that. You *know* you did."

Isaak scooted his chair away from the table and stood. If he didn't leave the room, he was going to whack something, which was both a waste of effort and beneath the dignity of anyone claiming to be a gentleman. "I'll get the cake."

He picked up his and Miss de Fleur's empty dinner plates and carried them into the kitchen. After setting the plates in the sink, he hauled some deep breaths in and out of his lungs.

Yancey came through the door to the dining room carrying empty dinner plates she'd cleared from the table. She laid them in the sink. "I thought you might need help."

She didn't add, *with serving dessert,* to the end of her statement. Nor did she apologize for saying he deserved to be humiliated in front of guests in his own home.

"I'm fine." Isaak moved to the counter and lifted the glass dome covering the remainder of Aunt Lily's chocolate cake. Thank goodness she'd brought it over yesterday afternoon out of concern that "her boys" were running low on sweets. He sliced a hefty piece and laid it on the topmost dessert plate he'd stacked on the countertop near where he was working.

Yancey walked over to him and lifted the top cake plate from the stack, clearing it out of his way. "No, you aren't fine, but I won't say another word."

He gave her a look to convey his skepticism.

Yancey's grin deepened on the left side. "For now." She took another plate from the stack and held it closer to him so he didn't have as far to balance cake on the knife while transferring it. "You know how you're always teasing about marking a day in the calendar when Jakob does something to surprise you? Well, I'm marking today."

Because? he asked with raised eyebrows.

"This past year has changed you. I don't know if it was being put in charge of The Resale Company or your decision to run for mayor, but we've all noticed your benevolent arrogance."

His jaw sagged. "My *what*?"

"You heard me. We've put up with you bossing us around because we know you mean well. However, it was only a matter of time before someone stood up to you."

How was he supposed to respond to that? It was unanswerable. Isaak dropped his gaze to the cake to conceal his dumbfounded silence. He sliced a smaller piece and laid it on the plate she held. "Forks are over there." He pointed with the icing-covered knife.

"Clearly," she sassed.

On any other day, he would have chuckled at the way she'd called him out, but he wasn't in the mood.

She took the plates over to where the forks were piled, added one to each plate, and headed back to the dining room.

Isaak set down the cake knife and let out a breath. Did people really think he was arrogant — *benevolently* arrogant?

164

If Jakob had heard the phrase, it explained why he'd been so argumentative of late. This whole mail-order bride business was likely another attempt to show he was responsible enough to handle the commitment of a wife and family, the same way he'd insisted he could get The Import Co. built, stocked, and opened by the first of week of May.

Ma had been convinced, but not Pa, or he wouldn't have told Jakob how important it was that The Import Co. open on schedule. Of course, when Pa said "schedule," he meant as soon as was reasonably possible, but no later than whatever date Jakob advertised as the grand opening.

Which was the fourth of May, nine days after Ma and Pa were planning to be home.

Who could be enlisted to make Jakob see reason and end the courtship before Ma and Pa arrived? Mac was away on his honeymoon, and given how Miss de Fleur had turned Jakob's brain to mush in a matter of two days, waiting two weeks for the sheriff to return was out of the question. Hale had already said he didn't consider it his business if Jakob wanted to order up a bride like another parcel to be delivered to The Import Co., and Geddes said pretty much the same thing. Windsor Buchanan? His penchant for saying he had Isaak's back meant Jakob would attribute any criticism Windsor voiced of Miss de Fleur to Isaak. Quinn Valentine, the city marshal, might be of some help. He was dedicated to serving the community, but he was also likely to say he had no jurisdiction to investigate Miss de Fleur without proof of a crime.

Isaak was on his own.

Yancey returned to the kitchen, her expression serious. "Why don't you like Miss de Fleur?"

Isaak cut a third piece of cake and laid it on a plate. "I don't want to talk about it."

"But you will." She leaned her forearms on the kitchen counter. "You always do."

He didn't want to, but there was something uncanny about Yancey and her ability to make people talk. With him, she was direct, but he'd seen her worm information out of others by doing nothing more than sitting next to them and remaining silent.

Like she was doing now.

Waiting for him to talk about something he *did* want to talk about . . . just not with the girl he considered his baby sister.

Who was still staring at him.

Waiting.

And watching.

Isaak sighed in defeat. "You of all people should understand my wariness when it comes to mail-order bride schemes."

"Because of the way I was deceived by Finn Collins?" She pressed her lips into a flat line.

She wasn't to blame. None of them could have known that Finn would team up with Madame Lestraude to lure a woman into prostitution by pretending to court her through letters — even going so far as to use Yancey as a proxy bride in Emilia's place. When Joseph Hendry wrote the newspaper article a year ago, he'd exposed the scheme without naming Yancey, but people had shunned her for weeks afterward anyway. She was still sensitive about it.

"We were all deceived on some level," Isaak acknowledged, and some of the antagonism drained from her face. He held out the chocolate cake. "Peace offering?"

She eyed the plate. "Not with a slice that small."

Laughter shook some of the tightness from his chest. He held the knife at an angle over the cake, moving it to indicate a larger and larger piece. When her scowl turned to a smile, Isaak cut. "I wish you and Jakob would make a match of it."

Yancey reached for two forks, exchanging one of them for the cake plate he held out to her. "I've wished for that, too, but I haven't been able to make myself fall in love with him."

Isaak cut himself a large piece and put it on a plate. "I've never agreed with the idea that people fall in love. It makes it sound like love is something you trip over and land in without any effort. Real love takes time and tending to develop."

"But sometimes even that isn't enough."

He frowned. "What are you talking about?"

"Joseph Hendry. He was a good man and I could almost love him, but he was always going to be second-best. I . . . I was going to break our engagement the night he died." She sniffed. "I decided I'd rather have nothing than settle for . . ."

Someone other than Hale, Isaak silently filled in the rest of her sentence. He took a bite of cake while searching for a way to move the conversation to something less upsetting for her. "What do you require in a husband?"

"Are you asking me for a list?"

He nodded. "Anyone who's contemplating marriage should know what's important to them in a spouse."

"Are you telling me you have a list?" Yancey shook her head as though clearing it. "Never mind. Of course you have a list.

And a timetable, no doubt."

"Which isn't a bad thing." Isaak took another bite of cake. Schedules and lists kept him from wasting time and effort. In business matters, they kept others from spinning in circles when, with a little planning, they could accomplish a great deal.

Yancey tapped her fork on his plate to get his attention. "Then tell me this: Why did you propose to Emilia Collins? You can't tell me you planned that."

"True, it wasn't on my timetable, but it wasn't an impulsive decision."

Her tilted head and raised eyebrows said, *Go on. Tell me all about it.*

Isaak pushed away his plate, no longer starving. "Before I proposed to Emilia, I analyzed the situation. She needed protection which I could have provided. She's a wonderful person, and we could have built a solid marriage and grown to love each other over time."

Yancey cut a piece of cake with the side of her fork. "My parents said the same thing about Joseph, but there was no spark of romance between us."

"Not all women require that. My mother didn't. She wanted a man who would help her raise her child — well, what she thought was one child at the time."

"*Pfft.* A tale a mother tells her sons. I bet she left out all the romantic parts."

Doubtful. His mother wasn't one to shy away from what others might consider uncomfortable topics. Even if she had, it didn't change the facts. "Romance is a fine thing, but it's not the same as real love."

"Says the man who's never even taken a girl out on a surrey ride." Yancey lifted her chin in challenge.

A somewhat valid rebuttal, but — again — it didn't nullify sound logic.

"Romance is like dessert." Isaak pointed to his half-eaten cake as an example. "It's a wonderful addition to the meal, but if that's all you ever have, you'll soon make yourself sick. True love is the meal. It's heartier, more nourishing, and — yes — takes some planning to put together a good one."

Yancey chuckled. "A good point, but maybe not the best example coming from a man who's notorious for loving his sweets."

"Touché." He grinned. "Do you think it unromantic to have expectations and then discover someone who meets them? Because I can't think of anything *more* romantic."

Yancey shook her head. "You and I have different definitions of romance. I remember the exact moment I fell in love with Hale. My feet left the ground. I knew in the deepest place of my heart that he was my future. People have told me I was too young, but it's been ten years, and no other man has ever made me feel that way."

"I want to feel all those things, too. I'm not heartless, despite what some people might think. But all that emotion needs to be balanced with cold, hard facts. For example, what if the man who made your feet leave the ground was Ole Olafson?" Isaak named the town drunk.

Yancey laughed merrily. "You've made your point. I suppose what we disagree on is the balance between emotion and logic."

"I suppose."

She set down her fork. "Then who's to say which one of us is correct?"

Isaak lowered his eyebrows. She was building up to something, and he wasn't sure he was going to like it.

"And" — she looked him straight in the eye — "who's to say you get to decide that balance for anyone else?"

The question felt like another punch. "You mean my questioning of Miss de Fleur, I take it."

She nodded. "Jakob isn't some flibberti-gibbet."

A matter of opinion.

Yancey scowled at him as though she

could read his mind. "He's not, and Miss de Fleur may turn out to be a perfect match for him."

Not when she was only out for his money.

Yancey picked up her plate and held out a hand to take his. "I know you consider me too young to have any wisdom, but mark my words, Isaak David Gunderson. If you choose to exercise your benevolent arrogance by separating Jakob from a woman he's falling in love with, you'll live to regret it." She walked to the sink and placed their dishes inside it. "I'll leave you to your thoughts. Thank you for dinner."

Isaak nodded to acknowledge her gratitude. She left the kitchen, and he heard her rounding up Geddes and Carline, convincing them to leave their dirty dishes on the table and leave without saying good-bye.

Once the house was quiet, Isaak started cleaning the kitchen. Perhaps it was somewhat arrogant to assume he knew better than his brother, but Isaak was sure of one thing . . .

Zoe de Fleur did not belong with Jakob.

CHAPTER NINE

Deal's Boardinghouse
Monday morning
De Fleur-Gunderson Courtship Contract,
  Day 3

How could anyone say Isaak Gunderson was a nice man?

Zoe sipped her lukewarm tea. No matter how many times she replayed yesterday's lunch in her mind, she found no reasonable explanation for his animosity, other than the rancor that was native to his arrogant personality.

You drop the R sound in words like people born and raised in New York do.

How dare he question her accent!

She had gone to bed thinking about how angry she was with him. She woke thinking how angry she still was. The last time she felt this angry at anyone had been —

She grimaced, unable to think of a time. She abhorred being angry at anyone; harmony with others made life sweeter. Isaak Gunderson bore not a sweet bone in his body.

"Something wrong?" Nico asked.

She met his curious gaze. "I am angry."

"Really?" He squinted at her. "I can't tell. You'd make an excellent poker player because you always look so calm and expressionless. My cousin's ears turn red and his neck swells when he's angry. It's kind of creepy."

That did sound creepy.

Especially because he had never before mentioned having a cousin.

"Zoe," he said slowly, "have you ever actually been angry enough to know if you're *really* angry right now?"

Zoe stared at him in disbelief. There was no other explanation for the emotional upheaval she had felt since meeting Isaak Gunderson.

"I know how I am feeling," she insisted. "My stomach aches like a million butterflies struggling to escape a vat of boiling water."

"That makes no sense."

Exactly. Which made it fitting to describe how the man made her feel.

"Well, because you're too *angry* to eat" — Nico's gaze flickered to her breakfast plate — "do you mind?"

Zoe looked down at her still-full plate of hot cakes made from overmixed batter, bland sausages, and fried-to-a-burned-crisp potatoes. None of it was palatable.

And yet Nico's plate had been scraped clean.

She put down her teacup. After giving him her plate, which he cheerfully accepted, she removed the linen napkin from the lap of her amethyst walking suit and laid it where her plate had been.

"What are you going to do today?" he asked before shoveling in a mouthful of potatoes.

"First, I need to open a bank account. Zen I would like to visit Jakob at Ze Import Company before Miss Palmer and Miss Pope take me shopping." She paused to remember what she needed to buy. "I must purchase a bottle of wine for Mr. and Mrs. Forsythe. Zey invited Jakob and me to join zem for supper tomorrow night."

"There's a bank a block south from here."

"Zat would be convenient." And far away from Isaak Gunderson, whom she was going to avoid for as long as possible. No more thinking about him, either. "What was ze name of ze bank?"

Nico cut the sausage with the side of his fork. "I don't remember, but there's brass everywhere and crystal chandeliers, so I bet it's a good one."

Unable to watch him eat the unpalatable food, she glanced around the wood-paneled dining room. Of the two cloth-covered rectangular tables, she and Nico sat at the one closest to the warm hearth. Three genteel-looking men sat at the table nearest the door, which led to the parlor and front foyer, because Mr. Deal had encouraged them to sit there instead of at Zoe's table. They had looked her way before returning to their breakfast and newspapers.

Yesterday, after lunch, while Jakob had taken her on a tour of Helena, she had noticed the number of boardinghouses in town. None had a wraparound porch or a wraparound second-floor balcony like the Deals' lovely, white-painted home. What a blessing Jakob had given her by choosing this boardinghouse over all others. The balcony rocking chair near the railing that separated the men's balcony from the women's was the perfect place to watch the sun ascend in its golden glory, as she had both mornings since her arrival in Helena.

She also appreciated Mr. and Mrs. Deal's upmost propriety in providing separate entrances for male and female boarders to ascend to their rented rooms. Nothing about this boardinghouse was pretentious. No, it was more like a hearty bowl of chicken soup. Comfortable, warm, and stable.

Except for the food.

Which was as unpalatable as what Isaak Gunderson had cooked.

Zoe groaned inwardly.

No more wasting thoughts on him. No more! She looked around for something — anything — to distract her. The glassware looked similar to the crystal goblets Mrs. Pawlikowski owned. In fact, Mrs. Deal's porcelain china, glassware, and white tablecloths were as fine as the ones in the Grand Hotel.

"Look what I found!"

Zoe turned to Nico, who was holding a hair between his fingers. She held back a gag. "Was zat in your food?"

He nodded, then flicked it to the floor. "Not the worst I've ever found in something I was eating. Once there was —"

"You will speak — *and eat* — no more."

The corner of his mouth indented. "Are you sure? It —"

"Hush."

He laughed. "You should have seen the look on your face. I didn't think a person could turn green, but you did. Green skin next to a purple dress . . . not a good look, even on you, although I'm impressed with your show of emotion. Disgust you do well. Anger, I'm still not convinced."

Zoe grumbled, "You would feel ze same if you met him."

"Your new beau?"

"No! Jakob is wonderful. His brother —" Zoe gritted her teeth. "I wish to not speak of him."

Nico's face scrunched on the left side as he studied her. He then tossed his napkin onto the table. "I'm full anyway. I'm sure tomorrow's breakfast will be better. Come on. I'll walk you to the bank before I start my deliveries."

Zoe hesitated. A trip to the bakery around the corner would provide a little sustenance, but she needed more than bread to maintain good health. Tomorrow morning's breakfast plagued her.

"Gee, Zoe, you want to say something about the food, don't you?"

Zoe found herself nodding. Mortified at what she had unwittingly admitted, she stopped nodding and looked at Nico. "It is none of my business," she said firmly.

"My employer says that sometimes the kindest thing we can do for someone is to be honest."

This was true. But the embarrassment from meal criticism would crush the kind-hearted Mrs. Deal.

"We will leave now for ze bank."

"Of course," was what he said. What he did was stack their used dishes one on top of the other and stroll toward the entrance to the kitchen. "Hello," he called out. "Anyone in here?"

Zoe dashed after him. "Nico!" She entered the impeccably clean kitchen in time to see Mrs. Deal and her niece, Janet, exit the larder.

"Can I help you?" Mrs. Deal asked.

"Hi, I'm Zoe's brother, Nico. Yesterday in church, the preacher said that sometimes the kindest thing we can do for someone is to be honest with him." He gave the dirty dishes to Janet. "We found a hair in the food and wanted you to know."

Janet's mouth gaped.

Mrs. Deal's face whitened. "I . . . I . . ." Tears pooled in her eyes and she broke into sobs.

Zoe gave Nico a look warning him to stay silent. Then she wrapped her arm around Mrs. Deal's shaking shoulders. "Madame, I must apologize for" — the words *my brother* refused to pass her lips — "for Nico. He wished no ill will about ze hair. Zis happens to even ze best cooks."

Mrs. Deal looked up. "How do you know?"

"I have been cooking with my papa since I could walk." Zoe paused, searching for the right and gentle *and* truthful words. "When I was young, he loved me enough to point out my error and to chastise me until I remembered to cover my hair. Papa taught all his chefs zat attention to neatness was essential in all cookery."

"You're a chef?" Janet asked before exchanging glances with her aunt.

"I am a household cook," Zoe corrected. "Or I was, before I moved to ze territory."

The moment Nico straightened his shoulders, Zoe realized how much he had grown from the scrawny ten-year-old boy she had met four years ago on a street corner across from Central Park. "My sister doesn't like to brag," he said proudly, "but she's one of the best chefs in the country. Trained in Paris. Worked for the European aristocracy before coming to America. She's cooked for Queen Victoria, the American ambassador to France, and, most recently, Misters Vanderbilt and Astor, and the mayor of New York City."

Zoe nipped at her bottom lip to keep from chastising Nico in front of Mrs. Deal and her niece. Why had he lied? There was no reason! Never had she cooked for Queen Victoria or the ambassador to France, although the rest had at least attended one of Mrs. Gilfoyle-Crane's dinner parties when Papa was alive, as had the American vice president.

Nico's grin grew as Mrs. Deal and Janet exchanged glances. "My sister can make anything taste like manna from heaven. If people in this town knew how good a chef she is, they'd be throwing money at her feet. Once Zoe cooks for you, you'll see she's a gold mine waiting to be tapped."

Mrs. Deal and her niece exchanged looks again. Mrs. Deal's brows rose in a silent question Janet must have understood because she nodded.

Mrs. Deal turned to Zoe, all tears gone. "Would you give us lessons?"

"Of course she will," Nico answered. "She can start immediately."

Zoe swallowed to ease the sudden dryness in her throat. She had other plans today. She needed to go to the bank, then she wanted to see Jakob before she went shopping with Misses Palmer and Pope. Nico knew this. She thought he was more considerate.

He and Mr. Isaak Gunderson would get

along mightily.

Mrs. Deal squeezed Zoe's hand. "I can't believe you cooked for Queen Victoria." The hopefulness in her tone rivaled that in her eyes. "Please say you'll help us. Please. I'm at my wit's end at how to make this boardinghouse profitable."

"We both are," Janet put in.

Zoe gave a half-hearted nod. "I can go to ze bank tomorrow," she said weakly. "I can also wait until zis afternoon to see Jakob."

Janet's sigh was utterly melodic. "What I'd give to marry him."

Zoe ignored Nico's curled lip and Janet's sudden dreaminess. "I am to meet Misses Palmer and Pope at ten-thirty. Zis is not negotiable."

Mrs. Deal looked to the wall clock. "That gives us an hour and fifteen minutes. Is there anything we should do to prepare?"

Zoe eyed the chestnut braid hanging down Janet's back. "To begin with, hair should be neatly combed, bound, and covered. Arms, hands, and fingernails, before beginning any meal preparation, must be scrupulously washed with lye soap." She noted the heavily soiled aprons over their work dresses. "Kitchen aprons should be used in ze kitchen only, daily, and —"

"Excuse me," Mrs. Deal said with a smile.

"Would you hold that thought while I go find a journal?"

As Mrs. Deal left the kitchen, Janet headed over to the sink. "I'll wash these dishes real quick and then find us some clean aprons."

Nico nudged Zoe's arm "Hey, um . . . Zoe, thanks for the breakfast," he said, walking backward to the kitchen door. "I'd like to stay, but I need to get on to work. See ya tomorrow."

"Wait!" She dashed to the door, grabbed his arm, and lowered her voice to keep Janet from hearing. "You must stop with ze lies."

"No more, I promise."

She released his arm. "Go to Ze Import Company after work. I wish to introduce you to Jakob."

"I can't wait." He gave her a cheeky grin and then disappeared into the dining room.

"You and your brother act nothing alike," Janet said from where she stood at the sink.

Zoe nodded politely.

It was the nicest response she could give at the moment.

Tuesday, March 20
De Fleur-Gunderson Courtship Contract,
  Day 11

"I am most displeased."

Isaak didn't have to finish rounding the

corner a few blocks from Gibbon's Steak House to know who was speaking. The French accent told him. Besides enjoying a productive campaign discussion over lunch with Hale, Isaak had the good fortune to be in the right spot at the right time to catch her in her lies. He edged closer, using the brick wall of the floral shop to shield himself from Miss de Fleur's view.

". . . meet Jakob zis morning, and I expect you to arrive zis time. I will have lunch for us."

"Sorry, Sis. Got work to do."

Sis? As in *sister*? Isaak's chest tightened with satisfaction. He'd known the woman was keeping some poor relation hidden away, and here was proof.

". . . don't want to meet him." Based on the tenorlike pitch to the voice, Miss de Fleur's brother was a youth. "And you don't want me to meet him either."

"Nico!"

At the sound of footsteps coming closer, Isaak flattened himself against the wall — a ridiculous waste of effort for a man of his size but instinctual. A flash of brown clothing whizzed past. The boy — Nico — ran straight across the intersection. Isaak waited for the sound of footsteps to fade before peeking around the edge of the brick wall to see if Miss de Fleur was still there. A blue ruffle disappearing onto Eighth Street was his only view of her.

He waited for a moment before stepping out of the alley onto the sidewalk and walking to the intersection of Eighth and Warren Street. He turned his head left and right. Which one should he follow?

Going after Miss de Fleur accomplished nothing. She'd already proven herself a worthy adversary by turning Jakob into a complete dunderhead within a few days. Nico, on the other hand . . .

Now that was a possibility. Younger and sporting something of a chip on his shoulder, according to the belligerent tone in his voice, the boy might be enticed into spilling the sordid plot to entrap a rich husband.

Isaak rubbed his jaw. His other option, according to Yancey, was to turn around and forget all about it.

He turned left, lengthening his stride as he headed south along Warren Street until he spied the same brown fabric he'd seen flash by the alleyway opening on a dark-haired youth who, with an almost imperceptible swipe of his right hand, stole a fresh roll from the bread basket outside of O'Callahan's Bakery.

Quite the brother Miss de Fleur had.

Isaak continued to follow the boy down Warren Street for ten minutes and into the red-light district. Nico walked straight into Madame Lestraude's *Maison de Joie,* a pseudo-hotel whose only residents were young women with names like . . .

Isaak's breath caught.

Everything in Madame Lestraude's business wore a fake French name: her hotel, her brothel girls, even her own pseudonym. And now she'd branched out into supplying fake French brides with names like Zoe de Fleur.

In the two years since laws were enacted to make prostitution illegal, brothel owners had begun diversifying their business practices to keep the money flowing. If he were a betting man, he'd lay odds Madame Lestraude and that matchmaker in Denver were in cahoots.

His blood heated. Who else had the madam and matchmaker targeted in Helena?

Whoever else they'd gotten their claws into, he'd figure out later and — when he was mayor — he'd shut Lestraude down so fast, she wouldn't know what hit her. Right now, he had a brother to convince, a business to run, a mayoral race to kick off, and a new storefront to make sure opened by

May 4. Jakob said his mail-order contract allotted him sixty days to evaluate whether he and Miss de Fleur were a good match. She'd been in Helena for eleven days. That left forty-nine on the contract — days Isaak would use to unmask her as a fraudulent schemer.

The brothel door opened.

Nico darted down the steps and was on the last one when Madame Lestraude appeared in the doorway and yelled his name in a tone Isaak recognized: maternal vexation. She pointed at the door. Nico's shoulders slumped and he stomped back up the steps, closed the door, and gave what Isaak presumed was an apology for leaving the door open.

Lestraude straightened the youth's hat. As she spoke to him, she slid a letter from the sleeve of her brown and burgundy dress.

Nico nodded, took the letter, then raced off in the direction of Main Street.

The madam watched him run away, a matronly smile on her face. She looked across the street in Isaak's direction. Her smile turned cynical when she locked gazes with him. *I knew your soul wasn't as lily-white as you pretend it to be,* she seemed to say, as though his presence in the red-light district meant he frequented its services.

Isaak glared back.

A flicker of unease crossed her painted features before she turned on her heel and reentered her den of wickedness.

Isaak spun around and headed north, back toward The Import Co. No wonder the Denver matchmaker could call Zoe de Fleur eminently suitable. No wonder Jakob, like other intelligent men who'd been taken in, fell for the woman. With Lestraude feeding the matchmaker information about Jakob, all Zoe de Fleur needed to do was play the role of the perfect bride for him.

Targeting Jakob was the only part of the plot Isaak couldn't figure out. True, he and Jakob were well-off, but they were by no means the wealthiest bachelors in Helena. It made more sense to target a Fisk boy, but — for whatever reason — Jakob was the women's chosen victim. Isaak was sure of it.

Now, he needed to convince his brother. Easier said than done.

As he neared The Import Co., raised masculine voices and the lack of pounding tested his resolve to stay out of Jakob's way. After Yancey's warning, Isaak had decided it was more important to let Jakob fail at opening the store than in marrying a fraud, although Isaak wasn't above making deliveries that took him close to The Import Co. to keep abreast of the progress.

He was ambling past, intent on glancing through the recently installed windows, when he heard Jakob shout, "They aren't straight!" followed a moment later by, "I don't care a fig about my brother or his precious schedule."

Isaak detoured to the open front door. Tin *fleur-de-lis* tiles littered the floor. Isaak stared at the mess, his blood heating and his determination to leave Jakob to his own devises crumbling like the plaster scraped from the ceiling along with the tiles. "What's going on here?" he asked, and every eye in the shop turned to him. "I thought these tiles were installed last week."

A few nods, a "Yes, sir," and several gazes dropping to the floor were all overshadowed by Jakob's, "They were crooked, so I tore them down this morning."

Isaak eyed the scattered tin, then his brother. "I hadn't noticed." He swung his gaze to the work-crew foreman. "O'Leary, how far will this set back the schedule?"

"It doesn't matter," Jakob answered. "It has to be done right."

"How far?" Isaak demanded, his focus never leaving the foreman.

Jakob stepped between Isaak and O'Leary,

cutting off their line of sight. "Don't answer him. This is my crew and my job."

"Which you clearly aren't handling well."

Jakob's face suffused with red. He jabbed his index finger toward the open door. "Get out."

"No. Someone has to make sure this store opens on time."

"Pa trusted me to open it, not you. *Me!*"

"Not enough!"

Jakob's cheeks filled with blotchy pink. "What did Pa say?"

"It doesn't matte —"

"What did he say?" Each word was clipped and emphasized.

Isaak wasn't about to speak in front of the crew. "I'm sure you men have something you can do on one of the upper floors."

Never had Isaak seen those five men move so fast. They scampered up the stairs like mice chasing after moving cheese.

When he and Jakob were alone, Isaak took a deep breath, then answered. "I overheard him tell Ma he was worried you might lose focus." It was a private conversation, something Isaak shouldn't have heard and certainly shouldn't have repeated.

Jakob swallowed, his neck tendons visible above his shirt collar. "Is that why you're here instead of doing your own work?"

Now was not the time to mention that Miss de Fleur had a wayward brother, although it was tempting, given how Jakob's question was a thinly veiled accusation that Isaak was neglecting The Resale Co. "I had different business that brought me your way. I was intending to pass by, but then I heard . . ."

Words he should have ignored. Maybe he would have, were it not for the way Yancey had poked fun at his lists and schedules nine days ago.

Still, as the older brother and the future mayor of Helena, it was up to him to set an example of —

Benevolent arrogance.

Isaak winced as Yancey's description stabbed his inner ear. "I'll leave. As you said, I have my own work to do." He turned around.

"Yes. You've done enough damage," followed him out the door.

CHAPTER TEN

Monday, April 2
De Fleur-Gunderson Courtship Contract,
  Day 24

"*Poisson* is fish. F-I-S-H," Zoe spelled aloud while covering the shopping list — written in both French and English — on her lap with both hands.

"Fish is *poisson*. P-O-I-S-S-O-N. If we remove an *s* from *poisson,* the word becomes poison. Hm." Mrs. Forsythe turned away from the carriage's right-side window to look at Zoe, who was sitting to her left. "What's the word for poison in French?"

"*Poison,*" Zoe answered without pause. "It is spelled P-O-I-S-O-N. *La méchante reine mit du poison sur la pomme qu'elle donna à Blanche-Neige.* Which means?"

Mrs. Forsythe's brow furrowed, her lips moving in silent speech. And then she smiled. "The wicked queen put poison on the apple she gave Snow White."

"Gave *to* Snow White."

"Oh, that's right. The word poison must have originated in French and the English adopted it, much like fiancé, chic, and . . ."

As Mrs. Forsythe shared additional words, Zoe's gaze fell to the sheet of stationery resting in the lap of her sapphire silk day dress. The sheet contained a list of foods she needed to cook for Mrs. Forsythe's breakfast party. Who would have expected that the first meal Zoe and Jakob had shared with the Forsythes three weeks ago would turn into an every-Tuesday-and-Saturday occurrence? Or that the divine and gracious Mrs. Forsythe would be the one to recognize Zoe's inability to read and write English?

Their agreement to help each other improve fluency in the other's native language had birthed a treasured friendship. Like Zoe, Mrs. Forsythe preferred attention on others instead of on herself. To watch and listen. Jakob and Mr. Forsythe always carried the meal conversation. Zoe appreciated that the judge never seemed put out with his wife's gentle demeanor or lack of opinions.

The judge would never demand his wife speak her mind.

The judge would never demand his wife explain her thoughts.

Nor would Jakob.

He was a good man. And kind. He knew how to laugh and smile and make a girl feel at ease in taking time to enjoy the beauty of the world around them. Whenever Zoe visited him at The Import Company, he would stop work and talk with her. She had seen him do the same with others. Jakob truly cared about people.

She had felt such happiness when they were together that first week.

But now? She must bore him. What else would explain his absence? In the last seven days, she had spent more than a few minutes in conversation with Jakob only twice: Tuesday supper and Saturday lunch with the Forsythes. During those moments, Jakob had been distracted. After she recommended a breakfast feast to welcome home Mrs. Forsythe's friend, Mrs. Pauline Hollenbeck, when she returned from her six-month European tour, Mr. Forsythe had been the one to declare it "unusual" yet "a novel idea." Jakob had heartily agreed.

Yet Zoe wondered if he had even been paying attention to the discussion. Perhaps he was more like his brother than she thought.

You drop the R sound in words like people born and raised in New York do.

Ha! The man's ability to distinguish accents was as poor as his palate.

Zoe shifted on the carriage bench.

"What's wrong, dear?" Mrs. Forsythe said gently. "You suddenly seem troubled."

"A disturbing thought came to mind."

"Ah." She said nothing more as the carriage slowed to turn a corner, and Zoe knew the elegant woman had no intention of pressuring her into offering a confidence. She also knew Mrs. Forsythe was not concerned about the "disturbing thought" being about her. Lily Forsythe never assumed the worst of anyone.

Nor did Zoe.

Except with Isaak Gunderson.

That familiar ache she had experienced of late started again in her chest.

Weary of it, Zoe shifted on the carriage bench so she could face Mrs. Forsythe. "A disturbing thought plagues me. I wish to know how to never zink of zis zing again."

"How often does the thought come to mind?"

"Mornings are ze worst times . . . except for when I try to sleep. Zen I lie awake unable to zink of other zings. I replay zee moment in my mind, and it causes pain" — Zoe touched the spot right over her heart — "here."

A long beat of silence passed before Mrs. Forsythe said, "And you've now started having this disturbing thought during the day?"

Zoe nodded.

"Most likely it is fear, worry, or unresolved conflict." Mrs. Forsythe fell silent as she studied Zoe's face. She spoke in a gentle manner. "My dear child, *love* could just as well be the culprit."

"Love?" Zoe blurted out in revulsion.

Mrs. Forsythe chuckled softly. "I take it Jakob isn't involved."

"Not at all."

"Then I recommend you face whatever's causing you this pain. Confront it head-on. Win the battle."

The carriage rolled to a stop.

A trio of ladies passed by the carriage window. One lady wore a calico day dress like the one Zoe had seen at breakfast on the newest boarder at Deal's Boardinghouse.

"Another French word zat is the same in English is menu. M-E-N-U." She handed the breakfast menu to Mrs. Forsythe. "Zank you for taking me shopping with you. I enjoy zese precious moments together."

"I feel the same."

Zoe nodded. "I will see you Sunday."

Mrs. Forsythe folded the parchment in

quarters, then slid it into her reticule, just as the carriage door opened. "The day isn't over yet. Before I return you to the boardinghouse, I need to see if the Minton china is still for sale."

"Ma'am," the hired driver said before taking her hand to assist her out of the carriage. He repeated the action for Zoe. The moment she stepped onto the sidewalk, her gaze caught on the words etched into the front window: THE RESALE COMPANY.

Zoe hesitated, having no inclination to face the cause of her pain.

Mrs. Forsythe wrapped her left arm around Zoe's right one. "This won't take long."

When Mrs. Forsythe walked forward, Zoe had no choice but to comply. Isaak Gunderson may not be at work. Jakob said his brother had many responsibilities, some of them requiring him to leave his employee to run the store.

She hoped now was one of those times.

The moment they strolled into the store, a petite brunette whom Zoe had yet to meet stopped petting the plump tabby cat resting on the service counter. Her curious gaze flickered for a moment on Zoe before she said, "Mrs. Forsythe, it's a joy to see you!"

"I heard you and Mac had returned. How

was St. Louis?"

"Wonderful," the brunette said, then cringed. "And rainy. Mac lost three umbrellas. I didn't know he was so forgetful."

"A man on his honeymoon is more likely to be distracted than forgetful," Mrs. Forsythe remarked with a smile. "Emilia, let me introduce Miss Zoe de Fleur of Paris by way of New York City. Zoe, this is Emilia McCall. She's newly married to our county sheriff."

Zoe and Mrs. McCall exchanged pleasantries.

"What brings you to Helena?" asked Mrs. McCall.

Mrs. Forsythe answered for Zoe. "Jakob is courting her."

Mrs. McCall blinked repeatedly. "Jakob, as in Jakob Gunderson?"

Zoe nodded. "I am his bride by mail delivery."

"Not his bride yet," Mrs. Forsythe clarified. "They met through the Archer Matrimonial Company in Denver. Zoe is helping me improve my French. Jonas promised me a trip to Paris for our tenth anniversary this December."

"That's wonderful!" Mrs. McCall focused on Zoe. "I was a mail-order —"

"— walk you to the door."

Zoe tensed at the sound of Mr. Gunderson's deep voice. She looked toward his office, where he stood half-in, half-out. Twenty-two days of avoiding him ruined. Ruined! Unless she ran. To her misfortune, dashing out of the store was impossible with Mrs. Forsythe holding tight.

Mr. Gunderson strolled out of his office, his attention on the talkative dark-haired woman in a gray-and-yellow-floral day dress. A mustached man holding a top hat and a wrapped package strolled behind them.

"I certainly will," Mr. Gunderson answered the woman.

And then he looked up.

If he was surprised to see Zoe, he was good at playacting, because nothing in his expression resembled the animosity she had last seen on his arrogant and, to her annoyance, handsome face.

Zoe raised her chin. She breathed slowly through her nose and let the air out just as slowly, hoping to calm her rapid heartbeat. If he could be so indifferent to her presence, she could reciprocate. And there was nothing to worry about. Manners dictated he would be kind and gracious because of the other women present, and because this was his place of business.

As the trio neared them, Mrs. McCall stepped to Zoe's side to clear the aisle. "Have a nice day," she said with a smile.

Instead of continuing past, they stopped. Or at least the unfamiliar woman did first; the two men, in good form, followed suit.

Her brown-eyed gaze settled on Zoe. "I don't believe we've met."

Mrs. Forsythe's right hand clenched her left wrist, thereby pinning Zoe's arm and keeping her from shaking anyone's hand. "May I present Miss Zoe de Fleur? Zoe, this is Mr. and Mrs. Kendrick. He is the *current* mayor of Helena."

Zoe dipped her chin in acknowledgment. "It is a pleasure to meet you."

"Oh, you're French!" exclaimed Mrs. Kendrick. "I've yet to meet someone truly from France." She looked at her husband. "Did you hear that accent? She's from France."

"I —"

"Zoe was born in Paris," Mrs. Forsythe interjected, cutting off Mr. Kendrick's response to his wife. "Her father was a chef for the . . ."

As Mrs. Forsythe shared Papa's culinary accomplishments, Zoe nodded. She should say something. She ought to take part in the conversation, but even without glancing up at the man towering over them all, she knew he was looking at her. She could verily feel Mr. Gunderson's gaze. She shivered; the action caused her shoulders to shift and squirm.

Mrs. Forsythe stopped speaking and gave Zoe a strange look.

"Miss de Fleur," began Mrs. Kendrick, "would you care to join Harold and me for Easter lunch? We would love to hear —"

"She and Jakob are spending the day with us." Mrs. Forsythe's words held a crisp edge. "Jonas will be giving Zoe lessons on how to ride a horse. Our godson is courting her."

Mrs. Kendrick's surprised gaze shifted to Mr. Gunderson, who stood as still and silent as a statue, and then to Zoe, and then back to Mrs. Forsythe. "Oh, you mean *Jakob* is courting her."

"Jonas and I are quite pleased with Jakob's choice, as David and Marilyn will be once they meet Zoe," Mrs. Forsythe said with great feeling. "We couldn't adore her more if she were our own daughter."

An awkward silence stretched.

Zoe's pulse raced.

Mrs. Kendrick kept glancing between Mrs. Forsythe, Zoe, and Mr. Gunderson.

Eyes narrowed, Mr. Kendrick tapped his

top hat against his thigh. He said nothing, but Zoe knew he was intently thinking. As his wife was. Why? There was nothing suspicious or odd or interesting about anything said.

Mrs. Forsythe drew Zoe back a step before saying, "We won't keep you."

The Kendricks nodded and continued to the door, Mr. Gunderson walking with them.

Zoe stared at the planked floorboards to keep from giving in to the desire to look Mr. Gunderson's way. Her heart continued to pound. Was he remorseful over his behavior? His bland expression had given nothing away, nor did he seem disapproving of her. Perhaps he realized how judgmental, unfair, and wrong his presumptions about her were.

Mrs. Forsythe released her grip on Zoe. "I can't believe their audacity," she said in a terse, low voice. "You'd think with Isaak running for mayor *against* Kendrick —" She broke off. "Jonas will want to hear about this. He distrusts Kendrick greatly."

A *humph* came from Mrs. McCall. "Mac warned Isaak that Kendrick or one of his supporters would try to bribe him to drop out of the race."

"Is Lestraude still backing Kendrick?"
"Yes."

"That can't please Mac."

"They've agreed not to discuss politics."

"How are things between the three of you?"

"As best as can be under the circumstances."

Zoe looked back and forth between the two women, expecting one of them to offer an explanation of who this Lestraude fellow was. Both stayed silent, which only added to Zoe's confusion. The Kendricks seemed a pleasant couple. Mr. Gunderson seemed at ease with them. How could they be political opponents? There was much about American politics she failed to — nor wished to — understand.

Mrs. McCall suddenly smiled. "What brings you two by?"

"Does Isaak still have that set of Minton tableware?" Mrs. Forsythe asked.

"Which ones are those?"

"White bone china with blue-printed, Chinese-inspired landscapes. Twelve place settings."

Mrs. McCall frowned. "I don't remember ever seeing anything like that." She glanced around the shop, which was strange, considering how her petite height limited her view. She looked to the front door, her eyes narrowing.

Zoe glanced over her shoulder. Mr. Gunderson stood outside under the portico talking to the Kendricks, his broad back to the store's entrance. Mrs. Kendrick's head turned in Zoe's direction. Zoe lifted the corners of her mouth in a polite smile. Mrs. Kendrick nodded, then returned her attention to the two men.

Mrs. McCall sighed, drawing Zoe's attention away from Mr. Gunderson. "Mrs. Forsythe, would you by chance remember when and where you saw those dishes last?"

"Last Friday," she said without pause. "That table that now holds clocks was set with four place settings, serving pieces, crystal goblets, and a silver candelabra. I first noticed the table arrangement the day after your wedding."

"No wonder I don't remember them. Isaak said he and Carline were adding new stock that weekend. Let me check the sales log." Mrs. McCall strolled to the counter, then pulled out a leather-bound book. After flipping through several pages, she said, "There's no record of a sale. Is there anything else you can tell me about the china?"

While the two women talked, Zoe glanced around the shop and up at the loft. Her breath caught. There on the second floor were several filled-to-the-ceiling bookcases.

"Zoe, dear, Emilia and I are going to check the storage room for the china. Would you like to stay here and look around, or come with us?"

Zoe continued to stare up at the loft. "Zere are books up zere."

"Isaak bought Edward Tandy's entire library," Mrs. McCall said. "Doubled our inventory, but I offer no complaint. Most of the books have been shelved."

"Any McGuffey Readers?" asked Mrs. Forsythe.

"We have at least one per level. They're a quarter each."

Mrs. Forsythe touched Zoe's arm. "McGuffey is spelled M-C-G-U-F-F-E-Y. If you're going up there, find us a second-level primer."

Mrs. McCall smiled at Zoe. "Look on the second bookshelf from the left, bottom shelf. Mr. Tandy's library begins on the far right."

"Zank you." After a glance to see Mr. Gunderson still outside with the Kendricks, Zoe hurried to the staircase. She raised the front of her skirts, then dashed upstairs. Two recipe books and Papa's Holy Bible were the only books she owned. While she would love to read anything written in her native tongue, she would settle for a children's primer to help her learn to read English.

The bookshelves ran along the building's west wall and curved onto the north wall, ending next to a closed door. Like the first floor, household goods sat on and below the tables, filling the loft.

Second case, bottom shelf.

Zoe knelt to read the book spines to be sure they were McGuffey Readers. She pulled out a second-level primer. For good measure — and because she could afford it — she added a first level and a third one, too. She stood and rested her reticule atop the pile of books on the nearest table before strolling to the far-right bookshelf. The door next to the bookshelf had intricate hand carving. She eyed the doorknob. It was likely another storage room.

"See something interesting?"

CHAPTER ELEVEN

Zoe flinched. She turned her head enough to see Mr. Gunderson leaning against the loft's iron railing, his arms folded across his broad chest. The tight fabric of his suit coat emphasized his muscular build. The man clearly did not spend his workday sitting behind a desk.

The tabby cat weaved around his legs, arched back and purring.

Mr. Gunderson's brows rose — a clear indication he knew she was studying him.

Cheeks warm, she turned back to the bookshelf. "I am looking for a book. Nothing more."

"But you *are* curious about what's behind that door."

"A little," she admitted in truth, "but it is none of my business."

"Have a gander. Door's not locked. I have nothing to hide."

At that, she turned to look at him again.

He was mocking her. She could feel it down to her bones. If Jakob were here, there would be no awkward silences. Jakob always knew what to say to make people feel comfortable. It was one of the traits she appreciated most in him.

Instead, she was stuck in the mire called Isaak Gunderson.

As his gaze stayed fixed on hers, it took every bit of confidence — and bravado — she had to lift her chin and smile at him.

His eyes narrowed in a silent yet clear *I know you are hiding something and I will discover what it is.*

"Zank you for ze offer, but no." She breathed deeply, then focused on the bookshelf to distract her mind from his disturbing presence. The first book that caught her eye was *William Shakespeare* by Victor Hugo. She pulled it out. Her heart flipped. It was in French! But it was about Shakespeare. As much as Papa liked Hugo's writings, Zoe's own dislike for the English bard propelled her to put the book back.

If Mr. Tandy had one book in French, surely he had more.

She tipped her head back for a better look at the top shelf. Was that — ? She eased onto her tiptoes, stretching her neck. It was! All twelve books of Jean de La Fontaine's classic work *Fables.*

Her heart pounding, Zoe glanced around for something to stand on. No ladder. No stool. She doubted the wooden crate could support her. The only option was the high-backed gold damask chair. Even if the bottom of her boots were clean, she could not stand on a chair. Doing so was gauche.

Leaving without those books was unacceptable.

She had no choice but to ask for help.

From Mr. Gunderson.

She pointed at the top shelf. "I would like to purchase ze books by Jean de La Fontaine. Ze red leather ones." She lowered her arm.

"It'll be ten dollars."

"Per book?"

"For the set."

The price was low. Almost an insult, actually. La Fontaine's works were a reading staple for every French schoolchild.

"I will take zem all."

"That's a lot of money to throw away on something you can't read." He pushed off the railing and strode over to her, looking none too pleased to be helping.

He was tall, as tall as Jakob, who was a foot taller than Zoe. She knew because Jakob had measured her after he refused to believe that she, in her stocking feet instead of her heeled boots, was exactly twelve inches shorter than his six foot, five inches. Mr. Gunderson seemed larger than his brother. No, not larger, because she had seen them side by side. More intimidating. More enveloping.

More the type who, once he decided to marry, would toss the woman he was courting over his shoulder and carry her to the nearest justice of the peace.

Miss Carline Pope would say that was so romantic.

That would *not* be romantic. It was inconsiderate, and something Jakob, thankfully, would never do. He was patient, kind, good, gentle —

Mr. Gunderson's throat cleared.

She looked up at him . . . and found herself struck mute. His eyes were as green as the valley north of town. The lovely flecks of brown in the center softened the green — like the barks of trees adding balance to a forest. Fitting because Mr. Gunderson was as unmoving and dependable as a tree.

Dependable?

"Ready?" he asked.

She nodded, her mind too confused to form words. She *liked* thinking of him as a man who could be relied on. Why? She disliked him as much as he disliked her.

With little effort, he reached the books, then handed them to her one at a time, building a stack that caused her arms to stretch downward. He laid the last one on the top.

Oof slipped from her lungs before she could stop it.

"Heavy?"

"A little, but I am stronger zan I look." The book stack reached her chin and weighed down her arms. She hesitated and then, with what little courage she had, she looked up at him again. "Why are you like zis to me?"

His gaze darkened. "You know why."

"Tell me."

"I need to protect my brother from a woman who isn't what she claims."

Mr. Gunderson stood there and stared at Zoe as if he could see into her deepest secrets. He believed she was a liar, a schemer, and a fraud. He was a truly handsome man . . . who, sadly, had the bullish manners of a goat.

This man — this arrogant brother of her suitor — would not get the better of her. She would wear him down with kindness and love until he welcomed her into his family.

"You are wrong about me," Zoe said softly.

He grabbed the top book and flipped it open, turning the page to her. "Read. In English."

She looked to where he pointed. " 'A lion of great parents born, passing a certain mead one morn, a pretty peasant maiden spied, and asked to have her for his bride.' "

"Continue."

Zoe resumed translating the lines. " 'Ze sire with dread ze lion saw, and wished a milder son-in-law. He was embarrassed how to choose, 'twas hard to grant, and dangerous to refuse.' Why must I read zis to you?"

"You're good," he said in a flat voice. "Polished, demure, with just the amount of naïveté for a man to find alluring. It's only logical to believe you're working with someone. I know about the boy."

"Ze boy?"

"Nico."

Zoe tensed. He knew about Nico?

"According to Alfred and Martha Deal, Nico's your brother," Mr. Gunderson continued. "You and I both know that's a lie."

"I never claimed he was my brother."

"Who is he?"

"Nico is a friend from New York. He traveled west with me." She intended to leave her answer at that, but Mr. Gunderson stood still, gaze suspicious, clearly expecting her to create an elaborate lie. She, though, was not Nico. "He calls me his sister because, like me, he has no other family. We are both orphans."

"Have you told Jakob about him?"

Zoe swallowed nervously. As long as Nico failed to visit The Import Company, she had no opportunity to introduce him to Jakob.

Mr. Gunderson released a wry chuckle. "I can tell from your silence you haven't." He closed the book and added it to the stack. "You can have the collection and every book on these shelves if you will leave Helena. I'll even buy you a ticket back to France."

"Is zis a bribe?"

He flinched. "What?"

"Like what Mayor Kendrick offers his political opponents so he can win."

"Who told you about him?"

"Zat is inconsequential. Zat you wish to bribe me is shameful. How can people speak so highly of your character? It is abominable." Emboldened by his gaping mouth, Zoe shoved the stack of books against him; one slipped and hit the floorboards. She scooped it up. "No man can purchase me," she said and slapped the book on the stack. "I will meet you downstairs to make payment. Unless you are too self-righteous to take my

213

money."

Zoe strolled to the table, grabbed the three McGuffey Readers and her reticule, and descended the stairs with her head held high. She was proud of not cowering before him. Mostly because she knew he was watching her walk away.

Her lips curved. Oh, how wonderful it felt to best him!

Isaak followed the woman down the stairs, his arms weighted down with her pile of books. Unease prickled along his neck. She was buying English primers like someone who needed to learn a new language, had translated the first few lines of the French book without pause, and hadn't blinked at the ten-dollar charge for purchasing the set.

Which didn't make sense.

She should have struggled to understand the foreign words, hesitated when he named the high price tag, and stammered some excuse about how she didn't have enough money with her but would be back later to collect them — with Jakob, of course, who would plunk down the funds on her behalf.

Then there was Aunt Lily's staunch patronage. She wasn't one to be taken in by a pretty face or fine manners. She'd spent the last several weeks with Miss de Fleur yet continued to sing her praises.

And just now, the woman had acknowledged that Nico wasn't her brother. Not with a blush or any other evidence she was uncomfortable, but a straightforward explanation.

Not the actions of a woman acting a part.

If that weren't enough, Mrs. Deal — whom Isaak had questioned extensively — had raved for a full twenty minutes about what a wonderful cook and teacher Miss de Fleur was. That and the return telegram from the culinary society in New York City confirmed that the woman told the truth about her father being a chef.

Evidence on top of evidence that perhaps — *perhaps* — Miss de Fleur was telling the truth.

Isaak reached the bottom step. He waited to see if she went to the counter to pay or to Aunt Lily to beg for money. To his surprise and dismay, Miss de Fleur not only went straight to the counter, she pulled money from the blue silk purse that matched her form-fitting bodice. She laid bank notes against the white-painted counter one by one until eleven dollars lay side by side.

"Mr. Gunderson, you may keep ze extra quarter as my gratitude for carrying my books down ze stairs." She gave him a cheerful smile before returning her attention to Emilia, who was gathering up the money.

No, not cheerful. Something more impudent, except without defiance or rudeness.

And there was something familiar about her smile, something that weakened his resolve to see her as nothing but his enemy.

How can people speak so highly of your character? It is abominable.

She wasn't afraid of him or his inquiries, which only made sense if she was telling the truth. He wanted to reject the notion out of hand.

"— listening to me?" Isaak heard his Aunt Lily's voice the same moment he felt pressure on his forearm.

He looked to his godmother. "I'm sorry. What were you saying?" Amazing how normal his voice sounded when his mind was vexed by a puzzle.

"I was wondering if you still had that Minton china. Mrs. McCall looked in your ledger and saw no record of a sale, but we couldn't find it in the storage room."

He set the books on the counter. "I have it in the back with inventory going to The Import Company."

Aunt Lily frowned. "I hope that doesn't

mean you've raised the price."

Isaak brushed his hands together to rid them of dust. "I'm sure we can work within your budget." There wasn't a more frugal woman in Helena than Aunt Lily. She entertained with great class without spending a fortune. Uncle Jonas said it was the reason he could contemplate the expense of running for a senatorial seat once Montana became a full-fledged state.

Isaak snuck a look at Miss de Fleur. Ten dollars was a large sum to spend on books in a foreign language, except if she was telling the truth, then they were written in her native tongue. Was paying ten dollars for a set of twelve books frugal or wasteful?

Miss de Fleur looked his way. Her lips curved again in that oddly familiar manner.

Isaak tugged at his shirt collar and turned his full attention on his godmother. "Would you like to come to the back room and look at the china?"

"I said as much, didn't I?" She looked to the other two women, who nodded their confirmation.

"I'm sorry. I —" He closed his lips over the rest of his apology. Admitting he was distracted by Miss de Fleur's smile was unwise. "I'll take care of Aunt Lily while you two finish up out here." He stepped back to allow his godmother to precede him.

Aunt Lily placed her hand on Isaak's arm as they walked toward the storage room. "I hope you'll still be coming on Saturday to discuss your campaign with Jonas. He's enjoyed planning how to beat that awful Harold Kendrick." She glanced around, as though looking for unseen listeners. "Losing the mayoral race to him — especially when Jonas knew Kendrick was bribing his way past a fair election — knocked more out of your godfather than he'll admit." She gave Isaak a significant look, one he interpreted to mean the information she'd shared was a secret between them.

"I understand."

She nodded. "I'll be forever grateful that Grover agreed to add a fourth territorial judgeship to Montana." Her right cheek indented with a conspiratorial grin. "Just as I've never seen Jonas as devastated by losing that mayoral race, I've never seen him as elated as when he recounted Kendrick's reaction when told the President of the United States was Jonas's personal friend from when they were law clerks together in Buffalo, New York."

It had been a rather stunning revelation to everyone in Helena, except Hale, who could also recount stories of personal interactions with President Cleveland.

"Now, about that china . . ."

For the next five minutes, Isaak assisted his godmother with her purchase. The instant she and Miss de Fleur left the store, he retreated to his office, where the same moment played over and over in his mind.

What was so familiar about that smile?

He sucked in a breath. Miss de Fleur's self-satisfied smile was just like the one Pa gave Ma on the rare occasions when he won an argument but was going to be gracious and not gloat.

Chapter Twelve

The Forsythe House
Friday, late afternoon
De Fleur-Gunderson Courtship Contract,
   Day 28

"What's your strategy for dealing with Kendrick?"

Isaak lifted the pencil off the journal page where he was jotting notes and looked across the desk between himself and his godfather. "Per Hale's advice, I planned to wait and see if Kendrick did anything underhanded first. If he does — and if I can prove it — I'll send proof to the papers."

"Hale is helping you with your campaign?" Uncle Jonas leaned forward and rested his forearms on the pinewood desk. Behind him was a wall of shelves from floor to ceiling, most of them filled with either law books or biographies of men he admired. "I thought Hale wasn't interested in politics. At least that's what he kept telling me last year, when I was pushing him to run for mayor. Has he changed his mind?"

Isaak shook his head. "No, sir. However, he's as concerned about Kendrick being mayor for another four years as the rest of us are."

"That's good to hear." Uncle Jonas grinned. "We'll make a politician out of the boy yet."

Not if Hale didn't want it — although Isaak wasn't sure that was the case. Hale had offered his help as soon as Isaak declared he intended to run. The way Hale spoke, he'd be happy to *be* the mayor of Helena; he just didn't want the hassle of campaigning. To someone like Uncle Jonas, who thrived on meeting people and persuading them to his point of view, Hale's reluctance to put himself forward was a foreign concept. Uncle Jonas thought it was a weakness he could force out of Hale with enough pressure.

His godfather usually had uncanny insight into people, but he underestimated Hale. Any man who could hold out against Yancey Palmer's incessant pursuit had more resolve in his pinkie finger than most men had in their entire beings.

The scent of baking bread wafted through the upstairs library.

Uncle Jonas inhaled. "Miss de Fleur is helping your aunt prepare for Pauline Hollenbeck's welcome-home breakfast tomorrow."

Isaak's mouth watered at the yeasty smell. Next to sweets, he loved bread best. Based on the aroma alone, he could have saved himself the trouble of telegramming Mrs. Gilfoyle-Crane in New York City to verify Miss de Fleur's employment as a household cook. After overhearing Yancey tell Carline the name of Miss de Fleur's high-society employer, Isaak had wired a telegram the following morning. A return telegram — one using a wasteful amount of words — arrived yesterday confirming Miss de Fleur's employment and heaping praise on her skill as a chef.

One more truth in a growing list of them.

Isaak tapped his pencil against his journal. "I'm afraid I misjudged Miss de Fleur when she first arrived."

"In what way?" Uncle Jonas looked up from the notes he was writing.

"I thought she was one of those women who pretended to be a mail-order bride to swindle money out of her gullible, would-be groom."

Uncle Jonas pursed his lips and nodded. "An assumption I shared, so I made a few inquiries to verify her story."

"As did I."

"A reasonable precaution. We both know Jakob is the type to leap first and look later." Uncle Jonas set his pen in its holder. A furrow deepened between his brows. "I'll admit I like Miss de Fleur a great deal — and Lily adores her — but even though I'm fairly certain she's telling the truth about herself, I'm not altogether convinced she's the best match for Jakob."

Relieved that his godfather had spoken his misgivings first, Isaak said, "Yancey cautioned me that trying to separate Jakob from the woman he was falling in love with would be unwise."

"Yancey's a smart girl." Uncle Jonas speared Isaak with a meaningful look. "And she's a born politician's wife."

Isaak's jaw sagged. "Are — are you suggesting . . . ?"

"Married men are apt to win more votes."

Isaak searched his godfather's face for some indication he was joking. No twinkle lit his gray eyes. No grin twitched the corners of his lips. "But she's like a sister."

"Only she *isn't* your sister." Uncle Jonas placed his elbows on the desk and intertwined his fingers. "Marriage is about more than romantic feelings. It's about building a life with someone who shares your goals and priorities."

The same thing Isaak had said to Yancey, or close enough to it. But *marry* Yancey?

"Fact of the matter is," Uncle Jonas continued while Isaak was still recovering, "Yancey and Hale are well-suited, although I doubt he'd consider it even if God appeared in a burning bush and ordered him to marry the girl." He shook his head. "Your father was almost as stubborn when it came to marrying your mother."

Isaak set his pencil inside his journal and closed it. "May I ask you a rather personal question?"

"Certainly."

Ever since hearing the story of how Uncle Jonas had proposed to his mother before she eventually chose his stepfather as her husband, Isaak had wondered something. "Did you ever regret my mother's rejection?"

"Of course I did." Uncle Jonas scowled, as if the question was an insult. "Your mother's a fine woman, and life in Montana was lonely at times. The Palmers and your parents did their best to include me, but evenings always ended with me going home alone." He smiled slowly. "When I met Lily, everything changed. She could give me a look and I'd swear I knew what she was thinking."

"Is that how you knew Aunt Lily was the woman you wanted to marry?"

Uncle Jonas leaned back against the brown leather of his wingback chair. "No, but it's a piece of it. My attraction to your mother stemmed from her willingness to enter into spirited debates with me, which was something I thought I wanted in a wife. Had we married, our home would have been full of arguments, some of which undoubtedly would have turned ugly."

Isaak had witnessed his godfather's and his mother's debating skills often enough to believe it. "Most of the time, Pa lets her argue every side of an issue without ever entering into it."

Uncle Jonas grinned. "Lily handles me in much the same way, and she always ends with, 'You're a good man. I'm sure you'll come to the right conclusion.' It's a show of respect. I married her because I fell in love with her. Since then, every decision I make is motivated by my desire to keep impressing Lily, keep her believing in my goodness, and keep that glow of respect for me in her eyes."

A much better defining moment than

Yancey wanting to feel as if her feet left the ground.

"I can be a hard man sometimes." Uncle Jonas crossed his arms over his chest. "Being a judge requires it. Lily's softness — which is not to be confused with weakness, mind you — balances me."

Isaak needed softness in his life, too. And someone who'd encourage him to stop and stare at clouds or put activities on his schedule other than work, church, and civic duties. He opened his journal and jotted "softness" and "clouds" in the margin of a page to remind himself to add the attributes to his list of desirable traits in a wife.

Uncle Jonas rubbed his chin. "We've strayed far from the topic of Miss de Fleur and your brother. What makes you question their suitability?"

Isaak took a moment to formulate his reasons. He knew Jakob better than anyone, even their parents. As twins, they'd shared everything from the very beginning. Yes, sometimes they fought, but most of the time they were each other's strongest defenders and best friends. Jakob came up with ideas all the time. Some of them wild and impractical; some quite good. Regardless, he could talk people into trying them. If it was a good idea, Isaak was the one who figured out the various tasks needed to accomplish their objective and which of their friends would be best suited for each. He was also the one to keep everyone on schedule because Jakob always lost interest or got distracted by details, to the detriment of the overall project.

"My brother needs a wife who'll challenge his ideas, as I often do, and then take on the role of organizer. Miss de Fleur values harmony over confrontation." It took accusing her of being a fraud and offering her a bribe before she'd pushed back. Even then, it was with grace and that soft smile Isaak couldn't shake from his memory.

"I agree." Uncle Jonas reached for his pen. "She'd be a far better wife for someone like you."

Isaak inhaled so fast he coughed. "For me?"

"Yes, although Lily is convinced Miss de Fleur and Jakob will be wonderful together. I've only observed them at a few dinners, so I'm reserving judgment as to their suitability for the time being."

Uncle Jonas dropped his gaze to the notes he'd been taking during their meeting. "I have one last thing to say about Kendrick."

Isaak coughed twice more, then focused on his godfather. "Yes, sir?"

"The man is a scoundrel and a cheat. You'll be tempted to sink to his level." He lifted his head to spear Isaak with piercing gray eyes. "Don't. Let me handle Kendrick. I'll expose his shenanigans to the papers while you remain above the fray. Your reputation as an honorable man is what sets you apart and will win you votes."

"Yes, sir."

"Now, about hosting a barbeque to announce your candidacy . . ."

Zoe rested the second pan of golden-brown croissants atop the cookstove to cool. "Come look! Zese are as perfect as ze first batch."

Mrs. Forsythe left the sink and walked over, using her white apron to dry her hands. She stopped next to Zoe and breathed in deep. "Mmm, I love the smell of freshly baked bread."

Zoe stirred the still-warm glaze in the saucepan. "I will add ze glaze while you go meet your friend at ze train depot."

Mrs. Forsythe rested her palm on Zoe's cheek. "You are so, so precious to me." She sighed, then lowered her hand. "Is there anything we may have forgotten for tomorrow?"

As Mrs. Forsythe untied the apron she

wore over her calico day dress, Zoe dug into her own apron pocket for the menu they had decided upon for tomorrow's eight o'clock breakfast party. While she had disliked being volunteered by Nico into giving cooking lessons to Mrs. Deal, Zoe had enjoyed helping Mrs. Deal learn to cook better. Partially because Mrs. Deal and Janet, before she returned to Butte, were cheerful and willing learners. Volunteering to cook for Mrs. Forsythe's breakfast party would show the depth of Zoe's appreciation for the Forsythes.

Their love for the Gunderson-Pawlikowski family was as apparent as their love for her. The Forsythes were as close to a set of doting parents as Zoe could dream of having.

Feeling the warm sting of tears, she blinked rapidly and focused on the menu. "For ze first course," she said, "we will serve individual bowls of warm oatmeal with baked apples, topped with fresh cream. All ingredients are stocked in ze larder."

Mrs. Forsythe nodded. "Next one."

"Ze second course is scalloped fish and cucumbers." Zoe looked up from the menu. Both baked round dishes filled with layers of flaked fish, bread crumbs, and butter were also in the larder awaiting reheating. The cucumbers were marinating in vinegar.

229

"All has been prepared. Do you remember seeing parsley in ze larder?"

"There isn't any."

Zoe looked back at the menu. "For ze third course, we will serve both sweetbreads and cauliflower with a cream sauce. All ingredients are in ze larder, but nothing can be prepared until ze morning." She followed Mrs. Forsythe's worried gaze to the counter on which sat a dozen jars of marmalade, olives, and pickles.

Mrs. Forsythe sighed. "I wonder if we should include a few relishes."

"Zere is no reason why we cannot serve zem." Zoe gave a cursory glance to the menu. "Ze forth course will include fritters and delicate griddle cakes. Coffee zat was first served with ze fish will be refilled."

"Then it sounds like the only thing we need is fresh parsley."

Nodding in agreement, Zoe slid the menu back into her apron pocket.

Mrs. Forsythe chuckled, a sweet, melodic sound Zoe had noticed never failed to bring a smile to her husband's face. "I have been trying to figure out all week what it was I couldn't remember I needed. *Buy Parsley* was it. Jonas keeps telling me to make a list. After nine years of marriage, he ought to know me better."

Zoe held up the saucepan as she drizzled glaze from a spoon over the croissants. "Ze grocer is two blocks away. I will purchase some parsley."

"Oh, don't do that." Mrs. Forsythe removed the black netting covering the back of her ash-blond hair. "Marilyn grows herbs year-round in her greenhouse. Isaak can take you over there while I go to meet Pauline at the depot."

Zoe blinked, hoping she had misheard. She scooped another spoonful of glaze. "Mr. Gunderson?" she said, her heart beating faster at the mere mention of his name.

Mrs. Forsythe's gaze shifted to the pan of croissants.

Zoe looked down to see she had drizzled the last spoonful of glaze on only one croissant, soaking it. She dropped the spoon into the saucepan, then set it back on the cookstove.

Mrs. Forsythe gave Zoe a strange look as she said, "He and Jonas are in the library. Jonas surprised me by returning home early from his trip to Bozeman. He leaves again on Monday, so he sent Isaak a note asking him to reschedule their campaign-planning meeting to today."

Zoe glanced at the kitchen door in panic. *In the library* meant Mr. Gunderson was in the Forsythes' home. What was he doing here? He should be at home resting after a day of work, or be at The Import Company checking up on Jakob or — or — be anywhere but here. Where she was.

Mrs. Forsythe gripped Zoe's elbow. "What's wrong?"

"He dislikes me."

"Isaak?"

She nodded.

"Of course not," Mrs. Forsythe insisted. "Isaak is a nice young man."

"He zinks I am a schemer who wishes to rob his brother. He" — Zoe lowered her voice — "zinks I am a woman ze newspaper warns about."

Mrs. Forsythe's eyes widened. "Does Jakob know this?"

Zoe nodded.

Mrs. Forsythe shook her head in a disapproving manner. "Isaak's problem is he's jealous." She spoke with an impressive amount of assurance that she was right. "Jakob has always been the one girls flocked around and fawned over. Once Jakob marries, Isaak will be alone for the first time in his life."

"He has his mother and stepfather."

"Parents aren't the same as a sibling. I was devastated after my sisters married.

They were in their twenties. I didn't marry until I was thirty-four." Mrs. Forsythe twisted her wedding ring. "The most caring thing I can do for Isaak is to intervene."

"Intervene?" Zoe wanted no part in this.

"Yes, dear. The best way to help Isaak is to find him a lady to court. Doing so will keep him out of Jakob's courting of you."

The idea was tempting. But what did Zoe know?

"The problem with this whole plan," Mrs. Forsythe mused, "is if there was a girl for Isaak here in Helena, he would've already found her. The man plans everything months and months in advance."

"Jakob has told me of ze calendar his brother keeps," Zoe remarked, because she felt increasingly unsure about Mrs. Forsythe's impulsive idea. "His life is full with family, church, work, and running for mayor. Where is ze time for him to pursue a girl?"

Mrs. Forsythe sighed. "I know. I'd hoped he'd fall for Yancey or Carline or even Miss Snowe. Isaak Gunderson is the type of man who'll fall in love once he decides doing so fits in his schedule. There's no joy in that. Love is too wild, too unexpected, too grand an emotion to limit it to a timetable."

Or expect it to occur by Day 28 of a

courtship contract.

Unlike during the first weeks of their courtship, work now consumed more of Jakob's time. Whenever Zoe inquired about his plans for the future — marriage, children — his answers had been vague. Sometimes she wished Jakob would be a little more decisive. And focused.

All courtships reached a point of stagnation, did they not?

Her heart felt no pull toward Jakob. Maybe Jakob's lost interest was the confirmation she needed to end the contract.

Zoe managed a small smile. "I wish you well, but zis is none of my —"

Before Zoe could say "business," Mrs. Forsythe grabbed her hand. "Come. You and Isaak need to clear the air."

CHAPTER THIRTEEN

"I do not zink —" Zoe bit off her argument as she hurried to keep in step with Mrs. Forsythe's determined pace to the front foyer and up the stairs.

They stopped at the second door on the right.

After a quick knock, Mrs. Forsythe opened the door. She pulled Zoe inside the library, breathed in deep, and smiled as if she had just sniffed the bouquet of roses. "Jonas, have you and our godson finished with your campaign planning?"

Mr. Forsythe, who was standing next to a wall of books, slid the one he held back onto the shelf. "We haven't, but what do you need done?"

Zoe did her best not to look at Mr. Gunderson standing next to the library's window. She had seen his scowl when they entered the room. She felt his gaze upon her. She must look unladylike to him, dressed in her serviceable gray work dress and her hair hidden by a white kerchief. And yet her heart fluttered, truly fluttered. Why? He usually made her sick with nerves.

Mrs. Forsythe squeezed Zoe's hand. "We need parsley."

"Parsley?" Mr. Forsythe echoed.

"Yes, darling. We need parsley from Marilyn's greenhouse."

"I'll ring over there," Mr. Gunderson said in a genial tone. "Mrs. Wiley is cleaning today. She can bring you some."

"Thank you, dear, but no." Mrs. Forsythe was smiling; Zoe could hear it in her tone. "Zoe needs to go herself to select the amount we need. You will escort her to the house so she isn't molested, as Miss Rigney was on her way home from school last week. It will be dark soon."

"In three hours," he clarified. "The greenhouse is only a couple of blocks away. There's no need for *me* to accompany Miss de Fleur. Marshal Valentine arrested the perpetrator."

"The *accused* perpetrator," Mrs. Forsythe corrected him. "Until the man is proven guilty in a court of law, I am *not* putting my daughter's virtue at risk."

"Miss de Fleur isn't your daughter."

"Isaak David Gunderson, do not take that

tone with me." Her grip tightened on Zoe's hand. "As far as I'm concerned, she is."

Silence descended.

Zoe twisted the bottom edge of her apron. Whatever looks they were giving each other, she had no desire to see. Her life was more pleasant without Isaak Gunderson in it.

It was Judge Forsythe who finally spoke. "Isaak, do what Lily asks. We can continue this discussion tomorrow, after you've finished with work." He paused. "And *if* we're fortunate, there will be remainders from my wife's breakfast feast for us to enjoy."

"Oh, Jonas, I've repeatedly said you are welcome at the party."

"Yes, dear, I know."

Silence descended again.

Zoe tipped up her chin enough for her to see both men still stood where they had been when she entered the library.

Mr. Gunderson made no response to the judge's order.

Zoe said nothing either, but she suspected Mr. Gunderson, for the first time ever, appreciated her silence.

"Now that we've got that settled . . ." Mrs. Forsythe released Zoe's hand. "You'll love Marilyn's greenhouse. She designed it herself." To her husband, she said, "I'm leaving to meet Pauline at the depot."

"I'll go with you."

"There's no need."

"I know." He strolled toward his wife, the corner of his mouth indenting. "But a man would be a fool not to indulge in a private carriage ride with a beautiful woman. Heed my words, Isaak." He wrapped his wife's arm around his and escorted her out of the library, but not before Zoe noticed Mrs. Forsythe's blush.

Mr. Gunderson cleared his throat. "I have a Widows and Orphans Committee meeting to go to. Let's make this quick."

Zoe nipped on her bottom lip. This was her fault. She should never have confessed what she had about Mr. Gunderson's dislike to Mrs. Forsythe, or complied with her insistence about going to the greenhouse for the parsley.

"Well?" he prodded in that I-dislike-you-more-than-the-plague voice of his.

Zoe opened her mouth to apologize for putting him in this awkward situation. She wished to be kind to him, but — oh, how he unnerved her! So she pursed her lips tight. She should draw comfort in knowing Mr. Gunderson was no more pleased to be accompanying her than she was at this moment.

And yet tears pooled in her eyes.

Without waiting for Mr. Gunderson, Zoe hurried out of the library, removed her apron as she descended the stairs, hung the apron on the hall tree, and then ran out the front door and across the lawn. She reached the first intersection — and rid herself of tears — before he caught up to her.

He slapped his black hat atop his head. "I can't protect you if you run off."

"You should return to work," she said, suddenly warm at how close he was standing. His arm could easily wrap around her waist and draw her against him, holding her close, never letting her go. Mortified at the thought, she blurted out, "I need no assistance."

"Your self-reliance is admirable."

As much as she wished to be immune to his biting honesty, his words stung.

"I prefer you leave me alone," she whispered.

Mr. Gunderson did not respond.

They stood there silent, waiting for a surrey to roll past.

Zoe looked anywhere but at him, hoping for a sudden outbreak of hives. Or a megrim. Or a plausible head cold. As fate would have it, nothing happened. She felt as healthy as ever.

The street cleared, and Zoe released a grateful breath.

Mr. Gunderson held on to her elbow and escorted her across the street without first asking if she needed assistance. He dropped his hold. They continued down the street.

She said nothing.

He said nothing, that perpetual scowl on his face.

Or perhaps perpetual was too harsh a word.

He looked happy to see some people. Just never her. Or his brother. She had yet to see him pleased with Jakob. That could be from concern and worry over Jakob's handling of the building of the store.

There — two houses away — was his three-story home. She again did not wait for him. She hurried up the street, turned onto the house's side path, and entered the white-picket gate leading to the back property.

She gasped at the heartbreaking sight of the neglected garden.

Jakob said his mother's beloved garden and greenhouse were the first two places everyone looked when wanting to find her. April was past the ideal time to cultivate the garden for spring planting. Why had this not been done? Mrs. Pawlikowski would wish to come home and see her garden loved and cared for.

Not this!

Ashamed of the brothers' disregard, Zoe moved past the pitiful garden bed to the grand wood-and-glass building. She opened both double doors and stepped inside, just over the threshold, expecting to find the same neglect.

"Oh," she breathed in awe.

Both paths on either side of the center table had been swept yet held an occasional dropping from the little brown birds resting in the feeders hanging over them. None of the raised beds contained weeds. Dozens of sprouts and tomato plants grew from clay pots. The greenhouse smelled heavenly of lavender, rosemary, and roses from the three times as many aroma plants than budding ones, all looking lovingly tended to. Against the farthest wall a trio of citrus trees bore abundant fruit.

What she loved most were the birds.

"Zey are happy to live in zis heaven," she said as she sensed Mr. Gunderson quietly drawing up behind her.

"Are you talking to me?"

"Of course. Who else would I be talking to?" When he failed to answer, she asked, "What kind of birds are ze?"

"Finches." Then he was silent again for a long moment. "How can you tell they're happy?"

"Close your eyes and listen to zem sing," she said, and she did exactly that. "Zey sing with wondrous joy and with hope and loveliness." Curious to see if he had done what she asked, she looked over her shoulder. He stood there, right behind her, his eyes closed. Like his brother, he had thick lashes, darker and —

His eyes opened, and he looked sheepish at having been caught listening to the birds. "They . . . uh." He cleared his throat. "They chirp because that's what birds do."

"Oh, Mr. Gunderson, you are most —"

His hand rested in the middle of Zoe's lower back, sending a tingle up her spine, and it took all her fortitude not to move and give him any cause to believe his touch affected her so. Yet her heart beat so loudly she swore he had to hear it.

"Don't just stand there," he grumbled, along with a nudge, yet his hand stayed on her back, as if the action was natural to him.

Something tightened within her.

Zoe jolted into motion. She strolled down the right aisle to put needed space between them, peering at the various plants as she walked. He should not affect her so. He was the brother of the man courting her. He was the brother of the man who never made her feel uncomfortable in his presence.

She found the raised bed filled with fragrant herbs. Smiling, she ran the tips of her fingers along the tops, some recently trimmed. "Someone has been enjoying zese."

Mr. Gunderson drew up next to her, again closer than necessary. "Our housekeeper has access to the greenhouse," he said with none of the earlier gruffness. He offered a wicker basket.

Zoe took it. "Zank you."

"Fill it with as much as you want for . . ." His words trailed off as he stared at her.

As she stared at him.

It was the oddest, warmest, strangely familiar thing, standing there looking up at him and waiting for him to speak. Missing Jakob had caused her to feel this way. That was all the tingle was. That explained it.

Twins, yes. But not identical.

One could not be substituted for the other.

She lowered her gaze to Mr. Gunderson's tweed waistcoat, to the top button, the one that was directly eye level with her. "I apologize," she said in sincere penitence, "for keeping you from your meeting and for not being appreciative of your escort." She winced. "It has been two days since I have seen Jakob. I wish for his presence. And you are not him."

"I know."

It was not his words but his tone that drew her attention.

Zoe looked up at him, confused by the sadness she heard in his voice. Nothing about his vacant expression testified to him being sad. Or lonely. Or wishful for something more.

Yet his response had sounded . . . woeful.

Perhaps Mrs. Forsythe had been correct in her belief that he was jealous of Jakob. It was possible. People loved being around Jakob. Zoe had yet to see a crowd cocooning Mr. Gunderson like those that would seek out Jakob. Did Mr. Gunderson wish he had his brother's celebrity? What Zoe knew for certain was that Isaak Gunderson was unhappy. How she knew, she could not fathom. Nor could she fathom why that realization about him made her chest tighten or want to comfort him.

"I am sorry zat you feel a —" Zoe bit back her words before she embarrassed him by admitting she knew he felt alone. She gave him a weak smile. "I am sorry zat you were *forced* to escort me here. You should not have to be with me, should you not wish it."

He nodded in acceptance of her apology. Yet she knew *he knew* that was not what she had originally intended to say.

His gaze shifted to the herbs. "We couldn't have you molested."

Zoe studied his profile, unsure if he was jesting.

Mr. Gunderson stood there, saying nothing.

She glanced around the raised bed, searching for sheers to trim the herbs.

A pair appeared before her, held by Mr. Gunderson.

"Zank you." She took them from him, careful not to touch his hand. As deftly as she could, she trimmed the needed amount of parsley and added it to the basket Mr. Gunderson held with one hand while he checked his pocket watch with the other.

"That's all?" he asked, sliding the timepiece back into his waistcoat pocket.

"It is enough."

His troubled gaze shifted to the handful of stalks in the basket.

"Is something amiss?" she asked.

"You have a wealth of fresh herbs at your fingertips, and yet *enough* is all you choose to take. I don't know what to make of you."

Zoe stayed silent, unsure what to make of him. She wished to believe his words were a compliment, but for that to be the cause, his perception of her would have had to change. Isaak Gunderson, she had been told, rarely changed his mind because rarely was his opinion wrong. He was, though. Wrong about her.

She was not the schemer, liar, and fraud he believed she was.

That little pain above her heart returned.

She looked down at the herb garden.

One day, she would learn how to be unaffected by his words and touch. One day, she would have no care what he felt about her. One day, he would look her way and she would not sense his presence, because she had learned to be indifferent to him as she was to . . . to . . . to Yancey's brother, Geddes. Never did Zoe wonder anything about Mr. Geddes Palmer. Never did she hear sadness in his tone or see loneliness in his eyes or care what he thought of her.

Zoe laid the sheers next to the raised bed. "Papa taught me to live with *enough.* I am content with life."

"Are you?" she thought she heard Mr. Gunderson whisper.

Regardless if he had or not, she had to share the words bubbling from her heart.

"My life is good. What more should I want?"

"That, Miss de Fleur, is a question for another day." Perspiration beaded under the brim of his hat, his face glistening. Not surprising considering the temperature in the greenhouse. "We should go. I have a committee meeting."

"You are a kind and generous man for serving on ze Widows and Orphans Committee," she said as she followed him to the double doors. "Is it always zis warm in here?"

"It is."

"Your mother must enjoy zis in ze winter."

"She does. So do her chickens. I'll escort you to the boardinghouse."

"Zere is no need. I am staying ze night in ze Forsythes' guest room."

He stopped at the entrance, his scowl returning. "Why?"

"Mrs. Forsythe said it was unsafe for me to travel alone at five in ze morning. I must begin cooking before dawn."

"Jakob didn't offer to escort you?"

"I did not wish to impose," she explained. "He has been working late. He needs his slumber."

"He needs —" His words broke off. "Last chance, Miss de Fleur. Is there anything else you need for tomorrow's breakfast feast?"

She looked over her shoulder. Among the citrus trees at the southern end of the greenhouse stood a lemon tree. In gratitude for the Forsythes inviting her to stay in their home tonight — to convey the depth of love she bore for the couple who were as doting on her as Papa had been — she could make lemon *pots de crème* for them to enjoy after she returned to the boardinghouse.

She could make them *if* she had some fresh fruit. Because he was offering . . .

She touched Mr. Gunderson's arm. "May I have four lemons?"

His brows rose. "What are you going to cook?"

"Something wonderful."

"A dessert?"

Zoe nodded. "*Pots de crème.* It is a French custard zat can be flavored with coffee or a favorite liqueur, but I prefer lemon topped with fresh whipped cream best. I will make enough for you to enjoy, too, if you like."

After a quick "I would," he strode back into the greenhouse.

Zoe felt her lips curve into a smile. For all Isaak Gunderson's gruffness, he could be helpful and endearing when he wished to be.

Or he merely had a weakness for sweets.

CHAPTER FOURTEEN

Monday afternoon, April 9
De Fleur-Gunderson Courtship Contract,
  Day 31

"Which one *I* like doesn't matter," Jakob responded in a tone sharper than Zoe had ever heard him use before. "I want *your* opinion." He tapped wallpaper samples against The Import Company's eastern wall. "Which one of these do *you* like best?"

Zoe glanced back and forth between the samples Jakob held . . . and did her best to ignore the workmen standing on the stairs overhearing her and Jakob's conversation. "Zey are both lovely." She tried a new tactic to avoid answering because asking which wallpaper Jakob liked had failed to distract him from badgering her for an opinion. "But I zink you should ask your brother which he prefers."

"I don't care what Isaak prefers. I care what you prefer." There it was again — that why-won't-you-comply-to-what-I-ask edge to his voice. Jakob's blue eyes focused on her in expectation of a response. No, in expectation of a decision. A decision *he* should make.

Zoe clasped her gloved hands together and maintained a polite expression to cover her growing annoyance with him. His desire for her to choose from the wallpaper samples — like with the ceiling tiles and paint — in no way obligated her to give it, especially when his brother should be helping him decide. That Jakob continued to ask her opinion vexed her. Literally and figuratively speaking, this was the Gunderson brothers' business, not hers. Save for wallpaper, the store was ready to be stocked with cabinets and merchandise. If Jakob wished not to make decorating decisions, he should have left the choices to his brother.

Isaak Gunderson could be counted on to make an immediate decision. The man had proven to her how quick he was to rush to judgment about her being a schemer, a liar, and a fraud. Oh, but he had also been so kind and gracious in giving her lemons from his mother's greenhouse. Perhaps he now realized how he had misjudged her.

But if that were so, why had he avoided her yesterday at church? Why not sit next to her and Jakob? Why not join them for lunch with the Forsythes? She had prepared extra lemon *pots de crème* for Mr. Gunderson to enjoy. She wished to know what he thought of her cooking. She wished to know why he felt so alone. He had a family who loved him. He had friends.

In truth, she had no knowledge of his friendships. Having no confidantes could be why he felt alone.

"Zoe?" Jakob's voice drew her from her musings.

She looked his way. "Yes?"

"I don't know why you're making this difficult. Just tell me which sample you like best."

Was this what Jakob would be like if she married him? Insistent that she make the decisions he was too unsure to make on his own? Critical of her when she refused to comply with his wishes? Too focused on his own life to be aware of her obligations?

True, he had been appreciative earlier, when she arrived unexpectedly with lunch. True, he had cleaned up the remains. True, he had seemed sincerely apologetic about not being able to accompany her this afternoon to Mrs. Hollenbeck's home for tea.

What time was it? She looked to the grandfather clock Jakob had moved over from The Resale Company after she recommended bringing in a clock to help him better keep track of time while he worked.

"I need to leave," she said, "or I will be late."

"Mrs. Hollenbeck won't mind." Jakob waved the wallpaper samples. "Which one?"

"Ask your brother!" Zoe flinched at her harsh tone. No matter how vexed she was with him, she should not have been short. The poor man was upset about work, about deadlines, about his parents returning in a few weeks.

Shamed at her outburst, she began an apology. "Jakob, I should not have —"

Something between a snort and a chuckle came from one of the workmen.

Jakob's eyes narrowed into a targeted glare, first at the workmen and then at her. "I don't need anyone's help making a decision."

Zoe gave a sad shake of her head. "If zat was possible, you would not have asked for my opinion. It is not a sign of weakness to ask for your brother's assistance. He cares about you."

Hurt flittered across his expression. "Give Mrs. Hollenbeck my apologies, will you?"

Zoe nodded.

He turned his back to her and focused on

the samples.

"Which one costs more?" she asked softly.

He raised the cream one with the gold-foil stripes.

"Does cost matter?"

"We're under budget."

"Do either have to be ordered?"

"Charlie Cannon has both in stock, but only enough of the expensive one to cover two walls. I'd have to order more, which would put us behind schedule again." He paused for a long moment. "If I purchase the more expensive one, Cannon will spread the word that we're sparing no expense on this storefront."

"Zat would not be good."

"You're right, it wouldn't —" He swung around to face her, his eyes widening, the samples slipping out of his hands. "That's *exactly* what we want." He dashed to his notebook sitting atop a stool, grabbed the pencil he had stuck behind an ear, and began to write.

Zoe waited a few moments for him to say more. When he did not, she strolled to the door. After one final look in Jakob's direction, she stepped outside and headed down the sidewalk in the direction of Mrs. Hollenbeck's house. Zoe stopped at the first intersection, waited for a lull in traffic, then crossed the street and turned north.

She still had the train ticket to return to Denver if the courtship floundered. If? It was already floundering. The kindest thing might be to end it now, instead of debating whether she should end it.

She wanted love. She wanted marriage, a home, and a family. She had hoped she would find that with Jakob, but with each passing day she felt less sure she wanted a future with him. She liked Jakob. She did.

But nothing in her heart spoke of love.

What was the proper etiquette in America for ending a contracted courtship? Should she be the one to speak first?

Zoe stopped at the next intersection. Closing her eyes, she allowed the afternoon sun to warm her face.

Tomorrow night, if Jakob failed to join her for dinner with Lily Forsythe, she would seek Mrs. Forsythe's wisdom about ending the courtship. If only Mr. Forsythe were here, Zoe would ask him, too. Both a maternal and a paternal perspective would be helpful. Of course, if she ended the contract, then what? While she had the train ticket back to Denver, she was under no obligation to return to the Archer Matrimonial Company and consider other suitors. She could create a life for herself here in

Helena. Staying would be awkward at first, but she had the Forsythes, who had taken her under their wing. In time, she and Jakob could become friends, like he was with Yancey and Carline.

But Isaak Gunderson lived in Helena. If she stayed, avoiding him forever would be impossible.

Why did he dislike her so? She was likable.

While she would miss the Forsythes, returning to Denver was the wiser course of action. Because of Isaak Gunderson.

"Miss de Fleur?"

Zoe tensed. The sound of her name spoken by the very man she was thinking about increased the swish of her pulse. Unable to think of a logical reason to pretend she had not heard Mr. Gunderson speak her name — or to explain the breathless unease she felt in his presence — she reluctantly opened her eyes. He stood next to her, holding a crate of vegetables and looking none too pleased to see her.

In a voice that sounded as nonplussed as she intended, she said, "Good afternoon, Mr. Gunderson."

He dipped his head in acknowledgment. "Afternoon."

A wagon rolled past . . . and then two buggies and a youth pushing a wheelbarrow while they stood side by side in cumbrous silence, waiting to cross.

"Good day." She lifted the front of her red plaid dress and stepped into the street. To her surprise, he followed. Zoe stopped on the sidewalk and, in her annoyance that he viewed her as an obligation, swiveled to face him. "Zis is considerate of you to walk with me, Mr. Gunderson, but I have no need of an escort."

His face reddened. "I wasn't walking with you, Miss de Fleur. We merely crossed the street at the same time."

"Oh." Zoe moistened her bottom lip. "Mrs. Hollenbeck invited me for afternoon tea. And Jakob, too, but he cannot leave work."

"She invited you to tea *today*?"

"Yes."

"Now?"

"At four," she told him. "Is zere a problem?"

With a grim slant to his mouth, Mr. Gunderson shook his head, then started forward . . . in the same direction Zoe needed to walk.

She hurried to match his pace. "Did she invite you to tea, too?"

"No." He drew in a breath deep enough

to expand the wide chest beneath his black coat and matching waistcoat. "She has a dried ham to add to the food the Widows and Orphans Committee is providing to the Sundin family."

"I zink it is admirable, ze way you and your brother have worked together to provide for Timmy and his mother."

"Jakob often finds people in distress. I then take it to the committee to determine the next step. A problem at The Resale Company prevented me from delivering the food sooner." And then he said no more . . . which was Mr. Gunderson's not-so-subtle way of warning Zoe not to engage in conversation with him.

And so she stayed silent as they walked to the next intersection, passing numerous grand homes along the road. They walked another block in silence.

Zoe released a weary breath.

"What was that sigh about?" he asked.

She should have no care what he thought about her, but she had to ask. She had to know why he thought she was unlikable. "Why do you care so little for me?"

Isaak stopped walking before he tripped over his feet. "I care."

Disbelief flashed in her beautiful brown

eyes. "False compassion — zat is what zis is. Pretense." She said it with such assurance that his mouth gaped for a long moment in dumbfounded silence.

"Pretense? How in the world do you come by that?"

"If you truly cared, you would have been at ze train depot with Jakob to welcome me to Helena. If you truly cared, you would have supported Jakob's courtship." She poked his arm. "If you *truly* cared, you would treat me as if you are happy about ze prospect of my joining your perfect family and of me becoming your brother's bride."

Stunned at both the number of words that had left her mouth and how blatantly wrong she was with each one of them, Isaak offered no reply. He'd been busy the day she arrived and was justifiably suspicious of a mail-order bride. She was right about one thing, though. He *wasn't* happy about her joining his family as Jakob's bride.

"Indeed, Mr. Gunderson, you care nothing for me." Her indignation was at odds with her usual gentle manner. "You need not say ze words for me to know you still wish me to leave Helena and never return."

She was right. Being around her made him uncomfortable, which was better left unsaid at the moment. And because he couldn't justify it with a logical explanation.

Isaak started forward. He didn't want to add making her late for tea with Mrs. Hollenbeck to the list of his offenses.

Miss de Fleur fell into step next to him. "Zere is no reason to deny your feelings."

"I'm not denying anything." Her litany of complaints made sense from her perspective. So did his, but the middle of the street wasn't the place for this discussion. "Watch where you step."

She bumped into him in her quick avoidance of a manure pile. "You reject my overtures because you still zink I am a fraud."

When they reached the opposite side of the street, she stopped and rested her hands on her hips. "Be honest with me, Mr. Gunderson. Is it because I am French instead of American? Or because I answered an advertisement to be a bride delivered by ze mail?"

It was a natural opening into one of the things about her that plagued him. "Tell me why you left New York."

She looked away, but not before he saw embarrassment — or was it guilt? — in her dark eyes. She drew in a breath. "I was relieved of my position as household cook for a New York society hostess."

"Why?" Miss de Fleur's brief explanation

didn't match the glowing telegram he'd received.

"My employer said it was for my own good. She wanted me to open a restaurant."

Isaak conveyed his confusion with a look.

"Papa and I met Mrs. Gilfoyle-Crane four and a half years ago when she came to London for ze wedding of her daughter to ze nobleman who had hired Papa to cater ze reception. Mrs. Gilfoyle-Crane offered Papa double his usual pay if he would move to Manhattan and become her private chef. He agreed. Last year, after he passed away, I was promoted to household cook."

Isaak lifted his brows. "You really can't be called a chef because you're a woman?"

"Yes," she said matter-of-factly. "Zis past Christmas, Mrs. Gilfoyle-Crane had a dream in which I owned a restaurant. She began working tirelessly to help me bring her dream to life, so how could I tell her no?"

"Did you — *do* you — want to own a restaurant?"

"No." She spoke so softly he barely heard her response. She started walking up the Hollenbeck carriageway.

He followed. "You went along with what she wanted for your life even though it wasn't something you wanted? I can't believe you would have opened a restaurant, spent all that money and time, just to please this woman."

She shrugged. "I did not wish to be ungrateful for her kindness. She paid for Papa and me to come to America. She opened her home to us. She hired a tutor to help us speak English."

The magnitude of her response sank in. Even if she discovered she and Jakob were unsuitable, she would marry him out of gratitude for bringing her to Helena and providing her housing, food, and friends.

Isaak didn't want to believe it. "Why come out West to find a husband?"

"I want a home and a family," she said without pause. "I want a husband who will laugh with me but mostly just sit in lovely, companionable silence. Together. Faithfully together." Her voice grew raspy. "I want until death does us part."

His heart kicked inside his chest. He wanted the same thing.

Isaak tromped up the carriageway to Mrs. Hollenbeck's house. "You could have found that there. In New York. Or anywhere. You didn't need to come to Helena. You didn't have to agree to be a mail-order bride. You didn't have to sign that" — he caught himself in time to substitute a more suitable word for her ears — "*foolish* contract with the matrimonial company."

She walked beside him, silent until they reached Mrs. Hollenbeck's porch steps. "Not foolish. Ze contract is prudent for all."

Isaak clamped his lips over a contradiction.

"When Papa asked if we should move to America, I happily agreed. It was another exciting adventure, but no longer do I have Papa to journey to ze unknown with. I am weary of being alone, Mr. Gunderson. I ache —" She looked away and whispered, "I ache for something more."

He paused on the fourth step. "Does Jakob know this?"

"He knows of my desire to marry."

"But not that you feel alone?"

Her gaze turned to his, and he read the answer in her eyes. She had shared her heart, her deepest desire, with him. Not Jakob.

Isaak's heart pounded. People confided in Jakob. Went to him for solace because he could cheer up a lemon. People came to Isaak for decisions — which travel trunk to buy, what gift to give a bridal couple. They didn't tell him they felt alone or what they ached for. It was a gift. One he didn't deserve after the way he'd treated her.

He turned away from her and continued up the stairs to Mrs. Hollenbeck's house.

Miss de Fleur climbed alongside him. "I am sorry zat I burdened you with my feelings. I should be sharing zis with Jakob."

If she intended to marry him, yes, she should. But saying as much was the exact opposite of what Isaak knew she should do. "That's not why I walked away."

"Zen why did you?"

Because he kept picturing the two of them sitting together in lovely, companionable silence. "I need to get this box to the Sundins before dinner tonight."

"I will take you to ze bank in ze morning and show you what is in my account."

Isaak stopped on the top step and stared at her. How her mind jumped from feelings to finances made no logical sense to him. "Why?"

"So you will believe my reason to marry is not for financial security." Her tone held equal amounts of innocent sincerity and how-is-this-not-obvious-to-you?

"I know that's not your reason." Although he was taking that on faith. He'd not verified her accounts.

She looked hopeful. "You no longer believe I am a schemer, yes?" Before he could answer, she said, "You seem unhappy with zat realization."

He was . . . because he now thought of her as an honorable woman. Shame heated his chest as he recalled their previous encounters. He'd been rude, accusatory, and distant. Arrogant.

He ducked his head, staring into the vegetables as if they could absolve him. Pa had taught him that a man admits fault while looking the person he's wronged in the eye. So Isaak raised his chin and gazed into her deep brown eyes. "Miss de Fleur, every complaint you have against me is justifiable. I had my reasons. They no longer apply." Except for thinking she and Jakob didn't belong together. "Please allow me to apologize for my treatment of you."

She gasped. "Zis is a new beginning for us. No more dislike. No more distrust. We shall become friends, Mr. Gunderson, you and I." She held out her hand to him in a show of amity, her face glowing with delight.

He glanced at the box he held, preventing him from shaking her hand. "Sorry."

Undaunted, she laid her hand over one of his. "Zis is nice, yes?"

"Yes." And some other emotion he couldn't quite place.

CHAPTER FIFTEEN

The next morning

"Ze sky is sunshiny here and yet grimy over ze mountains," Zoe remarked in awe at the gray-and-white clouds in the distance. Without looking away from the window, she sipped the warm coffee Mrs. Deal said had too much cream in it to still count as coffee. "Nico, have you ever seen such a beautiful storm?"

"Stop being so happy," he grumbled in response.

Zoe turned to face him. Instead of looking at her, he aimlessly pushed his food around on his plate. Even the usually friendly male boarders seemed morose. None had smiled in her direction or offered anything more than a polite "Mornin', Miss de Fleur" and "Mornin', Nico."

"I am happy, but . . ."

Nico finally looked up. "But what?"

She wanted to say her spirit was as con-

265

flicted as the sky — part joyful, part turbulent. But a boardinghouse dining room was no place for an intimate confession.

Zoe rested her china teacup on its matching saucer. "Mr. Gunderson and I became friends yesterday."

"I thought you already were friends."

"With his brother, Jakob, yes" — she sighed — "but with Mr. Gunderson, no. Until yesterday. Our spirits are now in harmony."

Nico's brows furrowed. "Which one is courting you?"

"Jakob. His brother is Mr. Gunderson. Zat is how people keep zem separated," she explained. "Zey are twins."

"Oh, I get it. You're now bosom friends with your suitor's twin brother." Nico tapped his fork against his plate. "That's not strange at all."

She frowned. "What is zat supposed to mean?"

"Nothing," he insisted. He resumed pushing the food around on his plate. "I'm happy for you."

He was *not* truly happy for her; that was clear. Once he met Jakob, Nico would see what a good man he was.

Or she could end the courtship contract today. She could walk away and not look back, as her mother had. The other option was for her to hope for renewed interest, as Papa had with *Maman*. Zoe nipped at her bottom lip. Could she live with walking away? Probably. She disliked how sad Papa's longing for *Maman* kept him from finding a new love.

Zoe refused to miss out on love. She could live with the regret of not giving Jakob a second chance. She could not live with not honoring her promise to give Jakob sixty days to court her.

For the remainder of the contract, she would give a wholehearted effort to this courtship. She would be understanding, patient, and supportive. She would show Jakob what a wonderful family he could have with her and Nico, too.

"You must meet him," she announced.

Nico stared at her, his eyes narrowed with suspicion. "Your new friend, the brother?"

"Not him. Jakob. It is past time you two met."

"You're right." Nico looked to the window. "Maybe the meeting should wait until the rain passes, though. I owe you another chance to beat me at chess. I'll spot you two pawns and a knight. I'm sure you'll win this time."

As tired as she was of losing chess matches

to Nico, she felt no inclination to accept his offer. Nor had she lived in Helena long enough to judge the rain potential of the clouds. It could be minutes before a droplet fell. It could also be hours. The storm may not be heading to Helena at all.

Nico, for too long, had avoided meeting Jakob.

Zoe looked at the gray sky beyond the window . . . and then back at Nico. "Finish your breakfast," she ordered, and then she stood. "I must go upstairs to claim my umbrella. When I return, I will take you to meet Jakob."

Nico muttered, "Sure."

With a jubilance in her heart, Zoe hurried upstairs to her room. Once Jakob and Nico were friends, she would take him to meet Isaak Gunderson, who would realize what an upstanding citizen Nico was and would offer him employment as the delivery boy for The Resale Company. Mr. Gunderson would then train Nico to manage a business, to speak with honesty, and to make the community a better place by helping deliver food to needy widows and orphans. Jakob could teach Nico how to be charming and adventurous. Maybe one day, Nico could become mayor. Or governor of the entire territory. *If* there was a governor.

Constable? Senator? Did territories have senators? Oh, she knew so little of American politics.

What mattered was that Nico's life would change for the better with the Gundersons in it.

As hers had.

Now that she had made things right with Isaak Gunderson, she needed Jakob and Nico to get along so all four of them could move closer to being a happy family. Zoe claimed her umbrella and smiled. For Nico's sake as well as her own, she would make this courtship a success. She had come West to marry the man of her dreams.

And marry him she would.

Eight minutes later . . .
The Import Company

"What do you mean, Jakob is gone?" Zoe said to Jakob's expert carpenter, Mr. Lucian Snowe, who stayed focused on the piece of crown molding he was measuring in the construction area on the building's ground floor. She tapped the tip of her umbrella on the sawdust-covered floor, her wariness growing. "Jakob always begins his workday speaking to ze crew. He should be here."

"Isaak sent a message saying he needed Jakob over at The Resale Company." Mr.

Snowe drew a line onto the molding stretched across two sawhorses. He stuck the pencil behind his ear, then met her gaze. "If you hurry on over there, you'll probably catch him."

"How long ago did Jakob leave?"

"Five minutes, tops."

Which was how much of a head start Nico had had on her. She should never have gone upstairs for her umbrella. She also should never have expected Nico to wait for her, not after the many other times he had promised to go with her to meet Jakob yet never had.

"Oh, Miss de Fleur, my wife asked me to invite you and the Gundersons over for a coffee-and-cake social next Monday evening. Would around seven work?"

"Zat would be nice. Zank you." Zoe started to leave and then stopped at the first twinge of suspicion. She looked back at Mr. Snowe. "Did a young man with walnut-colored hair, blue eyes, about my height leave with Jakob?"

Mr. Snowe shook his head.

"Might you have seen who gave Jakob ze message from his brother?"

"Timmy, the lad who cleans up around here."

Zoe glanced around. Another five men

worked. No little boy anywhere, but that could mean Jakob finally had convinced the boy to resume attending school. "Mr. Snowe, might you also have seen who gave Timmy ze message?"

"Now, that I don't know."

If she were a betting woman, she would place a wager on Nico. Since arriving in Helena, he had been resistant to Jakob courting her. Refusing to meet Jakob was one thing. Intentionally sabotaging their relationship by tricking Jakob into leaving this morning before she could arrive to talk to him . . . why?

She looked out a front window at the gray, cloudy sky.

Thunder rolled in the distance.

"I suggest you wait here," Mr. Snowe said with fatherly concern. "Storm's coming. The roof will keep you from getting drenched. Trust me; Jakob's bound to come back."

"Zank you, but —

"You're gonna chase after him," he cut in and then chuckled. "My daughter's been doing that for years with no success, so I wish you all the luck catching Jakob. I'll let my wife know you'll be at the coffee-and-cake social." Mr. Snowe grabbed the hand saw and went to work cutting the molding.

Zoe hurried out of the building and down the boardwalk in the direction of The Resale Company. She crossed the street and headed north. The store came into view. Zoe waited for a lull in the traffic before she crossed the street. Then she strolled past the shop's paint-chipped front door, which was propped open. The moment Zoe stepped inside the shop, Emilia McCall stopped dusting a table of lamps.

"Well, good morning, Miss de Fleur. It's wonderful to see you again."

"And you." Zoe glanced in the direction of Mr. Gunderson's office. "I was told Jakob is here. His brother needed his help."

"That's strange. I haven't see Jakob since yesterday." Mrs. McCall hooked the feather duster onto the white apron she wore over her serviceable gray dress. "Maybe Isaak knows something. I'll walk you back there."

"Zank you, Mrs. McCall."

"As much as I love hearing 'Mrs. McCall,'" she said over her shoulder as she walked, "please call me Emilia. I doubt there's much difference in our ages."

"Zen you must call me Zoe."

"It's such a lovely name." Emilia veered around a stack of leather trunks. "My parents named me Emilia after my mother's second cousin, who was more a sister to her than a distant relative." She stopped near the partially open door to Mr. Gunderson's office, then looked at Zoe, her brows raised in a silent *how did you come by your name?*

"*Maman* liked how Zoe sounded."

Emilia seemed accepting of that answer, which was good, for it was the truth as far as Zoe knew. Once she had asked Papa why she was named Zoe. *Your mother liked how it sounded* had been his exact and only response.

"I hope you don't mind" — Emilia withdrew a notebook from the pocket on the right side of her apron — "but I did a little research on your name after we first met. Several notable women in history have had the name Zoe, including . . . Let me find where I wrote the information." She turned the pages. "Here we go. 'Two empresses in the Byzantine Empire, and St. Zoe, a Roman noblewoman martyred for her faith during Emperor Diocletian's persecution of the Christian church.' " She looked up. "Wouldn't it be nice to think your mother named you after one of those ladies?"

Zoe's throat tightened. She looked away from Emilia, blinking repeatedly to stop the tears from forming. To have named her after someone notable would have meant *Maman* cared. If *Maman* had cared about Zoe — if

273

she had loved her — she would have stayed with Zoe and Papa instead of chasing her heart's desire.

"I lost my mother, too." The tenderness of Emilia's words drew Zoe's attention.

"How did you . . . ?"

"Know?" Emilia smiled gently. As her eyes welled with tears, she cradled her hand around Zoe's. "People whose mothers are alive don't tear up" — she blinked, then fanned her face with her notebook — "like we both have. Grief is sneaky. It hits us when we least expect it."

Zoe blinked away her tears. She liked the stability emanating from Emilia. Yancey and Carline exuded fun, but their golden beauty, spontaneity, and vivaciousness drew too much attention, too much focus. Like pastries, Yancey and Carline were enjoyed best in small doses. Plus, both still had their mothers to talk to. As much as Zoe would like Mrs. Forsythe to be her mother, how could she be a genuine substitute?

Zoe squeezed Emilia's hand. "Zank you for understanding."

Emilia gave Zoe a tentative smile. "We mail-order brides ought to stick together." Without releasing Zoe's hand, Emilia peered into Mr. Gunderson's office. "Well now, isn't this strange?" she murmured. She walked to the storage room, pulling Zoe with her. "Isaak?"

No answer.

Emilia released Zoe. "Stay there for a moment. I bet Mr. Jones arrived and they're outside negotiating a price on the plow." She walked to the double doors at the end of the hall. A brick kept the right door propped open. She stepped outside and, as she released her hold on the door, the door banged against the brick.

Zoe glanced inside the storage room, packed to the ceiling with household goods, yet all was neat, organized, and divided into sections. Two crates, almost reaching Zoe's shoulder in height and width, sat in the far corner with the red-stenciled words THE IMPORT CO. on the sides.

The door reopened.

Emilia stepped back inside. "I'm sorry. I have no idea where Isaak disappeared to. When he returns, I'll let him know you were looking for him."

"For Jakob," Zoe corrected, and ignored the sudden fluttering in her belly. "I am looking for —"

The black candlestick telephone on Mr. Gunderson's desk rang.

Emilia hurried into the office to answer it. "The Resale Company. How can I help

you?" Pause. "He stepped out for a moment." Pause. "Jakob's not here either."
Pause. Her gaze shifted to Zoe.

Something odd flickered in Emilia's
caramel-colored eyes and then it disappeared, replaced with genuine pleasure.

Zoe looked to the door, feeing a sudden
inclination to flee.

"What if I send someone else over?"
Emilia paused, again listening to whoever
was on the other end of the line. "Yes,
ma'am, I'll be sure to tell Mac how blessed
he is to have married me. You have a good
day, too." She rehooked the earpiece, then
turned to Zoe. "Would you mind doing me
a favor?"

The Pawlikowski House
A month ago, Zoe stood in this very spot at
the bottom of the steps, listening to Jakob
boast about the locally quarried blue granite
that framed his parents' three-story home.
While the raised first floor, wraparound
porch, and magnificent tower added a
whimsical beauty to the house, what ap-
pealed to her most were the front steps.
Painted red, the twelve steps matched the
porch columns, railings, gingerbread trim,
and the house numbers on the wooden
shingle hanging from the porch awning.

Four, perhaps, five people could sit across each stair tread.

A month ago, she had daydreamed about sitting on this porch with Jakob and their children, his brother, and his brother's wife and children for a family photograph. Mr. and Mrs. Pawlikowski would be in the middle, surrounded by their legacy. Love, so much love, would be captured in the photograph. For years, they would repeat this pose on these steps, well into the next century, when Zoe would be in the middle with her husband, surrounded by *their* legacy.

A month ago, she had hope.

Now she was determined to make her daydream a reality.

Smiling, she strolled up the steps to the double front doors and knocked.

The right door opened.

A bony woman with gray-tinged auburn hair cut close to her scalp stood there, curiosity in her blue-green eyes. "Can I help you?"

"Mrs. McCall sent me to provide ze assistance you requested."

The woman's amused gaze fell to Zoe's sapphire silk day dress. "You seem to be a woman of good breeding. I appreciate your willingness, but I need muscle, not beauty."

Zoe hesitated, unsure of how to respond, so she said the only thing that came to mind. "I am Zoe de Fleur."

The woman gasped. "Oh! You're Jakob's girl! Come in, come in." She pulled Zoe inside, tossed her umbrella onto the hall tree, and then shut the door. She leaned close and sniffed. "Jakob was right — lilacs at first bloom. His brother said you smelled like a bridal bouquet. I told Mr. Gunderson he needed to learn to be more romantic if he ever wanted to win a girl's affections, but he insisted he wasn't trying to be romantic, that the description fit."

Warmness spread under Zoe's skin. A bridal bouquet was far more romantic in her opinion than lilacs in bloom. The latter, to be fair, was the exact name of the perfumed glycerin soap she used — Colgate & Co.'s Lilacs in Bloom.

The housekeeper studied Zoe. "Goodness, you're so pretty. I took this job hoping to ingratiate myself so much into Jakob's life that he realized he couldn't live without me. My plan was to marry him this summer, but now that you're here . . ." She sighed. "You're fortunate I'm not fifteen years younger. I'm sure I could lure him away from you."

"I zink you are joking with me, but if you

are not" — Zoe smiled and gave the house-keeper's arm a consoling pat— "zen I am sorry I ruined your plan to marry Jakob."

Merriment danced in the housekeeper's eyes. "You're here, so I might as well put you to work. Come along with me."

Zoe removed her bonnet, hung it on the hall tree, and followed the good-humored housekeeper down the hall.

"I'm Mrs. Wiley, by the way," she said over her shoulder. "You may call me Sarah, if you like. I've been working for the twins since mid-February. Twice a week clean-ing." She opened the door and allowed Zoe to enter the kitchen first. "Mr. Gunderson gave me a list of what he wanted cleaned and the most efficient schedule to have it all accomplished by the time the Pawlikowskis return home."

As Mrs. Wiley continued on and on about what was on Mr. Gunderson's list, Zoe glanced about the kitchen, which was larger than the front parlor. Burgundy silk curtains lay across the corner table, next to the iron-ing board. On the back wall, between two tall windows, was a steel sink as wide as a drinking trough. Black soapstone framed the sink, leaving room on either side for dishes to sit. That same soapstone covered a counter in the center of the room.

And Mrs. Pawlikowski had two — two! — cookstoves.

Best of all, the greater size of the kitchen allowed people to enjoy each other's company while preparing a meal. And the two-person table under a window provided the perfect spot for one to look outside to the greenhouse, the what-should-be-lush garden, the carriage house, and the fenced yard for several horses, a cow, and chickens. If the Pawlikowskis no longer needed space for their animals, they could build two more homes on their property. Not that either would need a kitchen, considering the size of this one.

"She must enjoy cooking," Zoe said when Mrs. Wiley paused to take a breath.

"Who must?"

"Mrs. Pawlikowski. Jakob's mother."

"She prefers to call it *experimenting.*"

Zoe looked out the kitchen's window. "Zank you for caring for Mrs. Pawlikowski's greenhouse. Zis is kind of you."

"Oh, that's all Mr. Gunderson's doing."

Other than Mr. Gunderson's godparents and a small circle of friends, *everyone* Zoe had met in town referred to him as Mr. Gunderson and Jakob as Jakob. Why that bothered her, she was not sure.

She returned her attention to Mrs. Wiley.

"Why is ze garden untended still?"

"Fret not! Jakob will take care of it before his parents return." Mrs. Wiley patted Zoe's arm. "It's a good thing you learned about his minimal gardening skills before he proposed marriage, isn't it?"

Zoe laughed. "I see what you are about, Mrs. Wiley. You wish him to lose my favor so he will be free to marry you."

"Am I succeeding?"

Zoe let her answer be a smile. At that moment, she noticed a jar on the kitchen table.

Mrs. Wiley's gaze shifted to where Zoe was looking. "Those are Mr. Gunderson's."

Zoe frowned as she walked toward the table, her attention on the glass jar half-filled with strange kernels. "What are zey?"

"You've never seen candied corn before?"

She had made candied carrots, beets, fruit, lemon peel, ginger, and even horseradish, but never had she seen or heard of candied corn. "Are zey edible?"

Mrs. Wiley picked up the jar and removed the lid. "Here, try one. He won't mind."

Zoe chose one of the tricolored kernels. Instead of the crunch she was expecting, it was soft. How could such a sweet fondant have so little flavor? She tasted vanilla, butter, and honey, but the waxy texture was unappealing at best. This faux candy should be melted and turned into a crème. With a little cayenne and cocoa power —

No! This candy should be tossed to swine.

There was no polite way to spit it out, so she swallowed. "Zey are edible, but eatable?" She shook her head. "Zat is *not* candy."

Mrs. Wiley laughed. "Don't let Mr. Gunderson hear you. He has a serious sweet tooth."

"He eats candied corn because he knows not better. I could make him a treat zat would banish all desire for zis —" Zoe grimaced. "*Ick.* I have no words to describe it."

"The twins mentioned you're a chef."

Household cook, to be exact. Weary of explaining the difference, she looked at the curtains. "How may I help?"

Mrs. Wiley grabbed the hem of her calico skirt and tucked the edge into the waistband, exposing her white bloomers. "Pick up one end of the curtains here and I'll do the other. We can lay them over the divan. I'll climb the ladder; you certainly won't be able to manage it in that fancy gown." She picked up one end of the stacked curtains. "Once we're in the parlor, you can hand me one curtain at a time."

While Mrs. Wiley walked backward down

the hall, Zoe carried the other end of the stacked curtains, taking care not to let them wrinkle. They were midway in redraping the last parlor window when the rain began.

After hanging the curtain, Mrs. Wiley climbed down the ladder. She drew up to the window where Zoe stood watching the rain pound against the street, mud puddles everywhere. "I'll wager we have a good hour or two before this lets up. How about we — Miss de Fleur, is something bothering you? You seem distracted."

Zoe stared absently at the rain-splattered window. "Zis morning Mr. Snowe mentioned how his daughter had once favored Jakob."

"Miss Snowe is one of dozens who once favored him." Mrs. Wiley bumped her shoulder against Zoe's. "Or still do."

"Including you?"

"If I were fifteen years younger . . ." The besotted sigh that came from Mrs. Wiley seemed more fitting coming from Carline or Yancey. Zoe had uttered a few of those sighs herself after first meeting Jakob. Clearly, he had his choice of ladies who would happily allow him to court them.

Desperate for an answer to the question that had plagued her for weeks, Zoe turned to face Mrs. Wiley. "Why did Jakob write for a bride by mail delivery when zere are many eminently suitable women here in Helena?"

"I've wondered that myself." Her knowing gaze settled on Zoe. "For all Jakob's virtues — and that man has many virtues — he's impatient and can miss what's right in front of him. If the idea pops into his mind to put out an advertisement for a bride, he's going to do it. Why not? As he often says, *It'll be fun.*"

Zoe nodded, having heard him say that. "Jakob knows how to make a girl smile and forget her worries."

Mrs. Wiley chuckled. "That he does. I doubt his brother has ever done a spontaneous thing in his life without Jakob leading him on. Compared to Jakob, Mr. Gunderson is quite the bore. You should see the cleaning schedule he gave me. He plans *everything.*" The emphasis Mrs. Wiley put on *everything* made Mr. Gunderson's diligence seem a grave character flaw.

"Mr. Gunderson can be counted on to do what he says he will do," Zoe said in his defense, "to be faithful, to never leave because something new has caught his interest. Some women would find zat dependability as appealing as Jakob's *joie de vivre.*"

A wrinkle deepened between Mrs. Wiley's brows. "I'm not even going to try to repeat what you just said."

Zoe chuckled. "It means a cheerful enjoyment of life. Jakob has happy eyes because he has a happy spirit. He will bring laughter into ze life of ze girl he marries." She turned to look out the window, her smile fading as understanding dawned. The more Jakob separated from Isaak, the emptier Isaak felt. "Mr. Gunderson needs to find a girl with happy eyes and a happy spirit who will bring *joie de vivre* into his life, as Jakob has done for him all zese years."

"She'll have to storm into his life like a cyclone because Isaak Gunderson would *never* go looking for a female version of his brother. There's not a soul in Helena who tries his patience more, and that's by his own admission." Mrs. Wiley stepped closer to Zoe and lowered her voice, even though they were the only two in the house. "I think young unmarried ladies intimidate him."

Zoe opened her mouth . . . yet no words came out.

Isaak Gunderson carried too much confidence to be intimidated by anyone, least of all a young unmarried lady. If anything, he was too busy to realize he was lonely. What he needed was a steady, gentle rain — not a cyclone — to remind him to work a little less and have fun a little more.

"He's never courted anyone," Mrs. Wiley remarked.

Zoe snapped to attention. His brother was the first person to court her.

"Never?" she asked even though this was none of her business. No one's romantic pursuits — or, more precisely, lack thereof — fascinated her as much as Isaak Gunderson's did. "How do you know zis?"

Mrs. Wiley paused for a long moment. "I've only lived in Helena for six years, but I can't remember seeing him with any girl besides Yancey Palmer or Carline Pope . . . or Emilia McCall before she married. He's always at work or helping at church with the Widows and Orphans Committee. Every widow in town knows to go to him for help. There isn't a more generous man or a more dutiful son than Isaak Gunderson."

"You said he was a bore."

"That he is. He's a good man, even if he's not as exciting to be around as Jakob is."

Zoe nodded in agreement. She glanced over her shoulder at the clock sitting on the piano Carline Pope had lovingly played a month ago. Not quite an hour had passed since Zoe arrived to help. Yet the rain still looked strong and steady.

Zoe smiled at Mrs. Wiley. "Is zere anything else I can help clean?"

"Do you *want* to clean?"

Zoe grimaced. "I *always* prefer someone else do ze cleaning, but I enjoy helping someone in need. And I like you." She motioned to the window. "Plus, I cannot leave. Ze rain holds me hostage."

"As it does me," Mrs. Wiley said grimly. "The rain *and* Isaak Gunderson's cleaning list." She looked from the window to Zoe, and the corners of her mouth slowly indented. "Miss de Fleur, please take no offense when I say I don't believe you can cook a better sweet than candied corn."

"You *like* zat wretched treat?"

"If I say yes, will you feel compelled to prove my opinion wrong?"

Zoe realized where this was headed. "You are hoping I am competitive enough to rise to ze bait."

"Seeing we have Mrs. Pawlikowski's grand kitchen all to ourselves," Mrs. Wiley said smugly, "I'm hoping you are mercilessly competitive."

"I feel strangely compelled to prove you wrong about my cooking skills." Zoe followed Mrs. Wiley back to the kitchen. What could she make based on memory alone? It needed to be simple. With limited ingredients. As they entered the kitchen, Zoe glanced at the icebox, then at the closet door she suspected led to the larder. The best sweet to fit the requirements would be —

"I shall make *praline de café,*" she announced.

Mrs. Wiley walked to the wall-mounted coffee grinder. "What is a praw-leen do — I have no idea what you just said."

"All zat matters is zey are a million times more eatable zan candied corn." Zoe gave the housekeeper her most mischievous grin. "Every flavor of praline is as alluring to men as a siren's song. I shall make ones flavored with coffee. Zey were Papa's favorite candy."

Mrs. Wiley seemed sufficiently impressed. "Be forewarned: I fully intend on telling Jakob I made these."

Zoe laughed. Mrs. Wiley could tell Jakob anything she wished because Zoe intended on taking Jakob a jar of pralines, along with a personal invitation to join her for supper tonight with Lily Forsythe. He would say yes. She was a jarful of candy sure of it.

CHAPTER SIXTEEN

Later that evening
The Pawlikowski House

Isaak opened the front door. "Jakob? Are you home?"

Silence.

The scent of coffee and something sweet filled the air. Isaak's stomach rumbled in response. He'd gone straight from The Resale Co. to church to talk to the Ladies' Aid Society and missed dinner.

Isaak shut the door. Where was that heavenly smell coming from?

He headed straight to the kitchen. A small plate sat in the middle of the table; propped up in front of his candied corn was a note card. Isaak walked closer. Four caramel-colored blobs lay on a plate. He lifted one to his mouth.

Wow!

Sweet, crunchy, nutty, chewy. He ran out of adjectives while munching the savory treat. A note in Mrs. Wiley's scratchy penmanship rested next to the candy. He opened it and read:

Zoe made these pralines for you. I told her that you didn't care for coffee, but she insisted you would like coffee served this way. She preferred to use almonds. We could only find pecans. I finished everything on your list.

P.S. She says your candied corn isn't eatable. I wouldn't let her throw them away.

He smiled and reached for another praline, unable to remember the last time someone had done something just for him. He was self-sufficient, confident in his likes and dislikes, and busy being the man others relied on. All good things, but they left him lonely.

Not an adjective he'd applied to himself until Pastor Neven's sermon on Sunday describing how God created loneliness in Adam's breast by making him name the animals — each of them with a mate — before bringing Eve to him.

Isaak had seen himself in the story. He enjoyed a great relationship with his parents. He and his twin shared a special bond . . .

most of the time. He had meaningful work to do. And yet he was alone.

He scooped up the last two pralines, then crossed to the stove. With one hand, he stoked the fire, lifted the cast-iron pot onto the stove, and retrieved the covered bowl from the icebox while polishing off the candy. He might have to pay Miss de Fleur to make him a batch once a month.

Jakob breezed in half an hour later, just as Isaak was sitting down to his stew, bread, and Earl Grey tea with lots of sugar and a splash of cream. "Hope you ate," Isaak said, "because I didn't save any for you."

"I had dinner." Jakob peered at the stew, a smile tugging one side of his mouth higher than the other. "And I must say, I ate better than you."

Isaak shoveled a bite of stew into his mouth so he wouldn't say, *But you didn't get pralines,* out loud.

"By the way" — Jakob opened the bread box and took out a biscuit — "Jefferson Brady came by The Import Company today. He wants the big office, so I added two dollars to the monthly payment and sent him over to Hale to sign the lease."

"That's great, Jake. I was hoping to have all those offices leased by the time Pa got back. You're way ahead of schedule there."

291

Instead of appearing pleased at the compliment, Jakob stared at the biscuit in his hand. "Why was I about to eat this?"

"Instinct, I imagine." Isaak spooned stew into his mouth.

Jakob tossed the biscuit back into the bread box, then strolled to the table and sat down next to Isaak. He swiped his finger in the crumbs on the praline plate and licked it. "Did Zoe leave you some pralines?"

"Leave me?" came out in a tone of voice more suited to a ten-year-old.

"She brought a jarful down to The Import Company for me." Jakob held his hands six inches apart to indicate the height of the jar.

Jealousy stabbed Isaak in the heart. So she hadn't made the treat especially for him.

"You're in a cheery mood." Isaak bit into his biscuit with more force than necessary, making his teeth clank together.

"I had a great time at Aunt Lily's tonight."

Isaak didn't want to hear about it. Tuesdays were Jakob's night for dinner with Miss de Fleur at the Forsythes'.

Jakob circled his index finger around the praline plate. "Yancey and Carline joined us for dinner and helped us figure out what to serve at the welcome-home dinner."

Isaak held his spoon inches from his

mouth while trying to untangle his brother's sentence and why he was jealous again — this time because Yancey and Carline were invited to share dinner at Aunt Lily's with Jakob and Miss de Fleur.

Isaak set his still-full spoonful of stew back in the bowl. "What welcome-home dinner?"

"For Ma and Pa." Jakob stretched his arms wide and yawned. "I'm bushed."

Isaak picked up his teacup to give his hands something to do. "Come on, Jake. Give me the whole story."

Jakob yawned again. "Sorry. It's been a long couple of weeks."

Did that mean he was on schedule? The question lodged in Isaak's throat. He'd committed to staying out of what was happening at The Import Co.

Jakob rubbed his left shoulder with his right hand. "Yancey showed up at the store in time to claim the last praline. She'd never tasted Zoe's cooking, although she'd heard plenty about Mrs. Hollenbeck's welcome-home breakfast last Saturday."

Who hadn't? It was the talk of the town.

"Yancey suggested Zoe cater a dinner party for when Ma and Pa get back, only this one large enough to include us and our friends." Jakob held up his hand. "Before you say anything about how I'm behind and don't have time to add another thing to my schedule, I've already planned how it will work."

Jakob planned something ahead of time? Isaak was tempted to make some smart-aleck remark about marking the occasion in his calendar. Instead, he sipped his tea and listened while Jakob glowed with enthusiasm as he explained how tasting pralines at The Import Co. had set in motion a grand dinner on the Friday night eight days after their parents were scheduled to return to Helena. The guest list included twenty-five people and would be held at Mrs. Hollenbeck's, if she agreed, because her house was the only one with a dining room large enough to accommodate that many people.

Isaak listened while sipping his extra-sweet tea, which did nothing to abate the sour taste in his mouth.

Jakob was as committed as ever to his courtship of Miss de Fleur.

Wednesday, April 18
De Fleur-Gunderson Courtship Contract,
  Day 40
Isaak sat in his office staring at a Spiegel catalog. He was supposed to be studying prices of new items so he didn't overpay for secondhand ones. He was supposed to stop

thinking about Miss Zoe de Fleur and his improper attraction to her, too.

Neither of which was happening.

Isaak slapped the catalog closed with a huff. He needed advice, but he'd run through the list of possible people and disqualified every one of them. Right or wrong, his pride couldn't take admitting his preoccupation with the lady to anyone else. His heart leaped every time he saw a woman with black hair, whether it was curly or not. He looked for Miss de Fleur every time he delivered merchandise for the store or food to widows and orphans. And every time he returned home, he hoped to find a bowl of nuts or some other treat he could pretend she'd made special for him.

Meow.

"Hello, Harry." Isaak reached down and picked up the tabby cat Jakob had rescued when they were eleven years old. Jakob had lost interest after a few weeks of playing with the stray, so Harry had become Isaak's.

"You were the first time I realized it was up to me to follow through on Jakob's initial ideas." Isaak stroked the cat's head. "Not that I've minded much. We're a good team most of the time."

As they were with the Sundin family. On an impulse, Jakob had hired Timmy to work at The Import Co. Once Isaak heard about it, he'd added the boy and his mother to the list of widows and orphans who received food boxes. Which made him think of walking to Mrs. Hollenbeck's house with Miss de Fleur.

Why did every thought either start or end with her?

Isaak held the cat aloft so they were eye to eye. "What do you think of Miss de Fleur?"

Harry blinked his yellow eyes.

"I agree. She *is* a lovely person, which is my problem." Isaak lowered the cat into his lap and reached into the bottom drawer of his desk. He pulled out a piece of paper. "See this?" He laid the paper on top of the Spiegel catalog. "It's my list of qualities I require in a wife."

Harry wriggled free to jump onto the desk and paw at the paper.

Isaak picked up the cat and held him away from the list. "I'll read it to you. Item number one: godly character."

There was a check mark beside it because Miss de Fleur had demonstrated grace and mercy every time she didn't return Isaak's accusations with ones of her own. The day she bought the books, she could have run straight to Aunt Lily, telling her about Isaak's bribe offer. But no, Miss de Fleur had remained silent. She even paid full price for the books when she could have bested him again by offering a ridiculously low price. Adding the two bits extra was her only comeuppance, and it was given with a smile.

"Item number two: balances me."

It was also checked. Like Uncle Jonas, Isaak was hard around the edges with a softer middle than most people knew. Like Aunt Lily, Miss de Fleur was soft around the edges with an inner strength.

Balance.

"Item number three: shares some of my interests." Isaak pulled Harry's claws from his tweed vest to prevent snags. "Pay attention, because this one is important. See? No check mark. We both like to cook, but that's not enough for a strong relational foundation. The problem is, I don't know Miss de Fleur very well. I've been avoiding her, for obvious reasons."

Harry blinked his wisdom.

"You're right. The problem isn't my lack of knowledge, it's what happens if I get to know her better and she *does* share more interests with me." He looked at the list. "I take that back. My biggest problem is that I never should have taken this list out in the first place. I was trying to prove that my infatuation was unfounded."

Harry purred.

Isaak stroked all the way to the tabby's tail. "I believe I need to add one more item."

Meow.

"Yes, I should have thought of it long ago, but I never imagined this situation." After setting Harry on the floor, Isaak picked up a pencil and added a new item at the top of his list: **NOT JAKOB'S GIRL**.

Seeing the words failed to relieve Isaak's exasperation at his weakness.

Harry weaved his way around Isaak's ankles. "You're right again. Sitting here is doing no good at all."

Neither was talking to a cat. Isaak needed advice from someone other than himself. If only Pa were here. Or Ma.

Knock, knock, knock.

"Come in."

Mac opened the door, sidestepping to let Harry race past him.

Isaak checked the clock. Before Mac and Emilia married, they'd developed a habit of sharing their lunch hour together. "You're here early."

Mac closed the door and locked it. "I'm here to talk to you."

Isaak tucked his disobliging list inside the catalog. "Have a seat."

Mac hung his Stetson on the peg. "Remember that leveling foot I showed you last year after Finn died?"

"Yes."

He crossed the room and sat in one of the chairs on the opposite side of the desk. "Could you look through your father's ledgers and make a list of anything requiring one?"

"Why? Has something new come up about Finn's death?"

"What I'm about to tell you must remain between us. You can't tell Jakob, Hale, the Forsythes, or even your parents when they return home."

Isaak nodded his agreement to the terms.

Mac licked his lips. "Finn and my mother weren't selling women into prostitution. They were smuggling young girls out."

"What! I mean, yes. That makes sense." At least about Finn Collins. But rescuing girls with Madame Lestraude? That didn't make *any* sense. Isaak shifted in his chair. "What a relief to know your best friend wasn't deceiving you all these years."

Mac nodded. "Emilia has known since last June. She's been encouraging me to earn my mother's trust, so she'd tell me the story herself."

"Which I'm guessing was right before the wedding."

Another nod. "I showed my mother this a few minutes ago." Mac pulled the leveling screw from his coat pocket. "She gasped. It wasn't much, and she attempted to cover it with a cough, but she knows more than she's telling me."

Isaak harrumphed. Of course she knew more. A brothel owner who catered to the rich and powerful probably kept more secrets than a graveyard. "Do you need me to check my father's ledgers now, or can it wait until after the grand opening?"

"After is fine." Mac stood. "But then as soon as possible."

"Of course, but before you go . . ." Isaak opened the catalog. "I need your advice about something that also must remain between us."

Mac sat down again.

Isaak pulled the list he'd hidden from between the pages. "These are the qualities I require in a wife." He turned the paper around so Mac could see the bold print letters at the top.

Mac's eyes widened, then snapped to meet Isaak's gaze. "Oh, man."

Madame Lestraude stormed into his office, her burgundy silk skirt rustling like leaves in a windstorm. "You killed Finn

Collins."

"I did not."

She gripped the back of the chair opposite his desk. "Don't play a game of semantics with me. You may not have shot the bullet, but you're responsible."

The rancher's death plagued his conscience enough; he didn't need Madame Lestraude fanning the flames. "Whatever gave you such an odd notion?"

Her brown eyes constricted. "A certain metal object my son showed me earlier today. One found in Finn's barn last year."

Heat snaked up his spine.

"As soon as I saw it and heard it was a leveling foot, I realized it belonged to that printing press you're so proud of."

He closed the file on his desk to give himself somewhere else to look other than in her too-intelligent eyes. That press was churning out page after page of near-perfect counterfeit money, so of course he was proud of it. He'd purchased it for pennies on the dollar because it required extensive repairs. Dunfree was supposed to find someone far from Helena for that job, but Collins was the only man in the territory who could fix the thing "What did you tell your son?"

"Nothing."

He looked up at her, a mistake because any doubts she might have had were eradicated by whatever she saw in his face.

She came around the chair, placed her hands on his desk, and leaned down close enough he could smell the rosewater on her skin. "I have tortured myself thinking I was responsible for getting that good man killed."

So had he.

She pushed off his desk and straightened her shoulders. With a deep breath and slow exhalation, she transformed herself into the passionless madam who cared for no one. "You and I have coexisted in this town for twelve years because our interests have never conflicted until now. Edgar Dunfree deserved what he got, and I was no fan of Joseph Hendry."

He flinched, unable to maintain the same disguise of disinterest. But then, she'd had more practice. "How did you know about Hendry?"

"I didn't until now, but I knew he wasn't killed for meddling in the red-light district. Was he getting too close to your precious counterfeiting?"

There was no point in denying it, but he wouldn't give her the satisfaction of confirming it either.

She stared down her nose at him. "We have reached an important point in our peaceful coexistence. Finn is gone. For us to feud over his death now is a waste o effort."

He nodded. He should have stood when she entered the room, a tactical error he wouldn't make again.

She took a step back. "We shall let Finn Collins rest in peace, but I swear to you on his grave, if you ever threaten my family or cause them harm, I will tear every one of your illicit businesses down with my bare hands."

CHAPTER SEVENTEEN

Millionaire's Hill
Late afternoon, the next day
De Fleur-Gunderson Courtship Contract,
  Day 41

"Ma'am, I found these in the attic."

The sound of Miss Bloom's voice drew Zoe's attention away from the food crate she was filling in the shadow of Mrs. Hollenbeck's three-story mansion. Mrs. Hollenbeck's paid companion, with a jubilant smile that emphasized her deep dimples, stepped out onto the patio and gave the older woman three stacked baskets, each the size of a hatbox.

"Thank you, Miss Bloom." Mrs. Hollenbeck studied the stack. She took the largest basket, then handed the other two back to her assistant. "Choose the one you like best, then return the other from whence it came."

"I like neither," Miss Bloom said without

losing her smile, "so to the attic they both go."

Mrs. Hollenbeck laughed. "My dear child, you will never win a gentleman's favor with that attitude."

"Then my surliness is working."

"Not if I can help it. I vowed to find you a husband by year's end, and I mean to fulfill my promise."

"I am most grateful for your concern over matters of my heart," Miss Bloom responded, even though her lack of gratitude for Mrs. Hollenbeck's matchmaking skills was clear to Zoe.

Ignoring their bantering, she added the final two onions to the food crate. Since arriving to aid in packing crates for a dozen church families, she had listened to Mrs. Hollenbeck extoll to her assistant the virtues of numerous Helena bachelors, including Geddes Palmer and Windsor Buchanan, the latter seeming to hold a tenderness in the rich widow's heart. Zoe had spoken on numerous occasions with both gentlemen — the former being friends with Jakob and the latter with Mr. Gunderson. Either would make a suitable husband, so she had no idea why Miss Bloom resisted being courted.

"— is why you will fill a basket. End of

debate." Mrs. Hollenbeck strolled over to Zoe and the wooden patio table laden with food crates. "This one is yours."

Zoe reached for the basket.

"Don't take it, Miss de Fleur."

Heeding Miss Bloom's warning, Zoe lowered her hands. She looked at Mrs. Hollenbeck and the basket she held. Then she looked at Miss Bloom, whose perpetual smile had faded. Then Zoe looked back at Mrs. Hollenbeck, who wore an expression of mild disappointment at Zoe for not immediately accepting the basket.

"What is ze basket for?" Zoe asked with equal amounts of caution and curiosity.

"Lunch." Mrs. Hollenbeck moved the basket closer to Zoe, as if it were imperative that she take it. "Go on, dear. It won't bite."

"Am I to fill zis?"

"That is the plan."

Zoe looked to the table which had held food donations for the baskets. Nothing remained save for dusty burlap potato sacks. On her way home, she could stop at the grocer and bakery. The cost was little in light of helping a needy family.

The moment Zoe accepted the basket, Miss Bloom called out, "Miss de Fleur, you're going to regret not listening to me. Never feed a tiger. Oh, I hear the door knocker." At that, with her head held high, she sailed past the opened patio doors and into the mansion as if she owned it.

"One of these days, I shall relieve that girl of her employment with me." The flicker of amusement in Mrs. Hollenbeck's eyes belied her words.

Zoe smiled warmly. "I believe you like her . . ." She paused, trying to think of the right English word. "Cheek? Nerve? Oh, how do you translate *le toupet*?"

"Cheekiness?" Mrs. Hollenbeck offered. "Sass?"

"Yes! You like her sass."

"Like? No, I tolerate her sass because I don't wish to train another paid companion." In a softer voice, Mrs. Hollenbeck said, "You may be on to something, but let's keep that our secret." Her attention shifted to the crates of food. "All we need now are our delivery men." She grasped the pocket watch she wore on a pearl chain around her neck and clicked the cover open. "They should be arriving about now."

Zoe held up the basket. "For whom do I need to fill zis?"

"Oh, dear child, this isn't for a needy family. In two Sundays, on April 29, the Widows and Orphans Committee is hosting a lunch basket auction at our church. Unmarried ladies are to provide a lunch for men to bid on." At the sound of people talking, Mrs. Hollenbeck glanced toward the opened patio doors before refocusing on Zoe. "I've raved to everyone I know about the welcome-home breakfast feast you cooked for me. During past auctions, men have bid on baskets to secure the attentions of the lady who provided the basket. This year I intend to cause a bidding war for your food."

"A bidding war?"

"Indeed, Miss de Fleur. Jakob will obviously counter every offer." She chuckled. "This will serve him right after all these years of running up bids."

Zoe hoped he would bid on her lunch basket. Yet a tiny part of her wished otherwise. After five days of focusing on nothing but Jakob's courtship, she was now doubting her decision to give him another chance because, after five days of renewed courtship, Jakob again had no time for anything save The Import Company.

Why did her heart fight against committing to him?

She sighed. Falling in love should never be this complicated.

She understood when he said he needed to give his full attention to stocking The

Import Company because his parents were returning in a short seven days. Shelves needed to be arranged and stocked. Merchandise had to be priced. Decorations had to be hung. But did he have to work more than nine hours each day? Jakob had canceled Monday's picnic trip to watch the construction of the new Broadwater Hotel. He was late to Tuesday's coffee-and-cake social with the Snowe family, and he forgot about dinner with the Forsythes entirely, even though Mrs. Forsythe repeatedly reminded him that Judge Forsythe wanted to talk to Jakob after eight days of travel.

At least, Jakob's brother had been at the Snowes' social and the Forsythes' dinner to carry the conversation, so Zoe could contentedly watch and listen. Mr. Gunderson was kind enough to include her in the discussion and not demand she speak. He was considerate enough to change the topic of conversation when Miss Snowe's brother embarrassingly goaded Miss Snowe about thinking she could steal Jakob away from Zoe, who, according to Miss Snowe's brother, was "a more swell girl" than his sister was.

With all the lovely young women in Helena, with ones like Miss Snowe chasing after Jakob, it made no sense why he had placed an advertisement for a bride by mail delivery. A man besotted with a girl would wish to spend time with her. Zoe wanted to believe Jakob was besotted. Nothing testified to it. Could he be using this courtship to dissuade the attentions of marriage-minded females in town?

Zoe tensed. He could be using her to make someone else jealous. Yancey? Carline? Both ladies were close friends with Jakob. Almost every time Zoe had stopped by The Import Company in the morning to see Jakob, either one or both had been there.

Mrs. Hollenbeck rested her hand atop Zoe's arm, putting an end to her wayward thoughts. "May I ask what troubles you?"

I want to love Jakob, but my heart refuses. What do I do?

She yearned to say the words. She yearned to talk to someone about her heart's struggle, but everyone would say she needed to give the courtship time, at least follow it through to the end. Jakob was a good man. A hard worker. Someone worth waiting for. Mrs. Hollenbeck adored Jakob too much to understand Zoe's dilemma.

Truth was, maybe she did not *really* want to love Jakob. Maybe she wanted someone else, someone she could rely on to help her not feel so alone.

"Whatever it is, you can tell me," Mrs. Hollenbeck prodded.

Something about her expression comforted Zoe. Maybe the older woman would understand. "How does a woman know if she should —"

The arrival of a quartet of men prevented her from finishing her sentence. Miss Bloom stepped out onto the patio, followed by Misters Gunderson and Buchanan, Deputy Alderson, and Dr. Abernathy's son, who had recently returned to Helena after medical school. John? James? Oh, she could not remember.

"This is a first," Mrs. Hollenbeck whispered to Zoe.

"What is?" she whispered back.

"The first time I've been disappointed at someone's promptness." Mrs. Hollenbeck turned toward the men. "Gentlemen, we have a dozen crates. Once you each load three in your wagons, I will give you a list of where to deliver them."

"I already distributed the lists per your earlier instructions," Miss Bloom put in. "And I exchanged the Nolans with the Bumgardens because Deputy Alderson told me the Nolans moved out to Mr. Fisk's old cabin this morning. Switching makes the deliveries more efficient."

For the barest second, Mrs. Hollenbeck looked unsure of how to respond. "Thank you for the insight. Mr. Gunderson, you should have the Ziegler family."

"I do," Mr. Gunderson answered. His gaze flickered from Mrs. Hollenbeck to Zoe. Was it her imagination or did he look somewhat uncomfortable?

"I should leave," Zoe said, because her work here was done.

Mrs. Hollenbeck gripped Zoe's arm, stopping her from leaving, and said to Miss Bloom, "Escort Mr. Gunderson to the stable. The brown goat with the yellow ribbon around her neck goes to Mrs. Ziegler. I need you to accompany Mr. Gunderson and help manage the goat. She doesn't like wagons."

Miss Bloom smiled brightly at Mr. Gunderson. "We're partners! Isn't that — oh!" Her smile fell. She grimaced, then gave Mrs. Hollenbeck an apologetic look. "Miss de Fleur needs to go in my place. Deputy Alderson asked for my advice in planning his marriage proposal to Miss Rigney. Discussing this with him while making the deliveries would look less suspicious to his soon-to-be fiancée."

"Indeed it would," Mrs. Hollenbeck muttered.

Misters Gunderson, Buchanan, and Abernathy all looked at Deputy Alderson, who looked caught in a trap.

"It's going to be the best," Miss Bloom said in that dramatic way of hers, "the most romantic proposal any woman has every received. I'm so honored Deputy Alderson asked for my help."

He nodded, like a man with no choice but to comply.

Mrs. Hollenbeck gave Zoe's arm a little squeeze. "I know this is asking a lot for someone of your tenderhearted nature, but could you help Mr. Gunderson manage a feisty goat?"

Zoe's chin rose a half-inch in offense at Mrs. Hollenbeck's pronouncement. She could outwit a feisty goat just as easily as Miss Bloom could outwit her I-vowed-to-find-you-a-husband-by-year's-end employer. "Certainly, madame. It is but a goat."

Miss Bloom leaned close to Isaak, shielding her mouth with her hand. "Miss de Fleur is a charming girl but a bit too malleable. I don't know what your brother sees in her besides a pretty face, excellent cooking skills, a sweet spirit, and a willingness to help others."

Isaak pressed his lips together. Miss de

Fleur was all that and more — including being concerned for widows and orphans. He could practically hear his pen scratching a check mark beside "shares some of my interests" on his list.

Had Zoe de Fleur arrived in Helena in any other manner than as his brother's mail-order bride, Isaak would revel in the way she made him feel. Over a long period of time — six months, at least — if her character still matched up with what it now appeared to be, they could have a romance that was a perfect balance of practicality and sentiment. But she *had* come as Jakob's bride, and Isaak would never betray his brother. When the time was right, Isaak would find another Zoe de Fleur who would fill his life with sweetness.

At least he hoped that was the lesson God was teaching him.

"The Widows and Orphans Committee needs your help." Mrs. Hollenbeck picked up a small basked and — were she any woman other than the most revered widow of his acquaintance — Isaak would describe the way she thrust a basket at Miss de Fleur as rude.

Miss de Fleur took it, but she seemed unhappy about it.

He took a step forward to discover why,

but it wasn't his place to ease her burden. To protect her. Or to sit beside her for the next two hours delivering food as Mrs. Hollenbeck had decreed, although he would do so rather than be rude.

Fifteen minutes later, he had three food crates loaded into the back of the wagon and the goat tied to the wagon wheel to keep it from running off. Miss de Fleur placed her small basket onto the spring seat. She frowned at the wagon's side, then looked up at him.

"How do you climb into zis?"

"May I?" He moved his hands to Miss de Fleur's waist, close but not touching. "It'll be easier if I just lift you into the wagon. Then the goat. You can hold it while I climb in. Between the two of us, it won't go anywhere."

"Zat sounds like a good plan." She smiled at him with such trust in her eyes that his heart began to pick up speed.

His reaction when she'd caught him listening to the finches sing in the greenhouse was nothing compared to this moment. Against all logic, his determination to overcome his attraction to her was replaced by a fierce desire to kiss her until she admitted her life would be incomplete without him.

Isaak choked on air. He coughed into his hand until he could swallow. "Sorry, I —" His mind went blank, so he focused on putting her and the goat into the wagon. He'd helped a woman into a wagon before, but this felt entirely different. Private. Intimate. And — heaven help him — splendid. Doing his best not to think about how his hands had encircled her waist, he hurried around the wagon, climbed in, and set off down the road with the goat standing between them.

His attraction to Zoe was madness. Madness! It would pass. It had to. In the meantime, he just needed to keep himself from saying or doing anything stupid. He had to get the food and goat delivered then get Miss de Fleur back to her boardinghouse before he did something he would enjoy but definitely regret.

She sat on the spring seat, petting the goat's head as she spoke to it in French.

They traveled another block before Isaak gave in to his curiosity. "What are you telling it?"

Miss de Fleur gave him a tentative smile. "What it knows but is afraid to believe."

"Which is?"

"She is a good goat. She does not fear where ze wagon is taking her because she is going to her new home. She will have a family who loves her and who she can love."

Isaak shifted the reins to his left hand so he could pet the goat. "How do you know this goat so well?"

"She is a girl. I am a girl."

Girl was too simple a word to define Zoe de Fleur.

Isaak drew the wagon up to the first home on their route, a two-room house on the outskirts of Chinatown. He left Miss de Fleur to charm the goat while he gave the food crate to Miss Marie Ying and her younger brother. After accepting hugs from the Yings, Isaak climbed into the wagon and turned the wagon in the direction of the Zieglers' house

Miss de Fleur patted his arm. "I am glad we are friends, you and I."

Isaak called on every ounce of self-restraint and honor to keep from confessing how her touch affected him. For a man to pursue another man's woman was treachery enough; for a man to betray his own brother in the same way was the deepest level of perfidy imaginable.

He gave her a steady look. "Everyone needs a friend." He motioned to the basket. "I take it Mrs. Hollenbeck wants you to contribute to the lunch basket auction."

She grimaced, her nose scrunching, something he'd never seen her do before. Something he never wished to see again because of how endearing she looked. "Mrs. Hollenbeck wishes for a bidding war — not for romance, but to raise money for ze Widows and Orphans Fund." She sighed. "Jakob will feel obligated to buy my basket. In no good conscience can I ask zis of him."

Isaak couldn't stop a burst of laughter. "It'd serve him right after all these years of running up bids."

"Zat is what Mrs. Hollenbeck said."

Which made him think of the way she'd thrust the basket at Miss de Fleur. "Instead of donating a lunch basket, you could make a monetary donation to the fund."

Her countenance brightened. "I did not know I could do zat. Yes! Zis is a wonderful solution. Zen Jakob will not have to be in a bidding war."

"You're more gracious to Jakob than he deserves." Isaak recounted the time Jakob had misjudged how angry his bidding was making a man intent on wooing the basket's owner, resulting in a round of fisticuffs before Sheriff McCall broke up the fight. "Your kindness in sparing Jakob retaliation is undeserved."

"If you were him, would you not wish for grace?"

Unsure of what to say, yet confident of what he *couldn't* say, Isaak turned the wagon onto the road leading to the Zieglers' ramshackle home. He listened to the rattle of the wagon's chains, the clomp of the horse's hooves, and the bleet of the goat to keep from thinking about things he shouldn't. Before he'd stopped the wagon and locked the brake, Mrs. Ziegler's two girls dashed from the house, only to stop and gasp when they saw the goat.

"Is that for us, Mr. Gunderson?" the older one said as their mother stepped outside.

He climbed down. "It sure is." After checking the rope around the goat's neck, he placed it on the ground, then led it to Mrs. Ziegler and gave her the leash. "The food is —"

Her gaze shifted to the wagon.

Isaak looked over his shoulder.

Miss de Fleur carried the food crate toward them. She placed it on the porch, spoke to the Ziegler girls about naming the goat, then shook Mrs. Ziegler's hand. "May zis be a blessing to you and yours."

"Thank you." Mrs. Ziegler's gaze shifted between him and Miss de Fleur. If she wondered why Isaak wasn't making the delivery on his own like usual, she kept it to herself.

Isaak said goodbye to Mrs. Ziegler then walked with Miss de Fleur back to the wagon. "You shouldn't have jumped out of the wagon. You could have twisted an ankle."

She laughed. "I am more clever zan you give me credit." Instead of stopping at the front of the wagon, she continued to the back. She turned her back to the wagon, placed her palms flat on the bottom board, then sprung in that fancy blue dress of hers onto the wagon box. She scrambled onto her feet. *"Voilà!"*

He folded his arms over the top boxboard. "You're pretty pleased with yourself."

She stepped around the food crate and over the bicycle, then leaned down and lowered her voice, as if imparting a secret. "You will be a gentleman and praise me for my ingenuity."

Isaak took his leisure in admiring the mischievous glint in her chocolate-brown eyes. The last time he'd been told to behave like a gentleman he was twelve years old and it had been a reprimand, not a pleasant bantering that made him desire to lean close to her mouth. Warmth filled his cheeks. "You can count on me to be a gentleman."

"And?"

And that needed to be the end of their

repartee. With Yancey and Carline, he could tease because their flirtations weren't personal. Yancey loved Hale. Carline loved Geddes, or so Isaak suspected. Playful bantering with Zoe —

Miss de Fleur.

Using her first name was a line he could not cross, not even in the privacy of his thoughts.

With a shake of his head, he climbed into the wagon and slid onto the spring bench.

She sat backward on the seat. With the lift of her legs, she swirled around. "Mr. Gunderson, zat was no compliment."

Not a compliment? The woman couldn't be more wrong. Being on his best behavior around her was the highest compliment he could give her. He didn't want mere friendship. Or playful banter. He wanted friendship and banter, plus her secrets, her hopes, and her future — the things she was dreaming about with his brother. Wanting what he couldn't have was turning him inside out. He should never have made that list. He should never have compared it to her. He should have insisted he could make these deliveries on his own.

She fit perfectly into his life. Too perfectly.

"We should get on to the Wileys." Isaak loosened the brake and flicked the reins, starting the wagon forward. "Sarah has four children from her first marriage — Alexander, Dante, Olivia, and Thaddeus. Did Sarah tell you she came to Helena as Hector Wiley's mail-order bride? She wouldn't marry him until he adopted her children."

When Miss de Fleur didn't respond, he looked her way.

She was watching him with a curious, studious expression, as if he were a puzzle she needed — dare he think *wanted* — to solve. How was it possible she grew more beautiful each time he looked at her? His heart pounded, urging him to touch her cheek. To discover whether her heart was beating as wildly as his. To —

Isaak jerked his attention to the road.

She inched a little closer to his side of the bench. "You cannot allow yourself to have fun. I wonder why zat is." Isaak opened his mouth to answer, but she waved him away. "No, no. Keep your secret, Mr. Gunderson. Ze bicycle is for ze Wiley children, yes?"

"It was in a wagonload of secondhand goods I bought."

"Ze people of Helena are blessed to have you. I would vote for you for mayor if I could." She patted his arm. "You will win ze election. I know it."

"Thank you." He scooted farther away,

her presence and touch too tempting for his peace of mind.

They sat in silence as Isaak turned the wagon onto the road to his parents' first home, Honeymoon Cottage, as Ma called it. His parents would adore Miss de Fleur.

"What do you do when you are unsure if you have made ze correct decision?"

"Pray. Talk to my parents." In the last year, he'd mostly sought counsel from — "Uncle Jonas is a wise man. You could talk to him or Aunt Lily. They love you like you're their daughter."

"If I talk to zem, zey may blame . . ." She sighed. "Ze fault is not one person's. I could not bear to have zem zink ill of him. But I feel sadness here" — she laid a hand over her heart — "and I know ze cause, but I fear I have not ze courage to do what I know I should."

Isaak tensed. This was about the courtship contract. It had to be. His heart pounded against his chest. "Is this about Jakob?"

She nodded. "I bore him. Next to Yancey and Carline, I am as bland as a flapjack. They know how to carry a conversation. They know how to make him laugh. I have not heard his laughter in days, not since I gave him ze jar of pralines." She sat still, not fidgeting, the blink of her eyes the only movement. "Zere are nineteen days left on ze contract."

And eight days from now was the welcome-home dinner for Ma and Pa that Jakob had talked her into catering — now a mere day after they arrived home because, according to the telegram Geddes delivered a few hours ago — Pa had sprained his ankle and needed time to recoup before traveling.

Isaak waited for Miss de Fleur to say she planned to end the contract before she was obligated to cook for the welcome-home dinner.

She said nothing.

"And?" he prodded.

"My spirit is torn asunder. You are right to point out I am cooking your parents' welcome-home dinner."

"I didn't mention the welcome-home dinner."

She frowned at him. "You did not?"

He shook his head.

"Well, I know it is what you were zinking. To end ze courtship contract before ze sixty days are over would be unkind to Jakob. He would feel crushed. I must carry zis burden, for I cannot lay it on him." She patted Isaak's arm again. "Zank you for being a

324

good friend and giving me advice about what I should do about your brother. I feel better now."

At least one of them did.

Zoe could not be sure how long they sat in companionable silence. It lasted until Mr. Gunderson stopped in front of a one-story house. Unlike the other ramshackle houses they'd visited, this one looked freshly whitewashed and had not a missing shingle or broken board. And the flowers — from what she could see — sprung along three sides of the house.

Mr. Gunderson jumped out of the wagon and made his way to the back to unload the bicycle. "Well?" he said, looking her way.

Zoe swiveled on the seat. She stepped to the edge of the wagon bed. In one gentle swoop, he placed her on the ground. She gripped the handlebars. He carried the food crate as she rolled the bicycle toward the house.

The door opened the moment they reached the porch.

"Mr. Gunderson!" exclaimed an auburn-haired girl, possibly six or seven years old. Her gaze shifted to Zoe. "Who are you?"

"Olivia Jane," scolded her mother. Mrs. Wiley leaned back inside the house. "Boys,

Mr. Gunderson is here."

Within seconds, three redheaded boys surrounded Zoe and the bicycle.

"Is this for us?" asked the oldest.

"Sure is," answered Mr. Gunderson. He then looked at her. "Miss de Fleur, let me introduce you to Alexander, Dante, Olivia — whom you've already met — and Thaddeus Wiley. Children, this is Miss de Fleur, a friend of mine and Jakob's. Miss de Fleur is from France."

Each child shook her hand and muttered polite nice-to-meet-yous before their attention returned to the bicycle. Soon an argument commenced over who would get to learn to ride first.

Zoe touched Mr. Gunderson's arm, drawing his attention. "Would you like to show zem while I help Mrs. Wiley with ze food?"

A chorus of *please* rang out.

He shook his head. "Not today. I need to return Miss de Fleur to the boardinghouse."

All four children turned their pleading eyes on her and called out another chorus of *please.*

Zoe glanced back and forth from the children to Mr. Gunderson. She was in no hurry. Her evening consisted of reading La Fontaine, but neither did she wish to impose on Mr. Gunderson's time. To him, she said,

"Ze decision is yours."

Mrs. Wiley took the food crate from Mr. Gunderson. "I wouldn't mind a few minutes of Zoe's company. I've been meaning to ask her for the praline recipe."

Mr. Gunderson leaned close to Zoe. The movement was not enough to cross the lines of propriety, but it caused flutters in her stomach. "How can you, in good conscience, conscript me into this great torment?" he asked.

Zoe pinched her lips tight so she could keep from smiling. "Were you not a child once?"

"Once," he conceded.

"Zen zis will atone for all ze people zat you, during your childhood, inflicted great torment upon."

A faint smile played across Mr. Gunderson's face. "*Touché,* Miss de Fleur."

She patted his arm again. "You will survive." She cast a slant-eyed glance at the snickering children. "Do not hurt him too much. He must drive me home." Leaving Mr. Gunderson with the children and the bicycle, Zoe followed Mrs. Wiley into the house. "Zis is a lovely home."

"Thank you. It belongs to Mr. Gunderson's parents." She set the crate of food on the small dining table. "Would you like tea

327

or coffee?"

"Whichever is easier."

"Then tea it is."

As Mrs. Wiley went to boil water on the cookstove, Zoe sat at the table, noticing the lavender tinge under the woman's eyes and the lack of neatness to her close-cropped auburn hair.

"Is zere anything I can do to help?"

Mrs. Wiley chuckled. "Entertain my children for a day."

Zoe sighed, wishing she could, but she had little experience with children. What the Wiley children needed was something to do, something adventurous while their mother worked. Papa used to say idle hands were the devil's playground.

Zoe glanced through the small house to the opened front door. Mr. Gunderson walked beside the oldest boy as he did a decent job of keeping the wobbly bicycle upright. The Wiley children clearly adored him. She smiled as he applauded Alexander. The lady who married Mr. Gunderson would be fortunate to have a husband so devoted to being a good father.

How was it he, like his brother, had yet to marry?

Any woman would be blessed to have Mr. Gunderson as a husband. He was kind-hearted, generous, dependable, and knew how to manage children.

Zoe looked back at Mrs. Wiley, who had confessed to having two jobs besides house-cleaning for the Gundersons. If Zoe remembered correctly from their conversation while making the pralines, with the twins' mother and stepfather returning next Thursday, Mrs. Wiley had a long list of Saturday chores.

Zoe gasped.

Mrs. Wiley sat the tea service tray on the table. "What is it?"

"Ze garden. I zink Jakob has forgotten his duty to cultivate it before his mother returns."

"You're right." Mrs. Wiley grimaced. "And Mrs. Pawlikowski loves that garden."

Zoe nodded. Her heart ached at the thought of his mother disappointed in Jakob because he had waited too long to complete his work. *She* was disappointed in Jakob enough for both of them. He should never have committed to courting her when he knew of his obligations to The Import Company. He should have put work and family above his quest to find a bride.

In addition to his obligations at the store, he had one to his mother.

Her mind was awhirl about the garden,

idle hands, and how to give Mrs. Wiley a day away from her children.

Taking a moment to let an idea form, Zoe added milk to her tea.

"Sugar?" Mrs. Wiley offered the sugar spoon.

"No, zank you." Zoe stared at her teacup for a long moment. "Mrs. Wiley, I would like to hire your children zis Saturday."

Mrs. Wiley tipped her head in question. "You would?"

Without pause, Zoe detailed her plan to cook breakfast and lunch for the children in exchange for their help cultivating Mrs. Pawlikowski's garden. But Mrs. Wiley must keep it a secret from the Gundersons.

"You want this to be a surprise?"

Zoe nodded.

Mrs. Wiley sipped her tea. "You may have to bribe me to keep your secret."

Zoe smiled, knowing exactly where this was headed. "I will feed you, too."

"You strike a hard bargain. But I accept."

CHAPTER EIGHTEEN

The Pawlikowski House
Saturday morning
De Fleur-Gunderson Courtship Contract,
  Day 43

" 'There's nothing better than surface soil from an old pasture,' " Alexander Wiley read loudly, " 'taken off about two-inches deep and thrown into a heap with one-sixth part well-decayed dung.' " He looked up. "I think this means we either need poop from an old cow or old poop from a cow that isn't necessarily old but could be."

Angling the brim of her straw hat to shield her eye from the midmorning sun, Zoe looked from Alexander to his snickering younger siblings — Dante, Olivia and her favorite doll, and Thaddeus — all four of them sitting on a wooden bench on the other side of the garden bed. Mrs. Gilfoyle-Crane's New York City mansion had comprised the entire lot, leaving no space for a garden, so Zoe had had to rely on making purchases from grocers and local farmers. While it had been over four years since Zoe had helped Papa cultivate a vegetable garden, she found suspect the amount of manure Alexander said they needed.

She reached into the apron over the faded calico dress Mrs. Wiley had loaned her and withdrew Mrs. Pawlikowski's gardening gloves. "Are you sure we need zat much cow dung?" she asked Alexander before selecting a hoe from the pile of gardening tools.

"One-sixth." He turned the worn copy of *The Gardeners' Monthly* in Zoe's direction. He tapped the page with his index finger. "Says it right here, if you want to read it."

"I believe you." Or at least she chose to believe him.

Zoe eyed the six-hundred-square-foot garden Jakob should have cultivated in February. With Mr. and Mrs. Pawlikowski arriving in five days, the garden needed to be prepared quickly and efficiently to be ready for planting season. Putting Jakob out of her mind, she focused on the Wiley children, still sitting on the bench.

"Gather your tool of choice," she ordered the quartet. "Who wants to have fun today?"

"I do!" Olivia laid her doll on the bench, dashed forward, and grabbed a shovel with a handle taller than she was, even though she also had the choice of three smaller shovels.

The two older boys, Alexander and Dante, exchanged glances, then chose rakes.

The youngest, Thaddeus, stayed on the bench. "I'm starving."

Of course he was. At six, Thaddeus had eschewed most of the breakfast Zoe had prepared for the Wileys in lieu of the day-old biscuits Mr. Gunderson had baked. Mrs. Wiley had insisted her children would trade labor for food. Once they finished consuming their *omelettes aux pommes* and potato cakes stuffed with trout, the Wiley quartet's enthusiasm for helping cultivate the garden lacked much luster. The only thing so far that had elicited any response besides apathy was when Alexander said the word *poop*.

Zoe refocused on young Thaddeus Wiley. He sat on the end of the bench, swinging his legs and looking as if he wished to be anywhere but there. "Zere is a remaining trout inside for you to eat," she offered to appease him. "Would you like me to warm ze lemon-butter sauce?"

He shrugged.

She looked to his brothers.

They shrugged, too.

His sister dragged the shovel to where Zoe stood. In a soft voice, Olivia said, "Thaddy only listens to Mr. Gunderson."

Zoe looked at Alexander and Dante, who both nodded, and then at Thaddeus. "You may go find your mother."

Thaddeus dashed to the back door leading to the kitchen.

Zoe glanced up to the second-floor window of what she believed was the master bedroom. As she hoped, Mrs. Wiley was still cleaning the window.

Mrs. Wiley waved.

Zoe waved back, then focused on the three remaining children. "First, we must cull all ze weeds and ze grass. I will begin in ze center. You will start on ze outsides. After we have broken up ze soil, we will work in ze compost and manure. When we are finished, we will wash our hands and eat lamb's stew, and zen you can help me crush ze fruit for ze marmalades I must make."

"Uh, Miss de Fleur?"

She looked at Alexander. "Yes?"

"*The Gardeners' Monthly* said a garden needs old poop." As Dante and Olivia snickered again, Alexander tossed his rake back onto the pile of gardening tools. "I'll run over to Vaughn's Seed Store. Do you think one bag of their finest manure will be

334

enough?"

"For a garden zis grand —" Zoe thought for a moment. "I wager Mr. Vaughn knows how much Mrs. Pawlikowski usually purchases." She looked to Alexander. "Better to take ze wheelbarrow."

"Yes, ma'am!" He slapped his brother's shoulder.

"I'll go, too," Dante blurted out. "Have fun, Ollie!"

Olivia waved vigorously. "Bye!"

Before Zoe could explain to Dante why the task only required Alexander's attention, the boys dashed around the greenhouse.

"Why did zey both leave?" she asked Olivia.

"They only listen to Mr. Gunderson."

Zoe studied the seven-year-old, who now chewed on the middle of one of her waist-length auburn braids. Surely all children were not as peculiar as these four.

The Resale Co.
"Thanks for the warning, Vaughn. I owe you." Isaak hung up the phone.

Zoe was supposed to be canning citrus marmalades this morning for the welcome-home dinner. Canning! Not cultivating Ma's garden. Why buy manure? There were bags on the east side of the greenhouse — bags he'd purchased in February, when, according to Ma's stated preference, Jakob should have cultivated the garden.

Instead, Miss de Fleur had sent Alex and Dante to Vaughn's. Unless the boys had lied and gone on their own.

An all-too-likely scenario.

Isaak pushed away from his desk, grabbed his hat, and strode out of his office. "Emilia, I need to go rescue —" What was Madame Lestraude doing in here? He stopped next to Emilia who held a paper-wrapped package to her chest. Did she know Mac had revealed the truth about Finn in Isaak's office three days ago?

Until he knew for certain, Isaak wasn't taking any chances. He offered the madam the same genial smile he gave to all his customers. "Good morning, Madame Lestraude. You're looking ever the proud mother-in-law."

The corner of her painted mouth indented. "That I am, which is why I brought Emilia my gift instead of sending it with my new delivery boy. Good lad. Some things, though, can't be entrusted to others." Her gaze fell to Isaak's loosened tie and unbuttoned shirt collar. "You're looking ever the politician."

Isaak tipped his chin. Uncle Jonas had warned him that Lestraude offered exclusives to all the politicians and judges in Montana and the surrounding states and territories. If Isaak had the authority, he would shut down her *Maison de Joie,* and all the brothels in Helena, which was why she vehemently politicked on Mayor Kendrick's behalf.

"It would be worthwhile for you to pay me a visit sometime." She looked at him as if she were sincere. "I hear the Forsythes are besotted with that household cook your brother is courting."

"Chef," Isaak corrected.

"Ah yes," she said with a brisk wave of her bejeweled hand. "We can all agree, a beautiful French chef is always worth more than her weight in gold. I doubt the Forsythes, Doc Abernathy's Book of Wagers, or even Miss de Fleur herself realize how *valued* she is. I, on the other hand, have no need for a French chef."

Isaak tensed. Lestraude had never crossed The Resale Co.'s threshold before, and nothing would convince him it had anything to do with a package delivery or with complimenting Miss de Fleur. Lestraude was trying to convey something indirectly. But what?

He took a moment to consider his answer. "I'll be sure to let her know."

To his surprise, Lestraude volleyed no mocking retort.

He stepped around Emilia. "Ladies, if you'll excuse me, I need to run an errand." With that, he slapped his hat on his head and strolled to the propped-open front door.

Isaak had one foot outside when he heard Emilia say, "What was that all about?"

"It's best, dear, if you don't know. I'm looking for anything a fourteen-year-old boy would enjoy reading."

"Try Jules Verne. Second bookshelf from the left, middle shelf."

Isaak glanced over his shoulder at Lestraude. Without looking his way, she strolled over to the stairs leading to the loft bookshelves. Whatever the madam was up to was no concern of his . . . until he was duly elected mayor and he could shut down her repugnant business.

Only, what if running her brothel provided the perfect ruse for rescuing girls?

Isaak frowned. He'd need to think more on that later. Right now he had a more pressing problem to fix.

He headed west in the direction of the house, his chest pounding. He was the only one who could handle the three Wiley boys.

Oliva Wiley would adore Miss de Fleur. The boys — Isaak knew their capabilities.

While Miss de Fleur was smart and clever, those boys would use her gentleness against her. She was too gracious, too lenient, and too tenderhearted for her own good.

And beautiful, which wasn't relevant.

Although his molars ached from gritting his teeth yesterday while trying *not* to stare at her beauty.

Isaak picked up his pace. He and Jakob had left the house at seven-thirty that morning because Miss de Fleur was to begin making marmalades for the welcome-home dinner at eight when Sarah Wiley arrived — which she'd clearly done with her children in tow.

He darted across the street.

The Wiley children — Alex and Dante, at least — would run roughshod over Miss de Fleur. Their mother had to be behind this: Find a meek and malleable person to tend to her children so she wouldn't have to. Twice now, Sarah Wiley had manipulated Miss de Fleur.

That was why, with hat in hand, he was running up the street to his home at nine forty-five when he ought to be at The Resale Co.

As he slowed to a jog along the pebbled

path by the house, the earthy smell of warm dirt greeted him. Isaak stopped at the picket fence.

And then he saw her.

Right palm turned up, Zoe knelt in the garden wearing a well-worn apron and a baggy calico dress, her straw bonnet shielding her face from view. Thad and Olivia knelt next to her, staring intently at whatever was in her gloved palm. She said something to them. They nodded and took turns touching whatever was in her hand.

She turned her head and saw him. Her smile stole the breath from his lungs.

He should have stayed at work.

"Mr. Gunderson!" Olivia exclaimed, to the piercing dismay of Zoe's right ear.

As Olivia and her brother dashed off to hug Mr. Gunderson's legs, Zoe gave her head a good shake to lessen the ringing. She slid the worm back into the dirt, then stood and looked at Mr. Gunderson. His jaw tightened. Oh, the action was minuscule, but she noticed how he now stood more stiffly, like when he was about his business. Not relaxed. Not at ease, even though Olivia and Thaddeus clung to his legs like husks around corn. Something worried him.

Zoe gasped, her heart pounding. "Did

something happen to Jakob or the Forsythes? Or —" She drew in a slow, calming
breath. "Is it Nico?" She had yet to see him
since his last failure to meet Jakob.

Mr. Gunderson's head shook. "Vaughn
called to say Alex and Dante stopped by the
store," he said in that direct, this-is-the-
problem-at-hand voice of his.

"Zat is why you are here?" Zoe waited for
further explanation. When none came, she
said, "Zey went to ze seed shop for manure
for your mother's garden."

Mr. Gunderson removed Olivia and Thaddeus from his legs. "Run inside and see if
your mother needs help." Then he strolled
to where Zoe stood in the middle of the
fractionally cleared garden and, after gripping her gloved hand, led her along the
greenhouse's south side to where a pile of
manure bags and a pile of soil bags were
stacked up against the brick wall. "Anything
my mother's garden needs is here. Or in the
shed. Or in the greenhouse."

"Yes, but —"

"Or three blocks away," he continued, "at
The Import Company, working to ensure
that all is ready in time for the grand opening." He released his hold on her hand.
"This is Jakob's job, not yours."

Zoe responded to his brisk tone with a

gentle, "If I were your mother — or even your brother — I would feel much love zat someone cared enough to cultivate ze garden for me because I had no time to do it myself."

"Jakob's had the time. He still has the time!"

"Zere is no need to yell."

His mouth opened, then closed, and then, in a moderate voice, said, "You're already doing enough for Jakob."

Zoe raised her chin. "I am doing no more for him zen I am doing for you."

He regarded her with a look that said, *I disagree with that statement, and as soon as I think of a suitable response to prove you're wrong, I will make it.*

Zoe merely smiled. She knew she was right . . . and knew he knew it, too.

He growled. "You're just like my father."

"Zen I know I will like him."

He blinked several times. "The point is, the next time Jakob or Sarah Wiley or *anyone* asks something of you, you will say no. You need to stop allowing people to obligate you into doing something you don't wish — or have the time — to do."

She looked at him in disbelief. "Isaak Gunderson, you have no right to tell me what I can or cannot do. I have everything under control."

Shock — or perhaps something in the lesser vein of surprise — at her outburst flickered in his eyes, and then it was gone. "You don't know how the Wiley children can be."

She touched his arm. "You worry for no reason." His brows rose, so she added, "I am providing food today in exchange for ze children's labor. I brought everything I need to cook both meals. If zey do not work, zey will not eat."

"You're cooking for them?"

"Papa said food can motivate a king to go to war."

"It can." His hand rested on the middle of her back, and he nudged her into walking. "What are you bribing them with?"

"Zis morning we had omelets, fried trout stuffed between potato cakes, and a lemon-butter sauce. Later we will enjoy lamb stew, fresh baked rolls, and —

He groaned. "Stop. Please, stop. I don't want to hear what I'm missing." As they neared the garden, he checked his pocket watch. "I need to get back to work."

"You want to." The words slipped out before she thought the better of them. But because they had been said, Zoe decided to go on. "Going back to work is a want,

343

something you choose to do, not something you *need* to do."

He looked at her intently. "I *have* to go. Obligation, not want. Emilia is there alone."

"Zis is true." She sighed. "Zere is also a telephone in ze house. You could call over zere and tell her to close ze shop. She may enjoy Saturday with her husband. Zey are newlyweds, yes?"

"But *I'm* not a newlywed, and I have a business to run."

"You are a dutiful manager."

He scowled. "What's that supposed to mean?"

Zoe stepped to the pile of gardening tools. She probably should have answered him immediately, but his arrival had put her in a cheeky mood, so she knelt and took her time examining the tools. She selected one and stood. With faux gravity, she said, "It means you must decide if you *want* to return to work where zere is no lamb stew, fresh rolls, and apple-raisin tarts with ze flakiest crust you will have ever tasted or if you *need* to."

One corner of his mouth lifted. "I'm fairly certain that's not what being a dutiful manager means."

As hard as she tried not to smile, she failed. Who knew she would have fun teasing him? "I am fairly certain zat what you will find at work will not be as enjoyable as what is here."

He glanced at the house and then back at her. "As much as I could agree with you, Miss de Fleur, there's the fact that I will find no children at work."

Zoe shrugged. "I see no children here."

"Oh, they'll be back. Trust me."

"How do you know?"

"Because you're here, and that's why my house is where they'll find the best food this side of the Mississippi."

"Zis is true." She stepped until she was right in front of him. Smiling — and ignoring the curious increase to her pulse — she offered him the hoe. "Take it."

"Why?"

"You need to work less and have fun a little more."

"Gardening?"

She nodded. "People call you Mr. Gunderson because zey see you as a benevolent king reigning over his subjects. Zey follow your lead because zey know you care. And you believe zis is all you are. A man with responsibilities. You can be Mr. Gunderson all day, every day. Or you take a holiday from ze job and ze expectations and just be Isaak." She gave him a flirtatious grin. "I will feed you."

"Apple-raisin tarts?"

"I will make extra for you to enjoy tomorrow."

He gripped the hoe's wooden handle just above where she still held it. "I'll stay . . . but *only* because you don't realize yet how much you need me to help you wrangle the Wiley children."

"Zat sounds like an excuse to escape work." His mouth opened, and in case he was about to change his mind, she hastily said, "Nevertheless, it is also one I will accept." She released the hoe, swiveled around, and as she walked to the overgrown garden, snatched up a rake. She stopped in the garden's middle. Although her heart pounded fiercely, she glanced his way.

"Isaak?"

"Yes?"

"I zink I can *wrangle,* as you call it, rambunctious children *and* grown men just fine."

CHAPTER NINETEEN

Isaak ran the entire eight blocks to The
Import Co. He shouted, and the crowd
gathered around the door parted like the
waters of the Red Sea. He slowed to bypass
them and cross into the store, shutting the
door behind him. Splotches of white paint
spilled down the walls, over wooden crates
awaiting unboxing, and puddled on the
floor. Isaak's nostrils stung at the fumes,
making it difficult to catch his breath. "Jake?
Where are you? Are you okay?"

"Iz?" Jakob's voice came from a distance.
Footsteps thudded overhead, then down the
stairs. He hustled into the retail space.
"How did you hear?"

"O'Leary barged into The Resale Company, shouting that you'd been vandalized."

Jakob nodded. "He was here when I

347

returned from lunch. He must have gone straight to you."

Isaak swung his hand to encompass the dripping mess. "Any idea who did this?"

"None, but I must have just missed who-ever it was." Jakob rubbed the back of his neck. "I was only gone for twenty minutes."

"Did you send someone to fetch Marshal Valentine?"

"No! I stood here wringing my hands, waiting for you to come tell me what to do."

Isaak bit back a retort. Watching the Wiley children bicker while they cultivated Ma's garden had been an eye-opener. The meta-phorical slap had come when Miss de Fleur said the children were as snippy with each other as he and Jakob were.

Jakob rubbed his forehead with the heel of his hand. "Sorry. I'm not angry at you, it's just . . ."

When he didn't continue, Isaak stepped closer and put an arm around his brother's shoulder. "It's just what?"

"You'll say it's irresponsible."

Isaak dropped his arm. Was he really so overbearing, demanding work without re-lief? Memories of gardening with Miss de Fleur and the Wiley children rushed back. After taking the afternoon off, he'd felt refreshed in body and spirit. There was something to be said for balancing work with relaxation . . . and apple-raisin tarts. "Whatever it is, Jake, I promise I'm not going to pull my big-brother act on you."

Jakob raised his head, his blue eyes searching for any hidden message. "You mean that, don't you?"

Isaak tamped down irritation at having his veracity questioned. "Would I have said it otherwise?"

After another searching glance, Jakob took a deep breath. "I'm supposed to be going to dinner and then *Romeo and Juliet* with Zoe, Yancey, Carline, Geddes, and Windsor tonight. I don't think I can make it now and stay on schedule."

Shocked by Windsor Buchanan's anticipated attendance at the theater — to see *Romeo and Juliet,* no less — and Jakob's worry over keeping to a schedule, Isaak chose to respond to the latter. "I can take over here. I just need to —"

"No," Jakob interrupted. "I need to take care of this."

"What about the play?"

"Can you take Zoe instead of me?"

Yes! No! I shouldn't. "If you're sure . . ."

Jakob's eyes glinted with a speck of humor. "Would I have said it otherwise?"

Isaak chuckled at the repetition of his own

question. Common sense pricked his conscience, prompting him to say, "I don't mind taking care of this." Not true, though it needed to be.

"No, but thanks for the offer, Iz. The Import Company is my responsibility."

The words, *I'm proud of you for doing the mature thing,* sat on Isaak's tongue, but to utter them would sound patronizing. Nor was it wise to throw stones at his brother when his own adherence to strict schedules and timelines was shifting.

A commotion outside drew their attention. Through the window, Isaak saw Marshal Valentine push through the crowd still gathered around as though they would be invited to view the vandalism the same way they would the store during the grand-opening celebration set for next weekend.

Jakob met them at the door. As he and the city marshal talked, Isaak slipped out the back. His brother had this well in hand. The best thing he could do was leave.

Besides, he was going to the theater with Zoe tonight. He needed to go home to make sure his dress shirt was ironed.

Deal's Boardinghouse
Despite the fact that she stood next to the warm cookstove, in a green-and-black silk

gown more suited for an opera house than a kitchen, Zoe licked the last bit of soup from the spoon. The sweetness of the tomatoes flowed effortlessly with the beef stock.

Thank the good Lord above for Mrs. Deal's friendship with her neighbor, Mrs. Hess, who had more canned goods in her larder than Zoe had ever seen in one. Thank the good Lord above also for Mrs. Hess's willingness to trade.

"Zis is perfect tomato soup." Even from tomatoes canned last year. Zoe gave the tasting spoon back to Mrs. Deal. "Mr. Deal will be pleased you have mastered his favorite dish."

Mrs. Deal's brown eyes grew teary. "I thought I was a culinary failure. The lessons you've given me have done wonders, enabling me to reduce food expenses by half."

Zoe acknowledged the compliment with a simple nod of her head. It saddened her to know a well-to-do French family, even without a household cook, could live on what Mrs. Deal had been discarding because of improper storage, overpurchasing that led to spoilage, and ignorance of how to use seasonal purchases in multiple recipes. Good cooking was less about costly produce and meats and more about knowing how to compound a good and palatable dish from a limited larder.

Not that the dear woman had any canning skills.

That, though, was something Mrs. Hess could teach Mrs. Deal, and would now that Mrs. Deal, admirably, had found the courage to admit to her friend that she needed help.

Zoe turned to the rectangular pan resting atop the cookstove. "Let us taste ze biscuits." She waited patiently for Mrs. Deal to find two forks. The biscuits looked as perfectly baked as the spongy sweetbread Mrs. Deal had served during lunch.

Mrs. Deal cut into a corner biscuit. "For years I've told Mr. Deal that my cooking is the reason we have so many vacancies. Today is the first day ever that the men's side is full of boarders." She handed Zoe a forked piece of biscuit. "Word has spread about the meal you prepared for Lily Forsythe and about the lessons you've given me. The prices you could charge —"

"I have no wish to find employment," Zoe cut in.

"Then what do you want to do?"

"I want to be a wife and a mother."

Mrs. Deal smiled sweetly. "Jakob Gunderson is a blessed man."

Zoe nodded, wishing she felt more joy

over Mrs. Deal's words. *Wait out the contract, and I recommend you don't share this with my wife* had been Judge Forsythe's advice Monday when she had stopped by his office after praying about Isaak's advice to seek parental wisdom. If Jakob had noticed Zoe had been keeping her distance, he had yet to say anything. All she had to do was make it through tonight, the welcome-home dinner the day after tomorrow, and the next thirteen days without him falling in love with her.

And then they could end the contract as friends.

Because things would be harmonious between her and Jakob and because Isaak was now her friend, she had no reason to leave Helena. She had friends. She had family in the Forsythes. For the first time since her childhood, she had a home.

Tomorrow she would find Nico and accept his offer to look for a house to purchase.

"Oh, dear," Mrs. Deal muttered. "I did something wrong. What is it you see that I don't?"

Realizing Mrs. Deal had assumed the worst from Zoe's silence, she quickly tasted the biscuit. The moment the flaky layers touched her tongue, she uttered an elongated, "Mmm." She returned the fork to Mrs. Deal. "You did nothing wrong. Good flour makes a better bread."

"You've said that repeatedly but haven't explained how I tell if the flour is good." While her words were clipped, Zoe knew they were not intended as a slight. In the last seven weeks of getting to know Mrs. Deal, Zoe had discovered how direct the woman was. And how benevolent and open to instruction.

"Place some flour in your hand, zen press your palms together." Zoe mimicked the action. "Good flour will adhere and show ze imprint of ze lines of ze skin. Good flour tint is also cream white. Poor flour may be blown away with ease and appears dull, as though mixed with ashes."

"So it'll look dingy?" Mrs. Deal supplied.

"Dingy?"

"Dull. Like when water has sediment in it."

"Dingy," Zoe repeated. She liked the sound of it. "Zat is a good description."

The kitchen door opened. Mr. Deal stepped inside. "Mr. Gunderson is here."

"You mean Jakob."

Mr. Deal shook his head. "Isaak Gunderson is here. Is there a problem?"

There had to be one, or Jakob would be

354

here to take her to the theater.

Mrs. Deal touched Zoe's arm. "If you ever feel things aren't working out with Jakob, Mr. Deal and I have friends all over this part of the territory who would pay richly to employ a ravishing French chef. Go on, dearie." Mrs. Deal motioned her forward. "I won't hug you and risk messing up your beautiful gown."

Zoe strolled to the kitchen door.

"I know I'm not your father," Mr. Deal said, "but if you need one, I'm here for —" His voice choked. "You're worth more than gold to me." He smiled a little as he opened the kitchen door for her.

"Zank you." Zoe stepped into the dining hall, where fourteen men sat at the two tables awaiting dinner. All stood. They smiled, as she had come to learn, in hopes of garnering her attention. She always strove to be polite in her response. This time she ignored them in light of how delighted she felt about Isaak's escort instead of Jakob's. Isaak made her laugh. He enjoyed silence, although not as much as she did. Best of all, he knew how to manage Yancey and Carline and their constant chatter.

With a friend by her side, the evening would be bearable after all.

Isaak stood by the door, as handsome as

ever in his black Sunday suit. Her ebony silk-and-lace cape lay draped over his arm, instead of over the chair where she had left it before going into the kitchen. He seemed as pleased to see her as she felt upon seeing him.

"Your carriage awaits," he said with a slight bow as she neared.

She stopped in front of him. "Where is your brother?"

"At work."

"Oh?"

"Someone vandalized the store. It'll take all night for him to repair to stay on schedule. He asked me to give you his regards."

"I am" — *partially* — "sorry he will miss ze play, but I am also happy to see you." She rested her palm against his exquisite green damask waistcoat and felt him tense, so she drew back. "Zis is nice you had something to match. Did Jakob tell you ze color of my gown?"

"Coincidental" was all he said.

Zoe studied Isaak's face as he reached around her to rest her cape across her shoulders, covering her green-and-black evening gown, the last dress Papa had purchased for her before they left Paris for America. When she had resisted the purchase, he had argued she would need it someday.

It had been worn twice, counting tonight.

Isaak's gaze settled on hers. At the curve of his lips, a strange, breathless, swirling feeling warmed her more than the cape about her shoulders.

"Zank you," she said and started to tie the cape's ribbon.

"Here, let me." As he knotted the ribbon at the base of her neck, she caught a whiff of his bergamot cologne.

It suited him. Why had she never noticed his cologne before? Perhaps this was his first time wearing it. Because of Carline? Or perhaps he favored Yancey. Both ladies were joining them for supper and the play. Those times Zoe had seen him talk to either lady, no time stood out as unusual. Or romantic.

But in one night, everything could change.

Not with Isaak, her heart whispered.

Jakob was fickle; Isaak was dependable. If he was going to fall in love with Carline or Yancey, he would have already done so. He had not, because he knew he needed some-one who would make him sniff flowers and admire sunsets. He needed gentleness. He needed tender strength to tell him when he was wrong.

With one hand, he opened the door. With the other, he touched the middle of her back and nudged. "Move along," he whispered, his minty breath warm against her cheek. "We're already late."

Zoe froze. His hand flinched; the movement was small, yet she felt the tingle it caused rise up her spine.

"Zat is because *you* arrived late," she said in her defense.

"That's because I struggled over whether I should convince Jakob to trade places with me. I could have done his work for him."

"Why did you not?"

When he failed to answer, she turned her head enough to see him. The moment their gazes met, her breath caught. Her whole being sparked to life with joy and with hope . . . and with a mind as full of clear understanding as was in her heart.

The person he needed in his life was her.

He needed her.

And she needed him.

Stunned, Zoe dashed to the Forsythe carriage, blinking away her sudden tears. She was never supposed to fall in love with Isaak Gunderson. She was supposed to love Jakob and his happy eyes.

Not Isaak.

Never was it supposed to be Isaak.

He was her friend. He was only supposed to be her friend.

Without a word, he helped her into the carriage. "The Palmer house," he called out to the driver before climbing in.

Zoe scooted to the far-left side of the bench. She faced forward, not turning her head to look up at him, not wishing to risk him seeing the emotions in her eyes. Isaak sat in the far corner of the backward-facing bench. Diagonally opposite.

The carriage lurched forward.

He turned from the window to look at her. "You seem distraught. Is something wrong?"

"I am unsure."

"Do you want me to go trade places with Jakob?"

She wanted to say yes. Her heart needed time to rest from the sudden tumult of realizing she was in love with him. But to say yes would be a lie. She abhorred lies.

"I wish for you to stay."

"Zoe, I . . ."

"Yes?" She waited for him to finish his thought. She needed to know what he was thinking and feeling because she needed him to be alive and imperfect. To be real. To be hers.

"I'd like to stay, too." He paused. "It's not like tonight will last forever."

"It never does."

Isaak said nothing more, and Zoe turned

her attention on the window, hoping they would reach the Palmer residence quickly. Yancey and Carline, like Jakob, could be counted on to add joviality and distraction to a gathering.

CHAPTER TWENTY

Ming's Opera House

Zoe stopped in awe on the threshold, gasping just inside Mr. and Mrs. Forsythe's box, where two additional chairs had been added to accommodate their group of six. Brass railing. Red leather seats. Elaborate draperies framed and hid the stage. At this level, they would have a perfect view of the sets and performers, and even of the Helena Orchestra in the pit below. Surely the spectacle of it all would atone for tonight's pedestrian play.

Perhaps this English version would be better than the French translation she had seen with Papa. If not, based on the warm and lush sounds of the orchestra tuning their instruments, at least the music would be enjoyable.

Isaak's hand rested on the middle of her back, as it had at the boardinghouse. There was nothing inappropriate or possessive in his action. He was merely being polite, she knew. But upon every touch, the tingles returned to race up her spine. And then her neck and face warmed.

Was she blushing? She hoped not.

"Miss de Fleur, your propensity to block entrances is a problem," he said before nudging her farther into the box.

Zoe stepped to the left, annoyed as much by his criticism and bossiness as his exotic cologne. Mostly, she was content to wait for everyone else to choose seats first. Including him. Her plan was to sit on the other side of the box from Isaak Gunderson, so she would not be distracted by his presence.

Isaak, to her surprise, did not seek out a chair. Instead, he moved to her side, maintaining a polite distance behind her left shoulder. "Ladies, take the front row," he ordered their group. "The gentlemen will sit behind."

Carline and Yancey thanked him as they slid past. Yancey, in her exquisite violet gown, settled in the front middle chair and Carline, in a rose-pink gown, took the right one, leaving the one on the left for Zoe. They rested their fans in their laps and immediately started talking. Mr. Geddes Palmer sat behind his sister. Mr. Windsor Buchanan sat in the chair behind Carline, leaving the two far left seats for Zoe and Isaak.

He motioned toward the empty front seat. "You're next."

She looked to where Carline and Yancey were huddled close.

Tonight is a night for falling in love, Yancey had proclaimed the moment the carriage had arrived at the opera house. Why had she said that? Carline, not Yancey, was the one to make rash pronouncements. For someone as outgoing and talkative as Yancey Palmer was, she was also impressively circumspect.

Yancey could have noticed something in how Zoe had looked at Isaak in the carriage. Equally possible was that Yancey and Carline had plans they had failed to share with Zoe. To match Isaak and Carline?

Zoe studied Carline's flaxen hair, pinned in a simple bun. Everything about the beautiful woman was understated. Even her pink silk gown was modest and unadorned. Carline would be a benefit to Isaak and his election campaign. Having lived all her life in Helena, Carline was well-suited to be the wife of Helena's next mayor.

Thinking of her marrying Isaak caused an ache in Zoe's chest.

Mr. Gunderson the mayor needed a wife

like Carline, but Isaak the man needed a wife like Zoe.

"It's warm in here," grumbled Mr. Buchanan. He stood. The bladesmith removed his suitcoat, draped it over the back of his chair, rolled up his sleeves, and —

Zoe felt her eyes widen. Goodness, the man's forearms bulged with muscles and scars. And he wore two knives sheathed on the back of his hips. At the opera! Not that he needed anything to make him more intimidating. Or physically impressive.

Carline should focus her flirtations on him.

A strange noise came from Isaak.

Zoe looked over her shoulder. "What was zat?" she whispered.

"What was what?" he whispered back.

"I heard you grunt."

"I saw you ogling Windsor."

"What does zis 'ogling' mean?"

"Looking at him."

"Why would my looking at your friend cause you to grunt?"

"You were drooling."

Zoe touched her lips. "Zere is no drool. Stop scowling at me."

"I will once you stop casting amorous glances at Windsor."

"Amorous?" She coughed a breath. "It is

impolite to grunt when ladies can hear." And because his eyes narrowed in response to her chastisement of his poor manners, she added, "Nor is it your business at whom I cast amorous glances."

"So you admit you were," he said with the startling smoothness of a man confident of the rightness of his opinion.

Her cheeks warmed. "Mr. Gunderson, I admit zat if I wish to admire someone, I will, but I was not admiring Mr. Buchanan. I was zinking Carline should flirt with him."

"Carline likes Geddes."

"She does?" Zoe whirled around to see that Mr. Buchanan had settled back down on his chair and was speaking to Mr. Palmer. Neither seemed happy to be there. Neither seemed romantically drawn to Carline. Although both men would make exceptional suitors for her.

Far better than Isaak.

A throat cleared.

Zoe peeked over her shoulder again to see Isaak watching her with an expression of pained tolerance. "I was zinking," she admitted.

"I could tell." His head cocked a little to the left, and he blinked, as if suddenly realizing something. "You think more and talk less than any woman I know."

She parted her lips, intent on defending her penchant for silent thinking, but as he continued to look at her as if she were an oddity, she closed her mouth and returned her gaze to the four other people in the box.

Zoe moistened her lips. "I suppose I should sit."

"What an innovative idea," Isaak whispered, his voice near her ear. His hand rested again on her lower back, and with a familiar gentle nudge —

"It is warm in here, is it not?" Zoe blurted out. Realizing how true her words were, she untied the black ribbon at the neckline of her lace cape.

"Let me help." Isaak removed it from her shoulders.

"Zank you." Zoe turned to take her cape from him. A mistake, because he stood closer to her, almost as if she was in his embrace.

His throat cleared. "We should sit."

"Sit?"

He motioned toward the empty chairs. "Before they notice and wonder why we aren't. Sitting," he said abruptly. "With them."

"Of course." She snatched her cape from his hold, then found solace — and comfort — on the chair next to Yancey, who immediately studied Zoe, then Isaak.

Her blue eyes narrowed. "All right, Isaak, what mean thing did you say to Zoe this time?"

"He said nothing," Zoe blurted out in his defense.

Yancey coughed a breath. "Hell hath no fury like Isaak Gunderson's icy stares."

"Drop it, Yancey," was all he said. More like grumbled.

"Someone is in a foul mood," Yancey quipped, and then turned around to face her brother. "Geddes, would you trade with me?"

"You *want* to sit by Isaak?"

"Of course not." She grimaced at the brass railing. "Unfortunately, I don't think I can sit this close without —" She covered her mouth and cringed.

Zoe turned her head enough to watch the play of emotions on Mr. Palmer's face. Confused and annoyed, to be sure. Yet the considerate man complied with his sister's request. Why was Geddes Palmer still a bachelor? Not that his reason was any of Zoe's business. But he was a kind man, a good listener, and not one to demand his own way. Much like Papa had been.

Carline likes Geddes.

Zoe smiled in remembrance of Isaak's words.

Yancey sat in the chair between Isaak and Mr. Buchanan. She smoothed the lap of her dress. "Perfect. And we" — she leaned forward and touched Carline's shoulder — "can still talk."

Carline shifted in her chair. "But my neck already hurts turning around to hear you." She smiled at Mr. Buchanan, who sat directly behind her. "Windy, trade with me."

He stayed silent for a long moment before saying, "No."

"Must you always be so cantankerous?"

"I must."

Carline's loud gasp sucked the air out of the box. "I don't know why I keep trying to be nice to you."

"You may stop any —"

"Windsor," Yancey warned. "What is with you men tonight? Can't any of you be pleasant?"

Zoe jerked her attention back to the stage and ignored the lecture Yancey was giving to the men about manners. The only drama Zoe wished to be enchanted by was that from the orchestra. The lead oboe seemed exceptionally skilled. Was that a piccolo? She adored piccolos. She loved the high tone, the unique sound, and the utter happiness a piccolo provided in symphonic solos. If she played an instrument, she would play a piccolo. And a flute. They were too similar for her to choose one over the other.

"I'll trade seats." Isaak brushed against Zoe's arm as he slid between her chair and Mr. Palmer's. He leaned against the balcony railing, waiting for Carline to move.

Curious, Zoe turned her head enough to see Carline.

"I — uh . . ." The ever-confident Carline appeared unsure. "Of course. Thank you." She hurried to the seat behind Zoe. She touched Zoe's shoulder and Yancey's knee. "Wasn't that considerate of Isaak to afford us the closeness to talk?"

Zoe tensed. Talk? During the performance? Talking would hinder her from being able to hear the musicians. Talking occurred at intermission and after the performance. Not during. Never during.

Mr. Palmer, from what she could see, seemed enraptured with studying the playbill.

Isaak muttered something too softly for Zoe to hear.

"I agree." Mr. Buchanan leaned forward in his back-row, right-side seat. He patted

Mr. Palmer's shoulder. "Trade seats with me."

"Why?"

"She's *your* sister."

"Which is exactly why I prefer to stay in *this* seat."

"You owe me for distracting Miss Snowe," Mr. Buchanan countered.

Mr. Palmer groaned. Yet he stood. "This makes us even."

Zoe watched as the men switched seats, putting Mr. Buchanan directly in front of Yancey.

Before Zoe could silently celebrate the end of the chair exchanges, Yancey groaned loudly. "Oh, for goodness' sake, how am I supposed to see with this" — she motioned to the back of his head — "hairy mountain range in front of me?"

Isaak turned around in his front-row, right-side seat and scowled at Yancey. "This is why I said ladies sit in front."

"Why are you so snippy tonight?" she retorted. "This, Isaak, is why I don't enjoy social events with you" — she poked Mr. Buchanan's back — "or you."

That was all it took for Mr. Buchanan to turn around in his seat.

As he responded to Yancey, Zoe focused her attention on the black stage curtains.

Occasionally, they would puff out, likely from someone bumping them. She noted that the gaslights on the walls matched those in the foyer and how the house attendants wore elegant coats, the same red as the leather seats and with brass buttons that matched the balcony railing. The opera house was styled after the circular plan used in European theaters and brimmed to capacity. A thousand people? Fifteen hundred?

Perhaps Mr. Buchanan would know the exact number of seats.

She looked to him to ask, but he was still turned around in his seat and engrossed in a glare showdown with Yancey.

Isaak gazed at Zoe, and all she could think of was the rapid beating of her heart. Could he love her? She wanted to believe that was what she saw in his beautiful eyes. She loved him.

If he gave her any sign — any clue — he felt the same, she would happily run away with him.

Isaak shifted slightly in his chair. And then he looked away.

Zoe's chest tightened. What did his action mean? He reciprocated her feelings? Maybe it meant nothing at all. Maybe she wished for something not there. Her chest hurt.

Love hurt.

The orchestra fell silent. A hush descended.

"Tell him to trade with me," came in a whispered voice.

From Yancey or Carline? Zoe was unsure and more than a bit annoyed. As much from their behaviors as from having to attend a play she had no desire to see because she disliked William Shakespeare. Mostly because she was in love with a man who seemed not to return her feelings.

"Geddes," someone whispered.

Zoe jumped to her feet, clenching her cape with her left hand. She turned around and pointed at Carline, and then at her own vacated chair in the front row. As Carline moved to Zoe's seat, Zoe motioned for Yancey to move to the left, to Carline's now-empty seat. Once Yancey obeyed, Zoe patted Mr. Buchanan's shoulder. He peered up at her. She flicked her gaze to the center chair in the back row, silently conveying her wish for him to move to Yancey's now-empty seat. He moved. After he settled into his new seat, Zoe focused on Isaak and Mr. Palmer in the first and second row, respectfully. Both leaned against the wall.

"Stay," she ordered.

Mr. Palmer nodded.

Isaak's gaze lingered on her face. Nothing in his expression indicated his thoughts or feelings. But then the corners of his mouth curved. Once his smile reached his eyes, she knew he was impressed with her actions.

A familiar warmth inched up her spine and spread through her body, causing her pulse to skip a beat. Fearful the others in the box would see what she felt for him in her eyes, Zoe claimed the seat between Carline Pope and Isaak. She straightened her shoulders, rested her cape and then her hands in her lap, and tried fruitlessly to look at the stage.

"Here we go," Yancey said in breathless anticipation.

Carline squealed in delight.

Sounds from the orchestra permeated the opera house. The gaslights on the stage brightened, and the curtains opened.

Isaak sat in the dark paying no attention to the performance on the stage. The conflict raging inside him surpassed the enmity between the Montagues and Capulets. The air inside the theater thickened. He inhaled but couldn't satisfy his need for oxygen.

He loved Zoe. Had loved her for weeks now, although he'd kept fighting it as a mere attraction because nothing about their relationship fit the way he'd always planned to court the woman of his choosing.

He almost laughed aloud at his arrogance, deciding beforehand when and how he would allow love into his life. His certainty that a reasonable person didn't trip and fall into love. His pity for Yancey because she'd set her sights on Hale when, with a little effort, she'd find any number of men who were suitable husbands. Then Zoe de Fleur arrived with both a shout and a whisper. Isaak understood Yancey's tenacity now. He knew in the deepest place of his soul that he belonged — would always belong — to Zoe de Fleur. God must be laughing in His heaven. *Pride goeth before a fall.*

Isaak stole a glance at her. She was enraptured by the play, her lips parted and her chest rising and falling with rapid breaths. No artist's brush could ever capture what he saw. She was beautiful, yes, and so much more. Her gentle spirit urged him to soften his opinions. She'd talked him into slowing down to hear birds sing and to dig in the dirt. Her touch brought out the best in everything, from food to children.

He clawed his fingers into his knees, remembering how she'd confided in him that she ached for something more. He ached, too, in every joint and sinew holding his body in place.

I wish for you to stay.

Those six little words wreaked more havoc in his heart than when she'd called him Isaak last Saturday in the garden. He'd refrained from responding by calling her Zoe because it was a line he shouldn't cross, and yet he *had* crossed it less than an hour ago in the carriage.

Where was the line between love and duty? Between what he owed to himself and what he owed to honor? Because chasing after his brother's woman betrayed every code of decency.

Loving Zoe changed everything and nothing for him. If circumstances were different, he would pursue her until she fell in love with him, but what was the point? The only way they could be together was to run away — to turn his back on his family, the Widows and Orphans Fund, and his promise to make Helena a better place when he became mayor. But then what? A new job in a new town would be easy, but no woman should trust her heart to a man who gave up on his commitments.

Even if Zoe could, she valued family and harmony. Loving him in return would go against her gentle nature. She would never — *never* — make herself the cause of an irreconcilable rift between him and Jakob.

Isaak gripped his hands to keep from reaching over and wrapping an arm around her. To say without words how much he loved her. How much he wanted to protect her with his life.

He didn't know what he was supposed to do, and before, he'd always known the right and honorable course of action. *Always.*

Not now.

If only Jakob hadn't entered into that stupid contract. As usual, in thinking only of himself, his twin was making a mess for everyone around him while he skated off undamaged. Because, out of all the things Isaak didn't know, there was one he did.

His heart would vacate his chest if Zoe left Helena.

CHAPTER TWENTY-ONE

By the time Lady Capulet and the Nurse beseeched Juliet to consider Paris's suit, Zoe accepted the strange and shocking truth: This dark, bawdy, and tragic play was *not* the one she had seen in Paris. Romeo and Juliet married in secret, without — not with — their families' blessings. Their families were enemies! Juliet's cousin Tybalt killed Romeo's cousin Mercutio, and then Romeo killed Tybalt. What was all this killing about? And friar Laurence? Like the Nurse, he was absent from the play she had seen. What possessed a friar to convince Juliet to "borrow death"?

Somewhere between Juliet's parents demanding she marry Paris and the friar delivering Juliet's eulogy, Zoe's tears began. They did not stop when the curtains darkened the stage.

Or when the orchestra fell silent.

Or when the applause died a death befitting poor Mercutio.

Zoe fought to collect herself as she stared at the tear-soaked handkerchief she clutched. Someone rubbed her shoulder in slow, circular motions. Carline, most likely, because she was sitting to Zoe's left.

"That was so romantic," Carline said in a dreamy voice.

Zoe stared at Carline. How could she view the play as romantic?

"You must have slept through the ending," Isaak said matter-of-factly. "The play is a tragedy, not a love story."

"You say that only because the hero and heroine died," Yancey argued.

"That's one reason," he replied. "The lords Capulet and Montague should have learned their lesson by play's end. Instead, they continued the feud, the same thing that led to Romeo and Juliet's deaths."

Carline stopped massaging Zoe's back. "I still think it's a love story."

"Me, too," Yancey put in.

A cough of breath came from Mr. Palmer. Zoe turned around.

His gaze shifted back and forth between his sister and Carline. "You two do know you'll never convince Isaak to change his mind when he believes he's right?"

Carline and Yancey turned to Mr. Buchanan in hopeful support.

He held up his hands. "I'll always have Isaak's back."

"Zoe, what about you?" Carline asked.

Zoe dried her eyes with the handkerchief. What Romeo and Juliet felt for the other was infatuation, not love. Real love needed more than three days to develop. Real love was gracious and kind, while Romeo's "love" was envious, boastful, and dishonoring. Real love was patient. Infatuation led to hasty decisions. Marrying a man the day after meeting him epitomized haste. Marrying a person in secret epitomized selfishness. There had been enough quarreling tonight. Zoe would not add to it by pointing out the error of Carline's views. So instead, she offered a polite, "It was a nice performance."

"Surely you know what you liked," Carline argued in a tone that implied Zoe should grow a backbone and stand up for what she thought.

Zoe stared at the handkerchief's black monogram: Isaak's. She had enjoyed the play far more than she expected to. Shakespeare's work should not be gutted of its potentially offensive elements, which she realized had been done to the performance she and Papa had seen in Paris. Amid the tragedy and moral ambiguity of the play, a warning could be found, which was why she stared at her lap and said nothing.

"Let's give Miss de Fleur a moment to collect herself," she heard Isaak say. "Geddes, take the ladies downstairs. We'll be down shortly."

"I'll have the carriage brought around," came from Mr. Buchanan.

Isaak uttered, "Thank you," and then another, "Thank you."

How long Zoe sat there, she knew not. The voices of those in attendance lightened as the hall emptied until the only other sounds she heard were muffled voices and the closing of music cases and an occasional door.

"Here."

She looked up. Isaak now sat in Carline's chair. Two white folded handkerchiefs lay in his outstretched palm.

"They're from Windsor and Geddes," he explained.

She took the top handkerchief, then laid the tear-soaked one atop the second one. She glanced around the box. Of course everyone had left. People always did what Isaak Gunderson asked them to do.

He folded the dry handkerchief over the wet one. He laid it on the chair Yancey had vacated. "If you need a shoulder, I have one you can borrow," he said, but she could tell by his lighthearted tone that the offer was nothing more than an attempt to be polite.

Zoe dried her wet cheeks. "I am not usually so . . . emotional."

"That's good to know."

She focused on the brass railing, unable to bear his scrutiny. She had never been easily moved to tears. Oh, she felt things. Sometimes she ached with loss, with heartbreak, with pride, joy, pity, loneliness, and even anticipation. When the tears came, she rarely succeeded in containing them. What she felt as the Montague and Capulet tragedy unfolded hurt terribly.

Grudges ruined families.

The welcome-home dinner was in two days.

Two days until she had to run away from Helena and the foolish de Fleur-Gunderson courtship contract.

Two days to hide her growing feelings from everyone she knew, especially Isaak. And Jakob. He could never know. The betrayal would crush him.

Zoe dried the last of her tears. "You need not feel obligated to sit with me," she said without looking Isaak's way. "I would prefer a moment alone."

"You need to talk."

Zoe shook her head. What was in her heart needed to stay *her* secret. As casually as she could, she stepped to the balcony wall to put needed distance between herself and Isaak. The lights in the opera house had dimmed. She gripped the railing, the brass cold against her skin.

"Please," Isaak said softly. "*I* need you to talk to me."

The entreaty in his tone drew her attention to him. Isaak Gunderson might not love her, but he certainly cared. For that, he deserved as much truth as her heart could bear sharing.

"I am fearful," she whispered.

"Of what?" Isaak sounded almost shy. This was not the Isaak Gunderson she knew — so confident, so in control of everything in his world. Nothing frightened him.

Though . . . maybe something did.

Zoe turned around. He was leaning forward, his elbows on his knees. And her chest tightened. "Of becoming my mother. *Maman* left Papa when I was nine to live in Italy with ze man she decided was the true mate to her soul. Every night, for years, Papa read First Corinthians before leading me in an evening prayer. He promised zat God would return *Maman* to us."

"She never returned."

Even though his words were a statement, Zoe responded with a small shake of her head. "Papa also promised one day I would find someone I would wish to spend ze rest of my life loving, as he loved *Maman* until his death."

"Have you found that someone?" Isaak asked in a painfully hoarse voice.

You, she wished to say.

And if she did, where would that lead them? She would never pit brother against brother. To the victor would go no spoils.

Better to leave now, before love had time to grow to full bloom.

"Would you . . . ?" He stared absently at the balcony, his lips moving as if searching for words. "Could you ever love a man who failed to live up to his commitments?"

"My heart would not be safe with" — *Jakob* — "such a man." Zoe released a weary breath. "I would never marry a man as fickle with his commitments as my *Maman* was with hers."

Isaak's hands were clenched so tightly, the whites of his knuckles showed. "You couldn't give him a second chance?"

"No. Zis play has confirmed zat Jakob and I are unsuited." The lack of feeling in her tone impressed — and saddened — her.

"Once ze welcome-home dinner is over, I will discuss with him ze reasons why we should agree to end ze contract before ze agreed-upon sixty days." And then in a softer voice, she added, "It is as you said — ze contract was foolish of us."

"Once the contract is ended, will you return to Denver?" Isaak turned his head to meet her gaze.

She nodded. "Better to leave now before anyone's feelings grow too deep to be contained. I will have no one's heart crushed because of me. Jakob will understand. I hope you understood, too." She hated how heartbroken her voice sounded. The words hurt to say, hurt to feel.

Isaak was looking at her most intently, studying her, likely measuring her words and tone to determine if all she had shared had been the truth.

"We should go," he said abruptly.

Zoe nodded. She stepped forward and reached for her cape, but he swiped it away. His right hand captured her left one. She tried to pull away, but he held firm.

"For once in your life, oblige me."

"Zere is no need to hold my —"

And then, just like that, they stood there. Looking at each other. His lovely green eyes had darkened, and when his gaze lowered to her lips, Zoe's breath quickened and her legs quivered. It was a strange sensation, one she had never felt before. But Papa had warned her about it . . . and what would likely follow. A kiss.

She would let Isaak kiss her.

Oh, she would still leave Helena with a broken heart . . . and with the glorious memory of her first kiss.

She waited in anticipation.

He turned away. "The lights are off in the stairwell," he explained, leading her forward out of the box and toward the balcony stairs. "Stay close."

With her free hand, Zoe lifted the front of her skirts to keep from tripping as they descended the steps. "Isaak, please. I am capable of —" At his growl, she fell silent. While the lights were indeed out in the stairwell, those in the foyer provided ample viewing.

There, at the bottom of the stairs, stood Jakob.

With unhappy eyes.

The accusation in Jakob's eyes sent Isaak's temper flaring. Zoe tugged to free her hand, but Isaak stopped it by gripping her fingers and holding tight. He wasn't risking her well-being on account of Jakob. There'd been enough of that already.

When they'd descended the stairs, Isaak was surprised to see Windsor standing a few feet behind Jakob. "I thought you and Geddes took the carriage."

Windsor shook his head, his beard brushing against his chest. "I sent Geddes with the girls. I thought you might need some help." His gaze flickered toward Jakob.

Isaak led Zoe past Jakob and placed her hand on Windsor's arm. "Please see her back to Deal's Boardinghouse." In case Jakob planned to object, Isaak added, "I'm sorry the play upset you, Miss de Fleur. I hope you feel better in the morning."

She glanced back and forth between him and Jakob, her indecision evident. Windsor wrapped her arm around his and escorted her outside before she could utter a word.

Isaak turned around to face his brother. "Let's go home before we make a public spectacle."

Jakob fisted his hands. "Like you didn't already do that."

Clinging to his resolve to act like a gentleman by a solitary thread, Isaak looped his arm through Jakob's, pulling him toward the opera house doors.

Jakob yanked free. "I'm not a child who needs to be told what to do."

"Could have fooled me." The moment the words left his lips, Isaak wished he could take them back. Not because they weren't true, but because they would provoke Jakob.

Sure enough, his cheeks filled with splotches of red. "Am I about to hear another you're-so-irresponsible lecture? Because I'm tired of them."

"Then grow up," Isaak growled. "Think about the consequences of your actions before you embroil others in your messes."

"I just spent all day cleaning up a mess without embroiling you or anyone else, so don't pull that same trick out of your hat."

"That's not what I meant, and you know it. A little paint is nothing compared to the damage you've done by bringing Zoe to Helena."

Jakob reeled back for a punch, but Isaak was ready. He caught Jakob's fist with his open palm inches from his chin. They pitted their muscles against each other in a farcical arm-wrestling match.

Isaak exerted every ounce of strength to force Jakob's arm lower while leaning close to whisper, "Stop it, Jake. We're making a spectacle of ourselves."

"I think you already did that by cozying up to my girl in a theater box and holding her hand." Jakob stopped pushing against

387

Isaak's fist.

Isaak lurched forward. Gasps from the theatergoers who remained in the lobby and were being treated to a second show of family rivalry snapped his last thread of patience. Isaak righted himself, his nostrils flaring when he saw the smirk on his brother's face. He tugged his coat back into place, grabbed Jakob by the arm — this time denying him the opportunity to pull free — and dragged him outside into the cool evening air.

The instant they were beyond the cluster of people waiting for carriages, Isaak let go. He strode across the street, his pace too fast for anyone but Jakob to keep up. When they were alone on Fourteenth Street, Isaak said, "You don't get to play the injured suitor when you're the one who asked me to escort Zoe tonight."

"Escort, not steal her away from me."

Thinking fast to cover how close the accusation came to the mark, Isaak stopped walking, forcing his brother to do the same. "Steal her away? You've all but ignored her since she came to town."

"Because the great Isaak Gunderson decreed that I had to follow his almighty schedule."

"Hogwash." Isaak slapped the back of his

right hand into the palm of his left. "The schedule I made included plenty of time for you to go to dinner or attend the theater or do the thousand and one other things you'd rather be doing than work. You easily could have kept it and, using one-tenth of the famous Jakob Gunderson charm, made Zoe fall in love with you." Because, if she had, Isaak never — *never* — would have let himself picture a life with her. "But instead, you allowed yourself to be sidetracked by crooked ceiling tiles, the insignificant difference between one beige wallpaper and another, and whatever nonsense delayed the windows going in on time."

"You know what?" Jakob stuck his hands in the air as if he was surrendering. "I'm done trying to please you. I'm done trying to *be* you."

Isaak flinched. "Who has ever asked you to be me?"

"You!" Jakob stabbed a finger at Isaak's chest. "Every time you've given me one of your lectures or schedules or helpful hints on how I can do things better. I've had teachers, people at church, Uncle Jonas and Aunt Lily, and even Ma and Pa tell me what a fine example of a gentleman you are. It's their subtle way of saying that I should be just like you. I always come in second behind Isaak David Gunderson."

"Spoken as though I haven't heard similar praise about Jakob Matthew Gunderson. You have no idea how many times I've heard what a charmer you are, or how you light up a room just by walking into it. People think the moon and the stars hang on your wishes. It's how you get them to jump in the river with you before anyone has considered that there's a waterfall just around the bend. Amazing how you always get out of the boat just before it crashes. Everyone else is battered and bloody, but you walk away unscathed. You with your it'll-be-fun motto. Well, brother, you need to come up with a new adage to live by because no one is having fun right now."

"Meaning Zoe, I presume."

"How do you think she feels, having been brought to a strange city and forced to fend for herself?"

Jakob sneered and ran his eyes from Isaak's top hat to shined shoes. "Seems like she's made plenty of friends, and Aunt Lily has practically adopted her."

"Precisely my point." Isaak pivoted on his heel and marched toward their house. He waited for Jakob to catch up before continuing. "How do you think Aunt Lily is going to feel when Zoe leaves town?"

"What makes you think she's leaving town?"

Isaak snapped his lips together before he betrayed Zoe's confidence. Thinking fast, he rephrased her intention. "Do you think she's staying in Helena when your sixty days are up?"

"What makes you think I'm not going to propose?"

"Your inattention, combined with the fact that you haven't even told our parents about her yet. If you were seriously considering marriage, you would have sent a letter to one of the hotels on their itinerary. But no! Tomorrow, you're going to meet them at the train depot and say what? 'Welcome home. Meet Zoe. She's my mail-order bride, but don't get too attached because I'm returning her.' "

"Fine! I'll marry her."

Isaak stumbled to a stop, staring at his brother's retreating back. What had he done? This wasn't where he'd meant the conversation to go. "But you don't love her."

Jakob called out, "Since when have you ever thought love a necessary ingredient for a successful marriage?"

Blast Jakob and his sharp ears.

Waiting until his brother was way too far

away to hear anything, Isaak whispered, "Since I met Zoe and fell in love."

CHAPTER TWENTY-TWO

The next morning
Thursday, April 26
De Fleur-Gunderson Courtship Contract,
  Day 48

As Zoe stepped on to the boardwalk in front of the boardinghouse, she felt awful. She had had naught but bits and snatches of sleep in the last night, the look on Jakob's face haunting her. She had tried on four dresses this morning before settling on this yellow-and-white-striped day dress, the only one she owned that did not accentuate the gloomy lavender circles under her eyes.

She should have had more than one coffee this morning, although Mrs. Deal said the way Zoe drank it, it had too much cream in it to still count as coffee.

With a sigh, Zoe headed west.

She would hide today . . . if it were not for the fact that she had another long day of cooking to be ready for tomorrow evening's welcome-home dinner.

But at least today she could avoid Mrs. Forsythe's curious looks and subtle questions about Jakob's courtship and when Zoe thought he would propose. Whereas Mrs. Forsythe was subtle, her husband was astute. One look at Zoe and the judge would see right into her heart.

If possible, she would leave on the first train on Saturday morning.

Leaving before anyone noticed she was gone depended on the train schedule.

Decision made, Zoe readjusted her grip on the basket of sweets she and Mrs. Deal had prepared to welcome Isaak and Jakob's parents home. The paper bags filled with *pistachios in surtout, nougat de Montélimar,* and *nougat de Provence* weighed down the basket. They need not have made the white and black nougats in addition to the sweetmeat, but the two nougats were part of the traditional thirteen desserts at a Provençal Christmas feast Zoe had helped Papa prepare every year since she reached her thirteenth year.

She would never cook Isaak a traditional French Christmas feast.

But she could leave him a taste of it.

Eyes blurring, she crossed the street,

continued west, and ignored the ache in her heart.

Over rooftops, white plumes of smoke rose from newly stoked hearths. A chilly breeze likely reddened her cheeks on this, according to Mr. and Mrs. Deal, unseasonably cold April morning. Zoe disliked the cold, so it was good she was leaving. In two days.

For Denver.

For a new life.

For a time to forget about Isaak and what could have been were it not for his brother. Although were it not for his brother, she would never have met Isaak. Or fallen in love with him.

"Oh, ze irony," she murmured.

She paused at the next intersection, partially to admire the risen sun, partially for a trio of wagons to roll past. Even if the feelings she bore for Isaak had the potential to be true and deep and abiding, she refused to allow them to come between brothers. She refused to come between Jakob and Isaak. She would never ruin a family. The most loving thing she could do was to leave Helena. Broken hearts could heal.

Papa's never did, but she was not her papa. She would work away her feelings for Isaak. In time. Because she was hopeful and determined, unlike Papa, who never tried to stop loving *Maman.*

"Zoe, wait!"

She looked over her shoulder. Nico?

He raced down the block, hand gripping his newsboy cap, his arms pumping up and down as he ran. Why was he coming to her now? If he truly cared about her, he would have spent time with her. If he truly cared about her and their relationship, he would have met Jakob weeks ago. If Nico truly cared, he would have become involved in Zoe's life instead of staying on the breakfast-at-Deals' fringes.

Instead, he had made promises he never fulfilled.

And he lied. Too easily. Too readily.

Zoe sighed. She had tolerated Nico's behavior because she considered him her friend. In time, they could have grown as close as siblings, but he had used her to help him escape New York. He had used her to provide him free meals. She wanted to believe he could change. She had lost hope.

A means to an end.

Knowing that was how he saw her crushed her heart.

Nico stopped next to Zoe and bent over, hands on his knees to catch his breath.

"How are you zis morning?" she asked.

"All to the merry, I say." He regarded her,

his face scrunching. "I went to the boarding-house to meet you for breakfast, but Mrs. Deal said you'd left. Where are you heading at this time of day?"

"I have work to do."

He stood straight. "You have a job?"

"Ze Gundersons hired me to cater his parents' welcome-home dinner."

"When is it?"

"Tomorrow night. Zey arrive zis morning."

"Lemme get this straight. Your suitor and his brother, who is now your friend, *hired* you to cook for them?" The moment she nodded, his eyes narrowed and his head tilted as he asked, "How much are they paying you?"

"Zat is none of your business."

Nico's eyes widened. "Someone's testy. Is it because the Gunderson fellow hasn't yet asked you to marry him?"

Yes. No. The answer depended on which Gunderson the question referred to.

She chose to ignore the question. "What is it you want?"

"My employer gave me the day off," Nico said with a smile. "We ought to go do something together. I saw a couple of houses for sale in East Helena in that new addition Charlie Cannon is building. We should go find us one. Or we could go back to the boardinghouse and play chess. I'll even spot you three pawns and a knight."

"I have work to do today." *And tomorrow . . . until I leave everyone I love.* "Enjoy your holiday."

At the burn of renewed tears, Zoe resumed her pace to the Pawlikowski house. She clenched the basket handle until the wood pressed into her palm.

The first task of the day was to bake —

"I'm sorry I haven't been around in a while," Nico said, matching her steps. "My employer has been working me hard." Pause. "How come you've never asked me who I work for? And don't say it's none of your business. We're family."

Family?

The Forsythes had become more like family to her than he was.

And yet she made the half-hearted effort to ask, "Who do you work for?"

"Remember that grand lady sitting next to you on the train to Helena?"

Zoe nodded. She had admired the woman's lovely broach.

"That's her," he said proudly. "Miss Mary Lester. She's a wealthy, independent woman, much like you."

"What is ze nature of her business?"

"She runs a hotel, but she also teaches the young ladies who work for her how to improve themselves and be a positive influence in their community. She even requires I spend one hour a day reading. She says reading daily is the first step in becoming a gentleman."

"Zis is admirable of her." Not once could Zoe remember him speaking kindly of school and education. Were it not for the fact she was leaving Helena on Saturday, she would want to meet this Miss Mary Lester who seemed to have helped Nico make a home here.

After a quick glance at him, Zoe crossed the next intersection. He seemed happy, truly happy, more than she could remember in the years since they met.

"You like working for Miss Lester, yes?"

"Sure do!"

"And you like living here . . . in Helena." She did not phrase it as a question, yet he responded with a nod.

The realization of what she must do weighed down her heart.

She stopped, glanced around to see no one was within listening distance, and then looked at Nico. "I am returning to Denver Saturday morning."

His eyes narrowed. "Why?"

"Zere is no future for me here."

"I'm here," he said quietly.

"You know how important a home is to me." She rested her palm against his cheek. "You have one here." She lowered her hand. "I like seeing you happy. Zis is why I have no regret bringing you on my adventure."

He looked away, staring blankly at a nearby building. The muscles in his face flinched, then twisted into a frown. "Are you going to marry that guy?"

She shook her head. "We are unsuited."

"Ah, Zoe, I'm sorry he broke your —" His mouth gaped and his eyes grew wide in sudden realization. "That bad egg broke your heart and you're *still* going to cook for him?"

"I made a promise, a commitment." Something she doubted Nico would understand. "No matter ze pain I feel" — she rested a hand over her heart — "in here, I must be true to my word."

He uttered a string of ungentlemanly words.

Zoe stepped back, startled at his outburst.

"This is just like New York!" he snapped. His lips pressed tightly together as he glared at her. "Those swells mistreated you and you kept going back for more."

Zoe swallowed uncomfortably.

Nico looked at her in disgust. "Remember

the Nephew? You lost your job and he still demanded you cook for him. If I hadn't talked you into running away, you would've done it, even though you didn't want to. You have no backbone."

Zoe stood there. She had no words to say in her own defense.

"I warned you that Gunderson fellow was a bad egg." He slapped his cap atop his head. In that moment, the anger in his eyes faded. "This is why," he said in a softer voice, "you can't leave Helena on your own. You need a brother to protect you. You need *me*."

Zoe looked away. She was tired. She was tired of Jakob's courtship, tired of cooking, tired of hating herself for falling in love with Isaak, and utterly tired of being told she was weak and malleable or, as Mrs. Gilfoyle-Crane declared, unimposing. Being unimposing was the only way Zoe knew to please others, to keep the peace, to make people like her. If everyone demanded his own way, harmony would have no place to take root and grow.

Yet though she knew making things right with Nico meant inviting him to leave Helena with her, she felt unable to say the words.

"Miss Lester is nice and all," Nico said

suddenly.

Zoe focused on him, more aptly on his shockingly *wet* eyes.

"But you're" — his voice cracked — "you're my only family. I can't lose you. You're my sister and you'll always be my sister." He sniffed, then lifted his chin and spoke firmly. "We came to Helena together. We'll leave together."

To be accurate, they had arrived on the same train on the same day at the same time. Only one of them knew the other was there.

She gave him a weak smile. "I must go to work."

He responded with a terse nod. "Zoe?"

"Yes?"

If he noticed the sadness in her tone, he chose not to remark on it. "If you didn't have to cook for that dinner party, would you leave now?"

She released a weary sigh. "Yes."

"You're your own person. Why don't you just leave?"

"Zis is not like New York," she said roughly. "I cannot simply pack my bags and run away and no one will miss me. Zey are counting on me. Zey need my help."

"I suppose," he muttered. His hard blue eyes focused on a passing wagon. "The best thing that could happen is for that dinner party to be canceled."

Zoe sighed again. The Gundersons would never cancel the welcome-home dinner save a death in the family. Murder certainly was *not* something Nico would ever do. He had a good heart, however misplaced.

She gave him one of the paper bags filled with nougat. "Deliver zis to the kind Miss Lester and zank her for me for all she has done for you."

A slow smile curved his lips. "My mum used to say flowers were always worth the rain." He took the bag and then enveloped Zoe in an awkward hug, pressing the basket she held into her ribs. "You're my sister, and I'll do what I must to take care of this for you." After a quick, "See you later," he dashed back down the street.

Later that morning

Isaak gripped his lapels and stared at the plume of gray smoke edging north toward the train depot. Jakob stood beside him, but he might as well have been a mile away.

Had he proposed to Zoe? He'd not said anything about it this morning when they broke their silence to discuss the logistics of getting Ma and Pa home from the train station.

Isaak dropped his chin as the front of the train appeared in the distance. When his parents disembarked, would it be to the news that Jakob was engaged? He'd not had much time between last night's rash pronouncement and now, but he'd left the house without eating breakfast . . . and without saying where he was going.

Isaak shifted his weight from one foot to the other. He looked over his shoulder to where Mr. and Mrs. Palmer, Aunt Lily and Uncle Jonas, and Mrs. Hollenbeck stood, as eager as he was for Ma and Pa's return.

The chug-chug of the train's engine grew louder, accompanied by the hiss of brakes. Passengers poked their heads out of the windows while the loose crowd on the platform congealed into a line as close to the railroad tracks as the wooden boardwalk allowed.

Jakob's posture stiffened an instant before he lifted his right hand, waving it back and forth in greeting. Isaak squinted against the cloud of steam until he saw his mother's favorite blue hat and then her face. Pa leaned out the window, wind blowing his hair into his eyes while he kept swiping it away with one hand and waving with the other.

The train braked, the squeal painful to

Isaak's ear.

He kept waving and leaned close to Jakob's ear. "Remember, when they —"

"I don't need another lecture."

Isaak jerked upright as though he'd been slapped, even though Jakob's tone of voice lacked force. "I'm not lecturing. I'm confirming our plan to load luggage in the wagon that you'll drive back to the house while I bring Ma and Pa home in the surrey."

Jakob turned, his blue eyes icy. "I don't need a reminder, either."

Was this how it was going to be from now on? Every attempt at conversation rejected out of hand? "So glad we agreed to be cheerful today."

Jakob huffed but said nothing.

The train came to a complete stop. Ma and Pa ducked back inside the train and began to gather their belongings before disembarking.

Jakob stopped waving and walked to the stair portico to assist their parents' descent.

Isaak followed, frustrated that his brother would leave him standing alone when they'd agreed on presenting a united front after their near brawl last night. Sidelong glances and hands cupped beside mouths to cover whispers magnified his chagrin. He smiled and touched the brim of his black felt bowler, gratified when mortification pinked cheeks or hurried steps. The feud between him and Jakob wasn't something to be gawked at or exclaimed over as though they were the players on the stage.

Isaak stopped on the opposite side of the portico, his muscles tense. As soon as Ma appeared, his face broke into a huge smile. He bent his knees, and the instant her arms went around his neck, he wrapped his around her waist and lifted her off her feet. "Welcome home, Ma. It's good to see you."

He set her on the boardwalk, and she cupped his cheek with her palm. "It's good to see you, too." New lines creased the skin beside her blue eyes and a few gray strands of hair were intermingled with the blond ones, yet she seemed invigorated.

"You look remarkable. Travel agrees with you."

She laughed and patted his cheek. "You look like you're carrying the weight of the world, as usual." She turned and enveloped Jakob in a hug, trading places with Pa.

Isaak hugged his father tight. "I've missed you."

"I've missed you, too, son." The embrace was too short, but long enough for the sting inside Isaak's soul to melt under his father's love. Pa stepped back a pace, gripped Isaak's biceps, and looked him in the eye.

Isaak's throat swelled. Like his mother, Pa appeared older. The wrinkles around his brown eyes were deeper and his silvery hair was touched with more white. It wasn't much of a change, but enough to remind Isaak that his father wasn't always going to be around to settle disputes and mend hurts. "We have lots to discuss, but let's get you home and off that ankle. How is it?"

"Tender, but not so bad I can't walk on it a little."

"The cavalry has come out to greet you and Ma, so Jakob and I thought you should wait inside the depot where you can sit and chat while we load up your trunks."

Pa nodded. "Sounds like a plan." He reached inside his vest and withdrew the claim tickets. "I hope you saved a little extra room in the wagon." He gave Isaak a conspiratorial grin. "Your mother spotted a set of lamps on our way out of Denver."

Isaak chuckled. He looked over to where Jakob was ushering their mother toward the depot. Had he told her about Zoe? If he didn't say something soon, someone in the crowd of friends surrounding Ma was sure to bring up Jakob's mail-order bride — a scenario Isaak had mentioned a few hours ago. But Jakob had refused to say how he intended to introduce Zoe before leaving the house.

". . . a good thing we sent the items for the stores ahead of us on last week's train."

Isaak returned his attention to his father. "The crates arrived undamaged. I wanted to wait until you got home to tell us exactly which pieces you wanted in which store, but Jakob opened them all while I was busy with something else."

"I'm sure it will be fine."

Isaak held the door open so his father could precede him inside the depot. Ma was already seated, Mrs. Hollenbeck on her right side, Aunt Lily on her left, with Mrs. Palmer standing and gesturing with her hands as she described her eldest daughter's wedding. Pa chose to sit a few feet away so Mr. Palmer and Uncle Jonas could bookend him in similar fashion. The conversation jumped straight into Pa's opinion on steam-operated streetcars as opposed to horse-drawn ones. Mr. Palmer was firmly in the camp of steam-powered, while Uncle Jonas favored horse-drawn — although Isaak had heard his godfather argue the opposite with Mr. Hess, the blacksmith, because Uncle Jonas didn't care either way. He just loved a spirited debate.

Isaak glanced into the telegram office and waved at Yancey. She smiled but didn't wave back, her hand busy taking notes while Mrs. Watson spoke.

A burst of feminine laughter drew his attention back to where his parents were sitting.

Jakob leaned to touch Ma's arm. "If you'll excuse us, Isaak and I will go load your trunks. I'll see you at home."

She patted his hand. "Thank you."

Isaak followed his brother to where two burly men hoisted trunks, crates, hatboxes, and toiletry cases. Isaak and Jakob silently waited their turn, stepping forward as each customer claimed their baggage and moved on.

Either in agreement that they shouldn't get into another fight in front of a crowd or out of orneriness, Jakob didn't speak until they were loading the wagon. "Ma said the lamps she bought are for The Resale Company, so I'll drop those off on my way home."

"Put them in —"

"I know where to put them," he said with that same flat calm as the last time he'd interrupted.

Isaak set a wooden trunk in the wagon bed. "Is this how it's going to be between us now?"

"Until you stop commanding me with every sentence, yes."

"I'm not commanding."

Jakob's look said, *That's a matter of opinion.* " 'Remember to do this, put that there.' Sounds like commands to me."

They went back for two more large trunks. Jakob hefted his trunk into the wagon box.

Isaak offloaded the trunk in his hands. "Where is this coming from?"

Jakob walked back to where the rest of the baggage was piled on the platform. He picked up a hatbox and tucked it under his left arm, then picked up two more.

Isaak followed, picking up a fourth hatbox, a toiletry case, and a small trunk he didn't recognize but the porter insisted belonged to them.

Jakob laid the hatboxes on the front seat where they wouldn't get crushed. "Per Uncle Jonas's advice, I refuse to either obey you or fight with you."

"You talked to Uncle Jonas?"

"Yes, Isaak. I do take advice from other people besides you." Jakob looked down for a moment, huffed, and straightened. His face was impassive and calm again. "Uncle Jonas came to The Import Company this morning. He was furious about our altercation at the opera house. He said the next time we decided to kill each other, we'd better do it in private. I told him I didn't know how to handle you. That's when he suggested I call you out every time you ordered me around."

"He didn't say anything to me." Although Isaak wasn't upset about it because spending the morning talking to Uncle Jonas left Jakob no time to propose to Zoe.

Jakob took the hatbox from Isaak and set it beside the other three. "Not every conversation or decision has to be run through you for approval."

Isaak set the toiletry case and small trunk in the wagon box. "That's not what I meant."

"Isn't it?" Jakob turned away and walked back for two tapestry bags.

Isaak didn't join him. He was no longer needed. He returned to the depot and stood just inside the door, watching his parents as they spoke with friends who, despite being apart for a year, were as close as ever.

Did he have any friends like that?

Hale was more like a big brother. Calm, rational, brilliant, and organized in his own haphazard way, he was someone Isaak trusted to dispense sound wisdom, but they weren't really friends. Mac was becoming more of a friend, but he was a newlywed who would — God willing — soon be a father. Windsor and Isaak competed back and forth in friendly one-upmanship, but the friendship was only three years old.

None of them were — or ever would be — Jakob.

Oh, for the days of catching frogs and watching clouds.

Pa gave him a searching look. Isaak shook his head to say he was fine, but after a few more minutes of conversing, Pa limped over to stand beside him. "Something's wrong, and I'd like to know what it is."

"Jakob and I are fighting again."

Pa chuckled. "I figured that out just by looking at you as we pulled in. What's wrong this time?"

"He thinks I order him to do things."

"You've always ordered him to do things. Why is he opposed to it now?"

Isaak took a step sideways to look in his father's face. "You're serious."

"About you always ordering Jakob around? Of course I am. I don't know why that stuns you." Pa put a hand on Isaak's shoulder. "Son, you order me around sometimes. It's as natural to you as breathing."

"Yancey says I'm benevolently arrogant."

Pa chuckled again. "That might be the

best description of you I've ever heard."

Isaak's chest stung afresh. "I wish you hadn't left us to open this store without you."

"It was on purpose." Pa squeezed Isaak's shoulder. "Sometimes the best thing parents can do is get out of the way and let their children figure things out on their own. You and Jakob are good boys. Good men, I should say."

Not of late.

"Your mother and I knew we were taking a risk, leaving you with the responsibility of opening the new store, but we had faith we'd raised you well enough to do so without killing each other."

Isaak looked at his feet, summoning the courage to confess how close they'd come, when a shriek from inside the telegraph office snapped his head up.

An instant later, Yancey ran into the depot, her face white. "The Resale Company is on fire."

Chapter Twenty-Three

The Pawlikowski House

Leaving the stewed greens to simmer, Zoe scanned the menu she and the twins had agreed upon for the welcome-home dinner tomorrow night. With the last of the comfits and sweetmeats prepared, her next task was to make the brioche dough and puff paste for the morning's baking. She slid the menu into her apron pocket, then opened the right cookstove to check on the braised ham for the Pawlikowkis' return-home meal today, which neither twin thought necessary until she suggested it.

She breathed in the smell of garlic, thyme, carrots, wine, and brandy. Perfect! She closed the oven door.

A quick touch notified her that the baguettes had finally cooled. She stacked them in a basket, covered it with a napkin, and then carried the bread basket and a crystal butter dish into the dining room.

Zoe stopped and frowned. Why was the table set for five? She had asked Mrs. Wiley to set it for four — Mr. and Mrs. Pawlikowski and their sons. Perhaps Mrs. Forsythe had decided to join them. But why only her? Judge Forsythe would want to enjoy the meal, too.

After setting the butter and bread on the table, Zoe added a sixth place setting. Then she returned to the kitchen to start on the brioche dough.

You have no backbone.

Nico's words swirled around in her mind as she mixed salt and sugar into the bowl of flour.

Zoe poured the yeast mixture into the center of the flour mixture. She added eggs and stirred.

You have no backbone.

Zoe growled under her breath. She *had* a backbone. That was why she was leaving.

The telephone in the parlor rang.

On the fifth ring, it stopped. Presuming Mrs. Wiley had answered it, Zoe dumped the dough onto the floured counter. She kneaded in pieces of butter.

For her plan to work, she would have to leave without saying good-bye to anyone. With the side of her left hand, she pressed on her chest in a vain attempt to ease the aching. She wanted love now. She wanted a home now. She wanted family.

Most of all, she wanted Isaak.

"It can never be," she said because she needed to hear the words, to feel them killing any hope she may have otherwise. She had to leave Helena before her heart crossed the threshold into unrelenting love. She had to learn to forget him.

The kitchen door slammed open.

Mrs. Wiley looked horrified. "The Resale Company is on fire!"

Zoe could barely believe what she saw. Like knights storming a breach, firemen clambered up and down scaling ladders; two men leaned over the eaves pounding against the roof with their axes. On the ground level, a stately fireman bawled through a tin trumpet, telling the men where to direct the water hoses and where to chop vent holes. Zoe stepped over hoses, maneuvered past a horse-drawn water truck, and weaved through the hundreds of people whose gazes never wavered from the building, black smoke billowing from the second-floor windows.

Where were Isaak and Jakob? The depot?

Zoe grabbed the arm of the nearest person. "Do you know ze hour?"

The man checked his pocket watch. "Eleven-twelve."

The Pawlikowskis had been due to arrive on the ten-thirty train. Isaak and Jakob could still be there, loading luggage.

"Zank you," she said to the man, then hurried on, weaving through the crowd in hopes of finding someone she knew. Her gaze caught on a blonde standing next to a petite brunette.

Carline and Emilia! It had to be. Isaak left them to manage the store while he spent the day welcoming his parents home.

With "excuse me" after "excuse me," Zoe made her way to her friends. She touched Carline's arm.

"Zoe!" Carline enveloped Zoe in a tight hug.

Zoe pulled back. "Where are Isaak and Jakob?"

Carline's troubled gaze shifted to Emilia.

"I don't know where Isaak is," she answered, her voice strained. "But Jakob is" — she turned to The Resale Company — "in there."

"He went in after the cat," Carline explained before Zoe could ask why he would do such a foolish thing. Her heart managed to pound even harder.

Zoe looked to the front of the shop, where

417

a fireman stood holding a hose nozzle and directing it to the awning over the door. She looked up to the roof. Flames flickered from the section between where the two firemen were cutting holes.

Suddenly, a cry arose.

Jakob stepped outside, fairly covered in ashes, dust, and smoke. He cradled the tabby in his arms. A fireman followed, patting Jakob's back.

"Get back! Get back!" yelled the tin-trumpeted man who Zoe presumed was the fire chief. He waved at the crowd. "Back farther! I can't guarantee this roof won't crash in!"

Jakob spoke to the fireman with him as they moved farther into the street. Someone called his name. He looked around. His gaze settled on Zoe, and he grinned.

She dashed forward and into Jakob's arms. "Oh, Jakob, I was so worried."

He drew back. "You were?"

She stared at him. Of course she was. For goodness' sake, she did not have to be in love with him to be concerned about his welfare. He had dashed into a burning building to save the cat. A cat!

"You could have died," she said, even though her throat felt it could not get any tighter. "My heart could not bear zat."

The fireman patted Jakob's shoulder. "My father's by the ambulance. He's fairly proud of his doctoring skills, so don't leave without seeing him first. You breathed in a lot of smoke."

Jakob nodded. "Thanks, Frank."

Zoe released a long, slow breath, hoping it would lessen the tension inside. "Ze fire is horrible, but at least you are safe. And ze cat is safe, too."

"I'm sorry I've been distant of late."

"You had to work."

"I thought you — Forget it! That was the past." He slid the tabby cat into her arms. And then he knelt. "Zoe de Fleur, will you consent to be my wife?"

Isaak pulled the horses to a stop, tossed the reins to his father, and jumped out of the surrey. He didn't care about the fire, not when Jakob was safe and kneeling in front of Zoe, not when the cat was in her arms, and not when Emilia and Carline were part of the crowd waiting with breathless anticipation for Zoe to answer Jakob's proposal. The only thing Isaak cared about was getting to Zoe before she said yes because she couldn't say no.

The scene blurred. Only Zoe was clear. She was wearing a white apron with green

419

stains. She was beautiful and gracious and gentle and everything he'd ever wanted.

Part of Isaak's brain recognized that he'd stopped running and was standing before her, and that he had no idea how to tell her what was in his heart.

"Zoe, I . . ." He should get down on one knee. Everything about how he'd fallen in love with her was as far from tradition as it could get. At least one thing needed to be right. He kneeled, and the crowd gasped in unison. "From the moment I met you, my life went sideways. I think that's why I worked so hard to find fault. I wasn't ready — didn't even *want* to be ready — for love to upset my well-ordered world. I fought against you every way I knew how, but you slipped under my skin and into my soul. I've planned my future a hundred different ways, but now I know in the deepest place of my heart that you — and only you — are my future. Marry me?"

She stood there wearing an expression he couldn't read.

"Please say yes," he begged. "Please."

Firefighters sprayed water on the flames crawling up the sides of The Resale Co., but their gazes were locked on Isaak and Jakob kneeling side by side in front of Zoe.

Aunt Lily wept and clung to Uncle Jonas.

Ma and Pa stood still as statues, their arms wrapped around each other's waists.

Emilia had her hand over her mouth. Carline's mouth was wide open.

Mayor Kendrick was smiling as if he'd just won the election.

He probably had.

Isaak didn't care. He needed Zoe more than he needed to run the city of Helena.

She looked between him and Jakob.

Isaak knew her answer before she spoke, and it stopped his breath.

"No . . . to you both."

Minutes later

"Zoe, dear, please don't walk so fast."

She paused on the boardwalk long enough for Mrs. Forsythe to catch up to her. What Isaak and Jakob had done stemmed from pure selfishness. After a glance at Mrs. Forsythe, Zoe resumed walking. They had humiliated — *humiliated!* — her in front of her friends, in front of their parents, in front of dozens of people who would remember this moment for years. Years!

Two brothers proposing marriage to the same girl while their store burned. Not a good time. Not a good place.

Did they not care how foolish they looked? Or how foolish they made her look?

421

Now people would believe she had been flirting with both brothers.

They would view her as a strumpet.

Zoe let out a harsh laugh to release the painful pressure of anger growing within her. They had treated her as if she was nothing more than a bride-by-mail delivery. A prize to be won. If either of them truly cared about her, they would have considered her feelings. If they cared, they certainly would not have proposed to her in front of a crowd.

Was she *that* weak and malleable that they thought she would accept either proposal for fear of looking bad? She would rather look like a fool than agree to marry for the sake of appearances.

Never again would anyone say she had no backbone.

Zoe hurried across the intersection, then turned south toward the boardinghouse. She had known Jakob was hiding something. She had from the moment she saw him at the depot, but she had allowed herself to be swayed by his charm and happy eyes and she ignored her inner voice. She never had anticipated his secret to be as small and petty as feeling second-best to his brother.

And Isaak? From the day they met, she had recognized his arrogance. That should have been enough of a warning. If anyone was going to win a competition, it would be him. People listened to him. People followed him. People did what he said because he was Isaak Gunderson, a man who literally stood taller than them all. A king among men.

. . . you slipped under my skin and into my soul.

Pretty words, but how could he expect her to believe his profession of love while he was humiliating her in front of a crowd? If Isaak truly loved her — if he *knew* her — he would have known she was going to refuse his brother. If Isaak had truly listened to her words at the opera house, he would have understood her decision to end the contract with Jakob.

Isaak had heard nothing of her heart because his focus was on himself.

. . . you slipped under my skin and into my soul.

He loved her. Every word in his proposal professed his love. His desperation to stop her from agreeing to marry his brother professed his love.

And she had said no!

Good heavens, all she wanted was to say yes and marry him. But not like this. Not while there was no unity with his brother.

Her lungs grew tight and she fought to

breathe.

Mrs. Forsythe grabbed Zoe's arm, stopping her. "Zoe! Weren't you listening to anything I said for the last two blocks?"

Zoe stood there, jaw clenched tight. She would not waste a single word defending why she had refused both twins, or why she had been ignoring Mrs. Forsythe's lecture.

Tears suddenly welled in Mrs. Forsythe's eyes. "I'm so sorry. They shouldn't have done that."

"Ze damage is done."

"But it can be fixed," she said with blatant optimism.

Zoe gave Mrs. Forsythe a look to convey the exact amount of hope she had for that to happen.

"I know things look dour." Mrs. Forsythe cradled her hands around Zoe's. "Give Isaak and Jakob a few days to make things right between them and with you. Instead of cooking in Marilyn's kitchen, you can use mine. I'll help as much as I can. I'll keep the boys away from you."

Zoe felt as if she had been slapped. "You wish me to stay and *cook* for them?"

For a moment, Mrs. Forsythe looked unsure of herself. "I do."

"Why do you zink I would help zem after" — Zoe jerked her hands free of Mrs. Forsythe's hold and pointed in the direction of the still-burning building — "after *zat*? Zey humiliated me."

"I know, and I'm ashamed of their behavior."

"Zen why do you ask me to stay? Because of your love for zem?"

Mrs. Forsythe's lips trembled. "Because of my love for you."

Zoe flinched.

"I can't lose you." Mrs. Forsythe's eyes showed bright with tears. "I can't. I'll say and do whatever it takes to convince you not to leave me. I need you to be my daughter, Zoe. Jonas needs you to be his daughter, too." A sharp whistle cut through the air. Mrs. Forsythe looked in the direction of the boardinghouse.

Zoe did, too.

Mr. and Mrs. Deal stood outside, a handful of male boarders on the second-floor balcony looking in the direction of the fire, all using their hats or hands to shield their eyes from the midday sun.

"You can come live with us," Mrs. Forsythe said softly. "Jonas and I have already discussed adopting you. Oh, don't say you're too old to be adopted. What matters is, we want you to be a part of our family forever."

Forever.

No word could be more bittersweet.

She could have the parents she dreamed of — a father *and* mother who loved her. If she stayed.

No. Not *if she stayed.* She could have had the family and home she yearned for if Isaak Gunderson had done the considerate thing and not proposed because he failed to trust her to refuse his brother. Because he failed to believe she could say no.

He had ruined everything.

Zoe stifled the cry that rose from her throat. She held her breath, reining in her broken heart. "I treasure you and Mr. Forsythe" — she looked away, unable to bear Mrs. Forsythe's hopeful expression — "but staying in Helena is not possible for me. Your godsons saw to zat. I am sorry." She placed a kiss on Mrs. Forsythe's cheek. *"Je t'aime,"* she whispered, and then walked away.

As she neared the boardinghouse, Mr. Deal opened the front door. Neither he nor his wife said anything as she strode past them and up the stairs to her room.

Knock, knock, knock.

With strange detachment, Zoe turned her head far enough to look up at the doorknob but lacked the energy to rise from her seat. She rested her head against the door. "Who is it?"

"It's me, dear," came Mrs. Deal's voice. "I brought you some tea . . . and your brother. He's concerned. Said you were at the fire at The Resale Company."

Zoe sniffed, then, with the back of her hands, dried her eyes. She looked to the clock on the table beside her bed. Eight minutes of crying because, as angry as she still was with Isaak, if circumstances had been different, she would have said yes.

"I am pathetic," she murmured.

She scrambled to her feet and opened the door.

Mrs. Deal stood there holding a tea service. To her left stood Nico. Neither were smiling.

Zoe stepped back for them to enter.

Mrs. Deal took the service to the bedside table. Nico grabbed the wicker rocker and the chair from the secretary and dragged them to the bed. Once Mrs. Deal sat in the chair, Nico motioned to the rocker for Zoe to sit there. She closed the door. He sat on the edge of the bed.

With a sigh, Zoe sat in the rocker. "Milk, no sugar."

Mrs. Deal stopped pouring tea and looked

to Zoe. "You always take your tea with sugar."

"Zat is how you serve it." Zoe took the teacup from her. "I saw no reason to make a fuss. But in ze last few moments, I have come to realize I can say *milk, no sugar* if zis is what I want. I have no obligation to drink tea with sugar so you will see me as a nice person. I have a backbone. I mean no offense when I say I prefer tea with milk, no sugar."

Mrs. Deal's mouth opened, then closed, as she looked from Zoe to Nico . . . before saying to Zoe, "I appreciate your honesty."

Nico studied Zoe.

Uncomfortable with his perusal, Zoe looked away.

"Miss de Fleur, what's wrong?" Mrs. Deal spoke gently. "You look like the weight of the world is on your shoulders."

Zoe stared at the tawny liquid in her teacup. There had to be a way of saying, *I wish to be left alone in this pit of despair so I can bemoan my rejection of Isaak's romantic declaration of love,* and not crush Mrs. Deal's feelings.

"Zoe's been humiliated." Nico's teacup *ting*-ed against the saucer he held. "Her suitor asked her to marry him, but before she could answer, his brother ran over and asked her to marry him instead."

"I see." Mrs. Deal's tone was more grim than curious.

The silence was awkward, yet Zoe welcomed it. That a crowd of people had witnessed the most mortifying moment of her life was bad enough. Why relive it inside her mind?

She was about to say, *It has been a long day and I wish to be alone,* when Mrs. Deal looked at Zoe and asked, "Which one did you choose?"

"She turned them both down," Nico answered.

"Oh. Oh, my." Mrs. Deal sat her teacup and saucer back on the tray. "Isaak I understand. He's rather pious and snooty. If anyone deserves a comeuppance, it's him. But Jakob? Humph."

Nico's eyes widened. "You *like* him?"

"He reminds me of Mr. Deal" — she sighed — "twenty years ago."

Zoe stared stunned at the boardinghouse owner. Isaak, unlike his brother, was steadfast, organized, dependable, conscientious, and — Zoe clenched her jaw. She was still too angry with him to defend his better qualities to anyone.

"If I were you . . . ." Mrs. Deal's slow, deliberate tone drew Zoe's attention. "Oh, I don't know if I should say this, but . . . considering how people in this town talk, if I were you, I would want to leave without anyone the wiser."

"If I could leave immediately, I would," Zoe admitted.

Nico handed Mrs. Deal his cup and saucer. "I'll go get train tickets."

"The train to Denver left the depot at eleven-fifteen." Mrs. Deal set Nico's teacup onto the tray. "Better check the stage instead. There should be one leaving in a couple of hours."

Zoe released a weary breath. "I cannot simply leave today. Zere are things to pack. I must close my account at ze bank and collect my knives and rolling pin from ze Pawlikowski house." She shook her head. "Ze earliest I can leave is tomorrow morning. Nico, you also need time to pack and tender your resignation to your employer. Doing so is most gentlemanly."

Mrs. Deal twisted her hands together. "I hate to be the bearer of bad news, but I know the Gunderson boys. They don't give up easily. Miss de Fleur, you and Nico are treasures to me. If you wish to go somewhere the Gundersons can't find you, Mr. Deal and I have friends in Idaho we can send you to who will help you and Nico find good, reliable work."

Perhaps she should not go to Denver. Her heart ached too much to consider another man's courting now. In time, once her heart healed, she would be open. The Archer Matrimonial Company simply had too many connections to Helena.

Zoe looked at Nico. He had said nothing since offering to buy the train tickets. They had played enough chess matches for her to know when he was analyzing moves ahead of hers. According to him, he found it challenging to see how many ways he could fit the various pieces of the whole together. She always hoped his silence meant he saw no way to beat her. That was never true. His silence meant something bothered him.

His silence meant something failed to fit.

"Nico, what is it?" she asked softly.

He met her gaze. Something — she almost believed she saw anger — flickered in his eyes. "Nothing." He grinned. "I was thinking of the things I need to do before I can leave."

"Are you sure zis is what you want to do?"

He nodded. "We're family. We leave together, we stay together." He smiled at Mrs. Deal. "You're swell for helping us."

Mrs. Deal touched her chest, her eyes growing watery. "Breaks my heart to see you go, but I understand that it's for the best."

Zoe swallowed to ease the tautness in her throat. If Nico had no misgivings, she would choose to have none. "Mrs. Deal, Nico and I would like to accept your offer to help us find a new home where no one can find us."

"Wonderful!" Mrs. Deal stood and collected the tea tray. "To make things easier for you, I'll send Mr. Deal to the Pawlikowskis to collect your things."

Nico stood. "Meet you at the depot in the morning?"

She nodded, then watched as Nico and Mrs. Deal left the room. Once the door closed, Zoe slid onto the bed. She stared up at the white-painted tin ceiling. In all her twenty-two years, she could never remember calling one place home.

Until now.

CHAPTER TWENTY-FOUR

Later that afternoon

"There's nothing more can be done, Mr. Gunderson. I'm sorry."

Isaak nodded at Mr. Booker, the fire chief. "I'm grateful for all your work and that no one was hurt." At least not physically . . . and not by the fire.

The firemen had worked hard to save what they could, but when the roof caught, they shifted their efforts from The Resale Co. to the surrounding buildings. Four hours later, the store was a soot-stained stone shell with gaping holes providing an unimpeded view of charred rubble and shattered glass. Oddly, the stairs remained, only they led nowhere.

Isaak shook his head. Were he a poetic man, he'd say it was a perfect representation of his life. "Do you know how it started?"

Booker waggled his head, neither a nod to

affirm nor a shake to deny but somewhere in-between. "We suspect someone set it deliberately, but the damage is so bad, we'll have to wait a week or two to sort through the debris before we can say for sure."

First the vandalism at The Import Co. and now arson. Someone was intentionally sabotaging their businesses. To pressure Isaak into exiting the mayoral race? Or could it be a coincidence?

Isaak stuck out his hand. "Sir, thank you for all your work. You and your men deserve a raise."

Booker brightened, took off his leather glove, and shook hands. "Now that, young man, is the type of talk I like to hear from politicians."

"Again, thank you."

"My pleasure." Booker released his grip, then trudged toward his exhausted crew, who were coiling leather hoses back into the fire wagon.

Isaak swung his gaze left and right. Clusters of gawkers gathered on the south side of Helena Avenue, a few more at the point of Helena and Fourteenth Street. What was left of the store blocked any who might be on Joan Street.

He waved at the ones he could see, and they scurried off. He needed to be alone, a desire he'd expressed to the friends who'd stopped by to offer their condolences on losing the store.

No one had mentioned losing Zoe, either because they were too embarrassed or because they knew it was the deeper pain. No one except Nico, who — directly after Zoe had run off — had delivered hard punches to Jakob and Isaak's abdomens, along with a declaration that they were bad eggs for humiliating her.

Isaak spied his father driving the family wagon. After Zoe had stormed off, Pa had limped in between his sons, ordering Jakob to guard The Import Co. against more vandalism and Isaak to stay at The Resale Co. — the equivalent of being sent to their rooms until Pa was ready to dish out punishments.

Isaak stood straight. He'd take his scolding like a man.

Pa pulled the reins, bringing the wagon to a stop. He set the brake. "Climb on up here. My ankle is throbbing, and I promised your mother I'd stay off it."

Isaak obeyed.

"I've spoken with Jakob and heard his side of the story. Now I'd like to hear yours."

Isaak didn't know where to start.

"Why don't you begin with your first

impression of Miss de Fleur," Pa encouraged, as though he could read Isaak's mind.

"I thought she was a fraud."

"What changed your mind?"

Isaak spread his hands. "A hundred different things."

"Start with the first one."

He pictured her smile when she snapped the bank notes against the counter to pay for the primers and the set of La Fontaine books. "She gave me a dressing down that I richly deserved." And then the words flowed. For ten or twenty minutes — maybe more — Isaak recounted all the ways Zoe wriggled past his distrust until he'd recognized she was a ruby beyond price.

Pa nodded. "Between your story and Jakob's, I have to say I like this girl. She's exposed Jakob's feelings of inferiority and humbled your pride in less than two months, something your mother and I have been working on for years."

Isaak released the breath he'd been holding. "I'm glad you approve."

"Of *her*," Pa stressed. "Not of what you and Jakob did to the poor girl. I never thought I'd be more disappointed in the two of you than the day you stole money from the cash register because you wanted matching kites."

It was the day Isaak determined to never again fail his parents. "I'm sorry for being a disappointment both then and now."

"I expect you to also offer your apologies to Miss de Fleur and your brother."

"Yes, sir."

Pa nodded. "Jakob will be making his apologies, too."

"Good."

Pa's eyes narrowed. "Why do you say *good*?"

Isaak stared at his father. "Jakob should have known better than to write away for a mail-order bride. Did you even know about Zoe before Jakob decided to play the hero and pressure her into marriage?"

"Stop right there, because you" — Pa pointed his finger at Isaak's nose — "are the one most at fault."

Isaak's jaw sagged.

"Son, I can't imagine loving you more if you were my own flesh and blood, but it doesn't make me blind to your faults. You're so busy being a respected businessman, exemplary church member, and dutiful son, you've never considered that you take unholy pride in your righteousness."

The accusation left Isaak speechless.

"Have you ever considered," Pa continued, his voice softer but still convicting, "that God needed to humble you, so He used Jakob's impetuous nature as a tool?"

Isaak closed his eyes while wave after wave of shame crashed over him. If that had been God's plan, He couldn't have chosen a more effective means. Isaak pictured Zoe's face when she'd said no to his proposal. He was so afraid of her desire to please others, he'd used it against her by proposing publicly to force her to say yes to him. The very thing he was angry at Jakob for doing!

Oh, Lord. I'm sorry. I never saw it. I never . . . You know I didn't mean to . . .

Even his prayers were in shambles.

Pa put a hand on Isaak's shoulder. "You clearly love this woman. I've never heard a more eloquent proposal, so —"

"It doesn't matter." Isaak rubbed the back of his neck. "She's returning to Denver, and I can't leave my job or obligations here to chase after her." Which she wouldn't want, anyway. She'd already said she'd never trust a man who broke his commitments.

Pa chuckled. "Now you sound as daft as I was before deciding to court your mother."

Isaak swiveled his head to look at his father.

"When a man is determined not to love a woman he's already in love with, he uses excuses to shield his heart. I know, because

I did the same thing. In my case it was fear." Pa smoothed his mustache. "In your case, it's more of your pride. You think this town, the Widows and Orphans Committee, and even I can't function without you."

The loving rebuke burned inside Isaak's chest. "More of my benevolent arrogance?"

Pa squeezed Isaak's shoulder. "Yes, but all men are afflicted with some measure of it. And all men are fools in love, so you're in good company."

Isaak bowed his head. *Lord, cleanse me of my pride. Teach me to walk humbly before You.*

"Let's go home, son. You need a bath and some food."

With a big slice of humble pie as the main course.

Ninety minutes later

Isaak removed his bowler and stepped inside Hale's law office. The double doors between the parlor and office were wide open.

Hale looked over the pile of work littering his desk. "Isaak. A pleasure to see you. Come in."

Isaak crossed into the cluttered room, amazed, as always, that Hale knew the subject matter of every stack and could locate whatever he needed without wasting time searching. Knowing that didn't keep Isaak from testing his friend once in a while by pointing to a mound and demanding the subject matter of each.

Today wasn't the time for games, however, so Isaak sat down in an empty wooden chair, ignoring the one next to him except to place his hat on top of the paper heap occupying it. "I've come to convince you to run for mayor."

Hale sat back and touched his finger to the bridge of his wire-rimmed glasses. "If this is about today's . . ." He spread his hands but didn't finish his sentence.

Isaak's lips twitched. "It comforts me that a skilled lawyer who forms arguments for a living and reads the dictionary for fun can't find a word to describe this morning's . . . whatever it was."

"Debacle?"

"Too benign."

"Fiasco?"

"Too insipid."

Hale grinned. "Whatever it was, it doesn't disqualify you from running for mayor. As I told you before, voters have short memories."

Isaak shook his head. "This isn't about the voters or anyone else. This is about me stepping away from something that's feeding my pride."

A long, considering look. "I see."

Had Isaak needed further proof of his besetting sin, those two little words would have provided it. "I need to withdraw, but Kendrick needs to be defeated. The only man who can do it is you."

Hale pursed his lips.

Isaak gave him a moment to come to the same conclusion. "You know I'm right."

"Says the man trying to overcome pride."

Isaak snorted. "Oh . . . you don't know how much I needed to laugh."

Hale looked at the corner of the room, took a deep breath, and returned his focus to Isaak. "I don't want this. I've never wanted this."

"Which is why you're the man for the job." Isaak let that settle. "At the risk of being put in my place again, I repeat, you know I'm right. No one else has the skill, the reputation, and the political backing of a territorial judge."

Hale glowered. "I hate nepotism. It would gall me to win an election because of my uncle's connections."

"Is that what's held you back? Because you do yourself a great disservice in thinking that." Isaak leaned forward and put his

441

forearms on the slender line of space between the edge of Hale's desk and one of
his stacks of paper. "You're an excellent
lawyer, you have good ideas about what to
do and how to go about it, and we've
discussed the campaign multiple times. All
that's needed is to switch the man running.
Nothing else changes."

For another five minutes, Hale came up
with excuses and Isaak rebutted them. Hale
took longer and longer to formulate each
argument. He stared over Isaak's shoulder
for a full thirty seconds before releasing a
sigh. "This isn't a good time."

When he didn't elaborate, Isaak
prompted, "Why not?"

Hale tilted his head and stared Isaak in
the eye. "You're really going to drop out."

It wasn't a question, it was acceptance . . .
and an excellent change of topic. "And
you're really going to run." Isaak picked up
his hat and stood. "Be at the . . . Sorry.
Would you be amenable to announcing your
candidacy at the The Import Company's
grand opening a week from tomorrow?"

Hale came around the desk to walk Isaak
toward the door. "You're going through
with that?"

Isaak nodded, his throat tightening. "With
The Resale Company gone, I'll put my ef-

fort into making The Import Company a success." Because he needed to work and keep working until the void in his chest went away.

They reached the front door, and Hale opened it. "You're *sure* about this?"

"That you're the right man for the job? Absolutely." Isaak fit his bowler on his head. As he crossed over the threshold and walked into the street, he called over his shoulder, "I can't wait to see Uncle Jonas's face when he hears you've agreed to run."

Hale responded by slamming his door closed.

Isaak's good humor lasted until The Import Co. came into view. This was going to be a much more difficult sell. He and Jakob had twenty-two years of sibling rivalry to overcome. They also had twenty-two years of practice at making up after fights. They ought to be good at it by now.

Isaak rehearsed his apology as he covered the remaining distance.

Jakob was standing by a window waiting. He opened the door and swung it wide. He'd also cleaned up since the fire. "I'm glad you came."

"Did you think I wouldn't?"

Jakob's expression froze.

"Sorry." Isaak took off his hat and held it

with both hands. "Humility is going to be a learned skill. Let me try that again. I'm glad to see you, too." When Jakob cocked his eyebrow, Isaak chuckled and stepped into the store.

It smelled of milled pinewood, lemon oil, and fresh paint. Unlike The Resale Co., where an eclectic array of goods was displayed according to category, here they were placed with an eye toward showing each piece as it would be used. A mahogany dining room table set with china, crystal, candles, and linens, as though waiting for a Christmas feast. A sofa and two wingback chairs framed a coffee table holding a stack of three books and a pair of reading glasses. The accompanying sofa tables were set with matching Tiffany lamps. Behind them was a carved-wood grandfather clock, the pendulum swinging and the hands at the correct time. Farther back, a four-poster bed with slippers on the floor and a dressing gown laid over the quilted bedspread. Paintings were grouped on the walls so they didn't overwhelm but rather helped create the illusion that each designated space was its own room.

Isaak had helped uncrate a number of items, but he hadn't been around to help with the display. "This is incredible, Jake. I never imagined it would look this good." He sucked in a breath and turned. "I'm sorry. I didn't mean for that to sound like —"

"I know you meant it as a compliment." Jakob pointed at the living room display with an open palm. "I thought we could sit while we talked."

"Good idea." Isaak chose the wingback chair and waited long enough for Jakob to sit on the sofa before he said, "I'm at fault."

Jakob took a moment before settling back against the brown leather and crossing his legs. "All right. I'm listening."

Isaak began as he'd rehearsed. "I was born with an inflated sense of duty and responsibility. Because my diligence, organization, and planning have always resulted in success, I've viewed myself as superior to you."

"To everyone," Jakob corrected.

Isaak grimaced. "To everyone." He opened his mouth to continue, but Jakob held up a hand.

"Wait." The corner of his mouth indented. "I'd like to relish this moment a bit longer."

Isaak grinned. "Please, relish as long as you need. I deserve it."

The amusement faded in Jakob's eyes. "You don't deserve it. Not really."

"I do." Isaak tugged his shirt collar away

from his neck. "Every time you got in trouble for doing something impetuous, I determined to plan more. Every time I was rewarded for doing the responsible thing, it stoked the fire of my pride. Your failures reinforced my belief that I was the better son, the better person, the better man." He paused for Jakob to nod his assent. "I'm sorry for that, Jake. Truly sorry."

"Thank you." Jakob uncrossed his legs and shifted on the sofa. "Truth is, I've made plenty of mistakes through the years. I do need to think through consequences a little more and stop thinking every suggestion you give is a criticism of my character." Jakob gripped the V-shaped opening of his vest. "You have to agree my idea to bring Zoe here wasn't all bad."

"I'll concede that point." Isaak scooted forward on the chair. "Do you love her?"

Jakob inhaled and held the breath before exhaling with a whoosh. "I'd like to love her, but it's not the same thing as actually being in love with her."

No. It wasn't. "I never wanted to love her, but I do."

A twinkle lit Jakob's eyes. "I caught that."

The band of tension around Isaak's ribs loosened an inch. If Jakob was already finding humor in his loss, they were going to be fine. Isaak rubbed the knuckles of his right hand and looked around The Import Co. stocked with items from all over the United States and the world. He knew — was *almost certain* he knew — why his brother had chosen to send for a mail-order bride, but he was *un*certain how to balance his God-given talent for recognizing it with respect for Jakob as a man who had the right to come to his own conclusions.

Pa said Zoe had exposed faults. Had she done the same for Jakob?

Isaak looked his brother in the eye. "What is it about her that you find most attractive?"

Jakob jerked backward. "What?"

"Please, just answer." Isaak gripped his hands together. "I'm curious."

The room was silent except for the ticking of the grandfather clock. Jakob's attention swirled around the room, as though he was searching for inspiration. His eyes settled, and Isaak looked to see the painting of Notre-Dame Cathedral beside the Seine River. "I loved that she didn't grow up here, that she didn't know me as Isaak Gunderson's irresponsible twin."

"So you threw yourself into work and pushed Zoe to the side."

Jakob scratched an earlobe. "Told myself I

was doing the mature thing — the Isaak thing, so to speak."

"Is that why you proposed?"

Jakob shrugged. "I care for Zoe a great deal, and the thought of her with you stings."

Isaak swallowed against the tightness closing his throat. "I don't want to lose you, Jake. Not over Zoe."

Jakob was silent for long moment before he leaned forward, his expression sober. "What if I said you had to choose between her or me?"

Isaak's heart tilted sideways. What would he do? "I want to say I'd choose you, but" — he looked his twin in the eye — "I can't. Not if she'll have me."

Jakob grinned. "Good answer." He sat back again. "We sure made a mess of it. If I were her, I'd never speak to either of us again."

Isaak rested his elbows on his knees. "How do I win her back?"

"I don't know, Iz," said the man who persuaded people to jump into raging rivers using nothing but his charm.

A skill Isaak had underestimated until now.

Jakob touched his stomach. "But you might start with that young man who punched us both."

Isaak left The Import Co. intent on one more apology . . . the most humbling one yet.

The walk to the red-light district only took five minutes, but with the late afternoon sun providing no cover, he endured enough stares to last a lifetime. Last year, when Emilia and Yancey avoided people for fear of censorious glances after the article about Finn was published, Isaak told them to put on a brave face and look people in the eye. To make them back down.

Maybe he was right to offer them such wisdom, but it was equally likely he was wrong. He'd never walked that proverbial mile until now. Nevertheless, he followed his own advice. He kept his chin high and his shoulders straight. Yes, he was Isaak David Gunderson, and yes, he was walking straight to the *Maison de Joie,* Madame Lestraude's brothel.

He stopped at the door. Was he supposed to walk in or knock? When in doubt, err on the side of being a gentleman; he lifted his hand and knocked.

A massive Chinese man opened the door. He didn't speak. Or move. Or even blink.

And he was looking *down* at Isaak.

Intimidation was a new sensation. Isaak usually inspired that emotion in others. Evidently, God was pulling out all the stops for this lesson. "I'm here to speak to Nico."

A feminine "Let him come in" moved the wall of muscles out of Isaak's way.

He stepped inside and stopped in his tracks. It looked like a regular home with a huge parlor and grand staircase leading to a second floor. Six women sat on sofas and chairs dressed in plain, high-collared dresses reading what looked like school primers.

Not how he'd ever imagined — or tried *not* to imagine — a brothel.

Madame Lestraude looked up from where she was bent over a pretty blonde's shoulder. "Ah, Mr. Gunderson. What a pleasure to see you here."

He should return her greeting, but his tongue refused to come down from the roof of his mouth. He dipped his head in a polite bow only because his neck muscles remembered on their own that they were supposed to greet women with that courtesy.

"You've caught us at our lessons, as you see, but we were just finishing. Ladies" — she clapped her hands — "if you would give us the room, please."

"Yes, ma'am," was spoken in unison. The

women rose, gathered their books, and filed up the stairs. They greeted Isaak with polite nods and an occasional, "Sir," but didn't flirt or . . . or *anything.*

After the last woman left, he swung his gaze back to Madame Lestraude and was taken aback by the fury in her brown eyes. She glanced at his forehead. Heat flooding his face, he swiped off his hat. "I beg your pardon, ma'am."

"I see Mac never told you that I give my girls lessons. This group is new, so we're starting with basic reading, writing, and arithmetic."

Isaak didn't know what to think. It had stunned him when he learned the madam was rescuing girls from prostitution. It was almost as shocking to see her teaching lessons like a school marm. "I, uh, guess . . . I mean, I think that's . . . admirable?" His voice lifted of its own accord.

She laughed, though it lacked mirth. "Oh, Mr. Gunderson, you are a delight."

It was said like a compliment, but it wasn't. And yet it was. Which reminded him of how conflicted he was over Zoe and brought him back to his purpose. "I'm looking for Nico."

The fury she'd masked earlier flickered in her eyes again. "Why?"

"I need to ask him a question."

"What kind of question?" Her voice hardened.

Isaak looked at her more closely. She'd been beautiful once, but now she wore too many regrets for the term to fit. Her dyed blond hair appeared brittle, the skin at the corners of her eyes was crosshatched with thin wrinkles, and the lace around her high collar was unable to disguise the deep creases in her neck.

And she was afraid of something.

It pricked him the same way Zoe's discomfort had when he greeted her that first Sunday morning. He didn't brush past it this time. "I haven't brought law enforcement with me, if that's what you're thinking."

She didn't appear mollified. "That doesn't tell me why you need to speak with Nico."

Isaak gripped his hat brim tighter. "I need to ask him a question regarding Miss de Fleur."

Nico pushed through a door to Isaak's right. "What d'ya need to ask about my sister?" Belligerence filled his face and his question.

"Nico," Madame Lestraude bathed the two syllables with censure. "I told you to wait until I called for you."

"But he said this was about Zoe, not the —"

"Hush."

As if Isaak didn't already know illegal activity went on upstairs. "Madame Lestraude, might I have a word with Nico in private?"

"No."

He blinked at her rudeness.

Before he could think of a suitable response, Nico said, "It's all right, Miss Lester. I can handle Mr. Goon-der-son."

Isaak vacillated between astonishment and irritation at the names rolling off Nico's tongue.

Madame Lestraude remained rooted for another moment before speaking to Nico. "I'll be in my office. If you need anything" — she slid a meaningful glance at Isaak — "call me or Mr. Lui. Do you understand?"

Nico nodded.

Isaak checked to see where Mr. Lui had hidden himself, but the mountain of flesh had somehow slipped away unnoticed.

After squeezing the boy's shoulder, Madame Lestraude swished out of the room using the same door Nico had earlier.

Nico fisted his right hand and pounded it into his left palm as though he was imagining punching Isaak in the stomach again.

"Why're you here?"

"Because I need to apologize for the way I've treated both you and your sister."

Nico's eyes narrowed to slits. "You think wearing a fancy suit is going to make me forgive you just like that? I'm not a jellyfish, Mr. Goon-der-son, and neither is my sister."

Isaak swallowed his first response. Jakob had said winning over this young man was going to be nigh impossible, but the only way to do it was by treating him with honest respect. Good advice Isaak intended to follow, no matter how difficult Nico made it. "I'm not wearing this suit to make you forgive me but because it's what a gentleman wears to pay important social calls."

"You saying I'm an important social call?" Nico made it sound like an insult.

"I am."

"Why?"

Isaak lowered his chin so Nico could look him straight in the eye. "As Miss de Fleur's only family member, I should have come to you to declare my intention of courting her before asking her to marry me."

Nico's eyes widened for an instant before sliding back into narrow suspicion.

"May I have your permission to court your sister?" Isaak held the young man's stare.

Seconds ticked by.

Nico didn't move.

Isaak barely breathed.

"What if I say no?"

Isaak's heart pounded. This was the crucible. Unlike with Jakob, if Nico said he wouldn't give Zoe up, there was no going around him. "Then I'll honor your wishes."

"You will?" Nico's voice pitched an octave higher, a reminder that he was a boy on the verge of manhood. He coughed and said in an exaggerated bass voice, "I mean, of course you will."

The temptation to laugh at his attempt to appear older and wiser than his years was tempered by the seriousness of the topic. Isaak gripped his hat so hard, he was certain the brim would have permanent imprints of his fingers.

Nico shifted his weight from his right foot to his left. Stared. Shifted his weight back. Stared some more. "If I say yes, you'll just take her from me."

Isaak inhaled. This was the crux of the matter for Nico. Zoe once said he called her his sister because he had no other family. To win Zoe, Isaak needed to expand his future to include not only a wife but an imp of a brother-in-law who thought nothing of lying, stealing, and living in a brothel with a madam as a surrogate mother.

Nico would also defend his sister to his last breath.

Isaak could deal with that.

"I give you my word as a" — he revised his usual promise — "as the gentleman I hope to become that, should I be fortunate enough to win your sister's heart, you will always be a member of our family."

After a flickering glance at the door to the hallway that presumably led to Madame Lestraude's office, Nico said, "All right. You can court her."

Isaak took his first deep breath since seeing Jakob's proposal six hours earlier. "Thank you, Nico. I'll do my best to deserve the faith you're putting in me."

"You figured out how you're going to win her heart? Because you made her angry, and I mean an-gry."

Isaak cringed. "She has every right to be, which brings me to my second request."

"Go on."

"I need your help."

Nico stood taller. "You want me to help you court Zoe? You and me together?"

It wasn't exactly what Isaak was picturing, but he'd do whatever it took. "Sure. We'll court her together."

Nico beamed. "She likes surprises."

"And sunrises."

Nico looked impressed. "How'd you know that?"

"She mentioned it the first time she was in my home for dinner." Isaak winced, remembering his behavior that day. If he was lucky enough to win her love, he'd spend the rest of his life living up to the grace she'd extended to him that day . . . and the weeks that followed when, in his arrogance, he'd refused to believe his initial impression of her was wrong.

"We could tell her you're dying."

Isaak snapped his attention to Nico.

"Or that you'll hang yourself if she doesn't marry you."

The boy's line of suggestions needed to stop. Isaak searched for a gentle way to say it. "Your sister doesn't like lying."

Nico's expression soured. "It got her here, didn't it?"

"You lied to get her here?"

"She needed to get out of New York."

There was more to the story but pressing for details might make the boy change his mind about helping to woo Zoe, so Isaak remained silent.

Nico crossed his arms over his chest. "She can't read English too good, so I pointed at the advertisement for a mail-order bride and pretended it was for a cook instead. When she found out what I'd done, she asked that Archer lady about the man looking for a wife. She saw your brother's smiley eyes and decided to come here even though I told her it was a mistake."

Regardless of whether Zoe agreed to marry him, Isaak would never think of her coming to Helena as a mistake. She'd enriched his life, humbled his pride, and made him a better man. At least he hoped he'd be a better one from now on. "I'm glad she came, but I don't think lying to her now is our best plan."

Nico remained stony for a long moment before wilting. "Yeah. You're right."

Isaak waited for the boy to come up with another suggestion.

Silence.

Outside of lying, it appeared he didn't have any ideas. Isaak didn't offer any of his own, though, because it was important for Nico to take the lead.

He shifted his gaze between his feet and Isaak. "Way I see it, the problem is that Zoe doesn't get involved in what's not her business."

Isaak nodded. An idea struck. "What if we do things together that *aren't* her business, but we make sure she sees us together."

Nico nodded. "She'll get so curious, she'll have to come around to figure out what we're doing. I think this might work, but . . ." His expression grew serious.

"What is it?" Isaak curled his fingers into fists as he waited for another objection.

Nico's gaze flickered at the door to Madame Lestraude's office. "Miss Lester told me something, and I don't want to tell Zoe about it."

"Why not?"

"She's a girl," he said as though it explained everything. Nico shifted from balancing on his left foot to his right. "When I went to check on her after you'd humiliated her, Mrs. Deal said she knew a place where me and Zoe could disappear. It sounded funny, so I asked Miss Lester about it. She said the Deals sometimes sell women and children — even boys — into prostitution."

Isaak's jaw fell open. "Why hasn't she told her son?"

"She just found out about it." Nico's brow furrowed. "If I can get Mr. or Mrs. Deal to tell me the address of these friends in Idaho they're sending us to, do you think Sheriff McCall could arrest them?"

"No, but he could send the information to a sheriff in Idaho. Great idea!"

The boy beamed.

"But Nico . . . ?" Isaak waited until he had the boy's full attention. "While I understand wanting to keep Zoe from feeling betrayed by the Deals, sometimes we men assume" — *in benevolent arrogance* — "that we know what's best for the people we love."

"Yeah. So?"

Pa was right. All men, even those on the cusp of manhood, were filled with pride. A lesson Nico needed to learn over time as Isaak had. "If our plan to woo Zoe fails, promise me you'll tell her about the Deals. No lying to protect her."

Nico's posture relaxed. "Because people who love each other trust them with the truth."

Out of the mouth of babes . . . and young men.

"And we both" — Isaak pointed a finger at himself then at Nico — "love her very much."

Nico pivoted on his heel. "Let me tell Miss Lester I'm going with you." He opened the door and was almost through when he leaned back to add, "You and me courting Zoe together is good and all, but you might have to spend *some* time alone with her."

Isaak placed a hand over his heart. "I shall endeavor to make the sacrifice."

CHAPTER TWENTY-FIVE

The next morning

Zoe grabbed the quilt from her bed and then slipped out onto the boardinghouse's wrap-around balcony, careful not to make any noise to wake her fellow boarders. When she had first settled into her room almost two months before, she and Janet Deal had been the only females. Now nine ladies stayed one and two to a room. Zoe would be surprised if *her* room was not let by the time her last piece of luggage was removed.

Someone had turned her favorite wicker rocker to face the direction of The Resale Company fire. She adjusted it to face east, then unfolded the quilt and draped it over the rocker. Once settled in, she wrapped the edges over her head and around her amethyst traveling suit, leaving only her face to endure the nippy morning breeze.

Zoe closed her eyes and waited for what was sure to come.

Crickets chirped.

Horses clomped on the dirt-hardened street.

A dog barked from somewhere in the distance.

Finally . . . what she had been listening for happened: a rooster crowed. She smiled. Other roosters joined in.

How they knew it was dawn never ceased to amaze her. The first rays of light had yet to grace the Earth. The underbellies of the clouds had yet been lit to a glow.

Yet the roosters crowed.

Their hearts told them it was time.

. . . you slipped under my skin and into my soul.

Stop! No more reliving Isaak's proposal.

But if his brother had not proposed and The Resale Company not burned and the moment had been absent several hundred bystanders, she would have said yes.

She *might* have said yes.

She certainly would have taken a moment to relish the thought of saying yes and all the wonders that would come with it. A kiss.

Zoe pressed her eyes tighter. No sense dreaming about what she could have had with Isaak. This would be her last Montana sunrise. She would enjoy it to the fullest. She would enjoy it without regrets. Just as she had enjoyed watching last night's sunset after finishing letters of farewell to the people she was too cowardly to visit in person. Her own heartbreak hurt enough. She refused to live with the images of their tearstained faces as they looked upon her own tearstained face.

"I cry too much," she muttered before focusing on what she needed to do today before she and Nico could start a new life somewhere exciting.

Sunrise.

Breakfast with Nico.

Load belongings into Deal's wagon.

Bank.

See Jakob, despite the Deals' recommendation she avoid him. Ending the contract personally was the right thing to do.

Board train and —

Oh! Sensing the moment she had been waiting for, she opened her eyes. The blue-black of night eased up, a gentle escape from the approaching sun minutes from breaking dawn.

"Shhh."

After a second, louder "shhh," Zoe stood and looked over the balcony at the single-story home directly east of the boarding-house. She leaned forward, squinted, blinked. Only one person in Helena wore a flattened beige derby and a brown corduroy coat. Nico! But why was he sitting on the top ridge of the slanted roof? Who was that sitting to the right of —

The man in the black suit and bowler looked over his shoulder up at the boarding-house balcony.

Isaak?

Her chest tightened. What was he doing with Nico?

With the back of his hand, Isaak tapped Nico's shoulder and said something, all the while never looking away from Zoe.

Nico turned around. He smiled and waved . . . and then elbowed Isaak. He waved, too.

Zoe lifted her hand, but the quilt hindered her from waving back, so she smiled. At least she thought it was a smile. It may have been more of a toothy, what-are-you-doing-on-a-roof-at-this-time-of-the-morning gaping mouth.

She waited for an explanation, but both Isaak and Nico turned back to watch the sunrise.

Why?

She specifically remembered Jakob saying Isaak needed a good hour in silence and two cups of sweetened tea along with a hefty breakfast before he became tolerable. Nico, she knew, could put on a good and false show of morning joviality. Never had Isaak or Nico expressed interest in admiring the sun during any time of day. Not to her anyway.

Zoe worried her bottom lip. How did Isaak know where to find Nico? Unless Nico found him first. But why would Nico want to find Isaak?

Shadows inched west as the sun peeked over the horizon.

As Isaak and Nico sat watching.

As the rising sun cast a golden glow about them.

As Zoe leaned over the balcony and waited and waited for them to do something.

And then . . . both released a heavy breath, their broad shoulders rising and falling. Nico patted Isaak's back. They took turns climbing over the ridge, easing down to the eaves, and descending the ladder that rested against the house's west wall.

Unable to fathom what was going on, Zoe looked to where the sun had warmed the sky and turned the clouds into pink spun sugar. She growled softly. In her concern for why Nico and Isaak were together, she had missed what she had risen early to see. She dashed around the rocker and to the front balcony railing, looked down, and saw no one.

Where had they disappeared to?

Breakfast!

After ridding herself of her quilt cocoon, Zoe hurried into her room, ignoring her black traveling bonnet and the clothes on her bed that she had yet to pack, and scurried down the stairs to the dining room.

The *empty* dining room.

She walked to the parlor. Also empty.

She peeked inside the kitchen and found Mrs. Deal cooking.

Zoe returned to the front of the boarding-house. Upon looking outside, she saw neither Nico nor Isaak or the ladder against the house next door. What were they about?

It is none of my business. That decided, Zoe returned upstairs to her room to pack.

One hour and fifty-three minutes later

As Zoe gazed through the dining-room window, analyzing the view, she sipped her morning café au lait. She nibbled on a piece of buttered toast. Sipped coffee. Nibbled toast. Sipped. Nibbled.

Directly across the street, Nico and Isaak sat under the covered porch of the shoemaker's shop, the very place they had been when she sat down in her usual chair at the breakfast table, at her usual time of eight o'clock. Neither wore shoes. Between them was a chess set on a barrel. Not once had either looked in her direction.

Isaak's socked foot tapped the boardwalk under them as he studied the chessboard.

Nico moved a pawn. Or maybe a rook. From this distance the piece was difficult to discern.

Isaak's foot continued to tap.

Zoe let out a long breath. Her neck ached from how long she had been staring out the window. She focused on the breakfast in front of her, rested her teacup on its saucer, picked up a knife, heaped marmalade onto the last half of her toast, removed most of the marmalade from her toast, put down her knife, took a bite of bread, and chewed carefully. What Isaak and Nico were doing was none of her business. She had tasks to do before she could, in good conscience, leave Helena.

She had no care why Isaak and Nico were at the shoemaker's.

Or playing chess.

Or together at all.

Mrs. Deal entered the dining room carrying a coffeepot. She refilled cups at the other table. Someone said something that caused the men to laugh.

Zoe slanted her eyes toward the window.

"My dear, would you care for a refill?"

"No, zank you." She looked up to see Mrs. Deal's gaze flicker momentarily to the window, and then she smiled at Zoe.

"Mr. Deal has the wagon ready to load whenever you're ready."

"I am almost finished."

After a "Good, good," Mrs. Deal returned to the kitchen.

Zoe looked sideways.

Still there.

Isaak replaced one of Nico's pieces with one of his own.

Nico raised both arms. He pointed to the board and yelled something.

Isaak shrugged.

Zoe took another bite of marmalade and bread.

Whatever they were doing at the shoemaker's was not . . . not . . . *not* her business. Once finished with her meal, she would go to the bank and close out her account. And then she would make her peace with Jakob. Hearing her side of things, he would understand Isaak was not to blame for the failure of the courtship contract. She must do what she could to help repair the rift between the brothers and give them a more harmonious future.

You are my future whispered across her heart.

How could Isaak say that? How could a person know such a thing about the other?

She looked out the window.

The shoemaker exited his shop with two pairs of black boots. He handed Isaak one, then gave the other to Nico. They pulled on their boots.

Nico paid the man. Isaak did, too.

The shoemaker said something as he took turns shaking hands with them.

And then the new bosom friends walked away.

Zoe released the breath she held and ate the bite of bread. They were gone, and she was delighted to be able to finally finish her breakfast in peace. After the Deals loaded her luggage in the wagon to deliver to the depot, she would go to the bank and then . . .

Zoe frowned at the teller, a balding gentleman with rosy cheeks and a boyish voice that belied the streaks of gray at his temple. "You are holding my money hostage. Why?"

The man looked left, then right, then leaned closer to the ornate brass separating them. He spoke quietly. "Until we've ascertained that none of the greenbacks in the

469

vault are counterfeit, I can only give you the gross of your account in gold coins or a bank check."

Coins? Her luggage was already loaded into the wagons. There would be no way to stow away her gold without being seen. To carry a bag of gold across town would invite ruffians.

Zoe rested her gloved hand on the marble counter. "Other banks will honor ze check?"

He nodded.

She sighed. "Zen a check, please."

"Excellent choice. Have a seat while I have one filled out and signed." He took a step away from the counter and then looked back. "This may take longer than usual. If you don't want to wait, I can hold the check here for you."

"Zat would be helpful. Zank you." Zoe looped her reticule around her wrist. By the time she reached the double front doors, the right one opened.

Nico smiled at her. "Hey, Zoe."

She looked past him to Isaak. His eyes met hers, and she swore she could see right into his soul, feel his breathless longing. Or maybe it was hers. *Marry me.* Or maybe it was *Marry me!* Her heart beat too frantically for her to hear his thoughts — to hear *her* thoughts, not his. Indeed, she was no mind reader, despite her *grand-mère*'s Romany blood.

Zoe felt her cheeks grow warm. "I am sorry," she said to cover the awkward silence. "Did you say something?"

Nico backhanded Isaak's arm.

Isaak removed his hat and said, "Good day, Miss de Fleur."

They backed up and motioned for her to walk past.

She did. Before she could formulate a response, they walked inside the bank; the brass-covered door closed with a rattle.

Zoe looked at the door, then down the boardwalk to where Mr. Deal was standing beside the wagon, waiting to take her to The Import Company. He waved.

"Excuse me." A gentleman brushed past Zoe to enter the bank.

The door opened and closed before Zoe could catch a glimpse of Isaak or Nico.

With a growl under her breath, she strode to the wagon. Whatever they were about was none of her business.

"Zis truly is a beautiful shop," Zoe remarked, standing at The Import Company's entrance as she studied the grandeur of Jakob's creation. "Your parents must be proud."

Jakob nodded, his smile taking its own sweet time to grow. He gave her a mischievous sideways look. "My parents enjoyed yesterday's lunch. They were looking forward to tonight's dinner."

"Mrs. Wiley and Mrs. Forsythe can salvage dinner from what I had already prepared."

"Aunt Lily does work wonders with food." He gripped the lapels of his suit coat. "I know I don't deserve an answer, but I just have to know." He swallowed, his Adam's apple shifting. "Was it only Isaak for you from the moment you two met?"

"He was hard to love at first."

"It's not easy living in his shadow."

Zoe reached up and touched his cheek. "Jakob Gunderson, you are a *good* man. Just as good and kind and honorable as your brother is. Zere is a girl for you."

His eyes grew watery.

Zoe pretended interest in her reticule to give him a moment to collect himself . . . and for her to blink away her tears as well. Her heart hurt. Like someone had hacked a cleaver into her breastbone.

He cleared his throat. "Hey, um, how about a tour of the rest of the building?"

"Zat would be lovely, but Mr. Deal is waiting outside. I promised him I would be but fifteen minutes." She grimaced. "It has been twice" — she glanced at an ebony grand-father clock and corrected herself — "three times zat."

"Most of that time was spent listening to you apologize for ending our contract."

Zoe raised her brows. Jakob had talked and apologized far more than she had.

Jakob broke into that easy laughter of his that never ceased to make Zoe smile. "You're a good sport, Zoe de Fleur. Let me escort you out of here before I decide to charm you into staying in Helena." He opened the door.

Zoe stepped outside and stopped; Jakob bumped into her back.

"Sorry," he muttered, moving around to her side. "Is something wrong?"

She blinked. "I believe I saw —" She leaned to the right to get a better look at Dr. Abernathy's front window across the street, but all she saw through the clear glass was the dentist writing something in a book that rested on his counter. She could have sworn Nico and Isaak had been standing on either side of the man.

She looked at Jakob. "What is on your brother's schedule today?"

He shrugged. "I haven't seen him since last night. Best guess is he's organizing fire cleanup. Have you forgiven him?"

"Not particularly." Zoe looked back at the dentist.

He waved.

She did, too.

"Miss de Fleur?"

Zoe looked to where Mr. Deal stood next to the wagon. "Yes?"

"We should get moving. The train leaves the station in less than an hour, and I need to take you back to the bank."

Jakob placed a brotherly kiss on the back of her gloved hand. "I hope you find what you're seeking."

Zoe nodded and walked away before she gave in to her tears.

Northern Pacific Railway Depot

Zoe settled onto the two-person upholstered seat, impressed at how the gold baroque fabric matched that of the rolling shade. Mr. Deal had been more than generous to upgrade her ticket from second class to the plush Pullman Palace car. The ornate rococo style, with its gold accents, shell-like curves, and mahogany wood, made her feel like she was in a chateau.

She peeked around the shade and breathed a sigh of relief. Yancey had been too busy in the telegraph office to notice Zoe walking through the depot.

Saying good-bye to Jakob had been difficult enough.

The train whistle blew one final call for boarders.

The blue-uniformed railroad officer who had escorted Zoe to her seat stepped back into the car. His gaze moved past the two older ladies in the seat two rows ahead of Zoe. "Miss de Fleur?" he said, looking at her.

"Yes?"

"Excellent." He turned around, and after saying, "She's in here," he exited the car.

Nico dashed down the aisle, tapestry bag in one hand, rolled up sheet of paper in the other. "Sorry I'm late," he said breathlessly. "I had Mr. Deal write down the address for us to go to in Coeur d'Alene in case his niece is unable to meet us." He looked around and whistled. "Whoa, this is what I call first class."

"Sit down."

His gaze shifted from her seat to the one facing hers. "Does it matter where I sit?"

"I do not know," Zoe said with a sigh. "Never have I been in a car like zis. Ze railroad officer said zere is also a dining car and" — she pointed to the upper berth — "zat folds down and zese two facing seats fold over to make a bunk for sleeping."

"Humph. Seems like a lot of work just to have somewhere to lay down." Nico tossed his tapestry bag onto the seat across from her. He plopped down next to his bag. "Ready to start a new adventure?"

Zoe nodded. "Why were you late?"

"I had things to take care of."

"Oh?"

"Things," he answered, tapping the rolled paper on his thigh. "Important ones."

Zoe eased the shade back enough for her to see the boarding platform. Mr. Deal stood there. The remaining people milling about were unfamiliar to her.

The train jerked forward, momentum increasing with each turn of the wheels.

"You looking for someone?" Nico asked.

Zoe released the shade and the smidgeon of hope that Isaak would chase her down and beg her not to leave him because she was his *forever.* Life would be wonderful because they were together. Or so he would say, and so she would agree. *If* he had chased her down.

"Why do you zink I am looking for some-one?"

Nico shrugged. "You seem lonely."

"I am happy you are with me."

"We're a good team, aren't we?"

"Zis is true."

He shrugged off his corduroy coat, then laid it and his flattened derby next to his tapestry bag, which he then opened to remove a leather-bound book. He looked up and saw her watching him. "It's from Miss Lester. She said the author, Jules Verne, is French."

"Papa used to read his stories to me when I was a little girl."

Nico said nothing for a long moment. "I did all of this for you because we're family. We'll always be family. Always. Sometimes a team is better with three. Or four. Or twelve." And then he opened his book and started reading aloud. " 'Chapter one in which Phileas Fogg and Passepartout accept each other, the one as master, the other as man. Mr. Phileas Fogg lived, in 1872, at . . .' "

Zoe closed her eyes and listened.

When she lived at the Crane house, she had dreamed of her husband and the cottage where they would live with their children and a bird that talked. He would bring her fresh flowers every day when he returned home from work. She would love, feed, and cherish him. Not once had she imagined Nico in her idyllic dream. But here he was. And here she was. They would be happy.

Because they were together.

Carpe diem.

The tear slipped out of the corner of her eye, and the pad of a thumb gently brushed it away.

Zoe jolted and looked up.

Isaak stood there, gripping a traveling bag and a small paper sack. He reached inside his suit coat and withdrew a train ticket. "According to this" — his gaze flickered to the space next to her — "that's my seat."

His seat?

"Hey, Isaak."

"Hey, Nico."

"What took you so long? I've been stalling as best I could, but my sister is impatient."

Zoe stared speechless at them both.

"Sorry." Isaak set his traveling bag next to Nico's, then settled next to Zoe. "They put me in the dining car. There were pastries."

"Whoa. Could you eat as many as you wanted?"

"As many as they let me."

"That's less impressive." His eyes narrowed. "Did you really let free pastries delay you when the love of your life is waiting for you to sweep her off her feet?"

"I figured a little delay would make her miss me more. Did it work?"

Nico laughed. "Sure did."

Isaak tossed the paper sack onto Nico's lap. "Those are for you."

Nico gave Isaak the rolled-up paper. "Don't know if this'll help Sheriff McCall, but it's something."

"Sure is." Isaak tucked the paper inside his suit coat.

Zoe finally found her voice. "What is going on?"

Nico sent Isaak a meaningful look. "We'll tell you in a minute, but first, me and Isaak want to know if our plan worked."

"Worked?" Zoe repeated, still at a loss.

Isaak cradled her left hand in his right one. "Your brother and I have spent the day fishing."

"That was my idea," Nico put in.

"Fishing?" Zoe looked back and forth between the pair. Their smiles gave it away. "I am ze fish you were baiting."

They both nodded.

"But what makes you zink I wish to be caught?" she said with as much false indignation as she could muster.

Isaak looked at Nico.

"Excuse me, Zoe." He closed his book, grabbed his sack of pastries, and stood. "This is my cue to give you two some time alone." He eased past Isaak and moved up to the front of the car, sitting on the bench to the right of the car's only other passengers.

Isaak shifted to face Zoe. "After the way I mucked things up yesterday, I figured you'd never wanted to see me again. I used all my fine words in my proposal. I was out of ideas, so I found your brother."

She spoke softly. "You know Nico is not my real brother."

"He's as much your brother as Jakob is mine."

"You truly believe zat?"

"With all my heart." His gaze flickered to Nico. "He loves you."

"I know," Zoe whispered.

"Not as much as I love you." Isaak eased the glove off her hand, then placed a kiss on her upturned wrist.

Zoe's pulse quickened.

He threaded his fingers through hers. "Today has been torturous. Being that close to you yet unable to hold you in my arms. You'll never know how many times I imagined —" He cleared his throat. "I want to marry you, Zoe de Fleur. I started falling for you when you made me close my eyes and listen to Ma's finches."

"But for Jakob . . ."

Isaak sighed. "But for him . . ."

Zoe rested her head against the side of his

arm. "Your brother and I agreed to end our courtship contract. I zink we are still friends."

"He and I are still friends, too. Did I mention my train ticket goes all the way to Portland?"

She shifted to face him. "Why are you going all ze way to Portland?"

"I have tickets for you and Nico to go to Portland, too." Isaak looked hesitant, tense, worried.

"Are you moving to Portland?"

"I will if you will," he said firmly. "I'm running away with you and Nico, if you'll let me."

"I have no wish to live in Portland." Zoe moistened her bottom lip. "Or Coeur d'Alene, no matter how lovely ze Deals say it is."

"There are things lovelier than Coeur d'Alene. Trust me." His gaze fell to her lips. He slowly met her gaze. "Where do you want to live?"

Zoe dipped her chin, hoping the brim of her bonnet would shield her teary eyes. Her pulse raced as the words formed in her mind, growing from her heart, spreading out from her soul. She could no longer hide from him.

She breathed deep and looked him straight

in the eye. "I want to live wherever you are. I love you more zan you love sweets."

"Then how about we get married?"

"Married?"

"We can elope in Portland. Does that interest you?"

Her heart fluttered with thousands of yeses.

"What about Nico?" she whispered.

"He can tag along. We need a reliable witness."

"He *is* family."

"That he is. I love you," Isaak whispered, and then winked, "*almost* as much as I love sweets."

Zoe gasped. "You are most —"

"Wonderful?"

A host of adjectives rose to mind as a response, but Zoe chose to be harmonious and say, "Yes, you are most wonderful, indeed."

EPILOGUE

Saturday, May 5

He was admiring a set of silver candlesticks imported from Spain when Madame Lestraude strolled up, a primal smile on her rouged lips. She held out a folded piece of parchment sealed with burgundy wax imprinted with a solitary rose.

Furious at her bold approach, he took the letter. "I hope you're enjoying the grand opening."

"Immensely. Everyone is abuzz with the grandeur of the store and Mr. Gunderson's withdrawal from the mayoral race. I can only imagine your feelings on the matter."

"It came as something of a shock."

"Ah." The puff of air conveyed nothing. "As for me, the announcement was . . . enlightening. A pleasure to see you as always. I trust we will meet again very soon." With that, she bid him adieu and slipped back into the crush of people eager to touch, smell, and own pieces of the world outside Helena.

He snapped the wax seal while checking to see how many people noticed their exchange. No one was looking at him with shock or censure — why would they, when Big Jane, Chicago Joe, and several other wealthy brothel owners were shopping and exchanging pleasantries in their midst? — but his chest remained tight. He glanced down and read:

C'est guerre!
ML

Why declare war? He'd done nothing to her family. Emilia McCall had escaped the fire with no damage save a bit of ash falling on her hair and shoulders.

He crumpled the parchment between his fingers. The madam and her enigmatic message would have to wait. He weaved his way closer to the door. His lungs needed air untainted by scented candles, quarreling perfumes, and hair pomade. As he stepped into the sunshine, he saw Madame Lestraude step into her carriage. Her driver closed the door and mounted the box.

Madame turned, her eyes on him as deliberate as her slow pull drawing down the shade.

Did she think he would come to her now?

No, their next meeting would be the time and place of his choosing.

Only . . .

He craned his neck to look over his left shoulder and then his right. No one would think twice if he crossed the street to join husbands biding their time with cigars and conversation while their wives spent money on things they didn't need but could afford. From there, he could stroll to the shuttered bank as if he was returning to his office and duck into the carriage when no one was looking.

Fisk lifted a hand in greeting.

He waved back and stepped into the street, careful to avoid the dense piles of manure testifying to the success of today's grand opening.

He took his time chatting with Fisk, Cannon, Watson, and several other important men of Helena, relishing the way it kept Madame Lestraude waiting. Her carriage remained motionless except for an occasional horse's stamp of impatience. Anyone who had noticed her ascent was gone, and everyone else would think it empty.

He excused himself from the men after sparking a debate sure to consume their full attention. As he drew even with the door of her carriage, he stopped, pulled out his pocket watch, and pretended to check the time while skittering his gaze left and right to see if anyone was watching him.

No one.

He opened the carriage door and climbed inside. "I am not your lackey to command."

"Yet here you are." Madame Lestraude knocked on the wall of her carriage and it sprang to life. "Don't worry, we shall set you down somewhere close enough for you to walk back to the grand opening, but far enough away that no one will observe your descent."

"What if someone had seen me?"

"Then you should have taken even more care in your circuitous route." She inclined her head toward the curtains. "I find it quite useful to observe without being observed myself."

He picked up the cane he'd tossed inside before his hasty ascent to cover his embarrassment. "What is so important it couldn't wait until a more opportune time?"

"Ah." The syllable scraped across his nerve endings. "I shall enlighten you, because Helena has grown too large for one man to know all that goes on within it."

His pride pricked, as she'd meant it to. Once upon a time he had known everyone and everything that happened inside of Helena. Had campaigned on it, as a matter of fact.

The city was too large now. He was no longer at the center of every social circle as he once had been.

"Alfred and Martha Deal, in addition to running a second-rate boardinghouse, sell women who will not be missed into prostitution."

He jerked backward against the padded seat. "How long have you known this?"

"It doesn't matter. As long as people stay out of my business, I return the courtesy." She paused for a moment. "Sometimes the Deals ride the trains, offering their card and a shoulder to cry on to naïve young women who, when their rosy dreams are shattered, want to disappear to wallow in self-pity. They approached Emilia on her way into town last year."

"I assume they did the same for Miss de Fleur."

She nodded.

"Excuse my cynicism, but why do you care?"

"Were it just Miss de Fleur, I wouldn't. She made her bed, so she can lie in it."

Her callous answer didn't surprise him, but he was hard-pressed not to reach across the seat and throw her from her own carriage. "So why the dramatic declaration of war?"

"Because she dragged my Nico along with her."

"*Your* Nico?"

"He's a good boy. I'm thinking of adopting him when he gets back from his grand adventure."

He choked on a laugh. "Replacing Mac?"

"Nico loves me as the mother he's never known. Mac keeps telling me love can redeem any soul. Who knows, maybe it will." She pierced him with her brown eyes. "Nico is family."

"Fine, but I've not hurt the boy."

"Oh, but this was not our agreement. You were not to even *threaten* my family."

He gritted his teeth. He didn't see the connection and he didn't want to ask.

"Your fire at The Resale Company resulted in a breach of our . . . *understanding.* This was not your intention, but the consequences will be meted out just the same." She cocked her head. "I'm curious. Did you set it yourself or hire an underling?"

He'd used one of his best employees, a man who had followed instructions to the letter before slipping out of town unnoticed. Unlike Edgar Dunfree who, against orders, used his own name to purchase the printing press, a sale recorded and preserved in a cloth-bound ledger now burned to cinders. If anyone else made the connection between a man who used to boast of their once-close working relationship, the leveling foot found in Collins's barn, and a printing press, there was no longer any proof.

"Are you afraid your Nico will be accused of arson given his . . . other activity?"

Her patronizing smile mocked his mimicry of her dramatic pauses. "You refer to his vandalism at The Import Company, of course. I have chastised him and acknowledge that he played some part in the threat against him for which I blame you."

"Speak plainly, woman. I tire of your games."

"Very well. In plain terms, you pitted Isaak and Jakob Gunderson against each other by using Miss de Fleur to fuel their long-standing rivalry as a means to force Isaak from the mayoral race. As a result, in the literal heat of the moment, they humiliated the girl with dual proposals. She turned to the Deals for a solution. Nico, although he loves me, is more attached to his sister. He planned to flee with her and would have met with her same fate. My disgust for children conscripted into prostitution is well-known to you. It is for this that I will destroy you."

"How could I have foreseen such a convoluted turn of events?"

"*Ignorantia juris non excusat.* I laid down the law, and now I will not excuse you."

He tapped the gold-plated top of his cane.

"You've gone to great lengths to keep your little rescuing ring hidden from the other brothel owners, and with good cause. How do you propose to destroy me when I have the means to destroy you, as I did Hendry, by stirring up hatred against you?"

Her countenance held no fear. "When one side has all the weapons, it is a slaughter. That is why, my dear Jonas, this is war."

ABOUT THE AUTHOR

Gina Welborn is the best selling author of sixteen inspirational romances. She's a member of Romance Writers of America, American Christian Fiction Writers, and serves on the ACFW Foundation Board. Sharing her husband's passion for the premier American sports car, she is a lifetime member of the National Corvette Museum and a founding member of the Southwest Oklahoma Corvette Club. Gina lives with her husband, three of their five children, several rabbits and guinea pigs, and a dog that doesn't realize rabbits and pigs are edible. Visit her online at GinaWelborn.com.

Multi-published author, paper crafter, and Chai tea lover, **Becca Whitham** and her twelve-foot-long craft cabinet follow her husband of more than thirty years to wherever the army currently needs a chaplain. In between moves from one part of the country to the other, she writes stories of faith that touch the heart. She's a member of American Christian Fiction Writers and a Genesis Contest finalist. Connect with her online at BeccaWhitham.com.